NOW YOU SEE ME

NOW YOU SEE ME

Margaret Murphy

LARGE PRINT
Oxford

First published in Great Britain 2005
by
Hodder & Stoughton,
a division of Hodder Headline

Published in Large Print 2006 by ISIS Publishing Ltd.,
7 Centremead, Osney Mead, Oxford OX2 0ES
by arrangement with
Hodder & Stoughton,
a division of Hodder Headline

British Library Cataloguing in Publication Data
Murphy, Margaret, 1959 Apr. 14–
    Now you see me. – Large print ed.
    1. Police – England – Liverpool – Fiction
    2. Missing persons – Fiction
    3. Detective and mystery stories
    4. Large type books
    I. Title
    823.9'14 [F]

ISBN 0–7531–7561–4 (hb)
ISBN 0–7531–7562–2 (pb)

Printed and bound in Great Britain by
T. J. International Ltd., Padstow, Cornwall

For Murf

Acknowledgements

Thanks to all my net buddies, whose late-night conversations kept me sane when the going was tough. I am particularly grateful to Tabitha for her help with comic-book lore. And to the many sites I visited as a lurker: you were an inspiration. Neil Barrett's fascinating and eminently readable text *Traces of Guilt* proved a tremendous source of information on computer crime.

Once again, DCI Dave Griffin provided help, encouragement and procedural detail — thanks a million, Dave.

CHAPTER
ONE

Nine o' clock. Black sky, grey cloud. The street below Megan Ward's window gleamed ghostly pale after a sudden shower. Cars crammed the length of the street, jostling for space, some with their near-side wheels on the kerb, narrowing the gap between the facing yellow-brick houses.

A man stood on the opposite kerb. He was tall, powerfully built, the trapezius muscles of his neck so thick that his head seemed to be jammed down onto his shoulders. He had been watching the house for fifteen minutes, while Megan watched him from the darkness of her room, her breathing shallow, fearful.

Some youths approached, heading for the pubs in Lark Lane, loud and full of swagger, but as they passed the man they fell silent, taking care to give him space, avoiding his eye.

What did he want from her? She sighed, and it caught on the out-breath. *You know what he wants, and you brought this on yourself.*

The front door opened and light spilled out from the hallway into the street. *Oh, God — Sara!*

Megan ran from her study onto the landing, yelling Sara's name. Down the stairs, hearing the chink of milk bottles and the dull ring as one fell over and rolled.

"Sara!" She leapt the last few steps, stumbling and almost cannoning into her friend as she ran back inside.

"Megan, what is it?"

Megan slammed the door closed and stood panting with her back braced against it. "He's out there," she gasped.

Sara's hand went to her mouth. Her face, strong and clear-eyed in normal circumstances, looked small and pinched, but her terror was only fleeting. She quickly reached for the door handle, angered by her momentary weakness.

Megan spread her arms wide. "No. Sara — don't."

Sara wore her honey-blonde hair shoulder length, curling softly. Now she tucked it behind her ears and tilted her chin. "You can't let him terrorize you like this, Megan," she said. "You have to confront him."

Megan's eyes widened. "Please, Sara —" Sara didn't know — how *could* she know the danger in confronting this man? "Don't . . ." she said again, hearing the plea in her own voice, feeling tears prick her eyes. Sara's face blurred.

"He's stalking you, Megan," Sara said. "You have a right to protection."

You're wrong, Megan thought. *He isn't stalking me, he's watching me.* How could she explain to Sara that his blatant surveillance was far more threatening than a mere obsession? She tried to find the words, but could

2

find none. She trusted Sara as she had trusted nobody else in fifteen years, but she knew that Sara would not — could never — understand.

"At least call the police," Sara said, made impatient by Megan's silence.

"I did, remember? It did no good."

Sara's hand clenched and released. "I just — I'm concerned, Megan, that's all."

Megan knew that Sara believed in due process, in the fairness of the system, the protection afforded by the Law to the weak and defenceless.

Megan said, "I'll telephone tomorrow — talk to the detective." The one who was supposed to be handling her case. An exercise in futility. But who was she to challenge Sara's illusions — of safety, of a fair world in which violent men were brought to justice? Sara had relied on her beliefs for thirty-four years of life. They made her strong; her belief that goodness always had the advantage had given her the confidence to rebuild her life after her husband's slow death from multiple sclerosis. It had given her the courage to follow a career in a male-dominated profession, to allow Megan — a stranger — into her home, and to make a friend of her. Megan would do nothing to injure that confidence, or damage their friendship. "I promise," she said, "I'll talk to him."

Sara released her grip on the door handle and looked into Megan's face. "Don't let fear paralyse you, Megan," she said.

★ ★ ★

3

Megan knew fear; its terrain, its high crags that sparked energy and possibilities as well as its low silt marshes that stranded you, sucking you down and sapping your strength, turning fear to terror. She also knew how to use fear — even welcomed the familiar thrill of accelerated heart rate, the fast fizz of brain activity, the tunnel vision of an adrenalin high. It could work when, close to a breakthrough in the dead hours of night, exhausted beyond sleep, something clicked and the thick pulse of fear and elation screamed at her to go on or lose the chance for ever. At such times, it was this counterpoint between fear and elation that made her complete the arc, follow the logic through, make the connections when the end point proved difficult — even dangerous.

This time, though, fear made her sick and debilitated; dragging her deeper and deeper as she struggled in a quagmire of indecision. She was ready to give up. It had never been like this before. Sure she had been afraid, but in the past, she had evaluated the situation, basing her decision to go on or abandon the project on the balance of risk versus possible reward. Sara was the new factor in the equation. Though too young to act as surrogate mother, Sara had offered Megan her home and her trust, and with it a different view — one more generous than life had previously taught her, one which allowed the possibility of hope, and brought with it the cancer of weakness.

She kept vigil at her window, planning, dreaming, walking through each possible scenario and working out a course of action. Her face, faintly sketched in profile on the glass, was long and serious, the nose thin, delicate. Her dark hair broke like silk at her shoulders. She watched cars pass, the silences between them growing longer; a taxi rattled to a halt a few doors down and three girls tumbled out, laughing, drunk. Foot-passengers, then late-night drinkers, a dog-walker, patiently stopping at every lamp post, waiting while his terrier marked its territory. Finally the clubbers, paired off after the ritual of dance, booze and sweat. Pheromones and testosterone, the perfumes of sexual adventure.

But the watcher did not return.

CHAPTER
TWO

The central office of Safe Hands Security was unusually quiet; it was only a little past ten p.m. and night pick-ups were a feature: Patrick Doran believed in randomising schedules, from cash transport to perimeter checks on low-level premises. It reduced the risk of potential attacks and kept his men from developing sloppy habits. In the general run of things, technicians would use CCTV links to check that delivery and pick-up times were met, that hand-overs were efficiently enacted, and that protocols for signing off consignments were followed to the letter.

Tonight, he had sent the office personnel home. Computer monitors cast a moonlight glow in the open-plan office, and the low-frequency hum, normally imperceptible beneath the constant activity in the room, could be felt as an increase in pressure, a faint, subliminal sound: sea music, whale song. Nathan Wilde, Systems Manager, internet surfer and some-time hacker, a recent graduate in computer science, was used to working in a welter of noise from his MP3 player — techno-rhythms and the anthems of The Grateful Dead. He felt the silence as a void, and under it the dull sub-sonic drone of computers sounded like whispered warnings.

Nathan was joined by John Warrender, head of security, an ex-cop who trusted nobody and missed nothing. Warrender had retired early; he worked out and watched his weight and he was fitter in his mid-fifties than Nathan was in his twenties.

Not that Nathan was fat; a little soft, maybe — all those late-night sessions on the Net and a reliance on internet-prescribed pills to keep him functioning in the daytime. He was average height and build, with a sallow complexion that tended to flush brick-red when embarrassed; he wore his hair short and in waxed spikes.

Neither man spoke, which Nathan noted as a second anomaly: Warrender might not say much, but he did like to assert his position in any situation; generally he did this by asking a series of rapid questions, listening to the answers as though convinced they were a tissue of lies, and only then falling silent. Even before his arrival, they both felt the power of Doran's presence.

They stood outside Doran's office, Nathan, rumpled and glassy-eyed from working twenty hours straight with only caffeine, chemical cocktails and Cadbury mini-rolls to keep him going; Warrender clean-shaven and suited, fresh from the gym.

Doran came in, walking a straight line between the computer stations. If he was worried, he didn't show it. Nathan sensed anger, but could read nothing in his boss's face. Doran glanced at both Nathan and Warrender without speaking, then swiped his card key through the reader with a precision and force that made Nathan flinch.

Doran had the blue eyes and dark hair of the west-coast Irish, though he was born and raised in Liverpool, and had never even visited the mother country. Small, snub-nosed and slight, he looked younger than his forty-five years and could turn on the charm, smoothing the hard edges off his guttural scouse, blurring the "t"s and softening the vowels to a facsimile of his father's Westport accent. The girls in the office loved it; safe in the knowledge that he was a family man, and not one to take advantage of a little gentle flirtation.

He pocketed the key like a magician performing sleight of hand, then turned to his head of security and systems manager, still standing in the doorway of his office.

"Are you waiting for an invitation, or what?" Today, his accent was pure scouse; the words rattled off like hailstones on glass.

They stepped inside, Warrender first. The room was windowless, lit by strip-lights behind frosted glass panels. A dark wood desk took up a third of the room, a bank of CCTV screens occupied one corner — Doran was not a trusting employer.

"We've been hacked," Doran said, the "k" sounded at the back of his throat, like an expectoration. "My business account is wiped out."

Nathan looked at the tops of his Nike air trainers and said nothing.

8

Warrender sucked air through his teeth. "Okay," he said. "It's bad, but not disastrous."

"Well, I'm glad you feel like that, John," Doran said, an undercurrent of threat in the bass notes of his voice. "I was thinking of making up the shortfall out of your salary."

Warrender smiled weakly. "I meant to say that your business account is kept healthy but not flush — so the rest of your funds are safe, yeah?"

Doran watched him for a moment and Nathan, risking a quick glance up from his shoes, saw beads of sweat pop out on the security chief's forehead. While his female employees found Doran a reassuring, even avuncular figure, men received quite different signals. And Warrender, despite his easy authority and physical strength, was not immune.

"My personal accounts are safe," Doran said.

"You're sure about that, are you?" Nathan was horrified to hear his own voice. Doran turned his attention to him and he immediately began what he thought of as the Ritual of the Gibberish: any conversation with Doran always ended this way. "I mean he's in. Like, the system." He puzzled over it for a moment. "Maybe a Trojan, or a back door, but once he's in he's in — he can do . . . whatever — because these guys just like to mess with your head — and if he's got into the business account . . . 'Cos accounts — business, computer, bank — they're all the same, aren't they — I mean in essence?"

Doran waited a few moments. "Finished?" he asked.

Nathan nodded, his head not feeling entirely secure on his neck.

Doran looked at Warrender. "Translation?"

Warrender's eyes slid over Nathan like he was looking at something particularly nasty on the sole of his shoe. "He thinks the hacker can get into your personal accounts because he's got access to the system whenever he wants it, and computer and bank accounts both use the same process: a name and a password or PIN number."

Doran's eyes never left Nathan's face, and Nathan felt dark colour rising into his cheeks. "My personal accounts are not accessible from the business network," Doran said. "My home PC is not linked to the business network. So. Am I safe?"

"Ever use your Visa or Switch card for online purchases?" Nathan asked, forcing more courage into his voice than he felt.

"Not on the business network." Doran's voice was calm, but his eyes looked as deep and dangerous as Pacific waters.

Nathan looked away again. "Ever write to your bank, quoting account details in the text?" It was easier to remain lucid if he didn't have to look at his boss.

Doran had to think about this. "Not from work," he said after a short deliberation. "I always use my home PC."

Nathan nodded. "You're safe — from this guy, anyway."

"Meaning?"

"I can't guarantee immunity from hackers, boss."

"Can we stick to the present problem?" Doran said. "Just for now? How did he get in? You use a firewall, don't you?"

"Yes . . ." This was the one question Nathan dreaded most. The firewall worked on two levels: the first knocked back suspect requests to access the work system just as a bouncer might turn back undesirables at a night club; the second level warned the systems manager that an attempt had been made to breach security — equivalent to the bouncer radioing through to his colleagues to warn of trouble at the door.

Doran heard the hesitation. "Tell me you're operating a firewall," he said.

"Yes, Mr Doran, of course I am. It's just — I altered the config so it doesn't send me pop-up alerts."

Doran closed his eyes for a second. "Look at me, Nathan."

Nathan got a flash of Doran slicing his key card through the reader, like he was slashing the hacker's throat. Or maybe a systems manager who had fucked up and just happened to be close to hand.

Nathan looked at him, but not full-on.

"Do you see a ponytail?" Doran asked.

"No . . ."

"How about a pocket protector for all my multicoloured gel pens?"

"No, boss," Nathan said. *Taking the piss*, he thought. *They always have to take the piss.*

"No ponytail, no pocket protector — and you know why?" Doran waited until Nathan shook his head. "It's because I am not some anorak who might understand your meaningless babble."

Geek, you moron, Nathan thought, impotent rage and humiliation making him flush even more deeply. *I'm not a friggin' anorak, I'm a computer* geek.

"Okay," he said, so offended that he forgot his nerves. "I gave an instruction to the firewall not to bother me with every unauthorized attempt to access the system."

Doran looked ready to rupture something. "You did *what?*"

"We get fifty to a hundred of these attempts every day, boss," Nathan explained "— that's three thousand a month. It's just me and two computer techs dealing with technical problems, spam emails, archiving, tape backups, repairs, the lot."

"Next you'll be telling me you want a pay rise," Doran said.

Now you mention it, Nathan thought, but he knew when to keep his mouth shut.

"I accept you can't check every possible contact," Doran said. "But the firewall is supposed to keep hackers out, isn't it?"

"It recognises known hacker strategies and programs and keeps them out."

"So this was an *unknown* program or strategy."

"Maybe. It could've come in via an email, as a Trojan —"

"We've already had this discussion," Doran said, his face so close that Nathan could see the dark beard hairs beginning to show on Doran's carefully shaved cheeks. "Plain English only. Okay? You got that?"

He must shave twice a day, Nathan thought. *Neanderthal.* The insult, though unspoken, gave him courage. He decided to employ the KISS protocol — Keep It Simple, Stupid. *And you can kiss my lily-white ass, Mr Doran.* "Look at it this way," he said, keeping his tone even and reasonable. "You've been broken into."

"Well I *know* that, don't I?" Doran yelled.

"It's a *metaphor*," Nathan said, feeling a hot surge of answering anger, which he quickly quelled.

"Oh," Doran said, "A *metaphor* . . ." He placed a hand on his breastbone. "You should have said — and there was me, interrupting." He did fall silent, however, even went to the big cabinet behind his desk and poured himself a drink. He didn't offer one to Nathan or Warrender.

"An opportunistic burglar would try a door, find it open, raid the petty cash, grab a few portable items and run," Nathan went on. He was beginning to feel a lot better, and when he heard himself, it was more or less how he sounded in his head, instead of the messed-up crap he usually spouted when the boss got him rattled.

"But I think this guy's more of a planner — a strategist . . ." He saw that he had Doran's attention. "A strategist would sneak in, do a reccy, unlock a few doors, or maybe leave them on the latch, then get out and come back at his leisure to take whatever he wants."

"You're telling me the little shit who's ransacked my accounts left a few doors open so he can come back and do some more damage?" He laughed, and Nathan and Warrender exchanged a nervous glance. "This just keeps getting better." He took a mouthful of whiskey and swallowed it down with a grimace. "Damage limitation?" he asked.

"The surest way would be to shut down the internet connection and call the cops."

Doran looked aghast, but he quickly regained control and turned to his head of security. "Tell him, John," he said.

Warrender folded his arms and stood with his feet slightly apart, as if preparing to give a lecture. "Safe Hands is a security firm," he said, addressing Nathan like he was a particularly dense woodentop on basic training. "If it gets out that we can't protect our own money, how many businesses d'you think will trust us with theirs?"

Nathan swallowed. "Boss, this could be an inside job or it could be someone thousands of miles away — California or the old Soviet state. They could be anywhere on the matrix."

"*The Matrix?*" Doran left a silence during which the air seemed to hum. Then he turned away from Nathan and spoke to Warrender. "I've heard what *Neo* here has to say. What do you suggest?" His voice was so tightly controlled that there was a perceptible pause between each word he uttered.

Warrender thought about it for a few seconds. "Find out exactly which areas have been breached, change the passwords on all accounts — from yours, right down to the receptionist's email account. Close any back doors he's left open and trace the little shit."

"Can you do that, Nathan?"

There was no doubt in Nathan's mind that if he couldn't, Doran would have no qualms about replacing him. "Yes," he said, "but not in that order." He saw a look pass between Doran and his head of security. "We have to trace him first. If I lock him out, he's gonna know, and he'll shut down and ship out. He's not that sophisticated — he's used a pretty obvious exploit to get in —"

"'Exploit'. Is that *university* speak for the bloody gaping hole in my computer security? And if it's that obvious, how come you didn't spot it?"

Nathan smelt the whiskey, fresh and strong on Doran's breath. "There are sixty-five *thousand* ways in, if you know what you're looking for," he said. "But every time one computer connects with another, they exchange addresses in the form of a code number. He's probably tried to hide his, but my guess is this guy is relatively new to the game, so he won't have done it very well. I can trace him, give you a physical location in minutes."

"A street name and number?" Doran said, putting his drink down and looking at Nathan with new respect.

Nathan shook his head. "A city."

"Fuck." Doran snatched up his drink again and sat in the chair behind his desk.

"The point is," Nathan went on, determined to finish. "If I have his IP address — his computer code number —" he corrected quickly, "— I can hack *his* computer. That means I can get into every file, folder and document on his system. Like walking into an office with the keys to all the filing cabinets."

"Can you get my money back?"

"Maybe. If he's used internet banking I can try to crack his username and password."

"Never mind." Doran ran his fingers through his hair. "Find him for me, I'll beat the password out of him myself."

Nathan didn't doubt it. "If he's left any data on file with a home address on it — an email, a letter, anything — I'll find him."

"You'd better," Doran said.

CHAPTER
THREE

"God!" Sara Geddes slammed into the house, elbowing the front door closed against a gust of icy spring rain. "Mr Justice Partington-flaming-Jessop," she exclaimed, shedding her briefcase, shoulder bag, gloves, scarf and overcoat in a clatter of noise. "I could strangle him with his own sash, I swear!" In court, Sara was everything that could be expected of a court clerk, respectful, efficient, discreet, low-key; but that was a persona she shed with her dark suit and sensible shoes every evening.

The coffee machine gurgled in the kitchen and the house was filled with the nutty aroma of coffee. She kicked off her shoes, wriggled her toes into the carpet pile, and listened. Faintly, from Megan's office at the front of the house, she heard music: Fountains of Wayne — Megan's current musical passion. Sara padded up the stairs, talking all the way. "Four hours to empanel a jury, two more discussing evidence the defence weren't even intending to contest; then he starts the hearing at three-thirty, only to adjourn after barely half an hour. And he wants *me* to —"

She popped her head around the open door of Megan's office, her fair hair swinging across her face.

The room was empty. The band played "Hey, Julie", a song about an office worker with a tyrannical boss. "How appropriate," she muttered. Megan's computer monitor displayed a pretty good imitation of a tropical fish tank; the only other furniture was a sofa bed and a bookcase containing a few computer manuals and paperbacks, science fiction and technothrillers, mostly.

Sara turned and looked over her shoulder as if she might have passed her friend on the landing without noticing.

"Megan?" She knocked at Megan's bedroom door and eased it open, ready to apologise if she was intruding. The bed was made, the room neat and rather blank and bare-looking, as it always was.

The bathroom. Sara walked down the landing. The door stood open and the room was cool and dry; it looked like it hadn't been used since that morning. *She probably stepped out for some air*, Sara told herself. All the same, she felt a shiver of apprehension. The band moved on to a slower, more mournful tune, as Sara hurried downstairs and rummaged through her shoulder bag for her mobile phone, pressing the speed dial number for Megan's phone. A recorded message told her that it was switched off. She walked through to the kitchen, hoping to find a note on the kitchen table: perhaps she'd got a lucky break on the story she was researching and had to go out at short notice. The coffee-maker glugged, hissed and spat, then fell silent.

Sara stared at the machine. Freshly brewed for when she got home; it had become a kind of tradition during the six months Megan had rented rooms from her:

coffee, chat, then a glass of wine while they made dinner together.

A fresh gust of sleety rain blatted the house, rattling the kitchen door. It swung open, letting in a draught of cold air. Sara steadied herself against a falling sensation. Megan was gone.

CHAPTER
FOUR

Detective Sergeant Lee Foster was in a good mood. The sun was shining — at least for now. He had a clear desk and a clear head and all seemed right with the world. He strolled down the corridor, whistling, planning the next evening's enjoyment.

Detective Chief Inspector Jeff Rickman opened his office door as Foster passed, and invited him in. He was a little more lined and a half-stone lighter than the previous autumn, but essentially the same: quiet, a thinker, an observer.

"You seem cheery," Rickman said, motioning Foster to a chair.

Foster ignored it, folding his arms and leaning against the filing cabinet crammed in one corner of the room instead. "Got lucky last night," he said, grinning widely.

Rickman looked surprised. "Hart?" Naomi Hart's determined rejection was a source of real pain to Foster, though he would never admit it.

Foster blew air between his lips. "My manhood would shrivel and drop off waiting for the Ice Queen to come to her senses." He pronounced "my" as "me", and his scouse accent gave a rasp to his voice. "Now that new civilian computer operator is a much warmer prospect —"

"Spare me the details," Rickman picked up a pink flimsy from his desk and handed it to Foster.

"MisPer?" he read. "What d'you want me to do with this?"

"I want you to investigate it, Lee," Rickman said.

"She's only been missing fourteen hours," Foster said. "Maybe I wasn't the only one got lucky last night. She probably just stayed the night."

Rickman traced the line of his eyebrow, pausing at a scar that bisected it. "You really don't think of anything else, do you?"

Foster looked hurt. "Fair dooz, now," he said. "There's footy and ale — I care about them an' all."

"Megan Ward," Rickman said. "Twenty-five. Freelance investigative journalist. Tenant of the informant, Sara Geddes, a highly valued official at Liverpool Crown Court. The DCS has already had a call from Justice Partington-Jessop; apparently Miss Geddes is distraught — didn't turn up for work this morning."

Foster rolled his eyes. "So we're gonna waste resources looking for some soppy bint who'll turn up by teatime with a daft grin on her face, just because Justice Hyphen-Hyphen can't get a decent brew?"

"You can't judge everyone by your standards, Lee," Rickman said, frowning, though his hazel eyes gleamed with amusement. "Miss Geddes says that Megan Ward was being stalked."

Foster took a breath. "Okay, but you could've told me that before." Since the inception of the Protection

From Harassment Act in 1997, accusations of stalking were taken far more seriously. He folded the slip and pocketed it.

"It's further complicated by the fact that Miss Geddes says that the police ignored her tenant's concerns."

"Has she put in a formal complaint?" Foster asked.

"Keith Norton's dealing with it. Miss Geddes came in to give a statement earlier," Rickman said. "I had a quick word with her, and she's prepared to allow an informal resolution provided the investigation is given due weight from here on in." Rickman's face bore a few battle scars, and his nose had once been broken and never properly reset; at six-four, he towered over some of the newer intake. The hard men of Liverpool's criminal world were intimidated by him, but women responded warmly to Rickman, reassured by his aura of strength and gentleness. He had laid out the options to Miss Geddes and she had trusted him to do what was necessary to make sure nothing like it happened again.

"Take Naomi Hart with you," Rickman said.

Foster was already out of the door, but he took two steps back, his face a complex mixture of horror and incredulity. "You're winding me up, right?"

"Stalking, missing woman — Hart might be able to get more out of Miss Geddes than you."

"Meaning I'm tactless."

"You won't get any argument here." Rickman smiled. "But in this instance, it's insurance. Investigative journalists have been known to pull the odd stunt. You need to be aware that this could be a journo in search of a story: 'police insensitivity to stalker victim', that kind of thing."

"Well, okay," Foster said with a martyred look. "I'll take Naomi. But she's gonna smell it on me."

Rickman raised his eyebrows. "You know, it's a mystery how Hart could ever turn you down — a man of your obvious style and sophistication . . ."

Foster walked away laughing.

He called DC Hart from his office and gave her the abridged version. She was on her way back to base after attending a house burglary. She knocked at Foster's door as soon as she got in.

Foster opened it with one hand, holding the phone with the other. He had his feet on his desk and a notepad in his lap. He waved her inside, still talking into the receiver. His "office" was a small airless box, but Foster had a fan whirring quietly in one corner.

He finished his call and hung up.

"All right, Naomi?"

She noticed his appreciative look. Hart was a tall, confident blonde, and men noticed her; she was aware of it, but didn't dwell on it — it wasn't her problem. "Aren't you cold?" she asked. She'd had to dash across the car park in a sudden hail shower.

"I'm the outdoorsy type," Foster said. "I like some air movement. And anyway, it gets fuggy in here."

Hart found that hard to believe. Foster looked as fresh as usual, his dark hair glossy and sculpted into fashionable spikes. He was smooth-shaven and he smelled wonderful. She couldn't quite identify the cologne — Cool Water, maybe — light and not too spicy.

"Thanks for coming straight up," he said.

"Sounds intriguing."

"Probably a waste of time and energy," Foster said. "But it's the chance of getting the odd interesting bone to gnaw at makes the job bearable."

"Never had you pegged as a philosopher," Hart said.

"I'm full of surprises, me." He tore a leaf from his notebook, swung his feet off the desk and stood up, folding the piece of paper and slipping it in his pocket, next to the pink slip. Foster was lean and well-muscled, though not exceptionally tall; in her flat work shoes, Hart met him eye to eye. His were a searing cobalt, and many had fallen for his striking baby-blues, but his secret weapon was what women personnel called The Smile. He used it now, though Hart had proved immune for so long that she wondered why he persisted.

"You don't know what you're missing, Naomi," he said, reading her mind.

"That's kind of comforting," Naomi said. The corner of her mouth twitched.

Foster shot her a sharp look, but she caught an amused twinkle behind it. "The main thing is, the boss doesn't think it's a waste of time," he said.

"Who *is* the SIO?" Hart asked. "DCI Hinchcliffe?"

"DCI Rickman," Foster said, holding the door for her.

"*Rickman?*"

24

He let the door swing shut again. "What does that mean, 'Rickman'?"

Hart heard the note of warning in his voice. This was the time to be careful around Foster. His loyalty to Rickman had achieved almost mythical status, and rumours abounded as to the reasons behind it.

"Nothing, Sarge," she said, unconsciously pulling herself up to her full height. "I just didn't think he was working" — she shrugged, embarrassed — "proper investigations," she finished feebly.

"Think he's not up to the job, Hart?"

"I never said that."

"But the rumour mill has been running at full production, yeah?" The crux of most of the gossip was that Rickman had lost it since the previous autumn. "What version have you heard?" he asked.

Hart avoided his eye. "Just that he was doing a lot of committee work — planning and advisory stuff."

"Is that all?" Foster said, "Haven't you heard the one where he was suspended from duty after a drunken brawl with a superior officer?"

Hart flushed, wishing to God she'd kept her big mouth shut.

"How about the latest? He's been shoved sideways into education and school liaison?"

"Sarge, I didn't mean to —"

"To what, Naomi? Kick a man when he's down?"

"Look," Hart said. "I've got nothing against Rickman. I *liked* working with him. He was a good boss, but you've got to admit he hasn't been around much since . . . what happened — and I didn't expect to hear his name. That's all."

Foster didn't speak for half a minute, and Hart felt nervous sweat on her forehead. When Foster finally broke the silence, it seemed he had decided that she was telling the truth. He nodded to himself, then said, "He took personal leave. Now he's back. That's all anyone needs to know."

On the rare occasions that Foster was serious, Hart found herself liking him. Really liking him — not just as a colleague, but as a man.

She met his gaze. "Understood," she said.

He opened the door and waved her through. "This is between you and me, right?"

"About the DCI?" Hart asked, confused.

"About the fan," Foster said, closing the door firmly behind him. "I went to a lot of trouble — did stuff I'm not proud of to get the damn thing — and I don't want some light-fingered bastard sneaking in here and robbing it."

CHAPTER
FIVE

Sara Geddes opened her front door in a quick, decisive sweep, as if half expecting her friend to be standing outside.

She hasn't slept, Hart thought. Miss Geddes looked neat in her grey wool trousers and burnt-orange cashmere sweater; her honey-blonde hair was carefully tied back and she had even dabbed on a little make-up, but there was no mistaking the dark smudges under her eyes and the slight wince as she blinked in bright daylight.

"Miss Geddes? Detective Constable Hart." She nodded to Foster. "And this is Detective Sergeant Foster."

Sara looked from their warrant cards to their faces, matching the photos to the two people on her doorstep. Only when she was entirely satisfied did she let them in.

The hall was wide, and its warmth welcome after the chilly April sunshine. A long mirror with a beaten metal surround had been hung above the radiator; gunmetal grey and warm bronze. She led them to the front sitting-room and Hart realised that the juxtaposing of warm colours and hard lines was something of a theme.

The walls of the room were stark white but they were hung with abstract paintings; the largest was in aubergine and lilac, relieved by beige and cream. A rivulet of silver metal ran from left to right, thick and globular, smooth as solder. There were four more, in a range of colours and styles, three large, one small.

"Your own work?" Hart asked.

"Yes." Sara Geddes frowned. "Can we get on with this?"

Hart understood. This was a woman used to dealing with the police, she had no need for reassurance, and she had no time for small talk.

"Have you spoken to Detective Constable Frinton?" Sara asked.

Hart looked at Foster. "The officer investigating the stalking allegations," he explained. "Not in our remit, Miss Geddes. You'll hear in due course from Inspector Norton."

Sara considered this for a moment, then nodded. "All right. What do you need to know?"

"Let's start with the approximate time of Miss Ward's disappearance."

Sara glanced at the wall behind them, as though picturing the scene, her green eyes a little clouded. "The coffee had just finished brewing as I came in," she said. "That takes about ten minutes — she always has it ready for when I come home. I'd say she disappeared no more than ten minutes before I arrived, and that was at six p.m."

The contradictions of hard and soft, warmth and hard edges that Hart had seen in her artwork were, it seemed, reflections of the woman herself: she was evidently concerned for Megan Ward, had spent a sleepless night waiting up for her, and yet she was able to present a calm analysis of the facts.

"Could we see her room?" Hart asked.

"Rooms," Sara corrected her. "Megan has converted one for use as an office — she uses the smaller room as her bedroom."

They followed her up the stairs. "You say she's an investigative journalist?" Hart said.

"Freelance. I don't know what she was working on currently."

More of Sara's paintings decorated the walls in the stairwell and on the landing; oils, acrylics, even a collage which seemed to be made from left-over pieces of bronze and steel that made up the mirror frame in the hallway. By contrast, Megan's bedroom was as bare as a nun's cell. The bed was neatly made and there was no clothing on view — not even a pair of shoes or a discarded sock. No make-up or perfumes on the dresser, no paperbacks on the bedside table.

"Did she take all her stuff?" Foster asked.

Sara Geddes went to the wardrobe tucked into an alcove next to the chimney breast and opened the door. Blouses at one end, trousers and skirts at the other, boots and shoes lined up neatly on the floor of the cupboard. "It's all here," she said.

"When did she move in?" Hart asked, riffling through the clothing, not sure what she was hoping to find.

"Just under six months ago," Sara said. "She took the rooms in October."

"Not much to show." There was a curious absence of personal detail in this, a woman's most personal room. No photographs, no knick-knacks, no magazines; the only picture was one of Sara's abstracts in shades of yellow and blue above Megan's bed.

"She moved around a lot," Sara said. "She never really had the opportunity to put down roots."

Foster was behind Sara, checking through a chest of drawers to the right of the window. He glanced over and Hart acknowledged the look with the barest flicker. This seemed more and more like a set-up by the minute. Foster returned to his search and Hart began a thorough scan of the room, looking for places where a camera or microphone might be hidden.

"Bingo." Foster brought a faded shoebox from the bottom drawer of the dresser. He placed it on the bed, lifted the lid and carefully sifted through the contents with gloved hands.

"Do you know what this is?" Hart asked.

Sara Geddes shook her head. "I've never seen it before."

The box contained a random collection of bus and rail tickets, a couple of programmes for pop concerts, pull-outs from magazines, ticket stubs for various attractions. There was a prefect's badge, birthday badges, a butterfly hair-grip, a penknife and one six-by-four photograph.

"She was in care?" Foster said.

"For a short time, after her mother died," Sara said. "How did you —?"

"Kids in care get shunted around a lot," Foster said. "They've all got a little box of treasures like this — gives them a connection with the past. With home."

Hart eyed him curiously, but Foster moved on. "Is this her?" The photograph pictured a family group: mother and two children, the boy about fifteen years of age, the girl maybe five years old.

Sara studied the group. "It could be . . . She has the same colouring, the same fine features."

"Did she mention a brother?" Hart asked.

"Mm," Sara said, still distracted by the photograph. "He died."

"The father?"

"She doesn't remember him. He was killed in an accident on an oil rig when she was quite young."

"The Missing Persons Helpline has software that can age-up a photo," Hart suggested.

Foster tapped the photograph against the side of the box and after a moment's consideration dropped it back inside and closed the lid. "We've got an artist on hand," he said, smiling at Sara. "You must've done a sketch or portrait of her at some time or other."

"Yes." There was something in her tone that Hart couldn't identify. "I'm not sure it will be of any use to you."

She showed them through to Megan's office. It looked as if Megan had packed her belongings in a hurry, leaving a few unimportant items behind.

"This is . . .?" Foster began.

"How it always looks," Sara confirmed, looking sadly at the largely empty bookshelves.

"There's *nothing* missing?"

Sara's eyes skimmed the room. "I didn't come in here often. It was her work place, I didn't like to —" She stopped, checked again. "Her laptop —" She pointed to the bookshelves. "She normally keeps it there if she's not using it."

Hart was puzzled. "So she left — or was taken — within minutes of your arrival, leaving everything else but her laptop?"

"Her work is everything to her," Sara said. "If she had to clear out, she'd make damn sure she took her research."

"And you don't know what this research was?"

"I've already told you that." Sara was used to the cross-examination techniques of barristers, she wouldn't be so easy to trip up as the average witness.

"Was she a good payer?"

Sara frowned at Foster. "Payer?"

"Did she pay her rent on time?"

She eyed him coldly. "Always."

"'Cos freelance journos, irregular income . . ." He shrugged, palms up.

"*Always*," Sara repeated, fixing him with a glare that could melt steel.

"You spent evenings together," Hart said, drawing her attention from Foster. "Was she ever prone to mood swings? Did she seem overly anxious?"

"She was worried about the man who was following her, naturally — so was I."

32

"She's been here, what — six months?" Foster said. "You must've got to know her well. Was she —?" He broke off. "Did you ever worry about her . . ."

Hart saw that he was struggling for a suitably politically correct word. "Did you worry about her stability," she said. "Her mental state."

Sara straightened, looking from Foster to Hart with frank contempt. "You botched Megan Ward's complaint of stalking," she said. "So now you're trying to imply that she imagined it?"

"We're exploring all possibilities, Miss Geddes," Hart said.

"Except the very real possibility that Megan is in danger."

They were losing ground fast, and if there were recording devices in the house, they were going to come out of it looking very bad. Hart looked Miss Geddes in the eye; she was a woman used to rules of evidence, balanced arguments. She was analytical and, despite her evident dissatisfaction with the police's involvement to date, Hart felt she was a reasonable woman, too.

"People go missing for all sorts of reasons," Hart began. "Top of the list is family conflict — now you ruled that particular scenario out when you told us that Miss Ward has no family. Other factors are debt, substance abuse, stress, depression and mental illness." She saw Sara absorbing all of this, matching their questions to the relevant statistic. "Abduction might be the most feared, but it's also the least likely."

Sara seemed to be wrestling with some emotion; at first Hart thought it was anger — she was frightened,

33

and frightened people often felt the need to lash out —
but then Hart saw something glisten in the woman's
eye. She turned away and lifted a canvas down from the
wall.

"Megan," she said. The painting was done in
acrylics, the colours reminiscent of water and misty
light. Through milky greys and blues an occasional
flash of bright gold and red, like shafts of light, gashes
of blood.

Foster held the painting in his hands, a look of
surprised amusement in his face. "Not something you
could put on *Crimewatch*, is it?"

Sara smiled, even laughed a little. It came out in a
rush, as if she had been holding her breath; there were
tears in it, and rising panic. She seemed to catch herself
and made a visible effort to regain control. "I'll sketch
her for you," she said.

"I don't suppose you ever saw the man Megan said
was stalking her?" Hart asked.

"Once . . ." Sara frowned, evidently trying to recall
the details of his face, his height and built. "It was dark.
I could give you an impression."

"So long as it's got eyes and a nose where you'd
expect them to be," Foster said, squinting at the
painting of Megan. He glanced up at Sara, tried his
confused puppy smile on her, and it worked. She
positively beamed back at him.

"I'll go and make a start," she said.

"Before you do —" Sara stopped and turned to
Hart. "Do you know if Megan ever got any emails from
this guy?"

34

It was strange to see doubt and confusion on Sara's face. "I don't know. I'm sorry — I should have asked." She focused again on something slightly to Hart's left. "She did say that someone had got past her firewall, if that means anything." She closed the door behind her and they listened to her footsteps retreating down the landing.

Hart and Foster exchanged a look: people thought it was safe to talk behind a closed door. Had Sara closed it to give them privacy, or to give the illusion of privacy?

Foster shrugged. "What d'you think?" he asked, deliberately making the question ambiguous. For every action that had helped to persuade them that Sara Geddes was genuine, she performed another that made her look suspicious.

Hart sighed and shrugged. "Worth asking Technical Support to take a look?" She left him to decide whether she meant that they should check out the computer equipment for emails from Megan's stalker, or the room for bugging devices.

Foster got it. He smiled and said with equal ambiguity, "Can't hurt."

"Do we need to get clearance from the boss?" Hart asked.

"Nah — I'm making an executive decision," Foster said. "Let's see what this sucker's got to hide." He moved toward the computer system with a determined gleam in his eye.

Alarmed, Hart cleared her throat. It was enough to stop Foster in his tracks. He turned back to her, puzzled and a little impatient. Hart punched a number and spoke into her mobile, "Technical support?" she said, raising her eyebrows as she spoke. *Are you with me, Sarge?* From the look on his face, she guessed that he wasn't, but he was canny enough to keep quiet.

"DC Hart, Edge Hill Police Station," she continued. "I need some advice on treatment of computer evidence."

Thirty minutes later, the back seat of their fleet car was stacked with computer components bagged and labelled separately. They had also taken the box of memorabilia, but they found no disks, CDs, notes, diaries or passwords among Megan's personal effects.

"Thanks," Foster said, taking the last bundle of bagged leads.

"For what?"

"For not making me look like a total dickhead over this lot."

"No problem." There were protocols for gathering computer evidence, and the slightest deviation from procedure could destroy evidence or mean that it was rejected by forensic examiners.

Hart leaned her arms on the roof of the car and looked across at him. "You did do the seminar?" she asked, genuinely curious.

"Yeah."

"Were you even awake?"

"Daydreaming." The corner of Foster's mouth twitched. "About you."

Hart narrowed her eyes at him. He just never gave up. "It bothers me, there's no backup disks or notes, though," she said.

"Maybe she took them with her."

"Or somebody nicked them — people keep usernames and passwords close by their computer as a rule," Hart said. "Unless she's hidden them in the paperbacks or manuals . . ."

She took a couple of fresh evidence bags from the boot of the car and made her way back inside. Sara came out of a room at the back of the house as Hart reached the bottom of the stairs with the bags full of books.

"Megan," Sara said, tearing off a sheet from an A4 sketch pad.

Hart set one of the bags down on the hall floor and took the sketch. Megan had long hair, dark and straight; Sara had given it a glossy sheen. The face was attractive — a little long, perhaps, but the eyes were dark and luminous and the mouth full, suggesting sensitivity and perhaps vulnerability.

"Thanks," she said. "This will help. We found no passport or driver's licence." She posed this as a question.

"She always carries them with her," Sara said.

"What kind of car does she drive?"

Sara shook her head. "Something sporty. Silver. I'm not terribly good with cars. She bought it just after Christmas."

Hart looked again at the sketch. They didn't have much. "The stalker," she said. "Did you —?"

Sara tore off a second sheet. "It's not very helpful, I'm afraid."

The man was viewed from above. He was muscular, and he leaned forward on the balls of his feet, as though preparing for attack, but his face was a featureless shadow; for the purposes of identification, the sketch was useless.

"Not to worry," Hart said. "If you think of anything that might help, if Megan contacts you — or if the man appears again — call me, anytime." She handed Sara a business card with her mobile and direct line numbers, together with her email address.

Sara nodded, suddenly looking frightened and tearful, as if this small detail had made her friend's disappearance seem more real.

"Anytime," Hart emphasised.

Sara nodded again, unable to make eye contact, and Hart felt unhappy about leaving her alone in this big house, worried for her friend, and with the possibility of a stalker hanging around the place.

"If the stalker shows up, note the time. Dial this number, or the main switchboard, quoting the case number I gave you." Having some positive contribution to make to an enquiry often made people feel less helpless.

Sara Geddes looked into her face, understanding what she was trying to do. She offered Hart her hand. "Thank you," she said.

"Well, Naomi," Foster said as she got into the car. "You seem to have made a good impression. Think she bats for the other side?"

Hart sucked her teeth. "We shook hands, Sarge. And if you're suggesting that I must 'bat for the other side' because I turned you down —"

"Woah!" Foster exclaimed. "Pause and rewind there, girl. I never meant nothing by it. You know me, I just engage my mouth before my brain's in gear sometimes. Talking of which —" He slotted the key in the ignition and fired up the engine. "But say them two did have a — thing. They might've had a lover's tiff and Megan stormed off."

"Sara isn't gay," Hart said, amused.

Foster pulled away from the kerb, checking the rear view mirror. "How d'you work that one out?"

"For one thing, she's wearing a wedding ring on her third finger, right hand. I think she's a widow."

Foster glanced at her. "Doesn't mean she's not —"

"For another, she was taken in by the Foster charm." Foster frowned at her. "'So long as it's got eyes and a nose where you'd expect them to be'," Hart quoted, with a grotesque imitation of Foster's sad-puppy smile.

CHAPTER
SIX

Naomi Hart dragged her fingers through her hair and tugged at her shirt hem in an effort to smooth out some of the wrinkles. She knocked at DCI Rickman's door just as Foster turned the corner.

"Come in." Rickman's voice sounded strong and confident and she was encouraged. DS Foster hadn't been exaggerating: some of the gossip made Rickman out to be a gibbering wreck.

She stepped inside, followed by Foster. The DCI's office was only marginally larger than the sergeant's but it did have the benefit of a window, admitting the mingled sounds of afternoon traffic and the shouts and laughter of children playing in the yard of the day care centre nearby. Rickman rolled up some blueprints he had spread out on his desk and straightened up. His height was emphasised by the cramped conditions. His chestnut-brown hair looked slightly ruffled, as though he'd been running his fingers through it as he worked, and it was a little shorter than she recalled. It made him look vulnerable, despite his size.

"Sir." Hart's stance and tone were formal and respectful.

Rickman leaned across his desk and offered his hand. "Good to see you again, Naomi. You did some excellent work on the investigation last autumn."

Hart smiled, surprised he had remembered — there must have been fifty or more officers working that investigation. She was equally surprised that he'd mentioned the case at all, given its terrible outcome. He looked well, perhaps a touch thinner than when she had last seen him in November of the previous year, but that was understandable. The weight loss emphasised the sharp angles of his features and this, together with the warm hazel of his eyes, gave him a foreign, almost aristocratic look. He was a bit too bashed about for her taste, though: the bad set of his nose, broken in childhood, and the many nicks and scars on his face detracted from the Germanic nobility of his appearance.

"Sit down," Rickman said. "Let's hear what you've got."

Hart took the chair nearest the window, the cool, scented gusts on the back of her neck a welcome respite from the recycled fug of the building's air conditioning. Foster took up position by the filing cabinet, to her right and slightly behind her.

"I did an internet search," Hart said. "The only Megan Ward I found is a film star — and definitely not our Megan." They had divided the work between them, Hart on the computer, Foster working the phone. "Then I tried individual newspapers and Lexis-Nexis — her by-line doesn't appear anywhere."

"So," Rickman said. "Not a journalist."

Hart shrugged. "I suppose it could be her first big story — regional papers don't always allow cub reporters a by-line. But she did give Sara Geddes the impression that she was established as a freelance."

"I've had no luck, either," Foster said. "The DVLA gave me an address for a Megan Ward in Norwich. I faxed them Sara's sketch. The landlord says it could be her, but she moved out six months ago. No forwarding address."

"What about her car?" Rickman asked.

"The DVLA are gonna get back to me."

"If she hasn't changed the details on her driver's licence, she probably gave her old address anyway," Hart said.

Rickman nodded. "But at least we'd have a make, model and ID number to look for."

"Could we put Sara's sketch out on the regional news?" Hart asked.

Rickman tilted his head. "What if she doesn't want to be found? She's a right to her privacy and she's done nothing illegal."

"Do we know that?" The exchange felt like an interview: both men sizing her up, judging her reaction to Rickman, seeing if they could work with her, and Hart was determined to make an impression.

"I checked with NCIS," Foster said. "No previous form."

"Okay." Rickman folded his arms. "My turn. Inspector Norton has concluded his investigation into the alleged stalking incident —"

His phone rang, interrupting him. Rickman picked up and spoke a few words to the caller, then looked up at Hart and Foster. "You should hear this," he said. "Hold on, Tony, I've got Lee Foster and Naomi Hart with me now. I'm putting you on speaker phone. Tony Mayle," Rickman told them. Mayle was a senior investigator and crime scene co-ordinator with the Scientific Support Unit. "You're on, Tony," he said.

"I've just heard from Technical Support," Mayle's voice sounded grainy and muffled. "The data on Miss Ward's computer is corrupted."

Hart and Foster stared in horror at the machine. "No way!" Hart burst out. "We followed their instructions to the letter."

"Hold on." Mayle was an ex-cop; he knew how procedural cock-ups were viewed from both sides of the divide. Right now, he sounded conciliatory. "It's nothing you did or did not do. We think there was some sort of logic bomb embedded in the hard drive."

Foster looked at Hart, his eyebrows raised.

"Don't look at me, Sarge," she said. "I haven't the foggiest."

"It's a program," Mayle explained. "Very difficult to detect. Computers have an internal clock; if the system isn't accessed within a set time by the designated user, the logic bomb is triggered, destroying or overwriting all data."

Foster gave a low whistle. "She wrecked her own computer?"

"It may have been set up to protect sensitive data," Mayle said. "If you can't get to your machine — say it's stolen — the data's protected."

"It's a bit drastic, isn't it?"

"Not if you back up your files regularly," Mayle said.

"So she could have hidden files somewhere?"

"It's possible."

Hart shook her head. "We searched the place top to bottom."

"She could have taken the back-ups with her," Mayle said.

"Are you sure she planted this logic bomb?" Hart asked. "She thought someone had hacked into her system."

"Then they could just as easily have planted it."

"Is there any way of checking?" Rickman asked.

They heard a long sigh at the other end of the line. "There's bugger-all left *to* check, Jeff. A few fragments, maybe, in amongst the alphabet soup the bomb made of the files. But we'd have to find them first, and that could take months."

"Not worth it," Rickman said. "Thanks, Tony." He broke the connection. "Other lines of enquiry?" he asked.

"Her manuals and paperbacks," Hart said, feeling limp and disappointed. The computer equipment represented their best source of information about Megan, now all they had were a few dusty books. "Oh," she added, suddenly remembering. "And her box of treasures."

"Mementoes," Foster explained. "Miss Geddes says Megan was in care for a while. Didn't she say something about Megan's dad working on the oil rigs? I could check that out."

Rickman lifted his chin. "It might give us a family address, relatives, friends." He paused a moment. "But this is looking more like she walked away of her own accord: she lied about being a journo — which removes one major risk factor. Give it another day or two, then we shelve this one."

"What about the stalker, sir?" Hart asked.

"Oh," Rickman said. "I was about to tell you before Tony Mayle phoned. Inspector Norton has concluded there was no complaint. There's no record of a complaint being made in Megan's name: no report reference, nothing logged with Calls and Response. And this is the clincher — there is no DC Frinton on the Merseyside force."

"She made him up?" Hart said.

"Who d'you mean — Megan or Sara Geddes?" Foster asked.

"I'm not sure." Hart was stupefied; Sara had seemed so plausible, but if DC Frinton was a fabrication, maybe the stalker was — maybe Sara had even dreamed up Megan. "But I'll find out," she said, a flush of anger rising into her face. "I'll catch her before she leaves court."

Foster lingered after Hart had gone.

Rickman stared at the door, as if he could see her walking down the corridor. "What d'you think?" asked.

Foster lifted one shoulder. "I think Sara's a few cards short of the full deck."

"Don't be obtuse, Lee," Rickman said. "You know damn well who I mean."

"Naomi," Foster said, folding his arms.

Rickman's career had looked shaky since last autumn. At first, it didn't matter; at first, the major challenge was simply to get through each day. Now, he found it mattered a lot. His first major investigation in four months could make or break him. Which meant he needed people around him he could trust.

"She's listened to the Chinese whispers like everyone else," Foster said. "But she respects you and she liked working with you last time."

"I take it you didn't tell her I'm only covering for DCI Hinchcliffe's absence?"

Foster looked vague. "It didn't come up."

Rickman smiled. "Thanks." He could always rely on Foster to play a close hand.

"You're the boss, Jeff," he said with a shrug. "If I was the boss, I'd never explain myself."

Which was one reason why Foster would never rise above the rank of sergeant. There were compensatory aspects to his character, however, as Rickman had discovered over and over in the last year. Up until the events of the previous autumn they shared an office for two years, and had known each other for a while longer than that. It had taken him all that time to even begin to understand the true nature of Lee Foster, and even now, Rickman knew that this understanding was imperfect.

46

"When are you expecting the family?" Foster asked.

Rickman's heart gave a little jump. He had lived for twenty-five years with no family, and the discovery that he had a sister-in-law and two nephews was recent enough for it still to sneak up on him and poke him in the ribs if he wasn't ready for it.

"I'm picking Tanya and the boys up from the airport at six," Rickman said.

"They staying long?"

"Three weeks — right through the Easter holidays."

"They finish early — Liverpool schools are still in."

"Advantages of a private education," Rickman said. "They're staying with me." This represented a step forward, a development of trust and affection between them.

"Cosy." Foster said, with a big, vulpine grin. "You be sure and give Tanya a big kiss from me."

Rickman shot him a warning look.

"You're not telling me you haven't noticed what a cracker she is."

Rickman's gaze did not waver and Foster, embarrassed, slapped both knees with his palms and got hurriedly to his feet. "Reckon I'll hit the phones, Boss — can't leave it all to Naomi, can I?"

CHAPTER
SEVEN

The afternoon session was drawing to a close as Naomi Hart drove into the car park adjacent to Chavasse Park. The road surface was rough limestone hardcore and her tyres slewed a little as she made the turn too fast. She ran for the courts as a passing cloud cast a shadow over the building, staining the maroon concrete the colour of blood.

"Bugger," she muttered, feeling the first drops of icy rain on her face. She had hoped to avoid a drenching from the frequent showers that gusted across the Mersey. A two-hundred-yard sprint left her only slightly breathless and she pushed through the revolving doors into the foyer as the first wave of court rooms was beginning to empty. She checked her watch: three forty-five — early adjournments and Pleas and Directions, given their next court date and then dismissed. She hurried through the security checks, scanning the faces beyond the barrier; a reflex after ten years in the job. She saw relief on some, anger and disappointment on others; grief, too. The smokers moved with grim purpose towards the exit leading to the cold windswept plaza of Derby Square, anxious for their first hit of nicotine in hours.

Hart showed her warrant card at the enquiries desk and asked where Sara Geddes might be. She was in luck: the court was still in session. She slipped into one of the bench seats to the left of the court room, quickly locating Sara, sitting with her back to the judge, at one of the desks below the bench. The corridors and waiting areas were drab brown, and many of the courts shabby, the fold-down seats grey and threadbare, but this court had been refurbished with bright, honeyed wood and pink upholstery.

The defendant sat fidgeting in the dock at right angles to the viewing gallery, uncomfortable in a suit and tie. The jury shot furtive glances in his direction as the prosecution barrister gently questioned the key witness, a girl of no more than eighteen years. The left side of the girl's face was badly scarred, a lightning-bolt of livid tissue traced a line from her eye socket to the edge of her upper lip. The skin around it looked raised, almost quilted by the injury. The jury found it harder still to look at her than at the restless boy, tugging at his collar.

Sara looked all business; she was dressed soberly in a dark suit and her hair was tied back in a ponytail. Without the softening layers of blonde hair over her cheekbones, her jaw looked even more determined, perhaps even masculine. Over the suit she wore a black robe and clerical collar. There was a severity in her court persona that had been absent when Hart had first met her.

She saw Hart and her eyes widened. She lifted her chin in silent question and Hart shook her head. *No news*. Sara glanced at her watch and Hart saw a flush of impatience rise into the woman's face. By the time the prosecution had finished his examination of the witness and the judge had dismissed her for the day, Sara was visibly quivering. Another five minutes was taken up with decisions about running order for the next day, the recall of witnesses not yet examined and a stern admonition from the judge to members of the jury not to speak of what they had seen or heard to anyone but fellow jurors.

The court was finally adjourned at ten past four and Sara could barely contain herself long enough for the judge to leave the room before hurrying over to DC Hart.

"Has something happened?" she demanded, two bands of high colour staining her cheeks.

"Have you spoken to Inspector Norton?" Hart said in answer.

"I've been in court all afternoon."

Hart deliberated: it wasn't really her place to give this news, but she was here now, and she wanted answers. "Megan didn't lodge a complaint of stalking," she said.

Sara stared at her. "That's impossible."

"Is it?" Hart looked into Sara's face, trying to detect any hint of dissembling.

"A man was watching Megan," Sara insisted. "He was watching the house for days. She saw him — *I* saw him."

"Did you?"

"What the hell are you implying?"

A couple of heads turned; Hart returned their stares calmly and when they looked away, she studied Sara with the same composure. The anger seemed real, but anger, Hart knew, was often used as a cover for guilt.

"No complaint was ever made," she repeated, coolly assessing the court clerk. "And DC Frinton?" She clicked her tongue. "Doesn't exist."

Sara opened her mouth then shut it again. "I don't understand," she said, after a few moments of dumbstruck silence. "Megan said she had spoken to Detective Constable Frinton. She said he promised to look into it. She even had his card."

"Did you see it?"

Sara frowned, not understanding.

"DC Frinton's card — did Megan show it to you?"

"No . . ." Sara said slowly. "But she told me —"

"Did you see her make the call?"

The court was almost empty, now. Only an usher and a junior barrister remained, sorting through paperwork in preparation for the next day. He studiously avoided looking at them, but Hart felt him listening with breathless intensity.

"I —" Sara frowned, her gaze seeking that spot just to the left of her field of vision where images and memories seemed to come to life for her. "No," she said, after a few seconds. "No, I didn't stand over her and watch her make the call."

Hart still could not gauge if Sara was the liar or if she had been lied to by Megan.

"Why would she lie to me?" Sara asked, as if Hart had spoken her thoughts. "She's in trouble. I know it. Megan wouldn't just leave without telling me."

"You said yourself, she never stayed anywhere for long," Hart suggested.

"Because of her *work* — she had to go where the stories took her."

"What stories?"

Sara was about to respond impatiently, but she checked herself, sensing that there was more.

"Did you ever read any of Megan's articles?" Hart pushed, delivering this new deception before Sara had recovered from the last. She was trying to get a reaction, but all she read on Sara's face was confusion and worry.

"What are you saying?" Sara's said.

"That Megan Ward never wrote a news story in her life."

"But that's ridiculous!" The exclamation contained an implied question: *Isn't it?*

"I searched the internet," Hart said. "Undercover reporters might need to keep a low profile, but Megan is invisible."

A door opened at the back of the court room and a second usher called Sara's name.

"Coming," she said without turning; her voice, normally so strong and vibrant, sounded small and shocked. Half a minute passed and she seemed to be fighting with her emotions. "Something is badly wrong," she said at last. "If Megan lied to me there has to be a good reason. We're friends. We —" She looked away for a moment, as if trying to find something she had misplaced. "We trust each other."

Hart had come to the court furious at the thought that Sara might have played her for a fool, but she saw that Megan's lack of trust, and her lies, had wounded Sara. She looked bewildered and hurt.

Sara's eyes drifted back to her face. "You think she lied to me for the hell of it?"

Hart held her gaze.

Sara shook her head. "You're wrong. She didn't — she wouldn't lie to me."

"What makes you so sure?"

"Because she told me things she had never told anyone before." She paused, and her expression softened a little. "We talked once about childhood fantasies — you know the sort of thing — little girls dreaming of being film stars or dancers or models."

Hart nodded, regretting that she had been so hard on Sara.

"Megan said she never wanted any of those things," Sara continued. "She told me what she wanted most as a child was to be invisible."

CHAPTER
EIGHT

Tanya and the boys were waiting at the pick-up point at Manchester airport when Jeff Rickman pulled in to the bay. Tanya was as ravishing as ever. Even after a four-hour flight, her dark hair glowed as if the sun shone within it. She wore a sleeveless dress in pale cream, cut to just above the knee, and over it a jacket in matching suede. Her long legs looked slim and toned in low-heeled loafers. A single gold bangle on her wrist set off her tan and she wore simple teardrop diamond earrings that would have cost Rickman a month's salary. She slipped into his arms and kissed him on both cheeks. Her brown eyes showed a little tiredness and her face was perhaps a little strained, but she relaxed into a smile, turning to the boys.

Rickman eyed the trolleys stacked high with luggage, wondering if his Vectra would be able to accommodate all of it. Jeff junior, the older of the two, smiled, leaning with both arms on one of the trolleys. Rickman offered his hand and the boy took it, making eye contact, his handshake firm and confident.

"How's the revision going?" Rickman asked.

The boy glanced at his mother. "*I* think it's going just fine."

Tanya rolled her eyes. "He wanted to stay in Milan."

"She felt I needed to be supervised."

Tanya had to smile. "It's true."

The boy put an arm around his mother. "You're probably right," he said, adding, "I'm easily led," with just enough sharpness that he couldn't be accused of capitulating too easily.

He began loading the boot of the car under his mother's direction, and Rickman turned his attention to his younger nephew. As always, Fergus hung back; whether he was unsure of his reception or wary of overt shows of affection, Rickman still hadn't quite worked out. He was thin and rangy, and there was a quiet watchfulness about him that Rickman felt almost as an echo of his young self.

He offered the boy his hand, and Fergus seemed surprised and quietly pleased. He was at the age between childhood and adolescence when such small courtesies mean a lot.

"How tall now?" Rickman asked, squinting at him to try to gauge his height.

"A hundred and fifty-five centimetres."

Rickman whistled. "Half a foot since Christmas!"

Fergus grinned, blushing, pleased and embarrassed by the attention.

"At this rate you'll break my record," Rickman added. "Four-ten to five-ten in a year."

The boy absorbed this without comment, but his eyes glowed. Rickman understood: as a boy, he had been small and scrawny until the age of thirteen, when a growth spurt gave him a new perspective on life.

Fergus was very like him, with his nut-brown hair and hazel eyes. He seemed also to have inherited Rickman's youthful diffidence.

"Put on about twenty kilos and you'll look like a human being instead of a swizzle stick," Jeff junior added, ruffling his brother's hair. Fergus took a swipe at him and moments later Tanya had to intervene.

In the forty-mile trip from Manchester airport into Liverpool they talked about Milan, the business, which Tanya was now running, the weather — anything to avoid talking about the boys' father and his current state of mind.

Rickman lived in a large Victorian family house in Mossley Hill. High-walled gardens and mature trees shading the roadway gave the house a sequestered feel. The buds were beginning to plump on the trees and some of the shrubs in the garden were already showing their first flush of colour. He loved the place. It had been his rock, his place of refuge in a year when at times he thought he was losing his mind.

While the boys unpacked the car and argued over which bedroom they wanted, Rickman and Tanya retired to the quiet of the kitchen. It had always been the hub of the house and it remained the place where he felt most at peace. He opened the window to let in the sounds and scents of the garden before filling a kettle to make tea.

The kitchen was a marrying of modern utility and original features. The red floor tiles had been replaced by pink quarry tiles, the kitchen units were old pine but a big stainless-steel cooking range dominated one wall. An old oak table stood in the centre of the room, its bone-white surface and the slight dip midway along its length giving it an air of permanence: it had survived two world wars and a succession of families during its long history, and it would go on to serve many more.

"Simon will be here at eight," Rickman said. "It'll give you and the boys time to settle in. He's usually better in the evenings, anyway. Less excitable."

Evening sunshine glanced through the glass of the back door, burnishing the copper highlights in Tanya's hair. She ran her fingers through it and Rickman was dazzled for a moment. "I'm sorry you've been left to cope with all of this," Tanya said. "It's just I didn't want to disrupt the boys' education any further. They're settled in Milan — and the business —"

Rickman touched her shoulder lightly. "He's my brother, Tanya."

She took a breath. "And he's my husband."

"I know. I know that — but he couldn't have had better treatment. He's made huge strides since you last saw him. He manages the mood swings well — and the headaches are almost gone —"

"Does he remember me?" Tears stood in her brown eyes. "Does he remember his sons?" Since Simon's near-fatal car crash the previous autumn he remembered nothing of his wife, his children or his clothing business in Milan.

Rickman couldn't lie to her.

"Then forgive me if I'm a little doubtful of the 'huge strides' he's made."

Rickman stood facing her, the kettle boiling madly on the work surface behind him. He wanted to help her, he wanted to find some words of comfort. "He's recovering memories every day, Tanya. Maybe —"

Maybe what? Rickman wondered. Maybe a miracle would happen? Maybe the neurologists would come up with some new treatment? He shrugged, and Tanya smiled.

"His reality is in this city, in the past. In *your* past, Jeff."

Rickman looked away. "I don't know what to say."

Tanya groaned. "Oh, God, I had this planned. I'd prepared a speech and everything, and look what I've done." She looked into Rickman's eyes, her own earnest, anxious. "Can we start again?"

He smiled, relaxing. "Sure," he said. "You go and shower, I'll start on dinner."

He saw in her face the months of worry and hard work, a dozen visits from Milan to the UK and back again; too much time away from her boys and the family business to support a husband who neither recognised nor wanted her.

The clouds that had brought bursts of rain all day finally cleared around seven o'clock, leaving a washed denim sky and pale spring sunshine. The garden was sheltered and warm, and within an hour the barbecue was glowing nicely, the salad mixed and the dressing ready on the kitchen table. Tanya sliced bread in the kitchen while Rickman turned the meat, his face glowing in the heat from the barbecue, his eyes stinging with the smoke that rose in aromatic clouds from the coals. Jeff junior sat on the bench under the flowering cherry, his eyes closed, his arms folded across his chest while petals drifted around him. Fergus sat cross-legged on a rug on the grass, reading one of his comics.

The doorbell rang and the air around the boys seemed to contract and then expand again. Fergus glanced up at his uncle, then resumed his reading. Although Jeff junior did not stir, Rickman sensed the tension in the set of his jaw, and the tightness of the muscles in his upper chest.

Tanya appeared at the kitchen door, her face showing signs of strain.

"I'll get it," Rickman said. "Keep an eye on the barbecue will you, Jeff?"

The boy got up, stealing a look at his mother as he took the barbecue tongs from Rickman. "Okay, Ma?" he asked.

She nodded stiffly and disappeared inside again. Rickman followed her. She went back to the kitchen table and began piling sliced bread and ciabatta rolls onto plate. Rickman tried to catch her eye, but she wouldn't look at him.

Simon greeted his brother with his usual enthusiasm. The disinhibition had diminished somewhat and he stood on the doorstep grinning, waiting to be invited in, rather than barging past, as he would have done in the early days.

Simon was slightly shorter than his brother, lean and athletic, with a nervy energy that sparked around him like electricity. His hair was almost white, peppered with a darker grey, and it curled on his shirt collar. He had grown it out since the autumn, to cover the scar from the surgery to remove a blood clot on his brain. Rickman ushered him in, putting an arm around his shoulder. "Remember," he said, "they come first tonight. You and me, we can talk anytime. Ask the boys about the holidays — ask Jeff about his exams."

Simon nodded, the wide flat planes of his cheeks suffused with colour, his bright blue eyes sparkling with eagerness. "Jeff's the big one, right?"

Rickman inhaled sharply and Simon laughed. "Joking," he said, the sparkle in his eyes turning to mischief. "'Course I know the one from the other."

Rickman led the way through the house, into the garden. Tanya had finished laying the table. She came forward and kissed her husband lightly on the cheek. Jeff junior watched his father steadily, but said nothing. Fergus stood up to greet his father, looking shy and a little anxious.

"Hi, Dad," the boy said.

"Hello, Fergus." The hurt on the boy's face was plain, but Simon had never called either of the boys "son" since his accident.

They ate, Simon on his best behaviour, talking to the boys, asking questions, listening patiently to the answers. The silvery evening sunshine faded to coral, then mauve; the traffic sounds diminished, birds sought out their favourite roosts and the air was filled with the song of robins and blackbirds, chaffinches and the soft burbling of starlings gathered on the rooftops nearby.

By nine, the last glimmer of light had died. A chill set in, and Rickman began to clear plates, taking them indoors. Jeff junior picked up his own plate and wandered inside, depositing it on the table. He kept going and moments later, Rickman heard him bounding up the stairs to his bedroom.

Rickman stepped back out into the garden. Tanya was stacking dishes; she caught Rickman's eye. "He's not what you'd call a New Man," she said with a smile. "Washing dishes became *uncool* around his eighteenth birthday."

"What about young Fergus?" he asked, glancing over at his nephew. He knew immediately that there was something wrong. Simon sat next to the boy, talking rapidly, compulsively, while the boy leaned back slightly, angling his upper body to give the greatest distance between him and his father, his eyes fixed on Simon as if he was a snake about to strike.

"Simon," Rickman said.

Simon's head swivelled loosely on his shoulders. He focused on his brother only slowly, his expression increasingly perplexed.

"Help me with this, will you?" Simon looked from Rickman to his son and back to Rickman, and his face cleared.

"Sure," he said, getting clumsily to his feet, his co-ordination still a little off, despite months of physio.

He stacked a few dishes and took them through to the kitchen. Tanya glanced at Rickman, her face a mask of practised control, then she went to her son, leaving the two men alone. Rickman closed the door after her and turned to his brother.

"We talked about this, Simon," he said.

Simon seemed puzzled. "I did everything you said. I asked about school. I talked about Jeff junior's exams and university. I even kissed Tanya." He made it sound like a major sacrifice.

"Simon, think."

For a moment, his face was blank, then he frowned, evidently trying to process Rickman's words, replaying the last half hour in an effort to match his brother's disapproval to something he had said or done.

"Oh, God," Simon murmured, his hand going to his head, touching the scar hidden beneath his hairline. "I called him Jeff again, didn't I?" He immediately went on the defensive. "People do that all the time, calling one child by another's name."

"You were talking to Fergus like it was me — like it was me and we were still kids. You *frightened* him."

Simon's eyes darted right and left in tiny movements, a sign of his distress. "I — I got confused." He focused on his brother's face. "He looked so sad, sitting there all alone and I kind of lost track of time."

Rickman exhaled in one long breath. When Simon lost track of time it could be measured in decades. It was true that he could tell the boys apart, now. The difficulty was in keeping his son, Fergus, and the ten-year-old Jeff straight in his head. Talking to Fergus, Simon had slipped back to their childhood, when he was the champion, the protector of the family, and

Rickman was little brother Jeff, a scrawny kid in need of protection.

"You've got to stop this," Rickman said.

"Okay," Simon said, his head nodding in repeated jerky movements. "I'll go and apologise." He reached impulsively for the door handle.

Rickman touched his arm lightly. "Best not."

"Best not," Simon repeated, a touch of petulance creeping into his voice. "Best leave the boy's mother to explain that the crazy man doesn't mean any harm."

"Do you care?" Rickman asked. How could he refuse to acknowledge his sons and yet feel bitter that they trusted Tanya more than they trusted him? "Do you care *at all* what Fergus thinks?"

"Why should I?" Simon seemed to regret the sharpness of his reply and took a breath before going on. "I don't *remember* him, Jeff. But I remember you. I remember how scared you were."

"It's like arctic white-out," Simon had said once, in an effort to explain. He described vividly the melding of snow and horizon, the dizzying bewilderment of a world in which sky and land were inseparable, in which up and down had no meaning; but he had no idea where this memory had come from. It was there, as real as his own reflection in the mirror, but like his own reflection, now inexplicably old, it had no context, no past; he did not know its heritage. It was fossilised, like a fly in amber.

For a full minute Simon didn't speak. He stood with his hand on the door knob, gripping it as though it was the only thing preventing him from fleeing the house, his brother and his difficult questions. At last, he let his hand drop to his side. "I shouldn't have left when I did, Jeff. You were too young to cope with all the shit from Dad. I don't want to — I *can't* make the same mistake twice."

Rickman placed a hand on his brother's shoulder. "You didn't abandon your family, Simon. You had an accident. It's not your fault."

"Tell that to the boy."

"Your *son*," Rickman corrected, squeezing Simon's shoulder lightly. "Fergus is your son and you are his father."

"Am I?" Simon frowned, trying to make sense of what for him seemed like insanity. "Am I really a father? A husband? You tell me I am, but I don't feel it." He shook his head. "I tell myself over and over, but I can't make myself believe it. *They* don't even believe it," he said, jerking his head in the direction of the garden where Tanya was talking to Fergus, trying to explain. "They don't believe it and they didn't lose their minds."

"Don't talk like that!" Rickman exclaimed. "You didn't lose your mind, you lost your *memory*."

"Isn't that the same thing? It feels like I'm still seventeen and you're my brother. That feels real. But then I look in a mirror and . . . I see a stranger." He gazed at his hands, turning them over, staring at them as though repulsed by the faint mesh of lines and wrinkles that had begun to form. "It's like somebody stole all the years we should have had together."

His head nodded in a constant rhythm and Rickman knew that every beat of Simon's heart pulsed pain through his skull. The headaches had become an increasingly rare phenomenon in recent months, but today, it seemed his brother had regressed several steps.

"You're tired," Rickman said, dragging out a chair for his brother, guiding him to it. "I'll ring for a taxi, get you home."

CHAPTER
NINE

Sara Geddes checked her mobile phone for messages as soon as the court broke for lunch. She took the stairs down, too impatient to wait for the lift. As she strode across the long carpeted foyer on the ground floor, she phoned her home number and keyed in her pass code for the answering machine. There were no new messages.

At the main entrance she kept walking; she couldn't even think about getting changed to do her usual laps of Chavasse Park, but neither could she bear to stay in the dark depressing confines of the courts complex, so she turned right after the revolving doors, down the side of the huge, maroon-coloured building. It funnelled a fierce draught at this point and she held her jacket closed against its bitter chill; but the wind dropped as she reached the park and she walked on, under the alder trees, past the custard-yellow mock-up of the Beatles-inspired Yellow Submarine, heading towards the river.

At Strand Street, she stopped at the steel crash barrier and took in the waterfront: ahead, across six lanes of traffic, the brown brick warehouses of the Albert Dock stood solid and squat beyond the twinkling water of Salthouse, and to the right, the Liver and Cunard Buildings shone white against a crystal blue sky. Sara lingered for a few minutes, leaning on the barrier to take a few cleansing breaths, feeling a brief moment of contentment; but the gnawing anxiety quickly reasserted itself, and she fished in her handbag for the card Detective Constable Hart had given her. Perhaps they had discovered something new — if they had examined the contents of Megan's computer drive . . . She hesitated and the impetus deserted her, and after another glance at the number on the card she slipped it into her trouser pocket.

At the far end of the little park, she turned right again, onto the brick-blocked path. She barely registered the man jogging towards her, the hood of his navy-blue sweatshirt pulled up, feet pounding a steady rhythm on the pavement. He ran on, keeping an easy pace, passing her as she walked thoughtfully up the path, the regular thump of his feet on the bricks sounding like the inexorable tick of a clock in her mind. As she reached the top of the hill, he turned and stared after her.

There were no messages for her when she finished in court that evening, either at the reception desk or on her phone. She drove out of the car park, acknowledging the security guard with a brief wave. Ray would like to chat, she knew; he was recently divorced and liked to feel a part of other people's lives. She thought he also missed the canteen gossip of his co-workers on the police force. Ironic that he had left the force to please his wife, but she had walked out on him because she found him dull outside of the world of crime and imminent danger. Sara felt bad that she hadn't stopped, but didn't feel up to Ray's questions, or the excitement that sparked in his eyes when he asked her about Megan.

So she escaped without saying a word, turning left at The Strand and skirting the southern edge of the city, towards home. The sun was still shining, and the blue sky created a stunning backdrop to the pink-and-white cherry blossom in a few of the gardens along the route.

Megan had been afraid, she was sure of that, and she hadn't been lying about her stalker. After working in the courts for fifteen years, Sara knew genuine fear when she saw it. If Megan had lied about going to the police, it was because she didn't trust them, and being in care was enough to make most young people distrust any agency, especially the police.

The street was already crammed with cars and she had to park fifty yards from her house. Unable to stop herself, she dialled her message service as she walked back. Nothing — no messages — not even a missed call. In her hall, the LED on the answering machine was flashing and she pressed the new messages button eagerly, offering up a silent prayer. It was her mother, wondering why she hadn't been in touch. She cancelled the message halfway through, feeling a pang of guilt. The phone rang immediately and she jumped, giving a yelp of surprise. She picked up on the second ring, unable entirely to control the tremor in her hand.

"Hello?"

The line was silent.

"Megan?"

She was about to hang up when she noticed a faint sound, like the hiss of wind or the distant roar of the sea. *Traffic*, she thought. "Megan, is that you?"

She heard a click and the line went dead.

She punched one-four-seven-one, her hand still unsteady. Number withheld. Sara stood in the hall, listening to the house. It seemed too still, as it often felt after she woke from a bad dream.

She picked up an umbrella from the hall stand and went from room to room, opening doors, looking behind furniture; she rattled the door handle of the back door to establish it was secure and moved on to the upper floors. Every room and every cupboard and wardrobe was opened and checked for intruders — she even flung back the shower curtain in the bathroom, brandishing the umbrella in a heroic gesture. The house was empty.

"Idiot," she muttered, dumping the umbrella in the bath tub.

She had left the door to Megan's office open. Now, she returned to it and looked around the room. This was where Megan worked, where she spent most of her day, and yet it was as blank and featureless as if she had moved in days before, rather than months.

The desk was empty, except for the phone extension; the police had taken everything else: the monitor, the CPU, even the cables and power leads. All that remained was a thin film of dust where the keyboard had been.

Sara believed in God, she was versed in the emblematic and symbolic significance of dust in the Church's history and dogma, but she pushed these thoughts aside — she *would not* believe that Megan was dead. This dust was nothing more than dead cells, sloughed off by life and living. Impatient with herself, she swiped a hand across the surface, then clapped her palms together.

She snapped off the light and went into Megan's bedroom, standing for a few moments with her hands on her hips, while she decided where to start. She began with the bedside cabinet. The top was clear of clutter, its interior held only a paperback novel and a half-finished Sunday crossword. Megan liked the cryptic ones.

She went next to the large chest of drawers to the right of the window; they contained clothing: sweaters, jeans, underwear, but nothing that might indicate why Megan had disappeared. The same was true of the wardrobe — everything neatly organised, revealing an ordered mind and nothing more. The top drawer of the dresser clinked and rattled as she opened it. Inside, she found Megan's cosmetics, laid out on glass dishes, ready to be lifted out when they were needed: make-up, perfumes, nail varnish, lipsticks — everything she would have expected to see cluttering the surface of the dresser.

The bottom drawer contained T-shirts, but there was a gap at one end, and Sara remembered the sad little box that Sergeant Foster had found there. Stuffed with the sweepings of a young life, rubbish that most would have thrown out, but which Megan had hidden away as treasures.

She suspected Constable Hart and Sergeant Foster would dismiss the box as unimportant — and what if Megan came back, looking for it? The one possession she valued enough to carry around with her from place to place? Sara took the business card DC Hart had given her from her trouser pocket and looked at it for a moment. Hart hadn't exactly seemed concerned when they had last spoken. In fact she was pretty sure that Naomi Hart thought her a liar and a fantasist.

She sighed, moving back through to Megan's office. Standing in the dark, she tried to imagine where her young friend might be, wondering if she was afraid, willing her to be strong. She looked again at the card; she had the number by heart, she'd looked at it so many times. Down the street the lamps flickered on in twos and threes. A burst of noise from a motorbike speeding past brought her to the window.

A man stood under one of the streetlamps, staring up at the house. Sara gasped. Fear took hold of her, squeezing the air from her lungs, pressing on her chest till she couldn't breathe. It was the man who had been following Megan.

She staggered back, catching herself on a corner of the desk, bruising her thigh. The pain shocked her out of her panic, and she took a moment to steady herself, leaning on the back of Megan's office chair. Then she reached for the phone and dialled.

"Naomi Hart." The constable's voice sounded crisp and confident; background noise suggested a pub or restaurant.

"Sara Geddes," she said, careful to keep her own voice level and unemotional. "He's back."

CHAPTER
TEN

Naomi Hart bought Jake Bentley into the interview room and sat him down without so much as a flicker of anxiety. He was six-two and fifteen stone of supplement-enhanced muscle, she was eight-stone-nothing and slender as a sylph, yet Bentley allowed her to guide him inside and direct him to a chair, sitting meekly when asked to.

He might be a big bastard, Foster thought, *but the power is all with her.* "You're looking sorry for yourself," he remarked.

Bentley looked up at him; only the eyes moved, the head remained rock-solid on his shoulders. There was no neck to speak of; the shoulders merged seamlessly with the jaw line, tapering only slightly inwards and upwards.

The eyes were dark and cold. Foster saw the danger in the man: he'd seen it a hundred times before in Friday-night bust-ups — hard men building a rep.

"Ooh," he said. "He's giving me the dead eye. I've come over all trembly — help me, Constable Hart."

"You boys behave yourselves," Hart said, breaking the seal on two cassettes and slotting them into the tape recorder. It buzzed as she pressed play. She gave Foster the arched eyebrow warning — which really did make him come over all trembly — then she sat down next to him.

Hart went through the introduction and caution and then sat back, staring at Bentley as a mother might stare in disappointment at a child caught out in a lie.

Bentley looked down at his hands. They were wide and thick, the palms and finger-pads callused from lifting weights. "It's not what you think," he said. His accent wasn't as broad as Foster's and his voice was lighter and softer than you would expect from such a big man. Foster was intrigued. Was all this muscle a kind of armour against the classroom bullies of his youth, and the nightclub boozers of his early employment? Those types could spot weakness from fifty yards, seemed to sense it and seek it out in a bar or pool-room.

"What do we think, Mr Bentley?" Hart asked.

Bentley shrugged one massive shoulder. "The pictures."

"The obscene photographs we found in your flat," Hart said.

"They're not obscene," Bentley said, offended. "They're art."

They had found hundreds of photographs of young women, naked or near so; they appeared to have been taken in sand dunes.

"You're a Peeping Tom, Mr Bentley," Hart said.

"I'm an artist."

74

"Then how do you explain the other photographs — the ones of young women entering and leaving their houses?"

"It doesn't do any harm."

"Yes," Hart said. "It does. You're a stalker, Mr Bentley."

"No!"

"Why don't you tell us why you've been following Megan Ward?"

His forehead creased. "I wasn't," he said.

Hart gave him the more-disappointed-than-angry look again. "You were seen, Mr Bentley. More than once."

"Following her? No!"

"You've been watching the house."

"No!" His gaze wouldn't rest, it lighted on Hart, the tape recorder, the door, then back down to his hands. "I was there," he admitted, "but I wasn't watching the place. I was just . . ."

"You were just . . . Sussing out the place as an investment?" Foster suggested. "Gonna put in an offer were you? 'Cos you know what, mate, it's way out of your price range — I mean what do gym jockeys earn these days?"

Bentley's right hand tightened into a fist and he covered it with his left hand, but he made no reply.

"Where is Megan?" Hart asked.

"How should I know?"

"Because," Hart explained patiently, "you've been watching her house and she was obviously frightened by your presence, so when she suddenly disappears, we naturally think you might be involved."

Bentley's eyes widened. "No," he said again. "No way." He was sweating, and when he glanced at the door again, Foster wondered if he was thinking of making a run for it. He felt Hart tense, readying herself for the onslaught.

But Bentley was the sort who talked himself into trouble by trying to talk himself out of it. "I know what this is about," he said.

"You do." Hart kept her tone neutral.

"Them other charges." He looked miserable and pissed off and seriously misunderstood.

Bentley had two charges of ABH on record; one dropped, the other resulting in a six-month suspended sentence. As interviewing officers, Hart and Foster weren't allowed to mention previous form, but since Bentley had brought it up, they let him run with it.

"You don't keep order in the clubs downtown by asking people to be nice," he said. "The lad come at me with a knife, I put him down."

Hart nodded without commenting.

"The other charge was dropped," he said. "Some dickhead injecting testosterone. Couldn't handle it — went all Tarantino on one of the clients at the gym, I stepped in." He leaned in to the mike. "I saved that guy's *life*."

"Thank you for being so frank with us, Mr Bentley," Hart said, bringing the subject to a close, for now. Foster understood what she was doing. Right now, Bentley was talking without a solicitor present, but if they pushed too hard too soon, he could turn nasty or demand representation — either way, they would get precious little out of him.

"Did you telephone Miss Geddes at six p.m. this evening?" Foster asked.

The diversionary tactic worked. "I don't even know her number," Bentley said, sounding more confident. "She's not in the book."

"So you did check," Hart said.

He sighed and glanced away, then back to Hart. "Look," he said. "If I tell you why I was there, it's not gonna get me in any trouble, is it?"

"That depends on what you tell us, mate," Foster said.

Bentley gave Foster the dead eye again, but when he looked at Hart, he reverted to the vulnerable schoolboy. "I didn't mean any harm," he said.

"You know you're entitled to a solicitor?" Hart asked.

Foster held his breath. Bentley had already been advised of his rights, but if he was about to come up with some sort of confession, they had to be on solid legal ground.

"Can't we keep this just between us?" His tone was wheedling, unsure of himself.

"We'll see," Hart said, falling easily into the role of matriarch. Foster marvelled at her, she knew exactly when to be tough, and when to conform to an interviewee's expectations.

"I work at the gym on Castle Street," Bentley began.

"Uh-huh," Hart said, still maintaining her neutrality.

"I go jogging on my lunch breaks. It clears my head."
They waited.

"I noticed Sara a few weeks back —"

"Woah!" Foster said "*Sara?*" Hart silenced him with a look.

Bentley raised his eyes tentatively to Hart's face. "I'm listening," she said, nodding encouragement.

"She likes to jog, too," Bentley said, his eyes sliding away from Hart. "I wanted to speak to her, but I . . ." He sighed again. "I'm not good with that stuff."

"Were you in the park today, Mr Bentley?" Hart asked. "Wearing that sweat top?"

A slight flush rose to his cheeks. "She recognised me, didn't she?"

In fact, Sara Geddes was convinced she had never seen Bentley except outside her house, but Hart let him assume she had.

"I wasn't following her — not like you think — I just wanted to . . . I don't know, ask her out, I suppose." He looked at her again, wanting her approval, her understanding.

Hart gave it. "That's why you went to her house," she said, gently.

He nodded.

"How did you know where she lives?"

"I —" He lost eye contact again. "I was behind her at the traffic lights on The Strand one night. I didn't think about it — it wasn't you know — deliberate. I just ended up sticking with her all the way to her house."

Foster had done surveillance work. Following someone in rush-hour traffic wasn't an easy thing to do.

You couldn't "stick with" a car without serious effort. He cleared his throat, but managed to curb his urge to butt in, and Hart continued:

"So you found yourself at her house. Then what?"

Bentley raised his hands and let them fall. "Nothing. I couldn't just go up and knock at the door, could I? I mean, how would I explain? I thought maybe I'd start up a conversation in the park one lunch-time, but —" He grimaced.

"Somehow it never happened?" Hart offered.

He seemed pleased that Hart understood his difficulty. "I wanted to, but *look* at her . . ."

Meaning a classy woman like Sara Geddes would never give a brainless hunk of meat like Bentley a second glance — and of course, she hadn't. Foster had to admit the guy was more perceptive than he appeared.

"Were you at Sara's house the night Megan disappeared?"

"No."

"I haven't told you which night it was, Mr Bentley," Hart said. "Now if you know anything — if you saw anything that might help us —"

"I was there," he interrupted. "But I didn't see anything."

Foster stared hard at him. "You need to make up your mind, mate."

Bentley's eyes darted right and left. "I saw Sara go in. I — drove home with her."

Foster glanced at Hart. It sounded so much better for the tape than "I followed her".

79

"You and Sara drove home together?" Hart asked, deliberately obtuse.

"Not in her car," Bentley said. "I was just *with* her, you know?"

"You followed her."

"I know where she lives," he said, looking a little flushed and agitated. "I didn't need to follow her. I —" He seemed to have a sudden inspiration and his face lit up. "I wanted to see that she got home safely."

"Very considerate," Foster said.

Bentley glared at him and Hart intervened again. "What happened after Sara got home?"

But Foster had needled him once too often. "Nothing," he said. "I saw her into the house." He gave Foster a hard stare. "Then I left."

CHAPTER
ELEVEN

"That was a bit of turn-up, wasn't it?" Foster said.

It was eight a.m. and they were in the CID Room, DC Hart typing up her report of the previous evening's interview, Foster distracting her. A check of Bentley's mobile phone SIM card and landline showed no record of his having telephoned Sara Geddes. Of course, he might have used a public phonebox — the call to Sara's house at six p.m. had been from a public phone — but proving he had been the caller would be difficult, so they'd had to let him go with a warning to stay away from Miss Geddes and her house and not to attempt to communicate with her in any way.

"Am I talking to myself, or what?"

"Hmm?" She continued typing at her computer keyboard. Foster leant against her desk, legs crossed at the ankles, arms folded across his chest. It emphasised the long, lean look and Hart suspected that Foster knew it.

"I said it's a turn-up, Bentley stalking Sara, not Megan."

"If you believe him," Hart said. *Damn, damn, damn — don't get drawn into a discussion, Naomi,* she told herself. *Ignore him — he'll go away.*

He frowned. "You think he's lying?"

"I don't know, Sarge."

"D'you think he saw Megan leave?"

Hart stopped for a second, her fingers resting on the keyboard. "I don't *know*, Sarge."

"How many times have I asked you to call me Lee?" Foster asked.

She started typing again, but slowly. "Dozens," she said.

"So what's the problem?"

"No problem," Hart said. "It just feels . . . odd."

"So it's got nothing to do with the fact that I pissed you off in the interview room?"

Hart stopped typing again and looked up at him.

"Well, something's bugging you," he said.

He really wasn't going to leave until they'd talked this through.

At this time of day, the CID Room felt big and empty, despite the untidy jumble of paper and personal belongings that littered the desks. Voices carried and it was easy to eavesdrop. There were three other officers in the room, all of them men. She noticed one of them watching her. "I need to finish this report," she said. "The DCI wants to see it, and I need to concentrate."

Foster unfolded his arms and gripped the edge of the desk. "You think I deliberately wound him up," he said. "You think I was argumentative and sarcastic. You think Bentley clammed up because I didn't make him *feel good* about stalking Sara Geddes."

Hart swung her chair around. "How do you think it feels for me, as a woman, interviewing a self-justifying creep like Bentley?" she demanded. "D'you think I *enjoyed* making him feel I understand his twisted mind?"

Foster leaned off her desk. "You're saying I screwed up."

Hart clenched her jaw tight against the temptation to apologise or make some conciliatory remark.

Foster studied her for a few seconds. "If you want to talk about this, I'll be in my office." He glanced around the room and the other personnel became suddenly engrossed in their paperwork.

It took Hart fifteen minutes to make her way to see Foster. She could lie — tell him she had overreacted, and avoid a show-down. Or she could tell him the truth — that with a little more cajoling she thought they could have had the full story from Bentley. She still hadn't come to a decision when she knocked and opened the door of Foster's office.

It was neat and bland, as before; in some ways it reminded her of Megan's office. The stolen fan stood in the corner, rotating backward and forward like a giant mechanised nodding dog.

Foster didn't look up immediately. He was staring at the shoebox they had found in Megan's bedroom. It was yellowed with age, except for a paler patch at one of the narrow ends, where it seemed a label had been stuck on with sellotape and later removed. The box was almost square — only a few centimetres longer than it was wide.

"Sarge," she said. Now was not the time to take him up on his offer of first-name terms.

Foster turned to her. He seemed a little unfocused. She took a breath. "Look —"

"You were right," Foster interrupted. "I screwed up." He leaned past her and pushed the door closed. "Arseholes like Bentley piss me off. I can see they would probably piss you off more — and I know I should've kept my big gob shut."

She exhaled loudly. "You could have told me that fifteen minutes ago — saved me a lot of angst."

"You're joking aren't you?" he said. "Did you see who was earwigging our little chat? It would've been all round Merseyside by tomorrow, DS Foster's a wuss who admits he's wrong to *girls!*"

Hart had to bite her lip to stop herself from laughing. "I see that could have serious repercussions," she said solemnly.

"You're dead right," he grinned. "Now will you call me Lee?"

That damn smile of his will be my downfall, she thought. She pulled a chair up and sat next to Foster.

"Okay, she said. "I believe Bentley. The sleaze is obsessed with Sara, not Megan."

"So why did she run?"

Hart thought about it for a few moments. "Bentley was stalking Sara, but Megan thought he was stalking *her*, right?"

Foster grunted agreement, slouching down in his seat as he sometimes did when he was thinking.

"So maybe she ran because he spooked her."

"Or maybe she confronted him and things went bad," Foster said. "We know Bentley's got a temper."

"Or," Hart continued, "there was something else she was afraid of."

Foster tilted his head. "That's plenty to be going on with."

"Maybe the answer is in there."

They both looked at the shoebox.

Foster sat up from his slouch and lifted the lid of the box, releasing a whiff of old paper and dust. He had to switch the fan off after a while, to prevent it whisking their carefully separated piles into a flurry of confetti. They worked together, sorting the brochures from the bus tickets, the pop-star pull-outs from the badges, the penknife and the lock of hair. Foster picked up the photograph of the family group and stared at it for a full minute as if it held some hidden clue, then he riffled through the papers in his in-tray and found the sketch Sara had drawn of Megan.

Something about the rapt way he concentrated on the two pictures sparked an unreasonable jealousy in Hart, and she said, "Falling in love with a spectre?"

Foster didn't respond to the jibe, instead, he put the two likenesses down and indicated the assorted memorabilia with a gesture of his hand. "What does this tell us?"

Hart studied the forlorn piles of ageing slips and cuttings. "She liked Take That and the B*Witched in her childhood; moved on to Indie bands in the late nineties." She stirred a pile of ticket stubs with one

85

finger. "She went to Blackpool Tower and Camelot, Granada Studios, Alton Towers —"

"Well that's something," Foster said.

She looked again. "I don't see it."

"All the attractions she visited as a kid are in the north of England," Foster said. "So, Megan was brought up in the north."

Hart raised her eyebrows. "Sarge, there's about twenty-five million people in the north of England," she said.

"But only about twelve-and-a-half million women."

Hart laughed, and Foster smiled, gratified, but he continued to study the stacks of paper hungrily. "There's nothing here beyond her late teens," he said. "No photo-booth snapshots of her with her mates, no membership cards, no bank account details — nothing."

"She must have money," Hart said. "She bought a sports car for cash."

"So where is it?"

"What?" Hart said. "The car?"

"The car, the cash — the rest of her life."

Hart thought about it. "She's into computers — and if she moves around a lot, it would make sense to bank on-line, rather than have to change her branch every time she ups sticks and moves to another town."

"Have we got anything on the dealer who sold her the car?" Foster asked.

Hart shook her head. "Sara didn't even know the make."

"Okay." Foster reached for a copy of the Yellow Pages from his desk drawer. "Let's start with Mercs and BMWs."

After an hour of working the phones in tandem, they had the dealer on the line. He had sold Megan an Audi TT 150 Roadster for twenty-one thousand pounds, six weeks previously. He confirmed she had paid cash — he'd thrown in road tax and she had talked him into paying for a year's insurance. He seemed unsure exactly how she had managed that particular feat of reverse salesmanship.

"D'you have the car's ID number — and Miss Ward's Driver Number would be really helpful," Hart said. The DVLA had come up with a Mercedes, registered to the Norwich Megan Ward. They had yet to send a photo. If they could match the Driver Number, they would have at least one definite connection. There was a pause. Foster arched his eyebrows in question and she gave him the thumbs-up.

"I'm not sure I can . . ."

"You're concerned about confidentiality," Hart said. Doing this the long way, using all the right forms, would take days, and she had already reached her frustration tolerance limits. "You respect your clients' privacy," she went on. "And that's commendable. But this is a missing persons enquiry, and Miss Ward might be in trouble."

The dealer still seemed unsure.

She took a breath. "Tell you what — I'll fax a request through to you on headed notepaper and you can fax me her details right back — how's that?" Coercion worked, where persuasion hadn't. Minutes later, the task completed, they waited, trying not to watch the fax machine.

"We could ask the Department for Work and Pensions for her National Insurance number," Foster suggested. "But we'd need clearance from the boss for that."

"For what?" Rickman stood in the doorway. They had been so intent on the phone call that they hadn't heard him knock.

"DWP request," Foster said. "Bentley's our stalker all right, but he wasn't stalking Megan."

Rickman nodded. "I know — I've had Naomi's report."

Foster couldn't hide his amused surprise that she had come to sort things out with him *after* filing her report with the DCI. Hart treated him to an arched eyebrow.

"You've got your clearance," Rickman said. "What else?"

"We're waiting on a fax —" Foster was interrupted by a single ring from the fax machine, then a copy of Megan's registration details hummed through. Foster and Hart glanced at it, then passed it to Rickman.

"It might be worth giving out her car ID to the traffic police," Foster said.

The DCI considered. "Let me think on that one — we still don't know if she wants to be found; an area-wide alert might be overkill. What about her treasure trove?" he asked, lifting his chin to indicate the shoebox, now lying empty on the desk.

"She was probably brought up in the north of England," Foster said. "Otherwise, there's bugger-all of any use in this little lot —" He lifted the lid to replace it on the box, and frowned.

"What?" Rickman asked.

"Dunno." Foster shook the lid. "Feels off." He set the lid down on his desk and picked up the penknife from the sorted paraphernalia.

Rickman gave a cough. Foster grimaced and put the knife down again, mouthing, "Evidence." Then he fished in his pocket, taking out a Swiss Army knife.

"Well, dib-dib-dib," Hart said, gently mocking.

He took it in good part. "Ex-boy scouts, ex-marines — we always like to be prepared," he said, teasing the blade of the knife under the lining paper. Though yellowed and brittle, it peeled away without tearing. Hidden beneath was a credit card in the name of Megan Ward.

CHAPTER
TWELVE

Nathan Wilde was tripping. Maybe not full-on, mind-blowing psychedelic oblivion, but an altered mental state, for sure. He was seeing things: cyber-bugs — oval transparent shapes, all light and no substance. They scuttled like beetles on the periphery of his vision, making him flinch, freaked for a second, till his head cleared, and they vanished, and although he looked really closely, there was nothing, not even a shadow that could have caused the apparition.

The sharpness of vision and the blinding insights of the first two days had given way to a frightening cacophony of sensory input. Flashing lights slashed the soothing velvet darkness when he closed his eyes. Sounds, too — loud buzzing sounds, like angry hornets, distortions of speech, a constant hiss like a burst steam-pipe in his right ear. Drug-induced or a product of sleep deprivation, he couldn't say, but he knew for sure that he was going crazy.

He had slept in two-hour breaks, sometimes involuntarily napping at the keyboard; this apart, he had been in Patrick Doran's office for almost five days. Imprisoned — or as good as — in the dark and darkened room. Doran and Warrender, sometimes one, sometimes both, acting as jailers. Was it night or day? He couldn't say. This room felt like a tunnel, a cave.

The hacker now had a name: Warlock. Not that Nathan had discovered it; Warlock had presented it to them as a gift and a taunt: *catch me if you think you're fast enough — or smart enough*. Nathan knew that he was neither.

Warlock was using a meerkat application, which worked a look-out rota similar to the little ground-squirrels, sticking its head up every few minutes to check who was on the system that might pose a threat. Every time Nathan got onto exactly which part of the operating system was under attack, Warlock would disappear, only to pop up somewhere else moments later. It was like trying to catch smoke.

"Can't catch smoke," he murmured.

"What?" Doran demanded.

Nathan looked at his boss. "What?" he echoed.

"You said something."

Nathan looked beyond Doran to Warrender, who was dozing in a chair. "Shut down." It seemed as good a suggestion as any he had made, so far. "You have to do what I'm telling you."

"No," Doran said. "I don't. You know why? Because I'm the boss."

"And I'm the systems manager," Nathan said. He knew the danger, but felt no fear. He was past fear, past pain, past anything but a hacker's instinct to survive this assault and learn from the experience.

"You pay me for — this." He waved a hand at the computers; the soft hum of their cooling fans sounded like the breathing of a sleeping animal. One that might awake and attack without warning. He lowered his voice, irrationally fearful that Warlock might hear. "Neither one of us has the final say here — Warlock does."

A muscle jumped in Doran's jaw. "I thought you said this 'Warlock' was an amateur."

"That's the trouble with amateurs." Nathan spoke half to himself as he scrolled through multiple monitors on multiple screens. "They really love what they do. They don't do it for the money, and they won't stop till they find a weakness, a flaw, an exploit. Some way around or over or under or through your defences."

"You're supposed to be a professional. Like you said, it's what I pay you for." The menace in Doran's voice was barely masked. "This guy is taking the piss — why can't you stop him?"

Nathan swallowed. He was jazzed on speed and the odd blast of vasopressin, his head throbbed and he was parched and nauseous. "I dunno," he said, almost feverish with heat and exhaustion. "Maybe he teamed up with somebody else — a mentor. Sometimes experienced hackers will help out a novice if it's an interesting enough project."

Doran stared with a dawning horror at the computers ranked on his desk as he began to appreciate the potential of this new threat. "Why are they doing this to me?"

"Because they can." Nathan had to make Doran understand, and for the first time since all of this started, he thought that his boss might listen — really listen, instead of blustering and giving orders. "It's about power and control," he said. "The bigger and more powerful the people you hack, the better it makes you feel."

"Speaking from experience, Nathan?" Warrender had spoken for the first time in hours.

"Well — yeah . . ." Nathan frowned at the stupidity of the question. "In cyberspace, it isn't money or muscle that matters — it's brains and energy and imagination. Synergy of man and machine."

"You're telling me those wankers on their PlayStations or whatever are about energy and imagination?" Doran demanded.

"Hacking is like PlayStation with real villains who could really rip your head off if they found you," Nathan said. "But small and weak as the hacker might be in reality, when he's lurking in your system, or messing with your files, he's the one with the power."

"You said you could do some mojo — get into his machine."

"I'm *trying* to," Nathan said. "I almost had him, then he switched computers — he's working from a laptop now."

"Well how d'you think you're gonna get a street address off a laptop, *moron?*"

Nathan looked into his employer's dark blue eyes and saw a whisper of insanity. "Documents," he said, scrambling for ideas. "Receipts? Letters?"

"When? Next year? My system has been under attack for five days. I want a result."

Nathan didn't respond. He was staring at the monitor closest to him with absolute concentration. His scalp tingled and an ice cold shiver ran down his spine.

"I'm . . ." His fingers hovered over the keyboard. "My God — I'm in."

It took Doran a few moments to understand the significance of what Nathan had said. Then he let his systems manager work and for nearly an hour, he watched, fascinated, as Nathan trawled through Warlock's files.

"Most of these files are encrypted," Nathan said after a long, eerie silence during which the only sounds were the rustle of his fingers over the keyboard and the whisper of the computers' cooling fans. "The rest he must read and delete."

Doran's shoulders sagged. "So you can't find him."

"Oh, I can find him," Nathan said, an unshakeable calm settling on him. He stared at the machine, his hands rippling over the keyboard by touch, stepping through the configuration like it was a series of rooms, which to Nathan it was — a three-dimensional space he could walk through and manipulate.

"Deleted files aren't really deleted, only hidden," he explained. "The first letter of the file name is erased, so it's hard to find." He smiled a little. "But not impossible."

Another ten minutes passed during which Nathan worked in almost a trance state, typing in commands, filtering and categorising files.

"Gotcha," Nathan said quietly.

"You've got an address?" Doran asked.

Nathan held up a hand. "Wait." The tone of command, the absolute confidence, was impossible to ignore, and again, Doran deferred to his young systems manager.

"You are good," Nathan murmured softly, "but you're not God." Then, with a glance to Warrender, who had roused himself from his torpor and now sat at the edge of his seat, "Printer."

Seconds later, the printer activated and a sheet of paper appeared. "It's a receipt for hardware," Nathan said, as Warrender handed the sheet to Doran. "The name's probably fake. But the street name might be worth checking."

Doran smiled broadly. "You got the fucker. It took a while, mind, but —" He laughed and slapped Nathan on the shoulder.

Something flashed on the nearest monitor, capturing Nathan's attention. He looked back and saw an animation: a sinewy figure, old, dressed in sub-Celtic tunic and cloak. The Warlock smiled and turned, the cloak swirling fluidly behind him.

"Uh-oh." Nathan grabbed the mouse.

"What. The *fuck*. Does that mean?" Doran's eyes bulged slightly as he spoke.

Nathan tried to access the applications folders. "Stay still you fucker," he muttered. "Just stay still one lousy —" Warlock vanished again. "Shit!" He clasped his hands behind his head, his hands shaking. He tried switching identities, hoping to sneak up on Warlock from an unexpected location on the system, but this failed, too.

"This is nightmare on friggin' X-Box," he said, his voice low and fast.

"Nathan," Doran said. "Talk to me. Tell me what's going on."

At first Nathan thought that Doran was part of a hallucination, a disembodied voice adding to the complexity of the problem, so when he looked away from the monitor it was a shock to see Doran's face, level with his; Doran's blue eyes staring at him, bloodshot, angry.

"You've got to let me shut down." He heard the pleading note in his voice and hated himself for it.

"Shutting down is not an option," Doran said. "Finish it, Nathan. I want this parasite out of my system."

Nathan laughed, feeling hot and flushed and near hysteria.

Doran looked past him to Warrender. "Has he finally flipped?"

"I may be a bit crazed," Nathan said. "But I'm not crazy. These guys don't live by your rules, or mine — shit — they make their own rules." The shaking was worse, it took hold of his entire body, convulsing in a series of spasms he couldn't control it. "They can rewrite whole programs to fit their own friggin' rules," he went on. "You can't control them, and you can't intimidate them." He gave another shaky laugh. "Because they don't exist. They're phantoms. Shape-shifters." With growing horror, he saw that the transparent cyber-bugs were back, too, crawling over

Doran's desk, flowing over the computers ranged on it. He blinked, flinching from them.

"What is this crap?" Doran straightened up and spoke to Warrender with absolute contempt. "He's off his face."

Warrender lifted an eyebrow. "That's how these geeks function," he said.

"Yeah? Well he isn't, is he? Functioning, I mean."

"Oh, God . . ." Nathan abandoned the mouse and tapped commands in on the various keyboards, his eyes flitting from screen to screen.

"What is going *on?*" Doran demanded, grabbing him by the shoulders and forcing Nathan's chair around to face him.

"I think I'm locked out."

"*Locked out?* What does that mean, you're *locked out?*"

Nathan could have used the analogy of the burglar again, only this time he would have to admit that their hypothetical burglar had broken every pass-code and had changed the numbers on every hypothetical combination lock in the building. One look at Doran's face told him that would be a stupid idea. He decided to go technical.

"He's got the Root usernames and passwords," he said, "Root is the highest level of access permissions. He's got mine, yours, Mr Warrender's — all of them — and he's changed them." He shot a frightened look at Doran. "He's booted us off the system."

"Well, you'd better just find a way back in," Doran said. Like it was that simple.

Nathan clenched his teeth. He looked up at Doran for as long as he could bear the man's hostile stare. "I can't tell what he's doing to the system while I'm locked out. Jeez, he could be doing *anything*." He pushed his chair away from the desk and stared at the computers as if they were possessed by demons.

"He needs to take an hour off," Warrender said. "Clear his head."

"I'll sort him out," Doran said. "You've got an address. Find this fucker, Warlock, or whatever he calls himself. Bring him to me."

As Warrender left, Doran slapped Nathan hard across the face.

No pain . . . Nathan thought. *No pain, no fear.* He knew it wasn't right, but he wouldn't have wanted to do anything about it now, even if he could.

What he needed was eighteen hours of drug-free sleep. What he got was a thirty-minute break and his smart drugs confiscated. It wasn't enough. It was nowhere near enough.

CHAPTER
THIRTEEN

"Naomi?"

"What's up, Sarge?" Naomi Hart sat cross-legged in front of her TV set, the lights turned low, the heating turned up, a glass of wine at her side. She kept one eye on the TV screen as she spoke into her mobile phone.

"Am I interrupting something?" Foster asked.

Hart glanced wistfully at the bowl of popcorn in her lap: a question like that from Foster, you knew he was about to. *Terminator Two* was running on the DVD, Sarah Connor was trying to break out of the insane asylum, while the latest in a line of evil robots was in the process of breaking in. Naomi clicked the "mute" key on the remote. "It'll keep," she said.

"It's Sara Geddes," Foster said.

Hart's shoulders slumped. "What now? I told her I'd contact her if —"

"She's dead, Naomi."

For a long moment, Foster's words made no sense. The images on the TV merged into meaningless colours, as amorphous and abstract as one of Sara's paintings.

"Naomi?"

"I'm still here," she said. "What happened?"

"Dunno, yet. Police surgeon is here, and the Home Office pathologist is on his way. He wants the body left *in situ* — his words, not mine."

Again, Hart had trouble grasping the reality of it: "Sara" and "body" — it didn't seem feasible, somehow. She clicked the TV's off-switch and frowned in concentration. "Where is she?"

"Her place."

"You want me there?" She was already up and searching for her keys.

"There's enough of us here to police a home derby," he said. "I'll meet you at Edge Hill in an hour."

The murder scene was awash with red and blue light, strobing incessantly from three patrol cars and an ambulance. A coroner's van was parked at a discreet distance away, next to the CSIs' van. A cordon had been drawn two doors either side of Sara's house on both sides of the street. Bursts of radio transmission broke into the quiet hum of shocked conversation from onlookers, staring in fascination from the borders of the tape.

Sara Geddes lay on her side. A pool of blood, black in the lights of the emergency vehicles, seemed to flicker like a dark halo around her head. Two CSIs, kitted out in white all-in-one suits and wearing plastic overshoes paced the area. Two more had begun erecting a tent to shield Sara from the curiosity of her neighbours and to provide some cover from the weather. The wind was cold and gusting, and squally

April showers threatened to wash away any evidence before the CSIs were able to collect it.

Rickman parked behind one of the patrol cars and scanned the people on the other side of the tape. Foster had already arrived. Good. He could take on the majority of the organisation. Rickman braced himself. He walked to one of the uniformed officers at the tape, dipping into his inside pocket to retrieve his warrant card as he identified himself.

"DS Foster's expecting you, sir," the young constable said. Foster noticed him and came over, one hand in his trouser pocket. He nodded in greeting and waited for Rickman to be allowed under the tape.

"We've got to stay on the boundaries till the CSIs have finished," he said, leading the way to a closer view of Sara's body.

Rickman's jaw worked.

"You all right with this, Jeff?"

"Yeah," Rickman said. "I think — yeah. I'm okay."

"Neighbours heard a disturbance, dialled triple nine."

"What did they see?"

"Depends who you talk to. Either Miss Geddes ran into the street, followed by one or two assailants, or she confronted a man on her doorstep. Either way, there was a struggle, she fell, he — or they — ran off."

"Description?"

"Nothing to hang your hat on. 'Tall', 'Dark clothing', 'It was too dark to see' — the usual. Her neighbour opposite is a bit more specific. Says she saw a stocky guy in a hooded jacket. She says he's been hanging around a lot."

"Bentley."

"Who else?"

"You've sent someone to pick him up?"

"Ten minutes ago."

A Mercedes pulled in behind Rickman's car and a large, middle-aged man hauled himself out, using the door frame for leverage; the Home Office pathologist had arrived. He opened the boot of his car and moments late he was squeezing himself into an oversuit. When he had slipped on a pair of overshoes, he showed his ID to one of the police constables at the tape.

He nodded to Rickman and then walked over to the body, exchanging a few words with the CSIs and the police surgeon, who was hanging around on the fringes like a groupie at a rock concert.

Rickman's eye was drawn to Sara once more, and to the corona of flickering ooze around her head. He swallowed and looked away.

"You don't need to be here, Jeff," Foster said.

In practical terms, it was true — he didn't. Rickman's role was managerial; to facilitate and oversee the work of DS Foster and DC Hart — as well as the others who would be drafted in to help now that this had become a murder investigation. But he needed to know if he could do it, despite the awful clenching pain below his heart. He had to prove to himself that he could attend a murder scene and still hold it together.

"You know, I think I do," Rickman said.

Foster looked at his friend, understanding how difficult this was for him, understanding his need to be there.

"I just wish they'd hurry up with that tent," Rickman said. It seemed indecent, leaving her exposed to the inquisitive stares of the crowd. He forced his attention back to the task at hand. "Okay. The neighbour opposite —"

"Mrs Langley," Foster said.

"Get a tech over to her to do an E-fit of the attacker. And as soon as we have Bentley in custody, I want a VIPER ID parade set up."

At last the CSIs finished the tent and pulled the door flaps closed. Rickman felt a huge wave of relief, short-lived, because moments later a small outside broadcast van arrived.

"Local TV," Foster muttered. "That's all we need."

Rickman exhaled. "Can you take this, Lee? I don't want them drawing parallels, dragging my personal life into this."

"Sure."

Rickman nodded, grateful, then he glanced around the crowd, talking low and fast. "If they talk to the neighbours, they're bound to pick up on the stalker angle. We're investigating all lines of enquiry. Keeping an open mind — you know the drill." He kept his back to the TV crew, who were setting up as he spoke.

"What about Megan?" Foster asked.

"No names — not even Sara's, until we get a positive ID. They won't be expecting anything more at this stage. I'll talk to a few people, see if we can get a team set up by morning. I'll see you back at the office."

Rickman slipped away while the TV crew were still preoccupied with lighting and sound checks.

CHAPTER
FOURTEEN

Rickman approached the newly designated Major Incident Room with mixed feelings: he felt ready to take on the investigation, but he knew that he would have his work cut out trying to convince some of the team of that. A babble of voices and some laughter pointed to a quick bonding between the team members — essential to an efficient start in the investigation.

The room's previous use was clear: the label "store" was etched in white lettering on a black background on the nameplate. He'd get that fixed pronto, before some bright spark found an alliterative alternative which included his first name and the word "junk".

He stood in the doorway and scanned the room; the cardboard boxes and broken bits of furniture had been cleared overnight and equipment shipped in from the central store in Mather Avenue. Additional electrical points had been installed and a couple of whiteboards attached to the longest section of wall, opposite the door. The grey tile floor was unpolished and the faintly musty smell of damp cardboard lingered; a couple of days' rotation would no doubt replace it with the smell of stale coffee and take-away food.

Rickman recognised many of the faces from the investigation into the refugee murders the previous year. He also noted that they were the co-operative types, the team players. He glanced over at Foster, who was flirting with DC Hart. Foster might play the fool, but Rickman knew that he had hand-picked each officer, matching experience and enthusiasm, balancing steady nerves against the eagerness of the newcomer, and discreetly making sure they were on-side, as far as Rickman was concerned. Hart's face was slightly flushed and her body was angled towards Foster. She fell silent when she saw Rickman and nodded in his direction.

The noise level dropped as more people noticed him. Some avoided his eye: those who had listened to the canteen gossip, he guessed — maybe even contributed to it. Most, however, seemed keen to make a start, gratified to have been assigned to a major incident, and excited at the prospect of being allowed to show their capabilities.

Rickman made the introductions for the benefit of the two or three strangers among them, and explained that this had been DS Foster's investigation until Sara Geddes was murdered. Then Foster ran through events to date.

"Bentley is AWOL," he said. "We've got a trace alert with his mobile phone service provider. They've tried pinging it, but either he's switched it off or it's out of charge."

"I want surveillance on his flat," Rickman said. "Sound out his place of work — see if you think they'd co-operate — give us the nod if he shows up there."

"Do we know Sara Geddes was the intended target?" somebody asked.

"The honest answer is no," Rickman said. "I expect you to find out." He turned to Foster. "What have we got on Megan?" Foster had, in fact, already updated him; this was for the benefit of the rest of the team.

"Inland Revenue checks show no record of Megan paying tax, National Insurance contributions or declaring income of any kind." His gaze flitted from one face to the next. "In *fact* there's no work record at all for Megan Ward." The catarrhal catch on the word *fact* emphasised the unusual nature of what he was telling them. "She's got a passport and driver's licence, but there's no record of medical registration, no hospital admissions, no university or college registration."

"I did find a school record for her," Hart chipped in. Rickman noticed the men in the room studying Hart; her finely made features, the pale fall of blonde hair, her slim figure. Hart, however, seemed oblivious. "She attended Tyndale Primary School in Colne from 1985 to 1991, and Colne High School from '91 to '97. Then — nothing. It's like she vanished from public records after that age."

"Except for the passport and driving licence." Chris Tunstall pointed this out. He was a beefy Widnesian who tended to engage his mouth before his brain was fully in gear, but Rickman had cause in the past to value Tunstall's rather pedestrian approach.

107

Rickman frowned at him for some moments and Tunstall became uncomfortable, shifting slightly in his chair. "Okay . . ." Rickman said.

Tunstall looked troubled, unsure if he was about to be praised for his sharp insight or criticised for stating the bleeding obvious.

"Get onto the General Registry Office," Rickman said. "Ask them to check with ELVIS."

"It were just an observation, sir," Tunstall said, evidently hurt by Rickman's unnecessarily heavy use of sarcasm.

There were a few sniggers from the officers who didn't know Tunstall. His broad Lancashire accent and big rugby-player's build meant he was often underestimated.

Foster rolled his eyes. "ELVIS, Tunstall. It's a database. Links deaths with birth records, compares them with passports issued."

"Oh," Tunstall said, his face a blank. Then a few moments later, "*Ohhh* . . ."

"Any other comments, suggestions?" Rickman asked.

"The DVLA still haven't got back to us with her photo. They should have it as a digital image," Hart said. "We could ask them to send us a jpeg — that's computer-speak for a picture, Sarge," she added.

Rickman smiled. Hart had always had a soft spot for Tunstall, and this was her attempt at drawing some fire away from him. It worked.

"She's not kidding," Foster said, laughing with the rest. "I don't know a jpeg from a tent peg."

"I'll see if I can get them moving on that one," Rickman said, when the laughter had died down. "Anything from the credit card?"

"It's a dummy," Foster answered. "The number didn't link to any VISA account."

"Yet she hid it in the lining of that box." Rickman absently traced a scar on his chin with his thumb. "Did you check the magnetic strip?"

"I ran it through the piece of kit in the custody suite — it came out with a load of rubbish."

"It might be encrypted," Hart said. "If there's sensitive numbers on there, and Megan's a bit of a techie." Everyone looked at her, and she shrugged. "It's what I'd do."

"Get Technical Support to have a look at it." Rickman was fast remembering why he had liked Hart the last time they worked together. "If there's any info stored on the magnetic strip, I want to know."

"D'you think Megan is involved?" Foster asked.

He was on his way back to his office to pick up Megan's VISA card. Tunstall had been charged with finding a suitable Exhibits Room, but for now, the shoe box and its contents were locked in the bottom drawer of Foster's filing cabinet.

He and Rickman walked down the back stairway, their footsteps echoing on the concrete steps. The rest of the team had been deployed on various tasks; Rickman's was to start costing the investigation, but the prospect of totting up fees for forensic procedures and surveillance schedules, of weighing costs against a woman's life, was less than enticing, so Foster's question was a welcome diversion.

"Megan's involved, all right," Rickman said.

"You seem pretty sure."

"Sara Geddes leads an uneventful life, work, home, odd theatre trips," Rickman reasoned. "She's respected by her colleagues and superiors, spends her free time painting — hardly what you'd call a high-risk hobby. Then Megan Ward comes into her life and suddenly she's being stalked, she's getting silent calls, Megan disappears without trace and, within six months of her arrival on the scene, Sara is dead."

"When you put it like that . . ."

"I'm not saying she's guilty, Lee, but there's got to be some reason for all of this, and the only thing that changed in Sara's life is Megan."

"You think she's on the run from something?"

"In one form or another." The rootlessness, the craving for anonymity pointed towards something, and it couldn't be good.

CHAPTER
FIFTEEN

Fay Doran watched her boys from the corner of her eye. They were engaged in a game of endurance, kicking each other under the table — the challenge was not to cry out. They were managing quite well, eating their cereal and supping weak tea with barely a flicker of the eyelids to show how much pain the one inflicted upon the other. She suspected Declan had the upper hand — he was precisely twenty-seven minutes older than Frankie, and the more assertive and aggressive of the twins, though few could tell the boys apart. For the moment, Fay let them be; she had more important things on her mind.

She toasted bread and plonked it in front of them, then set to work preparing their sandwiches for lunch. Occasionally her gaze would flit to the kitchen door, half-expecting Patrick to appear. He hadn't been home in five days, except to shower and change. Then last evening, without any explanation, he was at the front door, his key scratching in the lock as though he was drunk. He stumbled in and went straight to his study, refusing food and drink, refusing even to talk. She cooked an omelette and brewed a pot of tea despite his refusal. He waited for her to leave before opening the door to take in the tray of food.

She hadn't seen him like this in nearly twenty years. That time, he had come to her and wept in her arms like a child, but he had grown tougher since, and she rarely knew if there was trouble at work.

Just after midnight, she had heard a car pull into the drive. She hurried into the hall: if the doorbell rang at this time of night, they would wake the whole house, and once the boys were awake, there was no persuading them that it wasn't time to get up. Patrick came out of his study and waved her away.

"I'll get it," he said.

She didn't argue, nor did she leave.

Two men came through the door, one she didn't recognise, the other was John Warrender. Her breath caught in her throat and she glared at her husband.

He let the men go ahead. "Please," he said, placing his hands on her shoulders. "Not now."

She stiffened under his touch. "You let *that man* into our house, and you're telling me 'not now'?" Her west-country Irish accent was exaggerated by her anger.

"I have no choice, Fay." His voice cracked a little and she felt as if someone had slipped a knife under her ribs, into her heart. They hadn't spoken since, and as far as she knew, Patrick hadn't slept.

The kitchen door opened and Fay turned from the counter, a buttery knife in her hand and anxiety etched in the lines of her face. She exhaled loudly when she saw it was Maura. "Hurry up," she said. "You've barely time for breakfast."

Her daughter flicked a long hank of jet-black hair over her shoulder. Maura was like her in many ways: the glossy black hair and the blue-eyed Irish complexion — pale, and given to pretty blushes, but also prone to flush hotly when she was crossed.

"I've got guitar class after school," Maura said, as though her mother hadn't spoken. "We'll grab a pizza then go on to band practice. It won't finish till late, but Gray said he'll give me a lift home."

Fay raised a carefully plucked eyebrow. "Gray of the Celtic tattoos and body piercing?" she said. "Gray of the monstrous motorcycle?"

"It's a Kawasaki."

"Kamikasi, did you say?"

Maura huffed. "You're so judgmental." When she saw that contempt wasn't working, she tried wheedling, instead: "He's really careful . . ."

"Nineteen-year-old boys are rarely 'careful' on their motor bikes, Maura. One of us will pick you up — ten o'clock sharp. It's a school day," Fay added, seeing her daughter roll her eyes. "And you should eat something before you go."

Maura glared at her mother, and the boys stopped kicking each other, a more bloody sport seemingly in the offing. This was becoming a daily battle, but one Fay was determined she would win. She poured tea into a mug and placed a slice of toast on a plate for Maura.

The door opened again and Patrick stood on the threshold as if uncertain of his welcome. Suddenly, Maura was all smiles.

"Daddy!" She ran to him, flinging her arms around his neck.

Patrick Doran hugged his daughter, holding her to him as if he feared she might fall.

She pulled away from him almost immediately. "Gross!" she exclaimed. "You're all scratchy."

He lifted a skein of cool glossy hair and smoothed it over her shoulder. "Go and eat your breakfast, darling," he said, staring past her at Fay.

Maura almost danced to the table, pausing only to tweak Declan's earlobe.

"Stop kicking your brother," she said, transformed from sulky teen to responsible older sister by her father's presence.

Fay stared into her husband's face. He looked ill; pale as parchment. Every line around his eyes and mouth looked as if it had been etched five years deeper in the last five days. His eyes, hollow and shadowed, glittered with feverish intensity. He gazed into her face, his hands limp at his sides. That look made Fay afraid for them all: over the years, she had seen Patrick in many moods — elated, happy, excited, anxious, sad, drunk, angry, and sober, but she had never seen him despair.

"I need a cheque for my guitar lessons," Maura said, cheerfully munching her toast. "And there's a letter in my bag about the foreign exchange trip. I forgot about it."

"I'll write you a cheque tomorrow," Fay said, her eyes still locked on Patrick's. "Get your things, boys — your sister will walk you to school today."

All three turned to her in dismay. "*Mum!*"

"No arguments," Fay said.

"But I've got my guitar lesson — and it's going to rain," Maura protested.

"That's what the case is for," Fay said. "Please, Maura, just do it."

"I don't see why we have to *walk!*" Maura exclaimed, swinging back to petulance in an instant.

"*Maura.*" The edge to her father's voice silenced her immediately. She looked at him wide-eyed. "I need to talk to your mother," he said more gently. "Can you do this?"

She stared at the boys, her resentment at being asked to childmind still evident. Then she raised her shoulders and let them drop. "Let's go, you two monster-munchkins," she said, taking Frankie's hand.

They listened to the children arguing quietly in the hallway, heard the slam of the cloakroom door, the scuffle as Maura got them into coats and shoes, and organised bags. They heard the muted clang of chords as she bashed her guitar on the door jamb on the way out, her soft curse and the final jostle as she shoved the boys through the front door without calling goodbye. Doran waited for the clank and drone of the electric motor which opened the gates to the driveway, then he gave a long, shuddering sigh.

"God, Pat, what is it?"

Tears filmed his eyes.

He led Fay through to his office. She balked seeing that Warrender was still there, but feeling the gentle pressure of Patrick's hand on her back, she stepped inside against her will — against her better judgement. She greeted the head of security with a curt, "Mister Warrender." He acknowledged her with a nod and she felt his cold appraisal. Offended, she held his gaze until he looked away: she would not be intimidated in her own home.

Her husband introduced the second man as David Manning. His handshake was warm and firm. He had a round face, made for smiling, though he wasn't smiling now.

"Mr Manning is a technical forensics expert," Patrick said.

Fay was puzzled: they had already tracked the hacker down, hadn't they? Warrender and the boy who ran the computer system — she never could remember their names, didn't want to get to know the shy, obsessive boys Patrick employed to manage his computers; after the first one, she had made an effort not to get to know them.

Warrender asked, "Do you know what a technical forensic expert does?" That was his style — every conversation an interrogation.

"Forensic *and* technical," Fay said, replying to his patronising tone with waspish sarcasm. "Let me guess — one of the computers died."

Patrick looked at her sharply. Warrender puffed air between his lips and looked away; the contempt on his face made her want to slap him.

"I investigate computer crime," Mr Manning said. His glance into her face was kind and respectful. "Fraud, hacking, identity theft . . ." He left the last two words hanging and Fay's gaze strayed once more to her husband.

"Mrs Doran, we think that the hacker got access to your husband's business system via your home computer." Mr Manning's slate-grey eyes searched hers.

Fay frowned. "That's impossible — we're not — connected?" She didn't know the correct term.

"Networked," Mr Manning said, ever helpful. "But there are other ways of gaining access."

"Oh?" she said, a little on the defensive, now.

Mr Manning looked embarrassed. He glanced quickly at her husband, then back to Fay. "Did you —?" He tried again. "Is it possible that you —"

"Have you given out your online or phone banking username and password to anyone?" Warrender asked, barely deigning to look at her.

"No," Fay said evenly, "I'd have to be an idiot to do that, and since I'm *not* —"

"Nobody's saying you are, Mrs Doran," Mr Manning said, taking charge again. "And I'm sorry to question you like this, but if you can bear with us, it really would help, if only to rule out certain possibilities."

Fay looked at her husband. He stared back as though he didn't see her. He was dishevelled, his face coarsened with fatigue and beard stubble. Seeing no help from that quarter, she came to a decision. Mr Manning was only trying to do his job. "Ask away," she said.

"Have you ever visited an internet chatroom, or maybe given your email address to someone you later felt . . . uneasy about?"

She bridled immediately. "My teenage daughter visits chatrooms, Mr Manning." At such times, her soft Irish tones became clipped even prim. "I, however, have been all grown up for some time."

Mr Manning smiled apologetically. "You'd be surprised — there are specialist message boards for every kind of enthusiast. Every age."

Fay had the sense that she had hurt his feelings and she was sorry for that: he seemed a nice enough man, and she didn't think he was trying to catch her out.

Warrender had an amused look on his face, overlaid by contempt, and Fay realised that she was right — she had hit too close to home. She had a sudden instinct to protect Mr Manning from Warrender's cold scrutiny.

"Would it help if I told you how I use the computer?" she asked.

Mr Manning seemed relieved. "That would be very helpful."

"Business letters," she said. "Flights bookings, rail tickets, holidays — that sort of thing. I email my sister in New Zealand and my family in Ireland. I've bought DVDs for the kids, electrical goods for the house — and I look things up with the kids for their homework." She hesitated, knowing that Patrick wouldn't like what she was about to say, and Mr Manning nodded encouragement.

She sighed. "I . . . occasionally buy collectables from eBay." She focused on Mr Manning, not wanting to see her husband's disapproval.

He didn't smile, exactly, but a corner of his mouth twitched, as though he was pleased that she too had secret passions. "How do you pay?" he asked.

"Paypal or banker's draft."

He nodded. "Ever had any problems?"

"No . . ." A troubling thought crossed her mind. "No," she said again. "Not with Paypal."

The tension in the room wound up a notch. She sensed latent violence in Warrender, and even Patrick seemed to be trying to subdue something volatile and dangerous in himself.

"It's not like I lost any money," she said, on the defensive.

Mr Manning said, "Why don't you just run it past me — I can decide if it's relevant."

"I collect Guinness memorabilia," she said. "I saw a Royal Doulton toucan on eBay." She stole a guilty glance at her husband. "I contacted the dealer. He seemed a really nice guy — we had a lot in common." She was blushing now. "He didn't want any money up front — just asked me to set up an account with him so I could check the progress of the delivery. I could pay him if I was satisfied with its condition on arrival." She shrugged. "It seemed I couldn't lose."

"But the toucan never arrived?"

"No. I mailed him a few times after a couple of weeks went by, but I never got a reply."

"Mrs Doran," Mr Manning said, "how did you set up your account?"

"I gave my name and address, of course. A username and password, and I had to answer a couple of standard questions . . ." A creeping dread began to assert itself and she faltered.

"What were these 'standard questions'?" Mr Manning asked. "Mother's maiden name? First pet's name?"

She nodded, twice, her neck stiff on her shoulders.

"And the username and password?"

Her eyes widened with the horror of what she had done.

"Bloody hell!" Warrender exploded. "She gave her personal username and password!"

Anger flared in Fay's gut and she turned to her husband. "I'd prefer if he wasn't here."

Patrick looked weary, barely able to stand. "He needs to know, Fay."

She gritted her teeth and focused on Patrick's gaunt face. "Then tell him later."

After a moment's hesitation, he said, "Wait outside."

"Outside the house," Fay said, still holding her husband's gaze. There was a brief moment of silent struggle, then Patrick Doran lifted his chin, acquiescing.

Fay felt Warrender's eyes on her as he walked past her to the door. She waited until he closed the front door behind him before speaking. "He got to you through me, didn't he?"

120

Doran nodded, sinking at last into a chair as if his legs would no longer carry the awful weight of circumstances. She had given this destructive force a way into her husband's place of work, into his business accounts, his records, their lives.

"I don't understand how," she said. "Patrick doesn't use my password on his system, and we're not —" She frowned, irritated to have forgotten the term again.

"Networked," Mr Manning said.

"Your password —" Doran began, but he couldn't go on. He covered his mouth with one hand and gestured for Mr Manning to take over.

"Your username and password gives access to correspondence, emails and so on. Does Mr Doran send you emails when he's away on business trips?"

"Yes."

"An email would carry information about the office system. It might be something as simple as how you configure email addresses: *p.doran@safehandssecurity.com*, for example. Some businesses use first name addresses, so *patrick1@safehandssecurity.com* might be an alternative. If he knows how they're structured, a hacker can create an email address for himself on the business system, then import viruses or Trojans to help him gain higher access."

"Which is how he got into the business current account," Fay said, feeling sick with regret.

Mr Manning nodded. "Then he backtracked."

Fay frowned. "Backtracked? To our home computer? What would be the point?"

"With bank account details stolen from correspondence to your bank he could do a lot of damage."

"Oh God." Fay sat on a chair opposite her husband and reached out her hand, then took it back again, appalled and half-afraid.

"How much did you have in your personal account?" Mr Manning asked.

For a second or two he sounded like background noise, barely audible over the buzzing in her head, then Fay realised he had asked the question of her and she blinked, trying to concentrate. "I don't know — ten thousand?" She tried to block him out, to focus on her husband. He was too still, too quiet. "Thereabouts."

"The account is now two thousand pounds in debit," Mr Manning said.

Fay felt sick and weak. What had she done? What had she *done*?

"He seemed so plausible," she said. "So pleasant — he didn't even want money. He just seemed to enjoy —" She shrugged helplessly, knowing how pathetic it sounded. "He seemed to enjoy talking to me."

Doran's eyes flickered, and he looked up slowly like a man waking from a terrible dream, "Are you saying that we've been stripped of all our assets because of a bit of internet flirtation, Fay? Is that what it was?" He sounded bitter and sick with fury.

"No! It was . . ." She looked to Mr Manning for help, knowing that Patrick was right — she had been lonely and frustrated after weeks of him working eighteen hours a day, and she had been flattered by the attention.

"You need some time alone," Mr Manning said. "I'll make a few calls, maybe brew some tea."

Doran laughed; the sound dangerous and high. "Yes, that ought to help. Let's all have tea."

Mr Manning left with a sympathetic glance at Fay, closing the door with a soft "click".

"Patrick —"

"Don't," Doran said. They sat in silence for some time, then Doran rubbed both hands over his stubbled face and through his hair. He stared at her, his fingers grasping tufts of hair, making him look slightly demented.

"There were other accounts," he said. "I set them up on your computer to keep them away from work. The auditors . . . the tax man."

"Accounts?" she said. "More than one?"

"Three." He sighed so heavily his body shook. "Three accounts, all wiped out." Then he brought his hands to the back of his neck, gripping it tightly. "It's all gone, Fay."

CHAPTER
SIXTEEN

Jake Bentley had returned to the place where he felt safe. He had booked into a B&B in Ainsdale, near the dunes. He wanted sand in his shoes, the wind in his hair; he thought it would make him feel better. It didn't.

His first happy memory of childhood had been playing in the dunes as a twelve-year-old. Till then, he hadn't known how big the sky was, that there could be so much space, that you could roll in sand and it would brush off clean. All of this seemed magical to him after the narrow streets of Walton. There, you saw the sky in mean strips, glimpsed between the huddled terraces, and when you played in the street, you stayed dirty, and Jake had always liked to be clean.

At twelve, he was skinny and sickly and his face was disfigured by acne. The other kids called him pizza-face and nobody would sit with him at lunch because they said the sight of him made them want to barf. His mother took him to a doctor, who prescribed antibiotics and suggested that sea air might do some good.

Every Sunday, his mother would pack a picnic lunch and they would take the train to Ainsdale. She would sit on a beach towel and administer his prescribed dose of sea air, grimly reading her magazines till they tore like tissue paper in the salt-spumed wind.

Jake didn't care — if it rained or the wind blew up a storm, he would insist on going. He put on muscle and developed a salt-brown patina, like waxed wood. The acne faded and his mother smiled with satisfaction that she had created such a handsome boy. The jibes and the bullying stopped at school. Some of the girls would even glance over at him and smile shyly, but he never spoke to them, and never felt forgiven for his past ugliness.

By the time he was thirteen, he was making the journey alone, enjoying the feeling of independence it gave him, the solitude amongst the car-loads of day-trippers. It was here he first began watching women; it was easy to observe without being observed on a beach, in the dunes. He came to know the hollows where they would go for privacy, slip off their bikini tops to catch the sun.

A gull sobbed on the rooftop of the B&B. It sounded like a demented mother grieving for her lost child. He went to the window and looked out onto the street below. Sand devils skirmished on the tarmac, whipped to a frenzy by the April wind. If he pressed his cheek against the glass and looked to the left, he could just make out the dunes. With their ragged tufts of marram grass they looked like herds of dromedaries marching to the sea.

It made him sick to think what had happened to Sara. He had seen the men pull up outside the house.

125

Two got out, one stayed in the car. Sara had not yet arrived home. He had scrunched down, cramping his knees against the steering wheel. He fired off a couple of frames — not very good ones because he was unprepared: it was Sara he was waiting for. The two men went inside — no more than thirty seconds playing with the lock and then they were in, closing the door behind them. He saw a light go on in Megan's office. They moved quickly, searching under bookshelves, in drawers. Lifting pictures off the walls and wrenching the backs from the frames.

Suddenly, Sara was outside the house, taking her keys from her handbag, letting herself in. Intent on the damage they were doing to Megan's room, he hadn't seen her arrive. He would have warned her, but he didn't want to frighten her — she wouldn't have understood. He had a restraining order against him; what would she have thought if he got out of his car and started shouting to her?

She went in. He thought about going after her, but there was no time. She reappeared, running out of the house, her eyes huge, her face contorted with fear. They were after her. Again, he hesitated: should he intervene? Would it make things worse? She might think he was with the men.

A vivid flash of recall: Sara running, her eyes wide. He almost went to her; had his hand on the car door-handle. One of the men grabbed her. She screamed, lashed out with her feet. Broke free. Fell.

He flinched, hearing again the crack of her skull on stone. Not so hard as a plant-pot's fall, not so soft as an eggshell. But there was a definite *crack!* The screams. The ugly sound of bone impacting on brains and blood. The terrible, terrible silence.

It was too late — there was nothing he could do. Even so, after the men left, he got out of his car and went to see if he could help.

"Fuck it," he muttered. He would have done anything for Sara, but now Sara was dead and he had to start thinking about himself. And he did his best thinking on the move. Minutes later, he was out of the house and jogging down the street, taking it slow at first, the sand like tiny ball-bearings under his trainers making the pavement treacherous.

Soon he was into the dunes, rediscovering the soft yield of sand underfoot and soothed by the insistent cry of gulls on the wing. On the beach, the long stretch of flat yellow sand and the wide sky beckoned him, and he fell into the old rhythm of those childhood seaside excursions: his feet pounding the sand, the roar of wind and surf a constant, drowning the sound of his breathing, his thoughts, his worries, his fears.

He knew one of the men. This was a revelation: he had pushed it to the back of his mind, not wanting to confront it, but the calming rhythm and the pain of pushing himself on an unfamiliar surface had a cleansing effect, making difficult truths somehow easier to face.

The man was a regular at the gym. He worked for Patrick Doran. Bentley knew this, just as he knew the make and model of Doran's car, that Patrick Doran had a pretty Irish wife eight years younger than him, twin boys aged eight, and a seventeen-year-old girl who took after her mother.

The man he had seen outside Sara's house was a relative newcomer. His mates called him "Cap", but Bentley knew he could find out his real name quite easily — that wasn't a problem. The problem was what to do with the information.

He looped off the beach and into the dunes. Out of the wind, he sweated freely, drenching his hooded sweat-top. He could hear himself here — the push of his breath, the salty hiss of his trainers in the soft sand. At the end of another two miles hard slog he had made up his mind.

He ran on, jogging down side roads until he reached Liverpool Road. He went into the first phone box available. He hadn't brought any spare change, but he wouldn't need it for this call.

"I'm not in the habit of accepting reverse charge calls from strangers," Doran said. His voice sounded cracked and old. "So this better be good."

"I saw what happened to Sara Geddes, Mr Doran," Bentley said, excited and terrified. He was talking to Patrick Doran and Mr Doran was listening. "I'm about to go and report what I saw to the police, but I thought I should get my story straight, first."

CHAPTER
SEVENTEEN

He had it all straight by the time he walked into Edge Hill Police Station at four p.m.

Naomi Hart sensed the difference in him immediately. She seated him in the same interview chair and went through the formalities as she had done before. Bentley listened carefully, alert and watchful, rather than miserable and guilty as he had seemed on the previous occasion. Despite his size and bulk, he had seemed to shrink in the chair when they had first brought him in about the stalking accusations. Now, he filled the room with an exuberance, a warped energy that Hart found unsettling.

"Right off the bat," he said, before either Hart or Foster had the chance to ask him a question, "I'm not proud of running away. I should've stayed."

"So why did you run?" Hart asked.

"I was afraid of what people would think."

"You worry a lot what people think of you, don't you, Mr Bentley?" Foster asked.

A troubled look crossed Bentley's face. "I'm just saying —"

"Nothing wrong with that," Foster interrupted. "Good citizens care what people think. That's what makes them do the right thing."

Bentley was confused. If he agreed, that meant he did things because they were expected of him, which would then make him a sad case who had no opinions of his own. But if he said he didn't give a toss, that would make him a bad person — a bad *citizen* — and for the purposes of his interview, he was Joe Average, law-abiding, unimaginative, reliable.

"I just knew you'd jump to conclusions," he said, sticking to the script. "But I ran, and that was wrong of me."

"Okay," Hart said. "You've made that clear. Now, why don't you tell us what made you decide to break the terms of the restraining order?"

Bentley took a breath. "I was worried. When you said Sara's lodger — Megan? — had vanished, yeah, I was worried. So I went to check that Sara was all right." He opened his hands, palms up — no weapons, nothing concealed.

Foster shook his head, smiling. "You were obsessed with Miss Geddes," he said. "You couldn't break that obsession."

"I was *concerned* for her safety," Bentley insisted.

"A witness identified you as one of the attackers," Hart said.

"No." He shook his head vehemently. "No way. I was there to protect her."

"Right . . ." Foster said. "So what went wrong, Big Man?"

Bentley looked at his hands. "I was too late."

"Did you see the men who attacked Miss Geddes?" Hart asked.

"I caught a glimpse. But it was dark, you know? I was in shock."

"Tell us what you saw."

"She was struggling with one of the men." He fiddled with his shirt cuff. He had worn a shirt and tie, smart trousers, knowing that he might be required to stand before a magistrate for committal, wanting to create the right impression. He took another breath. "This is *hard*, you know?" He looked to Hart for sympathy.

"I know, Mr Bentley," she said. "In your own time — whenever you're ready."

He took a breath, then started again. "She was struggling. She kicked him. He hit her. She fell . . ." He shuddered, recalling the sickening soft splat of her head on the pavement. He looked into Hart's eyes, his face intent, sincere. "If I'd reacted quicker — if I'd got there a minute or two earlier . . ." He sighed and clasped his hands in front of him.

Hart sucked her teeth. "Describe the men," she said.

"Big. Dark clothing." He shrugged. "Didn't get a look at their faces."

"The car?"

"I wish I could help," he said, shaking his head slowly. "Like I said —"

"Yeah, you were in shock," Hart said. Her tone more sharp than he would have liked and he began to protest. "We'd like to do an ID parade," she said, cutting across him.

This was not in the script. They hadn't even considered it. "I don't know about that," he said. "I mean, these people could pick me out because they've seen me in the street . . ."

"You want to help Sara?" Hart said, still with that unfriendly edge to her voice. "You say you were concerned for her. Help her now — agree to the ID parade."

He looked from one to the other, calculating the risks. A good defence council would tear a parade identification to shreds for exactly the reasons he had just given — and Bentley knew for damn sure he would get the best defence.

He lifted his head up and looked Hart in the eye. "All right," he said. "For Sara."

"He's a changed man, isn't he?" Foster said. Bentley had been taken down to the cells, pending the arrival of his solicitor. Hart was on her way to the exhibits room, and Foster tagged along. "No denials. Taking responsibility for his actions."

"Yeah," Hart said. "A miracle."

"Almost like he grew a pair overnight."

"He'll sound good on the transcripts," Hart said. "D'you think he's been coached?"

"Only as hard as Liverpool FC for the FA cup final."

"Do we know who he's asked for?" Hart was referring to Bentley's belated request for a solicitor.

"I checked with the custody sergeant." Foster paused and Hart looked at him, waiting for an answer. "Keiran Jago."

Hart stopped dead and a clerk hurrying behind them bumped into her, apologised and then squeezed past on.

the narrow corridor. "How can a no-mark like Bentley afford Keiran Jago?" Hart asked.

"Good question. I'll have a word with him when he arrives."

Jago was the son of Irish immigrants, educated at St Edward's Grammar School before it took fright at the prospect of being forced into comprehensive school status at the end of the 1970s and went private. He gained a double first in history and law at Oxford, funding himself with grants, bursaries, prizes and scholarships which he applied for almost indiscriminately. In recent years, he had become a solicitor-advocate, and law lecturers advised their students to attend trials he was defending and take notes.

"He agreed to the ID parade too easily," Hart said, moving on again; she had to log the interview tapes with the exhibits officer before getting on to calling in the witness who identified Bentley at the scene.

"'Course he agreed — we'd need a rock-solid witness to make that one stick — and even if we use VIPER, it'll take a couple of days to set up."

"You're saying Bentley's gonna end up back on the street."

"I'd put money on it," Foster said.

"Can't we hold him on the breach of the restraining order? He's admitted to being there."

Foster shrugged. "It's not like Sara's under threat any more . . ."

They pushed through a fire door and took the back stairs to the top floor. The corridor was crammed with cardboard boxes filled with yellowed papers, broken lamps, body armour, batons, sports kit, dusty folders containing out-of-date guidelines and faded copies of Home Office codes of practice. Tunstall stood at the entrance of the first room on the left, trying to manhandle a broken office chair through the narrow doorway. The big man sweated profusely, angling the chair badly so that he caught his elbows on the doorframe. He swore loudly and colourfully, throwing the chair down in temper and stepping back into the corridor berating it as though it had a life and will of its own.

"Need some help?" Hart asked, keeping her face straight.

"Oh, hell," Tunstall said, wiping the sweat from his face with his shirt sleeve. "I am sorry, Naomi. Didn't see you there."

She gave him the tapes to hold and edged past him.

"You'll not shift it," Tunstall said. "I reckon they must've built the room around that chuffing thing."

She tilted the chair and eased the backrest through the door, scraping the one remaining wheel on the paintwork, but otherwise had little problem with the manoeuvre.

Foster laughed and Hart gave him a look.

"What're you going to do with this lot, Chris?" she asked, indicating the chaos around them.

"God knows," Tunstall said. "I think the boss has ordered a skip or summat."

"Better check through the paperwork, make sure you're not chucking case files out with the dross," Foster said, patting him on the shoulder.

134

Tunstall looked despondently at the jumble around him.

"Maybe you could ask the boss to send some clerical staff to help out with that, Sarge?" Hart suggested.

Foster rolled his eyes. "Oh, all right then." He glanced at Tunstall. "You know, she's not this nice to everyone."

Hart smiled, surprised, Foster had sounded almost plaintive.

"Have you checked with the General Registry Office, yet?" Foster said. "Asked them to run Megan's name through ELVIS?"

"Do me a favour, Sarge," Tunstall complained. "I've been up to me armpits in crap all day."

Hart thought there was a hint of malice in the question and stepped in. "I've got a minute — I'll see what I can find out."

Foster checked his watch. "You'll be lucky. It's already after five." He shook his head. "You've got to learn to prioritise, mate."

"DCI said this *was* a priority," Tunstall said.

Hart waited until Sergeant Foster's footsteps were no more than a faint echo retreating down the stairwell. Then she turned to Tunstall.

"Don't worry about it," she said. "I'll sort ELVIS in the morning. You know what to do with those?"

He looked at the tapes in his hand. "I write them up in the exhibits register," he said, as though reciting something he had carefully memorised.

"And put them where you'll find them again," Hart said. "Bentley's solicitor will be wanting a copy when he arrives." She stepped into the room. It was empty — rather dusty, but the shelving was clear and ready for use. "You might want to divide off the room into areas: tapes, paperwork and such separate from physical evidence," she said. "And If I were you, I'd scrounge a few boxes for the smaller, fiddly exhibits, otherwise they could get lost under stuff. Everything will come bagged and tagged, but make sure you label any boxed items clearly."

"Right-o," he said, assimilating the instructions in the slow-but-retentive way that she had come to understand was more effective than some of the bright terrier types who responded snappily and forgot what you told them five minutes later.

"Naomi . . ." he said, as she signed the register.

"Hmm?"

"What do I do about all the muck in here?" He stared soulfully into her face.

Hart smiled. *Bloody men! Give them an inch, they'll expect you to do the housework.* She handed him the pen. "Talk to one of the cleaning staff — they'll loan you a couple of J-cloths if you ask nicely."

CHAPTER
EIGHTEEN

VIPER, the Video Identification Parades Electronic Reporting procedure had been in use on the force for several years. It was fast, because the Identification Officer — in this instance a police inspector stationed at Edge Hill — didn't have to scrounge around for volunteers off the street. The system had a database of seven thousand faces, video recorded in front, left and right side view, so an approximate match wasn't difficult; the computer software did all the hard work of sorting and sifting according to race and physical appearance.

Bentley was a man of his word — he stuck to his agreement and submitted to the procedure before leaving the station. DC Hart contacted their witness, Mrs Langley, to arrange a day for her to come in and do the identification.

"I can send someone to pick you up, if you like," Hart said.

"Can't you come?" Mrs Langley sounded older, more frail than when Hart had spoken to her earlier in the day. The woman Hart had interviewed was robust, tall and athletic-looking, her grey hair cut short and brushed straight. Then, she had seemed gossipy and interested, the type who liked to know her neighbours and their business but whose interest was not malicious; now she sounded like an elderly lady in shock: vulnerable and fragile, as though something had broken within her.

"I'd feel happier if you were to come," she said.

"I'm afraid I'm not allowed to do that, Mrs Langley," Hart said. "It has to be an officer with no involvement in the enquiry. But I can send a female officer. She'll take good care of you."

There was a pause, and when Mrs Langley spoke, there was a tremor in her voice. "What if I see him, though? He might recognise me."

"He won't be there," Hart assured her. "We do it all with video recordings, these days. You'll look at a recording of eight different men and the officer in charge will ask if you recognise the man you saw the night Miss Geddes was attacked."

"And he definitely won't be there . . ."

"Only on the recording."

Mrs Langley agreed, but it took five more minutes of reassurance. Hart gave her the Identification Officer's name and told her to expect a call in the next twenty-four hours: DCI Rickman wanted this actioned as a priority.

The buzz of conversation dimmed to a hum as soon as Rickman entered the Incident Room for the seven-thirty debrief. At six-foot four, he was hard to miss, and by the time he reached the whiteboard, the room was silent. A photograph of Sara Geddes had been blu-tacked next to Sara's pencil drawing of Megan Ward. Her name, age, occupation and time of death had been written below with a dry-wipe marker. They had precious little on Megan: approximate age, a bogus occupation, approximate time of disappearance — even her picture was an approximation, an interpretation sketched from memory, and Rickman knew just how faulty that could be.

He started with the post mortem results. "Post mortem confirms the head injury as cause of death," he said. "Sara's mother has formally identified the body and her name has been released to the press. Jake Bentley's out of custody, but we've got a witness coming in who we hope can place him at the scene."

He located DC Garvey, sitting next to the water cooler. "Anything from his place of work?" he asked.

Garvey was in his early forties. He had worked with Rickman before and had proved solid and reliable. "He turns up on time, stays after to use the facilities himself. Nothing of interest in his locker, or at his home address." They still had the confiscated photographs as evidence.

"Okay." Rickman glanced around the room; the team looked tired and a little rumpled, but not desperate. It was important to keep morale up at this stage. "Who's on house-to-house?" he asked.

Garvey raised his hand, along with two others whose names Rickman hadn't yet memorised.

"We did most of them yesterday," Garvey said. "Shouldn't take too long."

"What's the sequence of events so far?"

"Shouts and screaming." Garvey referred this time to his notebook. "Sara on the ground, bleeding from a head wound. Two men standing over her — possibility three. They got into a car — Merc or BMW. Car sped off towards Lark Lane. A minute later a second car — possibly an old Nova — drove off towards Ullett Road at speed."

"Bentley?"

Garvey shrugged. "He owns a Nova."

Rickman related Bentley's confession and his denial that he had been involved in the attack. There was an exchange of disbelieving glances between members of the team. "Anything from the murder scene or the house?" he asked Tony Mayle.

As Crime Scene Co-ordinator, he had an overview of any and all crime scenes relating to the case. "Witness statements indicate they wore hoods," he said. Mayle was known by most of the officers present: as an ex-cop, he had experience which drew respect that was sometimes withheld from non-police CSIs. He was quietly spoken, but his voice carried well in the overcrowded room, and although his hair had begun to grey, he looked fit and active for a man in his mid-forties. "I'd lay bets they wore gloves as well," he went on. "The only prints we found were Sara Geddes's. We got a couple of footprints from the carpet —"

"Woah!" Rickman exclaimed. "Wait a second — no other prints except for Sara's?"

"None." Mayle saw where he was going with this and sat up straighter. "Nothing that might belong to Megan."

"Well isn't she the clean little house-elf?" Foster said.

Rickman was ahead of him. "You searched her rooms, didn't you?"

"Me and Naomi, yeah."

"Did you find a hairbrush, toothbrush —?"

"A used lipstick would do just as well," Mayle said. "Even a stray hair on a sweater, if it has a root bulb attached. I'll send somebody to check."

"If she's tried to eradicate her fingerprints, she might just be on the DNA database," Rickman said. The team caught the mood of excitement and perked up. "Who's doing the DVLA check?" A young DC with ruffled brown hair and smooth skin raised his hand. "Andy Reid, isn't it?"

"Sir." Reid seemed pleased that Rickman had remembered him from the previous autumn. "I put in the request yesterday. But nothing so far." His accent was almost impenetrable, most of the sounds formed — or half-formed — at the back of his throat.

"Give them a dig," Rickman said. "I want her driver's licence photo circulated to foot-patrols, traffic, community officers — anyone who might spot her in the street. She drives an Audi TT 150 Roadster sports car — silver. DC Hart will give you the ID number. The car is going to be more noticeable than Megan — but send the two out together, so they link them."

Tunstall began putting his hand up, then changed his mind and coughed instead. "Could we not send the photo to other forces as well?" he asked. "I mean, didn't Sara say she was from outside the area?"

"Good point," Rickman said, and Tunstall flushed with pleasure.

They ran through the rest of the day's tasks quickly and efficiently: logs of Bentley's mobile phone and landline confirmed that he had used neither to get in touch with Sara, so the mystery caller was still just that — a mystery.

"Bentley has appointed Kieran Jago as his brief," Rickman said. One or two people actually gasped.

"I'n't he a bit out of Bentley's league?" Tunstall asked.

Rickman was impressed: Jago was part of the folk-lore of Liverpool, but Tunstall was a Widnesian, and hadn't been steeped in the same traditions as the majority of the team.

"He's doing the work for gratis," Rickman said.

Foster snorted. "*He* says . . ."

"I think we'd all echo that sentiment," Rickman said. "So either Bentley's pulling more legal aid than he earns in a year, or he has a sponsor."

"It might be worth having a word with his office staff," Hart said.

"I might be able to help with that." Foster avoided her eye as he said it.

The men on the team who knew him chuckled: Foster's "help" would no doubt involve dinner and a bottle of wine with a female member of staff.

Rickman nodded, noting Hart's careful impassivity. She was seated to Foster's right, her long legs crossed and her blonde hair carelessly twisted into a knot at the nape of her neck. She looked fabulous.

They moved on to the enquiries into Megan's past. The search of oil rig deaths had come up with a list that needed further investigation.

"Trouble is, they don't usually keep records of family details," the reporting officer said. "Just next of kin. I've discounted some of them, but there's four already I haven't been able to trace."

"Keep trying. Tunstall — what did you get from ELVIS?"

Tunstall flushed and Foster hummed a few bars of "All shook Up". Hart stepped in before he could begin apologising.

"He was busy shifting boxes to get the Exhibits Room up and running. I told him I'd do it." It wasn't a lie. "Sorry, Boss — when Bentley showed up, I lost track of time. I'll get onto it first thing."

Rickman's flicked from Hart to Tunstall; the big Widnesian's colour deepened under his scrutiny. "Be sure you do," he said, then let his gaze track the rest of the room, making brief eye contact with each member of the team. "I know it's been frustrating. You've worked hard and have little to show for it — but stick with it, we'll turn up something. Sooner or later, we'll get the break we need."

CHAPTER
NINETEEN

The silence in Lee Foster's flat was uncomfortable. He flicked on the radio and tuned it to Rock FM. He knew he had lost points with Naomi at the briefing, even if he had gained a few with the lads. Why the hell should he care? It wasn't like him and Naomi were ever going to hook up — not in this lifetime, anyway. He shrugged out of his jacket and hung it on the back of one of the kitchen chairs, then reached for the cheap whisky he kept in the cupboard and poured himself a third of a tumbler. He took a swallow. He had noticed Jeff Rickman's quick appraisal of Naomi. Her studied indifference was almost worse than if she had disapproved.

The cupboard door stood open. As he debated whether to replace the bottle or pour himself another, something caught his eye. A biscuit tin, circa 1970s. He freshened his drink, then took the tin down.

It was silver, with a Victorian winter scene painted on the lid: a coach and horses on a snowy rutted road. He smoothed a hand over the surface before lifting the lid. It was pitted and scratched here and there, the colour faded.

144

He was seven years old when his mother was taken into hospital for the first time. He had found her asleep on the floor of the bathroom. That's what he told the emergency operator: "Mummy's asleep and she can't wake up."

They didn't give him time to pack. They had taken him, still in his pyjamas, to the foster home where he had stayed for six weeks.

The next time, he was prepared. When the ambulance arrived, he was already dressed and hugged his box of treasures tightly to his chest. Short-term placements became harder to find as he got bigger, and he had to admit, troublesome. More and more, he waited out his mother's depressions in council homes — although there was nothing particularly homely about them. Except for Black Wood. Mr and Mrs Shepherd ran Black Wood like a big chaotic family home. High on Woolton Hill, they were surrounded by woods and fields. Until then, he hadn't known there was so much green in the world.

Lifting the lid of the tin, he got a whiff of old paper and bubble gum. This was where he had kept his secret stash; the faint odour of tobacco that lingered was from his roll-ups, a later addition to his secret treasures.

He stirred the contents idly with his fingertips, finding the penknife, the Plasticene and lengths of string he had stored so carefully. He found his old pea-shooter, the plastic mouthpiece perished and cracked, the red faded to pink; panto tickets, photographs — of him and Mum on one of her better days, smiling into a camera lens. Who had taken the picture?

He tilted the tin and something rolled. His cat's-eye marble. He smiled, remembering the boy who had puzzled over the mystery of how they got the colour inside the glass. A few birthday cards — not many — and a couple of letters. One envelope was in his mother's handwriting. He turned it over in his hands, the smile fading from his face. Then he pushed the envelope back into the tin and closed the lid, shoving the container back into the cupboard and closing the door.

He took a couple more swallows, then slammed a microwave dinner in the oven and set the time. While the microwave hummed, he dipped in his pocket for his mobile and keyed through his contacts list. Hayley Usher. Hayley with the long brown hair and infectious laugh. He checked his watch: nine-thirty — too late for dinner. Just a drink tonight, then. She wasn't soft — she'd smell a rat if he asked her out for a drink at this hour and bombarded her with questions. So, leave the questions till dinner, tomorrow. He could meet her straight after the evening debrief, maybe go on to a club — he might even get lucky. Foster was feeling better already.

Jeff junior was arguing with his mother when Rickman got home. They were all in the front sitting-room, Simon seated in one of the armchairs, puzzling over his turn at Scrabble, Fergus sitting on the floor near the fire reading a book in comic-strip format. Tanya and

Jeff junior stopped when he opened the door and Tanya smiled, though it looked like an effort.

"I've saved you some dinner," she said. "I can reheat it in the microwave."

"Great," Rickman said, then, with the slightest hint of irony, "Good evening, everyone."

Simon noticed him for the first time and beamed a smile at him. "'Lo, little bro," he said. Though it was a relief that Simon had got past the stage of the tearful reunion every time they met, this new craze of calling him "little bro" was rapidly beginning to pall.

In Simon's mind, he was still a seventeen-year-old and Rickman had discovered that he generally responded like one, so ignoring irritating behaviour was the quickest way to extinguish it.

"Good comic?" he asked, nudging Fergus's foot with the tip of his own.

Fergus grimaced. "We call them graphic novels in the twenty-first century, Uncle Jeff."

Rickman laughed. It still gave him a buzz, being called Uncle Jeff. Nobody else seemed to find it funny, however, and Rickman realised that whatever he had interrupted, it was more serious than he had first thought.

"Is everything okay?" he asked, loosening his tie and taking off his suit jacket; the room was hot and humid — Tanya said she could never get warm in England.

"Jeff is —"

"Everything is fine," his nephew said, with a sharp glance at his mother. Jeff junior was very like her — the same oval face and dark brown hair; but in the months

147

since Rickman had known him, he had begun to fill out and had the broad shoulders and flat pectoral muscles of a swimmer. Rickman knew that this was a constant source of friction between Jeff and his mother — his frequent trips to the beach when they were home in Italy, weekends away with his friends, surfing and partying.

"Jeff is spending too much time on the internet, emailing his friends back in Milan, and not enough time revising," she said, firmly, holding her son's gaze.

"Oh." This was an argument Rickman thought it best to stay out of.

"See," Jeff junior said, with a little smile of triumph. "Now he wants to go out to a club."

"Tonight?" Rickman said. "Not a good idea tonight, Jeff — there's a big match on. Liverpool against Man U. Bound to be trouble in the city centre." He had seen too many mindless acts of violence after football matches to sit on the fence on this one.

"That settles it," Tanya said. "You're staying home."

"This isn't my home, Ma."

"Jeff —"

"It's okay," Rickman said. "He's right."

Jeff junior lifted his chin in defiance, then seemed to decide the fight wasn't worth it. "I'm going to bed," he said.

Rickman followed him out of the room. "Sorry, Jeff," he said. "But it really can be dangerous out there, nights like this."

"Whatever." He was already on the staircase and took a couple more steps.

"Jeff?"

His nephew stopped and looked down at him.

Rickman hesitated, closing the sitting-room door before he spoke. "Your mum is having a hard time of it," he said, quietly. "I know it's tough for you, too, but she could use your support right now."

"Don't do that." A flush of anger rose to the boy's face and his brown eyes sparked with anger. "Don't try to be the father-figure, okay?"

Bad timing, Rickman thought. "Okay," he said, already backing off.

"Don't patronise me," the boy continued, unwilling to let it go. "You're not my dad. You can't advise me — I hardly even *know* you."

"Your dad isn't able to advise you just now," Rickman said, quietly.

"No, you're right," Jeff's hand was clamped tight around the stair-rail. "Pathetic as it seems, *my dad* can't advise me because he's sitting in there oblivious to everything, playing Scrabble, getting the spellings wrong like some spaz —"

"Jeff!"

The shocked look on his nephew's face was as much a response to the boy's own horror at what he had just said as to the tone of Rickman's voice. Tears stood in his eyes, and the knuckles of his hand were white as he gripped the rail. "I'm going to bed," he repeated.

Rickman knew immediately he stepped into the room that they had heard. Tanya stood at the window, looking out into the dark of the front garden, the tension showing in her shoulders.

Simon tipped the letter tiles back into the Scrabble box, the frown on his face telling Rickman that his brother was close to tears. Fergus alone looked up at him, wanting him to make things right. But if Jeff junior hardly knew him, the converse was true — he barely knew his sister-in-law or his nephews. God help him, he barely knew his own brother — how could he expect to help them? He tried anyway, sitting in the chair next to the fire to be close to Fergus, to show him that, though he didn't have the words, he did want to help.

"Simon," he said, noticing the slight tremor in his brother's fingers as he lifted a stray tile and placed it with the others. The brain injury or emotion? He couldn't tell. "He's upset. He doesn't mean —"

"Doesn't matter," Simon interrupted, a little too brightly. "He's just a kid. It's not like I *know* him or anything."

Rickman felt Fergus flinch next to him. The boy made as if to stand, but Rickman put a hand on his shoulder to stay him. "*He* knows *you*, Simon. That's why it does matter."

He saw blank puzzlement on his brother's face; Simon's feelings had been hurt, but not as a father's feelings can be hurt by the contempt of a son. His efforts had been mocked, and for Simon, every day, every new memory, every word, every skill relearned, took an effort that could break him out in a sweat. That was what had hurt, not that his own son had derided him, but that *his* struggle, *his* pain were seen as paltry,

150

pathetic. For Simon, since his accident, it was all about Simon — how *he* felt, how *he* coped, what *he* remembered, what *he* needed. Rickman understood why, but he felt a stab of pity for Tanya and for the boys, too.

"May I be excused?" Fergus's voice was watery with tears.

Rickman glanced at Tanya. She still had her back to them and she hugged herself as if she was afraid that it she let go, she would fall apart. "Sure," Rickman said, giving the boy's shoulder a squeeze. "We'll talk later."

Simon struggled out of his armchair. "I want to go home now," he said.

Rickman nodded, still looking at Tanya, staring at her own reflection in the window. *His needs — always his needs first.* "Fetch your coat," Rickman said. "I'll drop you."

Simon closed the door after him, and Rickman hesitated a moment or two before going to stand behind Tanya. He wanted to comfort her, but he wasn't good at platitudes; he couldn't promise that everything would be fine, because he didn't believe it himself.

"You must wish you could walk away from all this," she said, staring at the glass.

"Never think that," he said.

Her eyes had searched out his face, the dim reflection of his eyes, but now they slid away from him, staring past their ghostly images as though she saw something fearful in the darkness beyond the window.

Rickman willed her to look at him, but she refused and finally he gave a sigh of resignation. "If it weren't for you and the boys," he said, "I wouldn't have got through these last seven months."

Her eyes lifted to his, but now he found it impossible to meet her gaze. She turned to him, forcing him to look at her, and he saw surprise and gratitude in her eyes. She placed one hand on his chest, just above his heart, then she left without a word.

Rickman drove his brother back to the flat he had rented, near to the neurological unit in Fazakerley. A mizzly rain fell, smearing the windscreen of Rickman's Vectra like oil. They drove in silence, weaving past the football supporters spilling out of the pubs at closing time, negotiating the narrow stretches of Rice Lane, finally reaching the quiet street and the two-bedroom flat that Simon now called home. It was in a Victorian mansion, and the BMWs and Lexus and sports Mercs parked in the forecourt testified to the exclusivity of the client base.

"I don't think I can do this, Jeff," Simon said, as they pulled up outside.

"Do what, Simon?"

"Pretend that this is ever going to be right."

"It takes time," Rickman said, feeling a queasy unease in his gut. "You know what the doctors said."

"Little steps add up to large strides — something like that," Simon said with a tired shrug. "But it's been how many months now?" He found it hard to keep track of time. For Simon, time slipped between their childhood, twenty-five years ago, and a nebulous present he couldn't seem to keep in his grasp.

152

"Seven," Rickman said. In fact, he knew exactly how many months, weeks and days: Simon's arrival had coincided with the most catastrophic event of his adult life. But it didn't do to appear too obsessive around Simon. "Just over seven," he repeated, feeling every hour of every day that had passed.

"Seven months, and look at me. Jeff junior's right — I'm pathetic."

"No," Rickman said. "No, Simon." He turned to his brother and looked into his clear blue eyes. It pained him that they seemed to hold less intelligence and spark at forty-three than they had at seventeen. "You're making progress every day."

"But I still don't remember them, Jeff. The people who are supposed to mean most to me mean nothing."

"They're grieving, Simon. Jeff junior and Fergus have lost a father. Tanya has lost a husband and confidant."

"You think I don't understand how bad it is for them," Simon broke in. "I do."

Rickman took a breath and let it out slowly. He had waited a long time to say this. He had delayed many times, thinking that Simon wasn't ready to hear it, but after what had happened this evening, he could wait no longer.

"Maybe you never will get your memory back," he said.

He saw surprise, shock, relief and fear chase cross his brother's features.

"Maybe you'll never remember falling in love with Tanya, your wedding, the birth of your sons, watching them grow up. But that doesn't alter the fact that you do have a family. That they love you and they want to help you."

Simon was shaking his head, but Rickman went on, "Maybe you have to accept the facts and rebuild a new life."

"With *them*?"

"Why not?" Rickman asked. "You learned to love them before."

"That was different — *I* was different then."

"I know," Rickman said. "But they're willing to accept you. Can't you accept them?" Simon looked afraid more than anything. Rickman understood: he was asking his brother to put his trust — his entire life — in the hands of strangers. Strangers that not even Jeff, his kid brother, could vouch for.

"Can't you at least *try* — for Fergus? I know you feel something for him."

Simon closed his eyes as if the orange light of the sodium street lamps and the intermittent swipe of the wiper blades were too much distraction. "I do — I feel something for him — but it's not real. It's . . ." He struggled to find the word. "It's in the wrong place."

"I'm sorry, Simon," Rickman said. "I don't —"

Simon tugged at the short crop of grey hair that still came as a shock to him when he looked in the mirror. "*God!* The bloody *words!*" He slammed the heel of his hand into the dashboard.

Rickman was used to these explosions of temper when the words wouldn't come. He waited.

"Shifting about," Simon said, frowning in concentration. His hands clenched and unclenched as if trying to grasp the word that was just out of reach. "Changing all the time . . . Transient!" he exclaimed triumphantly.

"Fergus is the same," Rickman said, quietly. "He hasn't changed."

"He's like you," Simon said, and at first Rickman thought he'd gone off on one of his tangents, but Simon continued, "You used to look like that. Like you'd just found out something terrible and you didn't know what to do about it. I think you saw the bad in people — the meanness — and it made you unhappy."

Rickman remembered how that had felt. You didn't know what it meant, which made it worse, because you wondered if what you sensed from people was because of you: that they were angry or pissed off or just plain depressed — because of something you did. All you knew was those vibes felt *bad*. He had learned to shut down just around Fergus's age. It had taken fifteen years, and a good woman's gentle coaxing to open him up again, and he didn't want see his nephew withdraw in the way he had.

"That's why I feel something for Fergus. Because he reminds me of you."

"You couldn't help me then, Simon," Rickman said, feeling they were about to make a breakthrough. "You were just a kid yourself. But you can help Fergus. You can help your own son."

A moment of bright hope flashed across his brother's face, then Simon's shoulders slumped and he said, "Jeff . . . Little bro. I can't even help myself."

155

Conflicting musical beats reverberated from the boys' bedrooms when Rickman returned home. It was comforting to hear the rhythms of other people's lives in the house, to sense the pulse of hearts and minds not his own, but he wanted nothing more than to sleep. He sighed, not even sure if he could tackle the staircase, let alone the conversation he was about to have, but he had made a promise: he had told Fergus that they would talk.

He knocked and waited. No answer. He knocked again, and went in. Fergus lay on his bed, staring at the ceiling. His eyes were red from crying.

"He's never going to get better, is he?" the boy said, before Rickman could gather his thoughts to speak.

"I don't know."

The boy frowned, then nodded, as if in acknowledgement of Rickman's honesty. "But he's not a spaz."

"No." Rickman took a breath. "Jeff didn't mean —"

"Then he shouldn't have said it." He saw a flare of anger in the boy's eyes; like Rickman's, they flashed amber when he was angry.

"We all say things we don't mean sometimes — when we're afraid, or upset," Rickman said.

Fergus's Adam's apple bobbed. "I just want everything to be like it was."

Simon wanted it, too, but in a different way. He wanted things as they were when he was seventeen, and the world seemed full of possibilities.

"I wish I could make that happen," Rickman said, sitting on the edge of his nephew's bed. "I wish I could fix things."

156

Fergus sighed. "But you can't." He looked at Rickman, a puzzled amusement on his face. "You're not Batman, you know."

"So your dad was always telling me — I always had to be the sidekick," Rickman said, responding to his nephew's change in mood, relieved to be able to postpone a repetition of the talk he had just had with Simon. "It drove me crazy when he called me Robin," he added, with a smile.

"That was just to cover up," Fergus said, sitting up and leaning on one elbow. "He wanted to be Batman because Batman was a normal guy who stood up to the bad guys. But Dad was never strong enough. He wasn't even brave enough." A spasm of emotion passed over the boy's face, as if this admission was too much for him to bear.

"No," Rickman insisted. "He's confused. Your dad *was* brave — he took the brunt of —" He broke off, realising that Fergus might not know the family history.

"It's okay," Fergus said. "Dad told us about your father." He looked away, awkward and embarrassed.

"What, recently?"

Fergus raised his eyes to meet Rickman's. "He barely speaks to us now," he said. "But before . . ." He looked away again and Rickman felt the burden of sadness the boy carried on his narrow shoulders. Fergus seemed to shake himself free of the morbid thoughts that preoccupied him. "He was always saying I'm like you." He looked earnestly into Rickman's face. "Am I?"

Rickman smiled. "You only have to look at the pictures." *Always saying . . .* It was a lot to take in: that through all the years he had thought he was alone, his name had been spoken with affection; that he had shared in an obscure and almost magical way in the lives of his brother's family.

"I know I look like you did at my age," Fergus said. "But am *I* like you? As a person?"

Rickman sensed that it was important to answer this question well. The boy was quietly attaching himself to him, he could see that. Fergus needed someone to look up to, someone to approve of him, but it wouldn't be fair to appropriate the boy's affections just because it would be easy to do.

"Yes," Rickman said. "I think you are like me. Reserved, quiet. I was more . . . wary of people than you are. But that was because your grandad . . ."

Fergus shrugged. "Hurt you."

Rickman took a breath. He had never spoken to anyone but Grace about this. "Your dad *was* brave," he repeated, wanting Fergus to think well of Simon. "Your grandad only had to look at me and it would set him off," he said, remembering the rages, the terrifying hatred in his father's eyes. "Simon — your dad — he would say something and your grandfather wouldn't know which one of us to start in on, and Simon would goad and goad him till he forgot all about me and . . ." Rickman didn't finish.

Fergus frowned. "He did that for you?" Rickman nodded. It was plain from the boy's expression that he had understood perfectly what Rickman was hinting at. "That was . . . cool," the boy said.

"Yeah," Rickman agreed, softly. "It was very cool."

CHAPTER
TWENTY

Naomi Hart looked in askance as Tunstall took the half-full jar of coffee from the battered tray that housed the jumble of Merseyside police-issue mugs, biscuits, tea and coffee makings. He smiled crookedly at her and replaced it with another which had the barest scrapings remaining.

She rolled her eyes and went to her desk, leaving him to get on with it. Reid came in with a newly rinsed mug, shook the kettle to check the water level, then switched it on, picking up the jar with his free hand.

"Ar, 'ey —" He peered into the dregs left in the coffee jar.

"What's up, mate?" Tunstall asked, half-standing and peering over the computer on his desk.

"Bloody coffee's run out again."

Tunstall clicked his tongue. "Looks like it's your shout, mate."

"What?" Reid was young enough and fresh-faced enough to flush when set-backs happened.

"You know the rule, Reidy," Tunstall said, keeping his face straight. "Use the last spoonful, you get the new jar."

"Yeah," Reid said. "But twice on the bounce?"

"Ooh . . ." Tunstall winced. "Unlucky."

A few faces appeared from behind computer monitors, enjoying the game. Hart heard a couple of stifled laughs.

Boys and their little pranks, Hart thought, scrolling through her email messages. She clicked on one marked urgent attention and felt a thrill of excitement as she opened the message.

Foster was working through a pile of paperwork; his door was open and the electric fan worked quietly in the corner of his tiny office, the circulating air ruffling the dark glossy spikes of his hair with each sweep of the arc. Foster was in his shirtsleeves. He looked up and smiled; not the full fifty megawatts — he kept that for women who responded to it — but the smile he gave Hart was warm and sincere.

"I said you were falling in love with a spectre, didn't I?" she said.

"What are you on about?"

"Megan Ward. She's dead. I've had the results back from ELVIS." She held the top sheet of her bundle of papers just beyond reading distance. "I'm off to tell the boss. Wanna come?"

He dropped his biro onto the desk without a second thought and followed her. Even teasing and difficult, Naomi was more fun than a whole month of his short-term flings. She was no strain on the eyes, for sure — he often fell back a step or two when they were walking together, just to look at the pale downy hairs at the nape of her neck, the blade-thin line of her jaw —

160

but that wasn't all of it. She frustrated him and she wound him up. But she could make him laugh, too, and more than anything, she intrigued him.

She caught him looking at her and said, "I must say, you don't seem too devastated by the news of Miss Ward's demise."

"I'm the strong, silent type."

"Ah," Hart's smile was playful. "I was forgetting your date with your old squeeze."

"It was a *meeting*, and she's a *contact*."

She bit her lower lip. "Did you get anything useful?"

He shot her a sideways glance. "You really wanna know?"

"Just the bits that are relevant to the case, please — if it starts getting squishy, I'm liable to throw up."

"We had a drink, exchanged pleasantries — not bodily fluids."

"Thanks, Sarge," she said. "Thanks a lot. I *know* that image will stay with me for days."

They had arrived at DCI Rickman's door. Hart smoothed her skirt unnecessarily before knocking at the door. Rickman was on the phone but he waved them in while he finished up. His desk was cluttered with papers, reports and stick-it notes that refused to stay attached to his computer monitor, and fell instead like fluorescent leaf-fall and were slowly buried under the mulch of mounting paperwork.

The printer on his desk hummed and whirred into life and Rickman said, "Thanks, Tony, it's here." He hung up and said, "DNA results."

"They took a while, didn't they?" Foster said.

"Thirty-six hours — they had to screen a couple of bodies found after an arson attack in a disused warehouse out towards Garston."

"Well, if you paid premium rate, you should get a refund."

"I've said it before — and it bears repeating — you're the soul of compassion, Lee," Rickman said. "Now, do you want to know what the results say?" He fixed Foster with a beady look that told him he was being more than usually annoying.

"I'm all ears," he said. Rickman's hair was tousled and he looked tired. Foster hadn't been around to the house since the family flew in, but he could have guessed things were not easy: he had spent enough time with Jeff and his brother to know that Simon was hard going, even on his good days. With Tanya and the boys around —

"Megan Ward isn't on the DNA database," Rickman said, breaking in on his thoughts.

"Now I'd've put money on her having form," Foster said, taking a seat in the far corner of the room, leaving the chair nearest the door for DC Hart.

Rickman frowned and his finger went to the scar that bisected his right eyebrow. "Witness Protection?" he wondered, half to himself.

"I don't think so," Hart said.

Rickman focused on Hart, all attention.

"Megan Ward was killed in a road accident in 1997, aged sixteen."

"Stolen identity?" Rickman said, taking the report from her. "That'd rule out my theory." The Witness

162

Protection Programme had no need to steal the identities of dead people: they could create new ones from scratch. "But let's check, just to be sure."

"So what *have* we got on her?" Foster asked.

"The driver's licence photo's arrived," Rickman said, sifting through the drift of papers on his desk to find the A4 prints. He handed a copy to both Hart and Foster.

"Horrible, isn't it?" Foster said.

"It's nothing like Sara's sketch," Hart agreed.

"Which means it's probably useless for identification purposes." Rickman floated the sheet back onto the pile and sighed. "I've sent a copy to the local TV stations; it should make the lunchtime bulletins." He paused. "A bit of good news wouldn't go amiss."

Foster glanced quickly at Hart. "I had a preliminary meeting with that contact I mentioned."

"The one from Jago's firm."

His "meeting" was a swift half at the Blue Bar in the Albert Dock before closing time. Enough to establish there was still enough attraction between them to go to the trouble and expense of dinner the following evening.

"She reckons Jago's client list reads like the court listings at the Old Bailey. There's a few soap celebs for a bit of culture, but Jago's clients are more Cat-A than A-list."

"So if Bentley has been bought off, it's a lucky dip who's paying the legal fees," Rickman said. "Can you arrange another meeting with this contact — see if you can find out more?"

"See —" Foster gave Hart a little nudge with his elbow. "'Meeting'. 'Contact' . . . I'm seeing her tonight."

Rickman looked from Foster to Hart, taking in the situation. His phone rang and Hart and Foster stood to leave. Rickman held up a finger. He was smiling. "Great," he said. "Thanks, Mark." He hung up. "Mrs Langley has positively identified Bentley," he said.

DC Hart made herself a coffee when she returned to the office. The Incident Room was almost empty, most people having gone out on enquiries. Reid struggled with a report, sighing between short bursts of typing. Rob Voce sat at his desk near the high, letterbox windows, slogging wearily through the list of deaths on oil rigs. It was a job Hart did not envy, phoning bereaved women and asking personal questions about their families. Admittedly, the deaths went back between eight and ten years, but even after so much time it could stir up memories and emotions they thought they had laid to rest long ago.

She listened as she poured hot water on the coffee granules; his voice was low and gentle, his shoulders were hunched as though burdened by the weight of sadness he was causing.

Hart tightened the lid of the coffee jar and splashed some milk in the mug, passing Reid's desk en route to her own. "Nescafe," she said. "You've spared no expense."

"The system isn't fair, Nay —" she raised her eyebrows and he added, "— omi — Na-omi," he

164

repeated, and she smiled with little warmth. Reid knew full well of her aversion to any abbreviation of her name.

"It's even less fair than you think," she said.

He frowned — Reid still had the round face and ruddy complexion of a boy, and it brought out the worst in some of the older men.

Hart glanced over in the direction of the drinks tray. "Not even this lot can get through that much coffee in a day."

The frown deepened, and then his face cleared and he flushed to the roots of his hair. "Bastards!"

"Don't get mad," Hart said. "Get even." It took him a few moments to work it out, then he smiled, went to the bin next to the clutter of mugs and used tea bags and dirty spoons, and retrieved the empty jar he had thrown away a short time earlier. He spooned enough for one cup of coffee into the empty jar and placed it on the tray, carrying the almost full jar back to his desk drawer.

Hart grinned. "Now you're learning," she said.

She sat at her desk to prepare questions for Bentley's interview — with Kieran Jago sitting in, it wouldn't be wise to try to wing it. Tunstall had gone to pick up Jake Bentley at the gym where he worked. She estimated she had an hour, all told, allowing time for them to fetch Bentley and for Jago to cancel his other appointments and get to the station.

Bentley was well rehearsed for the previous interview, but she remembered he had been rattled when they told him they had a witness. Agreeing to the line-up would look good to a jury, and his objections on the tape — him being a familiar face in the street — were reasonable. So, either he was banking on the witness not being able to pick him out, or he thought Jago would argue that the identification parade was flawed. What depressed her was she thought he was right. Still, Mrs Langley had made a positive ID, no quibbles, which gave her something to work with at least.

The phone rang.

"Raj Anwar, in reception, Naomi."

"What's up, Raj?" she asked, clamping the receiver to her ear with her left shoulder while she finished the sentence she was typing in.

"I've got Mrs Langley here — she says she's a witness on the Sara Geddes investigation?"

"Not my bag, Raj. She needs to talk to the Identification Officer."

There was a pause while Anwar relayed the information to Mrs Langley, and Hart noticed Tunstall clumping into the room. She checked the digital clock in the bottom right-hand corner of the monitor. It looked like she had less time than she had originally estimated. Tunstall shed his fleece on the nearest chair and shambled over to the drinks tray. Reid glanced at Hart, then picked up his own phone and began a murmured conversation with an imaginary caller.

Tunstall rattled through the crockery, looking for a clean mug, picked up the coffee jar and gave a grunt of surprise. He shook the jar, then turned, a look of bafflement on his face. Reid frowned in feigned concentration, making notes on a scrap of paper he quickly pulled towards himself.

Tunstall unscrewed the lid of the jar and exclaimed, "Blood and sand!"

She heard Reid's innocent question: "Don't tell me that jar's run out already?"

Then Anwar was on the line again. "She says she can't talk to the inspector — she has to talk to you."

Anwar was a probationer, and dealing with insistent callers was an acquired skill. Hart sighed and clicked the "save" icon. "Put her on for a minute, will you?"

Mrs Langley's tentative "Hello?" dispelled any irritation she might have felt.

"Mrs Langley, I'm not being difficult, but I explained — much as I'd like to — I can't —"

"But I *have* to talk to you, dear," Mrs Langley interrupted. "I think I've made a terrible mistake." She sounded breathless and tearful.

Hart felt a thud of apprehension. "Couldn't you explain to Inspector —"

"No!" The notion seemed to fill her with dismay. "Please, dear . . ."

Hell. This didn't look good. "I'll be right down," Hart said.

She took Mrs Langley into one of the interview rooms and seated her at the table. The woman sat pale and upright, her body turned a little to the right, as if this were a brief visit and she didn't intend to stay. She was neatly dressed, her short hair combed back off a face free of make-up. She seemed nervous, and the vigour

167

that Hart had seen in her on their first interview was gone — she looked frail and fearful.

"Mrs Langley, are you all right?" Hart asked.

Mrs Langley waved a hand in front of her face. "I'm perfectly all right." Hart was relieved to see a flash of the direct, robust woman she had seen before. Mrs Langley let her hand fall into her lap and stared at it. "I'm afraid I've been rather foolish and now it's troubling my conscience."

Hart took her seat opposite and waited for Mrs Langley to continue. She fiddled with her handbag, placing it on the table and then on her lap, then replacing it on the table.

"What exactly is it that's troubling you?" Hart asked at last.

The old woman sighed. "I'm afraid I haven't been entirely honest."

"You lied to the inspector?"

"No — *heavens*, no — I wouldn't *lie* to a policeman. Of course not but I didn't tell him —" Mrs Langley didn't seem the sort of woman who was naturally given to prevarication, but she was evidently finding it hard to say what was on her mind, and Hart had a sick foreboding.

"It was so formal, you see — and he didn't give me the chance ..." She placed her handbag on her lap again, holding it with both hands, like a protective barrier. "And I didn't think I was allowed to answer anything but yes or no."

"Did you recognise the man or not?" Hart asked.

"Yes," Mrs Langley said. "But that's the thing, you see. That's what *he* asked, and sometimes it's not as simple as that, is it?"

"*What* isn't, Mrs Langley? You're not being very clear. Was the man you identified at the scene of the attack or wasn't he?"

"Yes, he was. And as I told the inspector, I did recognise him from before."

Hart's stomach began to churn; she thought she knew what was coming.

"But he wasn't actually there when she fell. He went over to her afterwards."

"You saw her fall?" Hart asked, pouncing on this new piece of information. "If you saw the actual attack —"

"No!" she exclaimed. You're muddling me!" She gripped the handles of her handbag tightly, and her eyes were red with unshed tears.

"I'm sorry." Hart raised both hands, palms up. "I'm just trying to understand. Take your time."

Mrs Langley composed herself before going on. "I saw Sara on the ground, and then he — the man I identified — he went over and stood by her. He just stood there, *looking* . . . I kept thinking, 'Why don't you help her?' Then someone came out of one of the houses and shouted something. He ran off to his car and drove away."

Shit. Just the way Bentley told it. Mrs Langley blinked anxiously at Hart, her story told, her duty done. Now she seemed to be waiting for Hart to fix the mess she had made.

169

Hart sighed. "Wait here, she said. "You're going to have to make a statement to the Identification Officer."

"Where are you going?" Mrs Langley asked, a quaver returning to her voice.

"To call off an arrest," Hart said.

CHAPTER
TWENTY-ONE

"All right," Foster said. "Who's the joker?" He held up a practically empty coffee jar. "Where's the rest of it?"

"That's it, Sarge," Tunstall said. "Last spoonful, new jar."

"Don't be at it," Foster growled.

Tunstall and Reid looked at each other and Foster lost patience. "Look, lads. I've just spent fifty minutes with Kieran Jago, persuading him we aren't harassing his client. Fifty minutes. During which he threatened me — that's me, *personally* — with litigation for the 'distress' caused to his client. And you know what kept me going? Kept me polite and pleasant all that time?"

"No, Sarge," Tunstall said.

"I was thinking, 'Never mind, Lee, you can have a nice hot cup of coffee and a Jaffa cake when he's gone, settle down for ten minutes and do the *Sun* crossword.'"

Tunstall listened avidly as if unsure how to respond, but eager to appease the Sergeant.

"In that fifty minutes, Mr Jago was clocking up serious money. Me, I'd have to work a full day to make my cash worth counting — a whole day with overtime. But when I stopped the clock on our little chat, I reckon Mr Jago had earned the best part of two-hundred-and-fifty quid. Which, I have to admit, pissed me off a bit, especially when he was making out that *I* was the sleaze, trying to fit up his client for something he didn't do. So. Whoever's got the coffee better come up with it now, 'cos I need caffeine like a junky needs his fix."

He took a breath and looked at both Tunstall and Reid. It was a long speech, and Hart was inclined to applaud, but for once it seemed that Foster was in deadly earnest. She watched the two men, curious to see who would crack first. They made eye contact and by some unspoken agreement, opened their desk drawers simultaneously and took out a nearly full jar of coffee. Tunstall hesitated, then reached in again and brought out a second jar.

"Bloody infantile," Foster muttered, gesturing impatiently to Reid, who tossed the jar to him. He caught it neatly and spooned coffee into his mug. It carried the legend, "Plum Island Animal Disease Center", and had survived three years in two different police stations.

His pager beeped as he stirred milk into his drink. He checked it and went to the nearest phone. Hart heard Tunstall whisper to Reid, "Was there Jaffa cakes? 'Cos I didn't get none."

Foster keyed the number for the switchboard. "Lee Foster." He was in no mood for courtesies.

"Got a call for you, Sarge." The line clicked and, there was a pause. "Look, if you got the wrong cop, don't bother apologising, just do me a favour and hang

172

up. If you're selling something, do *yourself* a favour and hang up. If you've got something to say, say it — or HANG UP."

"My name is Megan Ward."

Foster froze.

"I believe you've been looking for me." The voice was warm and vibrant, a hint of the north in her accent.

Foster placed the spoon carefully on the tray and focused on the voice. "How do I know this isn't a wind-up?"

"I began lodging with Sara last October," she said. "I expect Sara told you I'm a journalist."

"And would she be right?"

"That's rather tricky of you, Sergeant Foster." He could hear the smile in her voice. "You must have checked my . . . credentials by now." Foster didn't reply and she continued. "It was a cover story."

"For?"

She remained silent and Foster said, "We've been concerned for your safety, Miss Ward."

Hart's head came up at the name and he mimed for a pen.

"I'm safe and well," the voice said.

"Can you say where?"

"I could, but I choose not to. And I'd be grateful if you would stop showing my picture on TV."

"We don't have power over the TV news," Foster said. "But I can make a request." He hesitated, then said, "If you feel threatened, we can offer you protection."

She gave a short laugh. "Forgive me. If I want your protection, I'll . . ." She stopped. When she began again, she sounded more subdued, perhaps even a little bitter. "I don't want your protection."

"So, what *do* you want, Miss Ward?" Foster asked.

"To help."

He jotted the two words onto the pad Hart had placed before him.

"It would help if I knew your real name."

Again he heard a soft chuckle, this time more genuinely amused. "Sorry, I can't help you there."

He wrote the words "No way" on the notepad.

"How exactly *do* you think you can help?"

"I can give you the person responsible for Sara's death."

"You witnessed the attack?"

"I didn't say that."

He shook his head in response to Hart's questioning look, then pulled the pad closer and wrote, "She's angling for something", and tilted it for Hart to read.

"I'm listening," he said.

Hart picked up a spare pen and wrote, "The card?"

"You have something of mine," the woman said.

Foster smiled, tapping the words Hart had just written. "We checked your computer drive. It self-destructed when our techs tried to get into it."

"The equipment is replaceable," she said dismissively. "There was a shoe box."

"Full of junk."

"That depends on your perspective, Sergeant Foster. Do you have it?"

"We've got it."

Her voice was tightly controlled. "I'd like it back."

Foster laughed. "I bet you would. And in exchange, you'll give us this name?"

"The name and proof." She paused. "This goes way back."

Foster wrote the phrase down. "You're gonna have to be more specific," he said, heavy on the phlegm. "What goes way back?"

"The killings." She ended the word on a rising note and Foster caught a hint of vulnerability.

"Is that why you go under a stolen identity?"

"Borrowed," she said. "And Megan won't miss it."

"Her parents might disagree."

She didn't answer immediately and Foster thought maybe he had touched a nerve.

"I'll call to arrange a meeting-place," she said. "Be sure to have the box ready." She broke the connection and Foster immediately rang the switchboard to ask for the number.

"Anything?" Hart asked.

"Number withheld," he said.

It was just after two p.m. The Incident Room was filled to capacity. Rickman had called an emergency briefing, pulling officers off interviews, investigations of reported sightings of the attackers and leafleting of local garages to keep an eye out for a silver Audi TT 150 Roadster. Sara's bosses at the courts were vociferous in their demands that progress be made, two DCs had spent the best part of three days talking to colleagues and police security at the QE II Buildings, and viewing CCTV footage in an attempt to rule out a link with court proceedings.

Most of the team had brought sandwiches and snacks to the briefing; a couple of men chomped slowly through pies and chips as Rickman talked them through the morning's events. The room reeked of food and damp clothing: it had rained solidly for two hours and anyone on outside business had come in drenched.

The possibility that Megan might be alive sparked a lot of interest. This could be their first real break in the case, and the atmosphere, despite the damp and the cramped conditions, was upbeat — almost convivial.

Rickman stood next to the whiteboard and scanned the room. The eagerness was easy to read on the faces of the younger officers. DC Reid was flushed and he leaned forward in his seat. Even the older hands like Garvey seemed refreshed and revitalised by this new development. Though he sat back, looking relaxed — almost insouciant — picking over the remains of his chips and listening with half an ear, Rickman saw a tension in him that belied the implicit disinterest. Naomi Hart had positioned herself with her back to one of the desks near the windows. She looked cool and unapproachable, her blonde hair tucked carelessly behind her ears, her flawless features betraying no emotion; but Rickman knew of old that she was ambitious, and the significance of this extraordinary turn of events would not have passed her by.

"Okay," he said. "What do we know?"

There was a pause while everyone waited for somebody else to start. Eventually, Reid spoke up, unable to contain himself any longer. "We've got an idea what she looks like."

"So I'll know who I'm looking for at the meet," Foster said.

"Stolen ID." Rickman didn't see who had called that one out.

"She's a computer whiz," Hart said.

"We've got her car details," Garvey said.

"A high visibility sportster," Rickman agreed. "But no sightings. She may have it garaged, or we might just have been unlucky — and there's nothing like hard work for making luck change." This was for the benefit of the unlucky few who were currently driving from garage to garage, circulating pictures and the ID number of Megan's car.

"Possible oil rig accident." Voce said this. He looked strained and a little depressed.

"How's that going?" Rickman asked. It was interrupting the flow of ideas, but he felt that Voce needed a bolster in front of the rest of the team.

Voce shrugged, a small gesture that seemed to cost him a disproportionate amount of effort. "Nothing so far — two more to go."

"Well, keep at it," Rickman said. "It could be part of her cover story — we can't take anything she says at face value. But even if it only eliminates the oil rig accident as a lead, it's important to the investigation."

"One thing she did say," Foster said. " 'The killings go way back.' Killings, plural."

"So we might be looking at other unsolved murders," Rickman said. "Bear that in mind. What else?"

"She's got us by the short and curlies." This was Tunstall's contribution, and it raised a laugh, mostly because it was said with such despondency.

"Except we have something she wants," Rickman said.

"The killers ransacked the house," Hart said. "So maybe they were after the card as well."

Rickman waited. Something magical was happening here. If you were lucky — if you got a good team and the right breaks — they began to think as one, voicing opinions, random thoughts, off-the-wall theories without embarrassment or fear of being shouted down. On these occasions extremely useful intuitive leaps could be made.

"What she said —" Foster's bad mood had evaporated with the heat of energy in the room. He tried to recall the exact words he had heard over the phone. "She didn't say, 'I'll give you her killer', she said, 'I'll give you the person responsible'."

"Suggesting that the killing may have been ordered," Rickman said.

"It'd help if we knew who's paying Kieran Jago's fees," Garvey said.

"I'm all over that." Foster was concentrating so hard he didn't even realise the potential for a cheap laugh in his last statement. "I think we should keep on looking for a criminal connection."

"Based on?"

Foster looked at Rickman, a slight frown creasing his forehead. "Nothing specific — but she sounded awful bitter about police protection. She doesn't like us, doesn't trust us."

"Maybe she doesn't trust us because she's a criminal," Rickman said, thinking aloud. "And maybe it's because she was placed under police protection and they botched it."

"We checked with Witness Protection, Boss," Hart said. "They've got no record of a Megan Ward."

"They wouldn't, if that wasn't the identity they gave her. If she had to reinvent herself because of some failing of the system, she would be bitter — wouldn't she?"

"Well, yeah," Hart agreed, "but . . ."

"But there's no way of checking." Rickman said, finishing the sentence for her. He sighed. "Another one for the back burner."

"She isn't on the DNA database," Foster said. "So either she's smart, and she's escaped detection, or if she was arrested, it must have been before the millennium." Since year 2000 an increasing number of DNA samples had remained on file even if no charge resulted.

Rickman ran his thumb down the scar on his chin. "What if we're looking for the wrong person on the database?" he said.

"I don't get you," Foster said.

"She's running from something — and so far, it doesn't look like it's from the police," Rickman said. He remembered Tanya's words the night before: *You*

179

must wish you could walk away from all this. "Maybe it's family she's running from."

Foster looked at him like he was taking this too personally. "Yeah, well, we won't know that until we know who her family is, will we?" he said. "In the meantime, I say we go with what we've got. Like finding out who's paying Kieran Jago."

Rickman nodded. Foster was probably right: he was probably reading more into the situation than was entirely rational. And he didn't want to get a reputation for irrationality. "What else do we need to know?" he asked, throwing the discussion open again.

"What the killers were after," Garvey said.

"I don't want to sound silly . . ." It was clear from Tunstall's tone that he meant Garvey's suggestion sounded pretty silly to him. "But, don't we know that already?"

"Do we?"

"They wanted the credit card, didn't they?"

"I don't work on assumptions, Chris," Rickman said.

"But that's what Naomi said —"

"She said *maybe* they were after the card," Rickman corrected him. "But just because Megan seems to think it's important doesn't mean the killers did. They might not even be aware of its existence."

"Oh, aye . . ." Tunstall was evidently trying to understand, but any other possibilities seemed beyond him.

"Maybe they were after Megan," Hart said. "They might have thought she was still there. Or maybe it was something else we discarded as unimportant — or

180

maybe it's something we already have as evidence, but haven't identified as such."

Tunstall nodded thoughtfully.

"It'd really help if we knew what's on the card," Hart added. "That computer of hers must be worth five-thousand plus. But she wasn't bothered about it. She wanted the shoe box — and the only thing of any possible worth in the shoe box is the card. So whatever's on the card must be worth a hell of a lot more than five thousand."

"What's the latest on that?" Rickman asked.

She shook her head. "Whatever's on there is encrypted. Technical Support is still working on it."

He looked around the room. "Anything else?" He waited a moment longer while they tried to think of some other killer suggestion, honest-to-god zeal and naked ambition battling it out on their faces.

"Final question," he said. "How can we find out what we need to know?"

These three questions *What do we know? What do we need to know?* And *How do we find out?* were the basic tenets of any good investigation, and Rickman was not ashamed to make use of them, even if it raised eyebrows amongst some of the old cynics. Rickman had his own ideas about which direction the enquiry should take from here, but he wanted to hear from the team.

"Keep on doing what we're doing," Garvey said with a shrug. "The interviews, the leg-work, the background checks on families involved in oil rig accidents —"

Rickman saw Voce shift uncomfortably in his seat.

"Unscramble whatever's on that card," Reid said.

"Put a trace on Sergeant Foster's mobile." Hart leaned comfortably against the desk, her feet extended a little in front of her; her long legs seemed to draw the eyes of the men on the team. "With triangulation," she went on, unaware of the unwarranted attention, "they could probably pinpoint her phone to within a few metres."

"That's if she uses her mobie," Reid said.

"Well, let's hope she does, eh, Reidy?"

"That'll do a lot of good, won't it — hope?"

Rickman saw irritation in Hart's face. She remained in her relaxed position, but her hands gripped the table and her jaw tightened.

"What would you suggest —" She stopped abruptly and scooped her own mobile from her jacket pocket. The men closest to her could hear the faint buzz of the vibration alert. "Sorry boss," she said. "I should take this."

Rickman debated for a moment. "Go ahead." He would talk to her about this later: he liked officers' full attention in briefings. But for now the interruption was expedient: team synergy was giving way to overly competitive points-scoring, and that would get them nowhere fast.

Hart ducked out of the room and Rickman was about to take up the thread when Foster chimed in. "I say we give her what she wants."

"The card?"

"The box."

"What's the point of that — aside from pissing her off?" Reid again.

"It might flush the cockroaches out the pantry, as me grandma used to say. And who's rattled your cage, Reidy?" Foster demanded.

Who indeed, Rickman wondered. He'd have to have a quiet word with Reid as well. "Perhaps you'd like to expand your idea a little," he said, addressing the sergeant.

Foster glanced around the room. "We don't know for certain she wants the card, right? I mean, if we're not making *assumptions* . . ."

Tunstall's eyes bulged, and in a couple of the other officers Rickman saw a mental folding of arms and cocking of heads.

"O . . . kaay," he said, with a hint of a smile. "So we give her the box without the card, piss her off and she demands the return of her flexible friend. What then?"

"I use my superior psychological skills to get her to give us something for nothing. The name, for example."

There was muffled laughter which Foster took as an opportunity to ham it up a bit. "What?" he demanded, all injured pride. "I'm more than just good looks and a dazzling smile, you know."

They laughed openly now, but Rickman was inclined to agree; Foster had seen the potential of the team dynamic disintegrating into a pissing contest as clearly as he had — and he had achieved several things with his little side-show. He had come up with a viable suggestion that would give Technical Support more time to work on the card. There was a better than even chance Foster would winkle the name of the a murder suspect out of Megan. And he had defused a slightly tetchy exchange between Reid and Hart, bringing the team together — admittedly by having a sly dig at the boss, but Rickman thought it was a pretty masterly piece of psychology.

CHAPTER
TWENTY-TWO

Jeff Rickman looked over at Foster and pointed at his watch, holding up his hand to indicate five minutes. Foster arrived at his office door just as Rickman turned the corner at the far end of the corridor.

"Go in, Lee," Rickman called. "It's open."

The office was littered with paper, sorted into piles on his desk, the top of the filing cabinet, as well as on both chairs: pink flimsies with hand-written notes of completed actions, Megan Ward's separate from Sara Geddes's. Computer print-outs relating to previous enquiries, requisition slips, letters and memos all took up space.

"Bit of a snowstorm in here, Jeff," Foster commented.

"One of the perks of promotion," Rickman said. "I think it's reached critical mass."

"So," Foster said, leaning against the filing cabinet for lack of a chair. "What's up?"

Rickman half-sat on his desk, taking care not to topple the meticulously sifted and classified stacks. "I don't have to tell you this is risky, Lee."

"No."

"Go along with her, but only as far as you absolutely have to."

"Right."

"And if you get the opportunity, arrest her."

Foster tilted his head. "On what charge?"

"Withholding information, wasting police time — use your imagination."

"And if I don't get the opportunity?"

"Buy time," Rickman said. "Arrange another meeting. If it *is* the card she's really after, we'll need verification on any names she gives us."

"And how am I supposed to tempt her to a second meeting?"

Rickman stared at Foster, waiting for him to work it out for himself.

Foster's eyes widened. "Bloody hell. You're not really thinking about giving her the card?"

A smart rap at the door prevented Rickman's response. It was Hart, and she looked like she had just won the lottery.

"That call?" she said.

"Yes," Rickman said. "I wanted to talk to you about that."

"Yeah, sorry, Boss — it was National Fraud Squad."

Rickman blinked at her brisk dismissal of his most baleful stare.

"Megan Ward isn't so invisible as she thinks," Hart said.

Rickman had to admire her sense of the dramatic. He waved her in and she eased into the cluttered space.

186

Foster seemed to catch himself staring and gave himself a shake.

"Well, don't keep us in suspense," Rickman said.

"After we circulated Megan's picture nationwide to police authorities, I got a call from a guy I know on the Fraud Squad," Hart explained. "He wanted to know if this enquiry was related to a scam. I was going to say no, but then I remembered that Megan told Sara she was a journalist — which she patently wasn't. He said he'd have a trawl through, put together a list of possibles."

"And?" Rickman said.

"I've got a web presence."

"You what?" This came from Foster.

"When you told me Megan wanted to bring Sara's killer to justice, I phoned Curtis — my mate — and asked him to factor it into the equation. He got all mysterious on me, told me to stay by the phone, he'd get back as soon as possible." Her normally creamy-pale skin was flushed and her eyes were bright with excitement.

"You still haven't got to 'web presence'." Foster used computers like they all did — for reports, searches and for email, but he didn't pretend to understand "geekspeak", as he called it.

"Best if he explains it to you himself." Hart handed a slip of paper to Rickman. "He's waiting for your call."

Rickman pulled the phone to him by the cord, then picked it up in one large hand and turned it to face him, punching in the number from the slip of paper.

"Curtis Miller?" A pause, then, "DCI Jeff Rickman, Merseyside Police. Curtis, I'm putting you on speakerphone — Naomi Hart and DS Foster are with me." He pressed the sp-phone button on the key pad and replaced the receiver.

"Can you hear me?" Miller's voice was a rich baritone, warm and toffee-rich, with a hint of Jamaican in his inflexion.

"We hear you loud and clear," Rickman said.

"Okay."

Rickman remained perched on his desk, his arms folded and his head slightly bowed. Foster rested with one elbow on the filing cabinet, he looked newly pressed and carefully groomed, almost shining with good health. Naomi Hart stood with her back to the door. All three listened intently.

"We've been monitoring the activities of a particular scammer for a while," Miller said. "She was selling stuff on eBay she never actually had, keeping the money small, so people couldn't be bothered with the hassle of chasing her down.

"She has several internet aliases, and honey traps all over the world-wide web."

"This is all very interesting," Rickman said, "but what makes you think it's our MisPer? What makes you think these different aliases are one person in the first place?"

"We have experts who specialise in computer forensics," Miller explained. "They can read the way you use the machine like a CSI can read a fingerprint — key-stroke and grammatical errors, common misspellings — whatever. They call it scene-of-habitation analysis. Megan Ward is a new alias, that's why I didn't make the connection immediately, but it's the same person."

"She's been using this alias for six months that we know of," Rickman said.

Miller took a breath. "Fair point. But you have to understand we're swamped with work. The Dutch lottery and West African scammers are cheating people out of millions — your suspect is small potatoes next to that."

"Okay." Rickman understood the impossibility of balancing the importance of one investigation against another. As a manager, he also knew that resources were limited, and he had learned to be pragmatic. "So, how does it work?"

"She advertises on one of the big auction sites — say eBay. Different aliases for different specialist areas. For Star Wars she uses O.B.1.K.N.O.B.," he said, spelling out each character. He seemed to be waiting for them to get the joke, and when they didn't he said, "I guess you have to be a fan. She also does collectable pottery and signed first editions. Different names — I won't bore you with them."

Miller continued: "She gives a postal address which looks legit — in fact it is — except she pays the legit business at the address to hold her mail for her until it's picked up. Sometimes she uses PO box addresses, but people are more suspicious of those."

"Why don't you keep watch on the business addresses?" Hart asked.

"We do, when we can. But not twenty-four/seven." He gave a short huff of laughter. "If I'm honest, we've done a few hours here and there, between jobs. We just haven't got the personnel. Which is why we've never been able to catch her picking up mail from the mail drops.

"Then, about a month ago, something weird happened. The Met gets a comprehensive file on a paedophile ring downloaded to their secure data files. The Met's security is Fort Knox — I mean it's air-tight. But she downloaded these files direct to the most secure part of their system."

"Using the Megan Ward Alias?" Rickman asked. Hart and Foster stood rock still, their attention completely focused on Miller's account.

"She was calling herself NorthStar, then," Miller said. "But the signature — the way she used the system, was the same as our minor-league scammer."

"So, what changed?" Rickman asked, thinking small scams to gang-busting — it didn't sound right.

"You ask me, she found a cause," Miller said. "Paedophiles are about the most sophisticated computer criminals I know. They know how to manipulate the internet, they know the law and they know how to cover their tracks. But she bypassed their security like it wasn't there. Hell — she bypassed the *Met's* security system like it wasn't there." There was awe and respect in Miller's voice. "She sent us complete date-stamped images of the two chief suspects' computers. Then she cleared every brass farthing from their bank accounts. Two days later, one of the big children's charities

190

received an anonymous donation — a large six-figure sum — which matched this missing money to the last decimal place."

"Couldn't their lawyers just claw it back again?" Foster asked.

"That was just it," Miller said, with an incredulous laugh. "We couldn't trace it back to either of the accounts. It just appeared out of nowhere."

Foster leaned back a little and said, "Huh!" It was an expression of surprise and admiration.

Rickman shook his head. "What I meant was, if she had that kind of expertise to start with, why wouldn't she make use of it? Strip a bank's assets, or blackmail a big insurance firm?"

There was a silence at the other end of the line and it wasn't difficult to imagine the Jamaican give a shrug before answering, "Banks and big commercial interests have a lot of resources. Mess with them, they're not gonna let it go — hence the small scams — and if she pushes the odd paed our way, well . . . we're hardly gonna bust our balls chasing her down."

It was an odd kind of morality that condoned one criminal act as irrelevant set alongside greater transgression, but Rickman had seen it time and again. Petty crimes committed by informants: theft, muggings, benefit fiddling and drug pushing quietly ignored because their intelligence was too useful to lose. Deals made with criminals who turned Queen's Evidence against their bosses. Selective amnesia. Noble cause corruption. Which was a charge that he could have levelled at himself, and not so long ago. He knew that what he had done was wrong and that it was illegal, but he did not regret it for one moment, and he would do it again in a heartbeat.

CHAPTER
TWENTY-THREE

"Nathan. Listen to me. We want to help. Nathan?"

The voice came from far off. Nathan Wilde didn't know how to get there. He used to live in that place, but now he was lost and he didn't know how to get back. They were staring at him. Every one of them in that room. In that other place. It was like looking at a play on a stage. It was real and yet unreal, the players intangible. Too far off to touch. But the bizarre twist was *they* were watching *him*, the actors intent on their audience of one. Staring. At him. *Into* him.

Can they see? Can they see what I did? Panic rose in him like a surging flood.

The room was large and light. Tan carpet tiles, cream walls. Steel-frame table against one wall. Five armchairs in a loose circle. The psychiatrist, the psychiatric nurse, two others — a man and a woman, youngish. Probably students. He had already forgotten their names. Blinds on the windows. No curtains. The faint hum of traffic beyond. Or maybe it was the buzz of beetles' wings. He caught a movement off to his left, turned to see, but it scuttled out of sight.

Oh, God, they're in.

He pulled his feet up onto the chair, then leaned across and dragged the table away from the wall.

The psychiatric nurse intervened. "Nathan. You don't need to do that." She spoke loudly, like he was deaf or stupid.

"It's okay." The psychiatrist watched Nathan calmly. "Let's see what he does."

He dragged the table a few more inches, leaving a space all around. Then he crawled from the chair onto the table top.

"Okay, Nathan," The psychiatrist repeated, "If you want to sit there, that's fine."

She smiled at him with her thin lips and he thought, *What the fuck is wrong with you? What are you smiling at?* He stopped. *They can hear you. They know what you're thinking.* Nathan wasn't given to voicing his opinions of others, and the notion that they had heard this minor rant appalled him. He felt heat creeping slowly from the neck of his T-shirt up to his cheeks until even his ears felt hot. He looked anxiously around the circle, but they were unmoved. No offence taken. The actors watching the audience, wanting a reaction, discussing him like he was a character in a TV show and they'd missed the odd episode. Playing catch-up, not following the story.

"His mother found him hiding in his wardrobe." The psychiatric nurse. She was short and plump. She lowered her voice now, as though afraid that he would hear.

The psychiatrist looked at him. *Into* him. "Why did you hide, Nathan?"

194

He looked from floor to walls to the faces of the people. He caught fleeting glances of the bugs, translucent, almost invisible. He heard the buzz and thump of their bodies against the windows. *The bugs. I was hiding from the bugs.*

"All the electrical equipment in his room was disconnected," the nurse continued.

They all looked at him as if waiting for an explanation. *I told you why. They're here! Why don't you do something?*

"The plugs were sliced from the wires."

"Nathan," The psychiatrist said. Her voice was warm and low, but she wasn't built for warmth; her body was thin and angular, her face empty of any sympathy. "Were you afraid of the electricity?"

Not the electricity — the BUGS!

He checked the ceiling. If you didn't watch it, they came in through the light cables. He looked down at the floor. It was alive with them. *Oh, God!* His eyes grew wide with horror. *I looked away for a second — one friggin' second —*

They massed on the carpet, a shimmering torrent of silver-backed creatures. They flowed around the doctor, the nurse and the other two, a torrent of silvery shapes, dividing and reforming into a single shining stream. They didn't want the others. They wanted him.

A low moan escaped him and he wrapped his arms tight around his legs. His breathing was irregular, fast, coming in short panting bursts. He looked right and left. Behind him. At the ceiling again, ready to bat them away if they got to him. He heard the little hooks on their feet catch in the carpet fibres, the faint metallic scratch as they tried to climb the steel tubing of the table legs.

"He threw all of the plugs out of the window." The nurse was relentless, her voice a low mumble against the increasing static roar of a million bugs, pale as crystal, transparent as glass. "Then he threw his computer keyboard and mouse out after them," she finished.

The psychiatrist hadn't taken her eyes of him the whole time. *Reading my thoughts*, Nathan thought.

"Do you know who I am, Nathan?" she asked.

"Psychiatrist," he said, embarrassed to have forgotten her name. Then a thought occurred to him and he chuckled. "Spychiatrist."

"You think I'm spying on you."

He frowned, irritated. "It was a *joke*."

She nodded. "Can you tell us why you're afraid?"

A shape skittered left of his field of vision and he flinched.

"What do you see, Nathan?"

"You don't see them?" He stared at the steady stream of flat, discoid creatures flowing around their feet and over their shoes and his eyes widened.

She made a pantomime of checking with the others. "We don't see them. What do they look like?"

He shook his head. *Horrible.*

"Nathan." The psychiatrist waited until he made eye contact. "Why can't we see them? Wouldn't we see them if they were real?"

196

Why couldn't they? It only took a moment — he saw the answer with blinding clarity. "You're not infected."

"By what?"

"The BUGS!" he yelled. The shimmering flow shuddered and retreated a second, before surging again, in a second wave.

"It's all right, Nathan," the psychiatrist soothed. "Everything is all right."

He looked at the swarming mass of creatures beneath him and gave one short bark of laughter. "I'm under *siege*, here!"

"Where did they come from?"

A loud buzz made him yelp and wave his arms around, but when he looked again, there were none flying. Not in the room. It was just the buzzing in his ears. It was worse when he was tired. He was tired now.

The psychiatrist waited for Nathan to steady himself, then she asked again, "Where did they come from?"

He stared at the psychiatrist, and then past her to the other three; the actors seated calmly in their armchairs, waiting for their audience to respond, while around them the floor seethed with movement.

"Warlock sent them after me. He infiltrated the network. Warlock is like, some kind of hackmeister. I've never seen anything like it. He's there, and then he's gone. He's, like . . . I don't know . . . He — he's a . . ." He tried to remember how he had described Warlock to Doran. "A phantom. That's it. I tried to take him on, but he was way too powerful. Too many back doors, secret passageways — too fast — too clever. He infected the system with a virus. It — the virus — it mutated to make a superbug." He used his hands as though placing the information like packages on a shelf. "The superbug reproduced." He stopped, his emotions almost overpowering him. "Now, they're . . . *everywhere*."

"And now you're infected?" The psychiatrist said.

Nathan took a breath and let it out in a long juddering sigh. She understood. "Yes." His lips moved, but he made no sound.

"Are they in your blood, Nathan? These bugs?"

He shook his head. The effort of concentration and vigilance was exhausting. He lifted his hand wearily and rippled his fingertips over his scalp, tracing the path the creature took.

"You have a listening device in your brain, Nathan?"

For a moment he didn't quite grasp what she was saying. Then he clenched his fists in anguish. "No. NO!" Hadn't she been listening to a word he said? He spoke fast, trying to block out the regular *click click click* of the bugs' feet gripping and slipping on the tubular steel legs of the table.

"It's a *bug*. Just one. Like a beetle — or — or maybe a woodlouse." His head ached and he could feel the bug moving around inside his skull, squirming from layer to layer of the cortex, seeking out his private thoughts. Broadcasting them to these strangers. He put both hands to his head, trying to stop it.

198

"I'm sorry," the psychiatrist said. "I'm trying to understand. How could something as big as a beetle get inside your head?"

He was tired of explanations. Tired of keeping the creatures at bay. Afraid to close his eyes for fear they would rush him.

"Nathan?"

Oh, God. He brought his hands down, rapping the table top to punctuate his answer. "It's *light* energy and digital *pulses*. It's *virtual*."

"Which is why you disconnected the electrical equipment."

"Yes." *Thank God — yes . . .* "I thought the infra-red was safe. No connection."

"Your infra-red keyboard and mouse?"

He nodded, near collapse. "It shouldn't have been possible." His skin twitched as he listened to the millions of glassy bugs looking for a way in. "The one in my head. It jumped the gap on an infra-red carrier wave." A spasm convulsed him and he said, "I didn't mean for anything bad to happen. I didn't mean to hurt anybody."

Dr Jane Pickering sat at her computer, her notebook next to Nathan Wilde's case notes which lay open on the desk. It was eight-thirty p.m., and she could hear the bucolic tones of Beethoven's Sixth faintly from the sitting-room below. She knew that a glass of Merlot was poured, waiting for her, next to the paperback she had started the night before. She sighed and looked again at the screen.

"Patient agitated, insomniac, delusional, but not delirious," she wrote. "Possible amphetamine psychosis. Mr Wilde has one previous admission for amphetamine poisoning."

"Elements of paranoid psychosis," she continued. "I believe he thinks we can read his thoughts — that these 'bugs' are after him."

Her fingers moved swiftly over the keyboard. "He explored different meanings of the word 'bug' in his narrative, viz: virus/bug — bug/beetle — bug/microchip — bug in the system. On one occasion, he called me a 'spychiatrist'. This play on words, together with the paranoia, giving a possible alternative diagnosis of schizophrenia."

She hit the return key twice, and began a new heading in bold type. "Recommendations: 'Droperidol as sedative.' She knew that this would be effective whether the delusions were triggered by drugs or schizophrenic psychosis. "Accelerate renal elimination of the amphetamines by acidification of urine with ascorbic acid for two days. When his system is detoxified, we'll reassess."

She hit the return key once more, followed by the caps lock. "BE VIGILANT FOR SIGNS OF DYSPHORIA. AS THE AMPHETAMINES WORK THEIR WAY OUT OF HIS SYSTEM THE PATIENT MAY BE A SUICIDE RISK."

She pressed control S simultaneously to save the work, and was about to shut down, when another thought occurred to her. She found the passage relating to a tentative diagnosis of schizophrenia and added,

200

"Patient indicated that he may have unintentionally hurt somebody. Recommend further exploration when the patient has stabilised."

CHAPTER
TWENTY-FOUR

The pavements glistened with recent rain and the air was chill and damp, but the showers held off on the drive to the park. Foster had received the call on his office landline only ten minutes earlier. She had demanded his mobile number, then given instructions.

"Grant Avenue," she said. "At the edge of Wavertee Playground." This marked her as an outsider: since the land was gifted to the city in 1895 by an anonymous benefactor the park had been known as "The Mystery". It had survived the great sell-off of the eighties and speculators' bids in the new millennium almost unchanged, except for the new sports hall and pavilion at the Picton Road end.

Megan told him to leave his car facing the junction with Smithdown Road, as close to the junction as possible, which meant that she intended to make her escape in the opposite direction.

"If I think you've brought company, the deal's off," she said. "If you're wearing a wire, deal's off. Try to stop me leaving —"

"Let me guess," he interrupted. "Deal's off?"

"We should get along fine," she said, and he could hear the smile in her voice.

Technical Support traced the call to a public phone box in Lime Street Station.

The surveillance team held back further than was the norm. It was agreed that Foster would stay in touch by mobile with Will Garvey who, as the most experienced in surveillance, was lead officer.

Megan contacted Foster again as he got out of the car. He put Garvey on hold, knowing that Technical Support would already be triangulating the connection, placing her call within a five-yard location.

"I see you have the box," she said without preamble.

"Man of my word," he said, tucking the shoe box carefully under one arm and scanning the street, his eyes sharp, but his posture relaxed, almost indolent. He saw a woman hurrying from her car to one of the terraced houses that lined one side of the avenue, facing the park. Inside the railings, walking away, a man exercised his dog, his shoulders hunched against the cold, the dog some way behind him, moving stiffly, like it had an arthritic hip. No glint of binoculars, no tell-tale movement at the windows of the houses.

"Cross the street diagonally left." There was no trace of nervousness in her voice; it had the same warmth and quiet control as before. "There's a steel bollard allowing access to the park."

He found it immediately: a narrow gap in the six-foot-high spiked iron railings, a hangover from the Victorian era when parks were locked and patrolled at night.

"Go onto the path and walk until I tell you to stop."

203

He did, keeping the phone clamped to his ear, wondering where the hell she could be hiding in this flat, open landscape. A clump of trees fifty metres away, maybe, or the electrical substation twenty metres further on. She could just as easily have been huddled in one of the thirty or more cars parked, nearside wheels on the kerb, along the length of the avenue. The park was unlit, but moonlight silvered the footpath, reflecting coldly from the rainwater that stood in puddles here and there.

"Okay, you can stop."

He turned full circle, and when he faced the railings again she was striding towards him across the street. He checked the side road opposite. No sign of a silver Audi TT. He made a pantomime of ending the call, holding his phone up for her to see, surreptitiously opening up the line to Garvey again.

It was definitely her. Sara's sketch was a close likeness. Megan had cut her hair a little shorter and she looked a little hollow around the eyes, but Sara had captured the delicate nose and full lips, as well as something subtler — a solemnity of expression that was born from something deep and painful.

"Are you alone?" she asked.

Foster looked around him. "You see anyone?"

She satisfied herself that she didn't before saying, "Open your jacket, please."

He unzipped his Berghaus, awkwardly juggling the box and his phone.

"Now the shirt."

"You're joking, aren't you? It's freezing!"

She raised one eyebrow but said nothing. She stood back from the railings, well out of reach, every nerve ending alert to the possibility of danger; she watched each car that passed from the corner of her eye until she was sure it wasn't a threat — if a cat sulked by against the walled gardens of the terraces, Foster thought she would see it. He sighed, unbuttoning his shirt and shivering involuntarily in a gust of wind.

"Satisfied?" he asked. "Can I get dressed, now? Only I wouldn't want get arrested for flashing."

A smile twitched at the corner of her mouth. "If you wouldn't mind switching off your phone . . ."

He considered for a moment, then shrugged. Whatever else Megan Ward might be, she wasn't stupid. He did as he was asked, keeping his eyes on her, giving her the smile at low wattage.

"Can we get on with it?" he said, slipping the phone into his pocket and fumbling the buttons of his shirt closed.

"When I have the box," she said.

Foster's smile broadened. "When I have a name."

A momentary uncertainty flashed across her face, then she smiled back at him. "It's a question of trust."

"And I don't trust you, Megan. See — we know who you are."

"Do you?" She seemed more amused than surprised and Foster realised that whatever they had, there must be much more.

"We know *what* you are, anyhow."

She watched him calmly enough, but Foster saw a slight wariness in her face. Her eyes looked dark in this light, though Sara had said they were grey.

"The National Fraud Squad have been taking an interest in you for a while," he said.

She stared past him, her vigilance slipping for a second as she seemed to focus on something distant. "It was the Fraud Squad dipping into my files?" She closed her eyes momentarily. "Oh, God . . . I thought it was — him," she said, almost saying the name in the horror of realisation. "That's why I ran."

"It probably saved your life," Foster said.

"Yeah? Well it cost Sara hers." She sounded sick and disgusted with herself.

Foster was used to liars. He had dealt with them on a daily basis for years. As a rule, he assumed people were lying unless they proved otherwise, but he thought he saw genuine emotion in her face.

"So that really is why you're here?" he asked.

"You think I'd risk prison for less?"

"Well," he said, "there is this." He rattled the contents of the box and as he watched her, he saw a slow transformation as she regained control, almost a *gathering in* of her emotions. Then she smiled coolly.

"You're right — I'm here to exchange information for some property that belongs to me."

Foster looked down at the box tucked neatly under his arm. After a moment's hesitation, he took it in both hands and lifted it towards her.

She reached up, gesturing impatiently for him to hand it over the top of the railings.

206

He took a step back. "The name first," he said, smiling.

She smiled back. "The box first."

He debated. They were as sure as they could be that there was nothing of use in the box, but so far he'd got no concession from her. She stared at him unwaveringly, and he knew he would get nothing until she had the box. Everything in it had been photographed, scanned and archived.

"Why not?" he said, handing it over. He saw how carefully she handled the box, holding it to her and easing the lid off gently; he understood that reverence and he felt a pang of pity for her.

She turned the lid over and felt inside, then lifted her eyes slowly to his. "What the hell are you trying to do?" she demanded.

He dipped his head. "You asked for the box — we gave you the box."

She turned without a word and began to walk away.

Foster pulled his mobile from his pocket and switched it on as he spoke. "Does that mean we don't get the name?"

She tensed, then increased her pace.

Me and my big gob. He considered climbing the railings, but they were slick with rain, and there were no footholds, and rusted though they were, the spikes looked sharp enough to do some damage.

"What about Sara?" he shouted. "You know she raised Cain when you buggered off. She wasn't gonna let go till she found you safe."

She slowed half-way across the road.

"She cared about you, Megan. But I suppose some people are just too trusting."

Megan faltered.

He moved closer and gripped the railings like a caged felon. "Just her bad luck she was the one ended up with her brains spattered on the pavement."

Megan stopped at the far kerb. "Did she —" She kept her back to him, but he could still see the effort to keep her emotions in check. "Did Sara —" She tried again: "Was she in pain?"

A car passed, the sound of its tyres like a sigh on the wet tarmac.

"Death was instantaneous," he said, falling back on jargon; then shaking his head at his own insensitivity, he added more gently, "She didn't suffer."

Megan spun round, taking a step forward. Foster held up a hand to warn her. A car horn blared. The driver braked, then sped on with another blast on his horn.

Megan stood still, and they looked at each other over a distance of fifteen feet. "Doran," she said, her voice carrying clear and strong on the cold air. "His name is Doran."

Another car passed, then she crossed back to him. Foster let go of the railings and waited for her.

"This is Liverpool," he said. "Take two steps, you fall over an Irishman. There was Aiden Doran, John Doran and Aloysius Doran in my year at school. God knows how many you'd get in a whole city."

"*Patrick* Doran," she said. "He runs a security firm."

"And you reckon he set up Sara's murder?"

"No . . ." She looked at him as though he had dropped a couple of dozen IQ points. "It was me he was after."

Foster lifted his chin a fraction, acknowledging his mistake. "Why would that be?"

She smiled slowly. "I gave you the name, now you owe me."

"We'll need to check it out," he said.

She opened her mouth to speak, but he raised his hand to stop her. "Fair dooz, Megan. You *are* a con artist, aren't you?"

She seemed ready to respond angrily, but then a comical look of puzzlement passed over her face and she laughed. "Yeah," she said. "I'm a petty crook and I want what I came for."

He sucked his teeth. "Not gonna happen."

She shrugged and began to turn away again.

"Give us a few days to check out this Doran character, we might be willing to deal."

She placed the lid on the shoebox while she thought, and a wave of mischief made Foster ask, "Don't suppose there's any point in telling you you're under arrest?" Nevertheless, he did glance left involuntarily, searching for a gap in the railings.

She smiled. "Not unless you can leap tall buildings in a single bound. You look the athletic type — but Superman you're not."

Is she flirting with me? He shrugged, "The boss told me I had to have a go." He decided to push his advantage and went for the rueful look. "You know, I'm not exactly known for my tact." The catarrhal emphasis on the "c" consonants was for comic effect. "Fact is, you've risked prison before to do the right thing."

She wasn't about to fill in the gaps for him, but she seemed intrigued, and she didn't seem in such a hurry to leave any more.

"Come on, Megan, the Met know it was you helped them out."

"What can I say?" She frowned, distracted, as if trying to work out what had given her away. "I'm a 'virtual' hero."

"The guy I spoke to seemed to think so."

"Nice of him to speak so highly of me. But —"

"How did they identify you?" Foster said, anticipating her question. "Apparently you've got some kind of signature. They've also got you tagged for a number of small-profit, high turnover scams all over the world-wide web."

She managed a smile. "Based on my 'signature'?"

Foster wasn't about to give her details of the Squad's part-time surveillance operations. He said nothing and let her come to her own conclusions.

"Why are you telling me this?" she asked.

"There's something we want to know."

She raised an eyebrow in question.

"What's on the card?"

She tilted her head. "What's on the table?"

CHAPTER
TWENTY-FIVE

The twins were sleeping. Frankie still sucked his thumb for comfort, curled up on one side. Declan, always the more confident of the two, was lying on his back, arms and legs splayed, limbs twitching like a puppy-dog dreaming of chasing sheep.

Patrick Doran had showered and changed. He was supposed to be resting, but sleep eluded him. Warrender had pulled in a few favours among his police contacts. If Bentley was a grass, they would know within hours. He stood at the door of their bedroom, watching the rise and fall of Declan's chest, the uneasy stirrings of Frankie, and thought about what he might have to do to keep them safe.

Frankie groaned and struggled, troubled by a passing dream, and Doran stepped over to his bedside, handing his son the Spiderman soft toy that had become a magic talisman for a good night's sleep. Frankie mumbled something, hugging the toy close, already comforted, and Doran kissed his forehead. He smelled of soap and earth and rain. He rumpled the boy's hair, whispering, "Everything's all right, sweetheart." As he turned he saw Fay in the doorway.

The look on her face said, *No, it isn't. It isn't all right. And it's all my fault.*

"I'm so sorry, Patrick," she said, tears standing in her eyes.

He felt something tighten around his heart. Despite his own fear, he couldn't bear to see her afraid. He opened his arms and she walked into his embrace. He kissed her softly and she answered more urgently, her lips hard on his mouth. He pulled away, glancing back at the boys, then he laced his fingers through hers and they tiptoed to their own bedroom and locked the door after them.

Fay almost fell on him, her fingers tugging eagerly at his T-shirt, his belt, the waist of his trousers. He kissed her, his lips hot on hers, finding the little hollow where the clavicle meets the base of the neck, teasing her nipples with kisses and little flicks of his tongue till she cried out, guiding him into her. His hands went to the firm curve of her buttocks and they moved together until they found their rhythm. At the climax she was sobbing.

He stroked her hair and kissed her face, murmuring over and over, "Don't Fay. Please don't." At last she was comforted and they slept for two exhausted hours.

The doorbell rang and Fay gave a little yelp, startled awake by the sudden noise.

"It's all right," Doran said. "Go back to sleep." He sat up, swinging his legs over the side of the bed and trying to force the grogginess out of his head.

"It's the middle of the night, Patrick!"

"No" he soothed. "It's only" — he squinted at his watch — "ten o' clock. We fell asleep. It's early, yet."

"Even so —" The bell rang again and she hissed, "They'll wake the boys, so they will."

"Probably just Maura, forgot her key."

"Maura's staying over with Rena tonight. They're clubbing it with a gang from school."

"I'll go." He insisted, staying her with a gentle hand. He struggled into his dressing-gown, feeling drunk and stupid, the brief hours of sleep making him desperate for more.

He hurried downstairs and opened the front door as John Warrender reached for the bell a third time.

"Go through to my study," he said, forgoing the formality of a greeting. "And for God's sake, keep the noise down."

He closed the door softly and turned to see Fay at the top of the stairs, side-lit by a shaft of light from their bedroom. She looked ghostly in the dim light, insubstantial, like she was bound to him only tenuously, and might vanish in a moment. She stared down at him in sullen disapproval, then turned away and Doran was filled with a superstitious dread that if she reached their bedroom he would never see her again. He took the stairs two at a time, catching her arm and turning her to him.

"I need help with this, Fay," he said.

"You have help," she said. "Mr Manning —"

"Manning can't know about the insurance accounts." That's how he thought of the secret bank accounts — as insurance, a safeguard for his family's future.

"I know," she said, avoiding his eye. "But, Patrick — the twins are asleep just along the landing — couldn't you meet him at the office?"

Doran felt a wave of relief that made him want to weep: he could win this argument; the danger had passed. "Manning is using my office machines to get the worms or bugs or whatever the hell you call them out of the network. He sent me home 'cos I was making his crew nervous." He pushed his fingers through his hair and laughed, then stopped, because he heard hysteria in it. It looked like they had lost only a day's-worth of data — the day of the computer crash: at least that leadless prick Nathan had made decent back-ups of the system.

"We're losing revenue every day the system is down, Fay. People are beginning to cancel because we can't guarantee security for their cash. Everything: bookings, schedules, invoices, rotas — *everything* is run from the network. I need to leave him to sort it out. And I need someone I can trust to take care of this other thing."

He did trust Warrender, as far as he trusted anyone. Warrender knew about the insurance accounts; he knew that Megan Ward had sucked them dry. What he didn't know was how much was in the accounts before Ward got to them. He could guess. But his guess would fall way short of the reality. Doran hadn't told Fay the exact amount. He hardly dared admit even to himself how much he had lost.

Fay closed her eyes briefly. "All right," she said. "Just . . . keep him the hell away from me and the children."

★ ★ ★

Warrender had seated himself in the leather armchair by the window. Doran felt a spurt of anger. "Make yourself comfortable," he said.

Warrender glanced up. "What?"

Doran quelled the flush of unreasonable irritation. Warrender was not the rightful target; Megan Ward was. Maybe Bentley, too. Warrender, on the other hand, was his most trusted employee — the employee he least wanted to piss off. "Drink?" he said.

Warrender seemed mildly gratified. "Whiskey."

Doran poured two of Bushmills — the good stuff — and handed one to Warrender.

Warrender held his up as if hypnotised by the play of light through the facets of the heavy crystal tumbler. Doran allowed him his moment of repose. After half a minute, Warrender sighed and took a sip. "Where do you want me to start?"

"Background checks," Doran said. "Work, family, driving, police."

Warrender still had a cop's facility for facts and he spoke confidently, from memory. "Jake Alexander Bentley. Age twenty-eight. He's worked at the gym for two-and-a-half years. Before that, as a bouncer — various venues. His work record is good, apart from a couple of rucks when he was a bouncer — he had a rep for being a bit heavy-handed. Two charges of GBH — one dropped, the other stuck — six months suspended. Since he's been working at the gym, he got into it with one of the clients — but he saved some fat lawyer's skin, so he got off."

215

Doran sipped his whiskey quietly, seated in the chair opposite.

"Parents both living."

"Where?" It might be useful to know.

"Walton. I've got the address. He visits once a week. Clean driving licence. Two further arrests in the last week."

Doran's head came up.

"Released without charge," Warrender said. "But he was warned off Sara Geddes."

Their eyes met for a second.

"What was the complaint?" Doran asked.

"Stalking. Only the original target was noted as Megan Ward. Sara Geddes put in the complaint after Megan Ward disappeared. Said he'd been watching the place. Megan was spooked, so she jumped to conclusions."

Doran nodded slowly. "The other arrest?"

"He was IDd at the scene of Sara Geddes's murder."

Doran took a swallow of whiskey. "He didn't lie about that then."

"So, what does he want?"

Warrender thought about it. "What if Ward and Bentley were working together? Ward made up the stalking story so Sara didn't guess that Bentley was part of her operation."

"Have you been popping Nathan's pills?" Doran asked. "You're sounding more paranoid than him."

Warrender looked into his whiskey tumbler. "Just covering the bases," he said, taking a sip.

"The scam is *over*, John," Doran said. "That bitch has walked off with a fortune of my money, tax-free, untraceable. Why the hell would she stick around?"

"Like I said, I'm covering the bases," Warrender said, not bothering to hide his resentment. "I haven't had a full night's sleep in a week — don't expect me to hit the mark every time."

Doran poured himself another drink, his movements neat and precise, giving himself time to cool down. He swallowed most of the drink before he trusted himself to speak. "Set up a meeting," he said. "Let's see what this little fucker has to say."

"I think that would be a mistake," Warrender said.

"Because?"

"The connection with Megan Ward for one thing."

"Connection?" Doran slammed the glass down on his desk so hard it left an indentation in the wood. "He was stalking the landlady, not shagging the tenant!"

Warrender kept his head down and looked slightly off to Doran's right. "Bentley approached the firm last autumn. I didn't like the guy, so I blew him off."

"And you saved this till *last*?" Doran stared at Warrender, trying to control a powerful urge to pick up the tumbler and smash the glass into Warrender's face.

"You wanted to hear about the background checks."

"Anything else you've been saving up for me? Any little snippet of information, like maybe you know where Megan Ward is?"

Warrender knew better than to answer.

"Stalkers are obsessive, John," Doran said, his voice exaggeratedly calm. "They don't like rejection. Now he's had what? Six? Eight? months to exaggerate this out of all proportion and develop a colossal grudge against me, the business — whatever. So now I'm wondering if maybe he *did* set this up. Only he's such a stupid fucker he got taken by his partner in crime. And now he's *really* pissed off and he's hoping to get some satisfaction from me."

"Which is why you shouldn't meet him," Warrender said. "I'm just thinking —"

Doran resisted the temptation to make a snide remark about Warrender's reasoning skills.

"We know he's a witness to —" Warrender left the rest unsaid. "He could be working with the police — getting himself off the hook by putting you on it."

"If I don't meet him, how am I going to know?" Doran asked.

"You don't need to know."

The silence filled the room. Warrender returned Doran's searching look for a few seconds, then his courage failed him and he looked into the bottom of his glass. They both knew what he was suggesting, and it wasn't simply to ignore Bentley and hope he went away. Doran had been thinking the same thing. Watching the boys sleeping, hearing his wife's sobs as they made love, he had wanted to lash out, to break something. To make somebody pay for the hurt to his family.

"And if he's got useful information about Ward?"

Warrender looked momentarily confused, then he said. "All right, I'll talk to him first."

"If Bentley's got anything on Ward, I want to hear it myself." The assertion fell just short of a declared lack

218

of trust. "Tell me you're not pinning your hopes on finding Ward's address under 's' for swindler in Bentley's little black book."

"We traced Ward before," Warrender said. "All we've got to do is wait for her to go online again."

"Assuming she will," Doran said. "Only our systems manager has gone off his head, and David Manning isn't likely to help us trace Megan Ward and say nothing about it to the police now, is he?" Doran stood over Warrender, the heavy whiskey tumbler in his hand a potential weapon, a putative threat.

Warrender finished his drink, avoiding Doran's eye.

"Set up the meeting for tomorrow," Doran said. "I'll talk to Bentley. If he looks like trouble, we'll deal with it."

CHAPTER
TWENTY-SIX

It was eleven p.m. The majority of the team had knocked off after the eight-thirty debrief, those that remained had been involved in tracing or surveillance ops. Rickman called the few to order: Lee Foster, Naomi Hart, Andy Reid, Will Garvey, as the surveillance team leader — the others he had sent home. They gathered around a TV and video Rickman had filched from the Parade Room.

"This is the CCTV footage of Lime Street Station concourse near the phone booths," Hart said. She looked pale and tired. "The initial call was made from the call box on the left.

"Megan's the one in the baseball cap and dark glasses," she said, pointing. The image was in colour, and it was clear she wore jogging pants and a matching jacket with hood, but the definition was poor. Megan came out of the booth, keeping her head bowed. The time lapse made her appear to jump from one location to another. At the glass doors leading to the taxi rank, she turned and waved and then she was gone.

"The Scientific Support Unit might be able to get something useful from it," Rickman said. "Height, maybe. Clothing — although it's easy enough to change that."

"She was wearing jeans and a fleece at the rendezvous," Foster said.

Rickman nodded. "Anything on Doran?"

"He's definitely a client of Kieran Jago," Hart said. "That's all I've got, so far."

"Mobile phone trace?"

Reid shook is head. "She switched it off as soon as she had eyeball with Foster."

"What about the service provider?" he asked. This investigation was a succession of frustrations and disappointments.

"We haven't traced it, yet — could be she's using pay-as-you-go, keeping us guessing."

Rickman rubbed a hand over his face, feeling stubbly growth on his chin. "Garve?"

Will Garvey rarely gave anything away: he had long ago learned to meet with triumph and disaster and treat those two impostors just the same. Tonight, however, he looked sorely tried. Perhaps he sensed Rickman's exasperation, and perhaps he was simply exasperated with his own failure.

"We had three cars to cover any one of a dozen ways out, Boss," he said.

"Nobody's blaming you, Garve," Rickman said. Putting people on the defensive was never productive. "Just tell us what you got."

"Nothing," Garvey said. "Nothing is what we got. The woman's like smoke," he added, unknowingly echoing Nathan Wilde's description of Megan.

"You're not kidding," Foster said. "I ran like hell when she walked off and I couldn't see any sign of her when I got out the park."

"Did you see where she was headed?" Rickman asked.

Foster's hand went to his hair, as it often did at moments of stress. "She walked towards Centreville Road. I ran down to the gap in the railings. By the time I ran back, the road was empty."

Rickman reached forward and switched off the VCR. For a second or two, they all stared at the snowstorm of static on the screen, then Rickman spoke. "All we can do is wait for her to get in touch. Meanwhile, we check the Doran connection, see if we can come up with something. Lee — why don't you fill the team in on the offer?"

"I told her I was authorised to give her a look at the card — under supervision — on condition she gives us any de-encrypted info, together with any passwords and the decoder."

"What's in it for her?" Hart asked, puzzled.

"That's what she said."

"What did you tell her?"

What Foster actually told Megan was that she would get to be the virtual hero again, but that would take too much explaining, so he said, "Justice. For Sara."

Hart was incredulous. "And she bought it?"

"She said she'd think about it."

Rickman had heard the conversation relayed via Garvey's phone after Foster had re-established the connection as Megan walked away. Foster had pushed

222

harder and harder, finally telling her that they would need further proof of Doran's guilt.

"You're the police," she said. "That's your job."

"You've got the information we need," he countered. "We call it information-gathering."

She didn't reply, and Foster later told Rickman he felt she was thinking it over. "Find something while you were poking around in his computer, did you?" he asked.

The pause lengthened and then she said, "Maybe."

"We want whatever you've got."

"And if I don't oblige?"

"Our technical support team'll crack your code sooner or later," Foster said. "And if we do it, instead of being the virtual hero, you get stuck with the label arch-villain."

"Nemesis," she said.

"What?"

"The villains — they're always the nemesis of the superhero."

"You don't get out much, do you?" Foster said. She smiled and he felt they had made a connection. "You don't want to be charged with conspiracy, Megan."

"*Conspiracy?*" She seemed outraged. "With Doran?"

"The longer you leave it, the more time Doran's got to cover his tracks." For now, he was content to let her think he believed her accusations against Doran.

After a few moments, she said, "You know I didn't get hold of this information by looking him up in the Companies Listings — I'd want some guarantees."

"Any help you give us would be taken into consideration," he said.

"Well *sod* that —"

"And there's the witness relocation scheme," he added.

She laughed, but there was little humour in it. "No thanks. I've made my own relocation arrangements."

There it was again: Rickman was convinced she'd had some experience of witness protection. And when they discovered that connection, he was equally sure that they would unravel the mystery that was Megan Ward.

Foster checked his watch. "Boss . . ."

Rickman glanced at the clock on the wall. "You need to head off," he said.

"Am I still supposed to arrest her?" Foster asked.

"As long as she's co-operating, let's play along with her," Rickman said.

Foster made eye contact with Naomi Hart. "Well, come 'ead, if you're coming."

Hart was startled. "Where?"

"My place. She's gonna phone me there."

Hart looked around, suspicious that this was a set-up. "What d'you need me for?"

"Back-up. Chaperone. Whatever you wanna call it," Foster said. "She wants safe custody and that means twenty-four/seven."

Hart wasn't convinced until she looked at Rickman and he nodded. "Sorry it's such short notice," he said.

"*Short* notice?" Hart complained as they clattered down the staircase. "More like none at all."

224

"We can stop off at your place on the way," Foster said. "Pick up a change of clothes."

Hart stopped dead. "I'm not gonna be stuck baby-sitting *overnight*?"

"Twenty-four/seven," Foster said. "It's kind of an overnight thing."

Hart had a two-bedroom flat in a refurbished Victorian warehouse at the top end of Duke Street. She left Foster waiting in her sitting-room, staring at her view of the Anglican Cathedral while she threw a few things in a bag. It seemed he had quickly tired of the view from her window, because when she returned, he was standing in front of her TV zapping through the digital channels.

"Plasma screen," he said, without turning round.

"Pioneer, HDMI."

"Forty-inch?"

"Forty-two," she said.

"Every inch counts," he breathed.

She laughed and he said, "What?" He hadn't been joking.

"Nothing. Can we go now?"

He flicked the off-switch reluctantly. "Have you got a boyfriend?"

"That's none of your damn business," she said, offended. Then, realising the significance of the question, she shook her head in disbelief. "Did you think a love of gadgets was exclusive to the Y-chromosome?"

"Nah," he said, with an appreciative glance at the rest of the room: hardwood floors, a couple of striking paintings, cosy furnishings, lack of clutter. "Just never had you down as a gizmo-geek."

He felt slightly abashed letting her into his own place. It was smaller and darker and lacked the stylish touches of Hart's flat.

"Not up to your standard," he said.

"It's clean."

"Did you think you needed two X chromosomes for that?" he asked slyly.

"No," she replied, without a pause, "But most guys I know who have clean houses are either gay or married."

He hated to admit it, but even joking, the gay jibe was hard to take, which was why he answered less guardedly than he would normally. "One of the first things they taught us," he said.

"They? The marines?"

She was sharp, and he'd given out more than he meant to. He didn't reply, but instead waved her towards the kitchen. "Tea's in the cupboard over the kettle, if you want a brew." He had noticed the red light glowing on his answerphone. He watched Hart walk away, taking time to enjoy the sway of her hips as he pressed the "new messages" key.

There was a lot of background noise and the occasional clatter of crockery and at first he didn't recognise the voice. "Are you there, Lee? Pick up, you bloody sod!"

Suddenly it hit him: Stacey — Kieran Jago's PA. "Oh, crap," he muttered.

"Don't you dare call me," she said. "I couldn't stand to hear your smarmy, insincere apologies." The next few words were muffled as she took the phone away from her ear, presumably looking for the "end call" button. But one word was quite distinct before the line went dead. "Bastard!"

He went through to the kitchen and dropped his keys on the work surface. Hart handed him a mug of tea and took a sip from her own. "You stood her up," she said, looking at him reproachfully over the rim of her cup.

"I was kind of busy," he said, on the defensive for a second until he saw the mischief in Hart's blue eyes and had to laugh at himself. "Who cares?" he said. "We know who Kieran Jago's working for now."

"First off — that's really callous," she said. "And second, you're assuming we can believe what Megan says."

"Let's see what she comes up with, shall we?"

The doorbell rang and Hart said, "Are you expecting someone?"

"Not unless Stacey's gone all *Fatal Attraction* on me." He placed his mug of tea on the counter and walked down the hall. His flat door opened onto a communal area: Victorian floor tiles and a big front door with stained-glass lights; the figure beyond was obscured by the rose patterning of the glass. He opened the door and Megan Ward walked past him into the main hallway.

"You were gonna phone," he said.

"I lied."

"How d'you get my address?"

She feigned vagueness. "Phone book?"

"I'm ex-directory."

She gave him a look. "Think you police are the only ones with access to reverse phone books?" She lifted her chin, indicating his flat door.

"Through here, is it?"

He stood at the door a moment longer, lost for words, then followed her, unsure whether to feel irritated or amused.

Megan headed for the light at the end of his hallway. She wore jeans and the fleece she had been wearing at their first meeting. She carried a square shoulder bag strapped sash-wise across her body. She seemed relaxed, at her ease, but she froze when she saw Naomi Hart. Foster held his hands up as she turned on him. She looked trapped — afraid and angry and ready to fight.

"Before you throw a wobbler, DC Hart is here for your protection and mine."

She held back the anger but he saw it in a rapid tic at the corner of one eye. *Sara was right*, he thought. *Her eyes are grey.* "You said you wanted protection," he explained. "DC Hart — Naomi — is here to see nothing . . . untoward happens."

She stood side-on, trying to keep them both in her field of vision. Hart raised one shoulder. *Take it or leave it.*

Gradually, by degrees, Megan regained her composure. "Is this it?" she said. "No more surprises?"

"We were hoping you'd provide the real excitement of the evening," Hart said.

228

The two women eyed each other coolly. Megan was as dark as Naomi Hart was fair. Megan's face was long and solemn, a face not used to smiling, whereas Hart, though she had learned the poker face as part of her job, seemed at times to look at the world and perceive it as a huge joke.

"Okay," Megan said, "let's get the party going. D'you have the card?"

Foster patted the breast pocket of his suit jacket and she held out her hand.

"Tell us how it works," he said. Hart raised her eyebrows. Evidently, she thought he was pushing it. But Megan was practically salivating — it would take a hell of a lot more to make her turn and walk.

She looked from Foster to Hart. "Not in here," she said. "It's claustrophobic." She went through to his sitting-room, taking the seat nearest the door, and Foster wondered if she always had an eye for an escape route.

She waited for them to be seated before she began. "This isn't my usual bag," she said, beginning cautiously. "But say you wanted to hack somebody's bank account online . . ." She glanced first at Foster, then at Hart. "This is off the record, right?"

"Look, Megan," Hart said. "We want whoever killed Sara. *You* want whoever killed Sara. We're focused on that, okay?"

She took a breath and nodded, smoothing her hair back from her face before continuing. "People are incredibly lax about security. They use the same passwords all the time: for email, their bank accounts

— and for their online ordering, which is where I come in.

"You said the Fraud Squad tracked me on eBay?"

Foster nodded.

"I get my customers to set up an account with me. Name and address, date of birth, and of course a username and password. I sometimes throw in a couple of key questions like mother's maiden name and important date — in case they've been creative and use different passwords on other accounts — you can usually predict their password choice from personal stuff like that."

"So you use the password they've given you for their order and check if they've used it on other accounts?" Hart asked.

"It's like trying a key in all the locks in a house. It might be it just opens the front door, but all the other rooms are protected with a different kind of lock. But sometimes . . ." She lowered her voice and Foster sensed a growing excitement. "Sometimes the key opens the strong-room, and you gain access to a bank account."

"How do you live with yourself?" Foster asked.

"Quite easily," Megan said. "I don't take anything unless they can afford it."

"And how do you judge that?"

If Megan heard the sarcasm in his tone, she didn't react to it. "I take a peek at their bank details. If the sums of money are big enough, I monitor their expenditure patterns and add a few outgoings of my own, making it look like the money is going to regular bills or legit. purchases — never huge sums."

"Next you'll be telling us it's a victimless crime," Foster said.

Megan slid him a look. "Do we have to have the commentary?" she asked.

Foster raised both hands in mock apology and fell silent. Megan continued looking at him for a few seconds longer, before continuing. "I got an order from Doran's wife, set up an account —"

"And she gave you her bank account password?" Hart said.

"No. But the wife's password got me into all areas of their home computer. They had a bit of money in their joint account — but not enough. I filched some useful info from her correspondence and used it to hack into the Safe Hands network. It took a while, but I have software that will crack just about any password, given enough time. I was able to designate myself as system manager, which meant I could do pretty much what I wanted with it."

Foster saw a gleam of pride in her eye.

"Then she let slip who her husband was."

She fell silent, and Foster saw her working through some memories she evidently found painful. "I got Doran's password, which gave me access to his business account — again, only piddling amounts. So I went back to their home computer and tried his password." She smiled. "It opened the strong-room."

"Secret accounts?" Foster said.

"Three."

"And how much was in them?"

Her smile broadened. "Substantial sums."

"So, what are you offering us?" Foster asked, "A nasty case of tax dodging? I thought you were gonna give us a murderer, Megan."

She tilted her head. "It's how the FBI got Al Capone . . ." Neither Foster nor Hart so much as smiled.

She sighed. "All right. I riffled through his document folders, as well. He deleted most of the incriminating stuff, but even deleted files leave a trace. I discovered copies of incriminating documents ghosted on his disk."

"And you brought proof with you." It was a question.

She raised her eyebrows. "You guys are greedy. I have copies of the data, stored safely. What I'm here for tonight is the card."

"And all you've given us so far is hints and suppositions. We know you tell a good story, Megan," Foster said. "That's why you're such a good con-artist. But we're cops."

"What he's saying is, it takes more than a good story and a bit of sleight of hand to impress us," Hart added.

Megan flushed a little in annoyance and her eyes darkened.

"Tell us what's on the card, then you'll get your look at it," Foster said.

Megan took a breath and exhaled in a rush. "I found over a million pounds in his secret accounts. Now I have it."

"But, you don't, do you?" Hart said quietly.

232

"Okay," Foster said. "This is foreign territory for me. So, you can do the translation anytime you like."

Hart kept her eyes on Megan as she spoke. "She set up new accounts and moved the cash across, but the account numbers and passwords are encrypted on the card. And she can't get at the money without them."

Foster looked at her. "You understand the deal, yeah? You give us what's on the card. You walk away."

Her eyelids flickered almost imperceptibly. "For Sara."

For a while nobody spoke. Foster knew it was his call, and he knew there were risks involved — if Megan destroyed vital evidence on the card, they were in deep shit. Megan still looked angry, but was that because they were suspicious of her motives, or because she still hadn't got her hands on the card?

"How will you read what's on the card?" he asked at last.

The release of tension in the room was palpable. Megan reached inside her shoulder bag and took out a small grey device. It just about fitted on the palm of her hand. It was hinged and folded flat, like an electronic alarm clock; she opened it up, pressing a switch as she did so.

"This is a card-reader," she said. "I swipe the card, type in a password and it will bring up the sort codes, account numbers and passwords on the screen."

The screen was maybe five centimetres by ten, and Hart said, "We're going to have to get really cosy in that case, 'cos I want to see *everything* you're doing."

CHAPTER
TWENTY-SEVEN

The main restaurant at Five Star was beginning to wind down. The clatter of plates and the clamour of conversation softened by degrees as diners finished their final courses and coffees and slipped out into the night, bound for clubs or hotels or home.

Five Star belonged to John Warrender's brother, the name a joke because he said he didn't intend to wait for Michelin to get around to awarding what he already merited. In the early days, it was the name that drew custom, but the food and the atmosphere of the place had ensured its continued popularity.

Patrick Doran was seated in the function room upstairs. Usually reserved for corporate bookings and weddings, tonight it was empty, the tables waxed to a honey gold, the lights dimmed, so that the voices of the customers downstairs sounded like ghosts at an ill-fated feast.

If Bentley was being watched — with or without his knowledge — Doran didn't want him leading the police to Safe Hands Security. Warrender had suggested one of the sites they were guarding, but Doran wanted somewhere neutral, a public place he could enter and leave without being noticed. He sipped a brandy and listened with half an ear to the rise and fall of conversation, as one listens to the rhythms of a foreign language, or the suck and hiss of surf on shingle, allowing the diminishing murmur of voices and the warmth of the liquor to soothe him.

The bars and restaurants of the Cavern Quarter were emptying and the street below had the spirit of carnival: loud, colourful and brash, with an undertow of menace rippling just beneath the surface. Doran felt a tinge of recognition, a wistful longing to respond to its tidal pull.

Jake Bentley strode through the narrow winding streets towards his destination, confident that the crowds would part and flow around him as a river flows around a boulder. His height was an advantage: he could look over their heads, only occasionally lighting on a pretty girl, and only if she was unaware of his scrutiny.

He wore loose-fitting cream chinos and a black T-shirt with a sports jacket over it. It had taken some time to decide on the right combination: smart, respectful, but not over-formal. He thought he had got the balance just right. He hesitated for a second outside Five Star, then shouldered though the steel-frame doors and waited just inside. A smiling waitress came towards him, already composing her apologetic face to let him know that they were finished for the night. A man intercepted her and said a few words; she nodded and went back to clearing tables.

"Mr Bentley?" the man said. He was a few inches shorter than Bentley and a little soft around the middle.

Bentley nodded and the man gave him a practised, professional smile. "This way." His voice was rich and clear, pitched to make himself heard above the hubbub of restaurant noise. He led Bentley to a spiral staircase at the rear of the restaurant and removed a rope barrier to allow him access.

He climbed the stairs into the gloom of the empty function room, and stood still for a few seconds, waiting for his eyes to adjust to the light. Two men watched him quietly from the other side of the room. He recognised Mr Doran immediately. He was small, but strong; a kick-boxer's build. He knew that Mr Doran had a gym at home, and that he ran ten miles a day on the treadmill.

He crossed the room in a few strides, trying not to look self-conscious. When he reached the table he held out a hand.

"Jake Bentley," he said.

Doran glanced at the offered hand with little interest and Bentley jammed it in his pocket, hoping that the lack of light would hide the angry rush of blood to his face.

Doran lifted his chin, indicating the man seated at the narrow edge of the table. "John Warrender, my head of security."

"We've met," Bentley said. But that sounded cold. *Stop it, Jake*, he told himself. *This isn't about last autumn — last autumn all you had to offer was muscle. Now you've got something Mr Doran needs.* He started again. "Last autumn. You probably don't remember, Mr Warrender, but I applied for —"

236

"I remember," Warrender said, cutting him short.

"Sit down, Mr Bentley," Doran said.

Warrender shoved a chair out from under the table with the toe of his shoe and Bentley sat facing Mr Doran, and with the security chief's gaze hot on the side of his face.

"How did your interview go with the police?"

"Great," he said, then corrected himself, "I mean, you know — it was okay. I offered to do the ID parade, like you said. The old lady has withdrawn her statement." Neither man spoke, and he continued, trying to find some common ground. "Mr Jago was fantastic — he knew exactly what to say."

"I'll be sure and tell him. He'll be made up," Doran said.

Talking too much, Jake, he told himself. *Shut up and listen, for God's sake.* "So, I'm all in the clear," he said, unable to stop himself. "Except for the stalking charge. But now Sara's, you know . . ."

"Dead," Doran said, his eyes not wavering from Bentley's face for a second. "No complainant, no witnesses — you're laughing, aren't you?"

Bentley looked at his hands, clasped in his lap, unable to bear Doran's penetrating stare any longer. "I never meant nothing by that. I was just —"

"Making conversation."

The way Mr Doran kept finishing his sentences was unsettling. "Well, yeah," he said, bewildered.

"So," Doran said. "I'm thinking we're done here. You got what you want, and now we're finished."

"Oh," Bentley said, disappointed, not quite grasping the reason for Mr Doran's hostility. Then in a flash of understanding, he did. "Oh! You think — Mr Doran, I wasn't trying to pull a fast one on you, I swear. It's just — I've always wanted to work for you."

"Always?"

"Since I got into the business."

"And what business would that be?" The latent threat was always there, like a moving shadow, restless behind Doran's eyes.

Bentley frowned. "Security."

Doran and Warrender exchanged a look.

"Whose security?" Warrender asked.

Bentley kneaded the knuckles of his right fist with his left. "I don't know — whoever I'm supposed to be protecting."

Doran narrowed his eyes.

Oh, God, this is going so bad. He thinks I'm trying to blackmail him. "Mr Doran," he said. "I'm not so clever with words. If I gave the wrong impression, I apologise. I'm just trying to tell you how much I admire you."

Doran folded his arms. "Well, if it's a fan-boy thing, maybe you should contact me via the website."

Bentley flinched. He didn't have to be so mean.

"Tell me what you want, Bentley."

"I want to help — really I do." *Bentley. He called me Bentley. I've pissed him off and now he's calling me Bentley.* He was sweating and fearful and sick that he had so badly misjudged the situation. "I've got these photos, you see," he blurted out.

238

Doran lifted his hand to silence him. At the same time, Warrender stood, gesturing for Bentley to do the same. For a while the sound of voices in the restaurant below was drowned by the roar of blood in his ears. Warrender patted him down, removed his mobile phone from his jacket pocket and switched it off, then turned to Doran.

"No wires," he said.

Bentley blinked, shocked and upset. "A *wire*? I wouldn't — honest to God, Mr Doran —"

"What photos?" Doran interrupted.

He blinked again, swallowed. "Of Megan Ward."

Both men relaxed visibly. *Oh, shit! You moron, Jake! They thought you had shots of the murder.* He had a horrible recollection: the photographs. Two or three he had reeled off without thinking as the men approached Sara's house; the one they called "Cap" and another he didn't recognise.

He stared, horrified at Mr Doran. He knew how it would look if he admitted that he had photographed Doran's men. It would look like a set-up. It would look like he'd taken the film to the police and now he was trying to extract as much information from them as he could.

"Who is Megan Ward?" Doran asked.

The question threw him. *They don't know? But they must know — otherwise why did they go to Sara's house? Wasn't it on the news?* Sometimes the stories in his head bled into the real world and he wasn't sure where one ended and the other began. "Megan was

239

Sara's tenant," he said. "She a bit of a computer freak — always in that office of hers."

Doran looked at Warrender.

"There was no computer," Warrender said.

"The police took it."

This time there was no eye contact between the two men, but Bentley knew he had said something important.

"You were arrested for stalking, Mr Bentley," Doran said. Bentley took the reintroduction of his title as a good sign. "The police must have confiscated your photographs, camera, film — the lot."

"They did," Bentley said. *Careful, Jake.* "I had a roll at the photolab." He had said it. Now there was no going back. Maybe it was the adrenaline, he couldn't be sure, but something was making him think a little faster that evening. *The shots of Cap and the other man were near the end of the roll. I'm sure of it. I can just take them out and nobody need know.*

Again, Doran glanced at Warrender.

Warrender shook his head. "The police would've checked with the photolab."

"I didn't go to the normal one, though," Bentley said. "I went to see my mum, and I found a couple of rolls in my pocket. She was going out to the shops and I asked her to drop them in for me at the chemist." He shrugged. "They're still there, waiting for me to pick them up."

Doran left a brief silence. "And what do you want for this film?" he asked.

240

"Please don't take this the wrong way, Mr Doran." Bentley glanced anxiously at Warrender. "I just want a job."

Doran eyed him for a long moment. "A job," he repeated.

"Something with prospects. I'm sick of handing out towels to flabby businessmen down the gym." He had pandered to middle-aged men and their pampered wives for two-and-a-half years, and that was two years too long.

Something flashed in Doran's eyes. Amusement, perhaps, and then he fell silent until Bentley began to squirm in his seat. "All right," he said. "But while we wait for your photographs, I want a description of Megan, and anything else you know about her."

Dismayed, Bentley struggled to think of something. "There wasn't nothing. Just the computer, really. She didn't go out much. Oh!" he exclaimed, remembering. "The car."

He gave Warrender details while Doran went to the window and looked down into the street at the crowds, jostling, some singing, more than a few staggering out of the bars.

When Bentley left, Doran turned back to Warrender. "I want him followed. Until we meet tomorrow night, I want to know his every move."

"You're not actually going give him a job?" Warrender asked.

"Depends how useful he is," Doran said.

"And if he isn't? Useful, I mean?"

"Like I said before, we'll deal with it."

CHAPTER
TWENTY-EIGHT

They drew up outside a double-fronted Georgian house in Rodney Street. The road was quiet this time of night, the doctors' surgeries and the clinics specialising in everything from laser treatment to liposuction were closed and the one small restaurant had long since disgorged its diners into the night.

Faux-antique street lamps cast a pinkish glow on the drying pavements, and the traffic lights at either end of the road changed from green to red and back to green without a single car passing through them. During the day, parking was pay and display only, though the machines were frequently vandalised by rebellious locals unwilling to pay the tariff.

The front door, painted deep blue, gave onto a gleaming hallway with several brass-plated doorways: surgeons, dermatologists, opthalmologists. They took the stairs to the second floor to a low-framed door with a crooked lintel.

"Servants' quarters," Megan said, unlocking the door. "You'll need to watch your heads." Both Hart and Foster had to duck to avoid the lintel, but once inside, the flat was roomy, though the boards were a little bowed and the accommodations not quite as airy as the offices on the lower floors. The sitting-room was furnished with a sofa and one easy chair in cream linen, a large stone-coloured rug in the centre of the floor, coffee table, mirror over the fireplace, blinds on the windows, no pictures.

"Why this place?" Foster asked.

"It's central," Megan said. "Views over the front and back of the house. People coming and going all the time during the day — new custom, new faces." She lifted one shoulder. "Effective invisibility."

Hart explored the doors off the main room. "Bathroom," she said identifying each room as she came to it, "galley-kitchen . . . bedroom . . . And another bedroom." The larger of the two rooms had been made up. "Neat as a prison cell," she remarked. There was a second door on the far side of the room. "Where does that door lead?"

"Fire escape," Megan said. "Another reason for choosing this place." Foster noticed she hadn't said "renting": he suspected that she was not officially occupying the flat at all.

"Good choice," he said. "I doubt if Witness Protection could stretch to these rents, though."

"They haven't the imagination to find a place like this," Megan said disparagingly.

"You don't have much faith in the Witness Protection Programme, do you?" Hart said.

Megan turned her gaze on DC Hart. "It's an under-funded government con — fooling people into coming forward on the pretext they'll be safe."

"You talking from personal experience?" Foster asked.

She didn't answer, only stared at him for a few moments as though trying to figure him out.

Foster continued his evaluation of the accommodation. "Bit low on comforts," he said, "But not bad as a bolt-hole."

"Home from home, eh, Sergeant?" She shot back.

Foster clasped a hand to his heart as though wounded.

"I haven't had time to nest," Megan went on. "How long have you been in your place?"

"It's a — thing," he said, feigning offence. "Minimalist, I think they call it."

"Minimalist is my place," Hart said, slipping off her jacket and flopping into the easy chair. "What you've got is a cave."

"You're ganging up on me, now," Foster protested, but he was enjoying himself.

Megan went through to her bedroom and returned minus her fleece jacket. "Coffee?" she asked.

Hart nodded, but Foster said, "Any chance of a brew?"

He followed her through to the kitchen and stood at the entrance to observe her. She worked with quick efficiency, sure of where everything was, focused on the task.

"So," he said, as she poured hot water into the mugs, "why would anyone want to be invisible?"

"Where've you been the last few days?" Megan asked. "My friend is dead — her killer is after me."

"We offered —"

"Come off it, Sergeant! You must have seen dozens of cases like this: someone comes forward with information, you say you'll protect them. Death threats follow, damage to property, physical violence — lives made hell because they trusted their safety to the law. Well — news flash — you can't stop evil people with a warning or an Anti Social Behaviour Order. You might as well use a sticking plaster to fix a slashed artery."

Foster was momentarily at a loss for words. She handed him his mug of tea and carried the coffee through for herself and Hart.

Foster frowned, annoyed with himself. As Hart took her mug of coffee, he saw mischief in her eye and he rallied to counter-attack. "Nice try," he said. "Only you're not exactly Mother Teresa yourself, are you? Don't you think you hurt people with you're little scams?"

Megan handed Hart her coffee and turned to him and he saw an ocean of turmoil in her eyes. "I'm not even a blip on the radar compared with Doran. You don't *know* what he's capable of," she said, her voice roughened with emotion.

"I'm listening." Foster glanced at Hart. "We both are. But you've got to stop pissing about with all this tax-dodging crap and give us something we can use against him."

"I will," she said, taking a seat on the sofa. "I'll get you everything you need. I just — I don't have everything in place, yet."

"Let us investigate," Hart said. "If it's there, we'll find the evidence."

Megan took a sip of hot coffee. "It's not that simple."

Foster had a sudden insight. "He really messed with you, didn't he? This isn't one of your crusades — Megan's personal war against evil — Supergeek gets her guy. Doran messed with you or your family."

Megan's hand jerked and hot coffee slopped out of the mug scalding her hand. She cursed, slamming the mug down onto the table and stood up. "You know the attraction of invisibility? This." She opened her arms, taking in the sweep of the room, the two of them, the situation she found herself in.

"If I screw up, it's only me I need to worry about. I can walk away free and clear. Turn up somewhere else. New name, new life, no baggage."

"There's always baggage, Megan," Hart said. "We lug it around with us no matter how far we run."

"She right about that, you know," Foster said. "And from what you've told us so far, you screwed up big time, letting Doran track you down, involving Sara —"

"Getting Sara killed?" She looked away from him as if it hurt too much to sustain eye contact.

Foster wasn't in the mood to indulge her self-pity. "Point is, you screwed up, and you're still here."

She made no reply.

Foster pushed a little harder. "All this crap about freedom: no past. No ties. I bet you've got that shoebox of golden memories stashed somewhere safe, though, haven't you?"

246

The anger seemed to light her up like a pulse of energy. "Yes, I have." She looked into his face, her eyes flashing. "Question is, where do you hide your store of childhood reminiscences, Foster?"

She went through to the kitchen and they heard the tap running.

"What was that about? Hart asked.

"Nothing," Foster said. "She's just firing buckshot, hoping to hit something." He snatched up a newspaper lying on the coffee table and sat on the sofa. Megan returned and wiped up the coffee spill, then sat in brooding silence a few feet from Foster.

You had to keep on at it, didn't you, Lee? You had to let her know you could read her. Didn't think she was just as sharp, did you? He thought he had buried his past, covering his vulnerability with jokes and superficiality, but Megan had seen through the shallows into the depths. When the phone rang, all three of them jumped.

Megan picked up and Foster flicked down a corner of his paper to watch. Hart widened her eyes at him. The question was implicit in her look: *What the hell is going on?*

Foster shook his head and returned his attention to Megan.

"For you," Megan said, placing the receiver on the table next to the phone.

"They've checked out the account numbers you gave us," he said after a brief conversation. "There's 1 million, 320,000, and some change." He was shaken by the news: some part of him actually thought that

Megan was a fantasist, that she had been lying to them and they would find that the "account numbers" she had given them were as bogus as the Visa card number embossed on the front of the card.

Megan tilted her head. "Did you doubt me, Sergeant?" She asked, the hint of a smile on her lips, good humour apparently restored by his discomfort.

She disappeared for a moment and returned with a DVD. "This contains an image of Doran's network, including his "black book" accounting. Compare it with his tax returns and you'll see a big disparity," Megan said. "He's working way under the tax radar on a lot of his jobs."

Foster took the disk and then skimmed it to Hart, who caught it neatly. "Tax dodging," he repeated. "You told us you had more."

"Like I said, it needs more work. And I've got to keep something back to keep you interested."

"There's a word for that," Foster said. "Obstruction. Think if we searched the rest of the flat we'd find more of those?"

"I *could* make you go through the tedious and time-wasting process of obtaining a warrant," she said. "But I want Doran as much as you do. Believe me, you'll get your proof. In the meantime —" She waved her arm in a grand sweep. "Be my guest." As she walked out of the room she placed a hand on Foster's shoulder and he felt the heat of it through his shirt. "Oh," she said softly, "I was forgetting — you already are."

CHAPTER
TWENTY-NINE

Their search of Megan Ward's flat turned up nothing. She worked on her laptop computer in the sitting-room, pretending not to notice as Foster and Hart turned out drawers and looked under furniture. She didn't even seem to mind when Foster asked her to move from her chair so that he could check the lining for hidden disks.

"All finished, now?" she asked when he set the chair upright again.

"You're not making any friends messing us about like this, Megan," he said.

"I don't need friends, Sergeant," she said. "Thanks all the same." She perched on an arm of the chair and continued working on her computer.

Foster looked over her shoulder as she clicked though several pages of an internet website. Something struck him as odd. It took him a few moments to work it out: there were no connectors going into or out of the sockets at the back of her computer.

"What?" she asked.

"I thought you had to connect to a phone-line to get onto the Net," Foster said.

"You do. And I am." He frowned and she added, "It's WiFi."

"Now I know you're winding me up," he said.

"I'm not. It's wireless. Uses radio waves to pick up a broadband connection."

"Yeah?" Hart stood watching them from the kitchen door. "Whose broadband connection? One of the offices downstairs?"

Foster saw a twinkle of amusement in Megan's eye. It lit up her rather solemn face, giving it an animation he found attractive. "In theory, it could be any connection up to a fifty-metre radius — it depends on the strength of the signal," she said. "Of course *in theory*, their firewall would protect them — or if they had any computer savvy, they'd have a scrambler to prevent parasites piggy-backing on their bandwidth."

"*In theory* . . ." Hart repeated, with a smile.

"Girl talk?" Foster asked, irritated and a little humiliated that he had understood barely one word in three of the exchange.

The women turned on him, eyes wide, ready for battle and Foster held up both hands defensively. "I'm apologising," he said. "Unreserved apologies, okay? Just don't suck the life-blood out of my bank account and blacklist my credit rating, *okay?*"

Megan was surprised into laughter and Foster tried the smile. She responded and Hart rolled her eyes.

"How did you get into this, then?" Foster asked, flopping onto the sofa, still smiling.

Megan shrugged. "Computing degree."

"I meant the fraud."

She thought for a moment. "I discovered that I didn't need to work for a living."

"It's no kind of life, though, is it?" Foster said. "Looking over your shoulder all the time. No friends, no family, no roots."

"I have friends," she said evenly, "And only vegetables need roots — I like my mobility."

Foster noticed she didn't reply to his comment about family. "Where are your friends now?" he asked.

"My friends are on the Net."

"Oh," he said. " 'Virtual' friends. Ever wonder how much of what they tell you is true?"

She shrugged. "It's true in the context of the Web. Not some neat little story somebody else made up for them."

"But it's not real," Hart said. She was still at the kitchen door, leaning against the frame, her arms folded.

"As real as any of the stories people make up about us." Megan countered. "It's what you do that matters, not what you appear to be."

"What you *do*," Foster said, "is steal other people's identities."

"I never stole a living person's identity."

"You stole their money."

"Most of them didn't even notice it was gone."

"Doran did."

She lifted one shoulder. "The money doesn't belong to him."

Foster smiled. "Doesn't belong to you, either."

"And Doran is a murdering bastard."

"*You* say."

Megan held Foster's gaze, her grey eyes unreadable. "I'll prove it."

"Would that be anytime soon?" Foster asked. "Because I do have a life, you know, and I'd like to get back to it this millennium."

"I gave you a million and a quarter pounds in unpaid taxes," Megan said.

Foster snorted. "You know what happens to men like Doran who don't pay their taxes, Megan? They bargain their way out, pay a percentage and the tax-man goes away happy."

"Sarge . . ." Hart seemed to think he was taking things too far, but Foster was unwilling to let it go.

"I'd like to know how *Mystic Meg* here is going to prove that Doran is a murderer. I mean why are we hanging on her every word? Why are we playing by her rules when we don't even know who she is?"

Foster saw something flare in Megan's eyes.

"It's late," Hart said, "and we're all a bit frayed round the edges. We can talk about this in the morning, but we won't get anywhere arguing about it tonight."

"She says she wants to catch Sara's killer, why doesn't she get on with it?"

Hart tilted her head. "He's got a point. How about it, Megan?" she said. "Why don't you just tell us what else you've got on Doran?"

"I told you —"

Foster saw a muscle jump in Megan's jaw. "Oh, yeah," he said, insincerity oozing from every pore. "You'll let us know in your own good time. Meanwhile

252

a murderer walks free. You're yanking our chains — admit it."

"It's . . . I'm not ready, yet," Megan said, sounding uncharacteristically unsure of herself. "I told you, I need to . . . to gather more information."

"Bullshit." Foster saw the look of warning on Hart's face, but he saw that Megan was rattled, and he intended to use his advantage. He took a step towards her and said, "What is this, Megan? Revenge?" He stared into her slate-grey eyes. "Did he do you and ditch you?"

Megan stood up. Her laptop slid off her lap and bounced on the chair cushion, tipping onto its side. "You want to know who I am?" She was angry, her skin pale except for two bright spots of colour high on her cheekbones. "You want a summary?"

Foster felt a thrill of anticipatory excitement.

"I'm not so easy to précis. I don't have a life CV for you to read and tick the boxes. You see me. What do you say I am?"

She was shifting the focus back onto him, but he was onto her; he'd used the trick often enough himself. "Why ask me?" he said. "Did you forget to leave a reminder on the fridge door, or something?"

Hart covered a smile. Megan seemed ready to retaliate, but then she caught herself, and the anger dissipated.

"Is that what *you* do?" she asked, coolly.

Foster got up and headed for the kitchen. "I need a brew," he said. "She does my head in."

Hart moved out of his way, into the body of the room.

After half a minute's silence, during which Foster rattled crockery and filled the kettle, Megan said, "He doesn't like me, much, does he?"

Hart said, "How can you like or dislike a shadow?"

She sighed and bent to pick up her laptop. "Don't you start."

"I'm just saying —"

"I like being invisible," she interrupted.

"I get that," Hart said. "I just don't get why."

"I like the freedom it gives me. We all do it, one way or another. We all put on different faces."

"Maybe, but we don't change our names and pretend to be something we're not."

"Of course you do," Megan said. "You pretend you don't see him watching you. He hides behind that big smile, pretending he doesn't give a shit."

Eavesdropping in the kitchen, Foster felt a prickle of discomfort.

"Sergeant Foster is a work colleague." He heard the carefully neutral tone.

"Because that's as close as you allow him," Megan said.

Oh, what? "How come your cloak of invisibility failed with Doran?" he demanded, coming back into the room.

Megan raised her eyebrows. "What makes you think it did?"

"How else would Sara end up dead?"

She chewed her lower lip while she decided how to answer. "I got complacent," she said after a while. "Doran's computer security was so sloppy I underestimated him. I should've used a laptop, changed locations regularly, used WiFi, but I'm more of a hi-tech grifter than a dedicated hacker."

"Don't be so modest," he said. "You knew how to wipe out your own computer records."

"The logic bomb *was* you, wasn't it?" Hart asked.

She nodded.

"And you locked Doran out of his own system."

She tilted her head, modestly declining the compliment. "Easy when you know how."

"And you stole info from his computer network and a sizeable wadge of money from him," Foster added.

"I do my bit for society." She caught his look and laughed, "Oh, don't look at me that way! You may be full of surprises, but don't expect me to believe you're the moralistic type."

Foster smiled. "I was just trying to work out *how* you did it, not the rights and wrongs of it."

She broke eye contact with him for a moment, and Foster thought she was struggling to hide a smile. "It wasn't that hard."

Foster gave her an incredulous look and she said, "I'm not being modest. Anyone with a basic competence in programming could do it."

"So you see yourself as a modern-day Robin Hood, do you?"

"I don't need that kind of recognition," she said, amused. "I keep telling you — I don't like to be recognised at all."

Hart was talking on her mobile when Foster staggered into the sitting-room at nine-thirty a.m. She had replaced him on duty at six-thirty, and he had caught three hours of dream-fevered rest, waking stupefied and grumpy.

"Is there no coffee on?" he demanded. Hart rolled her eyes and continued her conversation.

Foster blundered into the kitchen and opened and closed doors at random until he found the coffee. There was no cereal, but he found half a loaf of bread and put a couple of slices in the toaster while he washed the mugs from the night before and made coffee.

He brought their breakfast through just as Hart finished her call. She left him alone until he had finished his first round.

"Feel better now?" she asked, looking at him over the rim of her coffee cup.

"I feel like the hangover after a three-day bender," Foster said. "Except I can remember every miserable moment. Who was on the phone?"

"I got Reidy to do a bit of digging for me." Hart picked up her notebook from the coffee table.

Foster took a second slice of toast and sat in the armchair to drink his double strength coffee.

"Doran was an enforcer with the rag-tag army of lefties who ruled Liverpool City Council in the nineteen-eighties," Hart said.

256

"I remember," Foster said. "There was that speech by Kinnock — the shame of redundancy notices being sent around the city by taxi cab. Only decent speech he ever made, if you ask me."

Hart looked at him blankly.

"Come on, Naomi," he said. "You must remember being sent home from school — half the teachers were sacked to try and make the books balance after the government capped the rates."

"I'd be about eight years old, Lee," she said. "I wasn't big on politics in those days. I was more into *Star Wars* action figures and Duran Duran."

Foster eyed her with frank admiration and she said, "What?"

"Somehow I couldn't picture you with the Barbie dolls and the pink fairy outfit."

She grinned. "I did have a Luke Skywalker light sabre — does that count as a wand?"

He shook his head solemnly. "The light sabre is more of a masculine symbol of power."

"You mean an extension of the male . . . ego?" she said, arching an eyebrow.

Even sleep-deprived, without-make-up and wearing the clothes she slept in, Hart looked stunning. Her fine blonde hair was tousled and her fringe lifted off her forehead where she had pushed her fingers through it; it suited her.

"What?" she repeated, slightly irritated.

He blinked. "Sorry," he said. "Miles away. You were saying — Doran was an enforcer."

She narrowed her eyes suspiciously but then referred to her notebook again. "He was strictly strong-arm until 1985, when he started his own security firm: building sites and empty office buildings at first, but gradually expanding into bank security, cash and valuables escorts, events security. He even does a bit of body-guarding."

"For Kieran Jago's celebrity clients, I shouldn't wonder," Foster said.

She lifted one shoulder. "Liverpool's still small enough for that kind of cross-pollination."

"Cross-infection, more like. Any complaints, charges, stains on his character?"

Hart shook her head. "His right-hand man is John Warrender. Ex-cop. He took early retirement in 1990. Had a bit of a rep as a ducker and weaver."

"Anything else?"

"One or two charges of unnecessary force against a couple of Doran's heavies. Nothing serious and nothing that stuck to Doran personally. Since he set up the firm, he's paragon of the community: Rotarian, sponsor of the arts. Local lad made good. Family man."

"He owns a security firm and there's *nothing*?" Foster said, taking a swallow of coffee. "That's got to be suspicious."

Hart shrugged. "Reidy reckons the local scalls don't mess with Doran's boys."

"Okay . . ." Foster felt the caffeine hit at last, "that's the route we take: talk to the pond life, see what Doran did to earn his rep."

258

She nodded. "Do you want me to . . .?" He held up her mobile phone.

"We'll talk to the boss as soon as our replacements arrive," he said, checking his watch. "It's getting on for ten — where the hell are they?"

"Dunno." Hart went to the window and looked down on the street below. It was a shining spring morning. The silver light reflected sharply from a constant stream of traffic in both directions. Mercs and Lexus, BMWs and Honda SUVs were parked half on the pavement opposite while their owners called at the offices and surgeries, now in full swing. Every parking bay was filled.

"Naomi," Foster said, eyeing the curve of her buttocks with the appreciation of a connoisseur. "Now you're calling me 'Lee', does that mean we're friends?" The question was deliberately phrased so he could turn it into a joke: Foster knew every defensive strategy in the book.

"Lee . . ." Naomi said, her tone thoughtful, a little dreamy, even.

"Yeah?" He tried to sound casual. Naomi had a knack of talking in a honeyed voice while she prepared to kick you in the goolies.

"When does the 'pay and display' start?"

He felt a thud of alarm. "Nine, why?"

"'Cos there's a couple of traffic wardens showing a powerful interest in your car."

He grabbed his keys and ran out of the door in his stocking feet, swearing all the way down the stairs.

CHAPTER
THIRTY

It was morning playtime at the pre-school day care centre adjacent to Edge Hill Police Station, and Rickman stared down onto the small corner of playground visible from his office window. Children appeared and disappeared, like characters flashing in and out of frame on a CCTV monitor, momentarily present; vivid, real. Then gone. He thought of Megan Ward, wondering what she did when she was out of camera shot. It was hard to imagine her life, the shapelessness of her existence. Harder still to imagine why she wanted to live the way she did. To live alone because you had no choice was one thing — he had lived without family or ties for long enough to know that it was possible. But to choose to live such a blunted emotional life . . .

They had made no further progress in tracing her family, but Rickman felt sure that family was the key: an abusive childhood, perhaps, or —

A sharp rap at the door made him turn. Foster and Hart came in. They both looked tired, but Hart had fared better from her sleepless night: Foster's hair was slightly flattened, and Rickman wondered if the sergeant hadn't found the time to tease and style the spikes he usually arranged with meticulous carelessness, or if he had forgone his usual preening, embarrassed to appear too vain in front of Hart.

"Take a seat." He had cleared a couple of chairs in anticipation of their meeting. Foster dropped into his, slouching with his legs crossed at the ankles. Hart sat more decorously, with her feet tucked neatly under her chair. "We've recovered all of the money," Rickman said. "We're going to use it to have a go at Doran."

"We?" Foster's eyebrows twitched. "It's just tax dodging, isn't it? Wouldn't it be the Fraud Squad's baby?"

"We'll be lending a hand. We need Megan to set up a meeting at midnight tonight. Church Street. There'll be firearms officers stationed in the John Lewis and Littlewoods stores. There'll be more armed officers in the van stationed near the junction, ready for the shout." The van was a regular feature, so it wouldn't look out of place.

"I still don't see why we have to do their job for them," Foster said.

"Because they need our help, Lee. Interdepartmental co-operation." He waited until Foster made a grudging acknowledgement, before adding, "And because they've agreed to share intelligence gathered from a house and office search. They'll have access to his records, computer systems — the lot."

"Oh, well —" Foster said, still sounding aggrieved. "It's good to know there's still some co-operation between departments."

Rickman frowned. "Not at your best this morning, are you, Lee? Did someone steal your Weetabix?"

"Run-in with a traffic warden," Hart said, having the good sense to keep her face straight.

Foster muttered, "Scabby bastards," and Rickman rolled his eyes, though he felt some sympathy.

"One final thing," he said. "Megan will not make the drop."

"Boss —"

"It's too risky." Rickman could see that Hart was ready to launch into an argument.

"But —"

"Go home," Rickman said, firmly. "Get some rest. Report back for the evening briefing."

Hart left, looking troubled and frustrated.

"Who's OIC?" Foster asked.

"Me." As officer in overall charge, Rickman would call the shots.

Foster lifted his chin in neutral acknowledgement, then seemed to do a double-take. "Aren't you taking the youngest on his birthday treat tonight?"

"I was," Rickman said. "Now I'm not."

"How'd he take that?"

"He called me a name."

"Don't blame him."

"It wasn't that kind of name."

"You believe what you like, Jeff. Thirteen-year-olds never forgive," Foster said darkly.

Rickman watched him go, mildly amused. He suspected that it was more than the parking ticket that had put Foster out of humour. An overnight watch with

Hart and evidently no warming of their relationship was enough to spoil Foster's entire week. He recalled his conversation with Fergus at breakfast. He had been trying out different explanations in his head as to why he couldn't go on his nephew's birthday treat, none of which sounded even mildly convincing. He even entertained the idea (if only for a brief moment) that he might sneak out of the house and leave a note of apology.

Then Fergus appeared in the kitchen doorway, his face eager and intent and a little flushed with excitement.

"Happy birthday, teenager," Rickman said, taking two slices of toast from under the grill and carrying it to the table. "Did you get the L-plates I left under your pillow?"

Fergus grinned, darting forward and snatching up a piece before it hit the plate.

"I hope you don't mind losing," he said. "'Cos when it comes to go-karting, I'm no learner."

"Fergus . . ."

The boy stopped with the round of toast half-way to his mouth, slowed and the smile died on his lips.

"You aren't coming?"

"I'm sorry," Rickman said.

A light seemed to go out in his nephew's eyes. He shrugged his bony shoulders, and Rickman got a flash of himself at thirteen: dark wounded eyes and thick, unmanageable hair. He was skinny and vulnerable at that age, and on his thirteenth birthday he had been more fearful than excited by the prospect of the day's surprises.

"Doesn't matter," Fergus said.

"Yes, it does."

"Honestly," Fergus insisted, avoiding his gaze. "Mum'll take me."

"I'd like to explain."

Fergus shook his head. "It's no big." He dropped the toast in the bin and turned to leave.

He's right, Rickman thought, *It doesn't matter. When it's your thirteenth birthday and an adult breaks a promise to you, no explanation will suffice.*

"I'm trying to catch a killer," he said, needing to explain, anyway. "I have a witness who claims to have evidence that could convict a man — a suspect."

Fergus kept his back turned, his hand on the doorknob, but Rickman knew by his stillness that he was listening.

"The thing is, I don't trust the witness," Rickman went on. "She's a thief and a liar and she's playing games with us. But if she *is* telling the truth, we need to get this man away from where he can hurt people. We have the chance to find out tonight, and I need to be there, because if this man is everything she says he is, my officers could be in danger. And if something goes wrong and I'm not there —"

Fergus still refused to respond and Rickman nodded to himself. *No excuse would suffice.* "I thought you should know," he said, hearing the disappointment in his own voice.

264

"It's the Batman thing, again," Fergus said, turning to him.

Rickman tried to look like he understood, thinking, *Children really do speak a different language.*

Fergus must have read the incomprehension on his face because he said, "You do *know* the story?"

Rickman lifted his shoulders and Fergus said, "Okay ..." as if he was a particularly dense five-year-old. "Batman saw his parents murdered when he was a kid, and he always thought it was his fault because he wasn't strong enough to do anything. Same as you — you think have to be there, or you'd never forgive yourself."

Rickman smiled. The boy had more insight than was strictly comfortable. "I just can't help myself."

"So," Fergus said, "Could you get in big trouble for telling me about your investigation?" A mischievous light danced in his nephew's eyes.

Rickman scowled at him. "Are trying to blackmail me, you miserable rat?"

Fergus steepled his fingers in a parody of an arch-criminal. "Blackmail is an ugly word, Chief Inspector," he said in a cracked, evil voice.

"You read far too many comics," Rickman said ruffling the boy's chestnut hair. Fergus ducked, darting out of reach.

"*Graphic novels,* Unc!" Fergus shouted, then he went back into the evil criminal voice again. "And you haven't heard the last of this . . ."

Rickman gave Fergus his hardest stare. The boy cracked up, staggering backwards in helpless laughter and grabbing the doorknob for support. Rickman shook his head, "I'm losing my edge," he said, laughing with him. "I'm definitely losing my edge."

CHAPTER
THIRTY-ONE

Jake Bentley finished his shift half an hour early to make sure he got to the chemist's shop in time. It was a twenty-five-minute drive allowing for rush-hour traffic, which should give him plenty of time to pick up the prints and then go home to shower and change.

Once he'd forked right off Scotland Road and onto Kirkdale Road, it was more or less a straight run, one he had made hundreds of times. He knew where the traffic lights were, which stretches were likely to have traffic cops with speed cameras or loony pedestrians diving across the traffic. He simply slowed down or picked up speed as the conditions dictated while he planned what to wear. Black jeans, maybe the black blouson from Next. He thought that would do. Smart, toned, but also useful-looking. A rogue thought troubled him, *You don't want to look like a fugitive Ninja from a bad Nineties film.*

He drew up at a row of shops, parking illegally on double-yellows a couple of doors down from the chemist. The guy in the car behind him sounded his horn and Bentley checked him in the rear-view mirror. He didn't think he'd be a problem. He locked up, still pondering what to wear, and gave the driver a blank stare. The guy looked away, meekly turning on his indicator and making a big show of turning around to check out the traffic before moving out. *Yeah, that's what I thought.*

The shop was small and cluttered with stands and displays. The walls were lined with shelves and the centre of the shop divided into two by a double row of metal shelving, back-to-back. It smelled of aspirin and soap, just as it had when he was a boy. He told the girl at the counter that he had lost his slip.

"Happens all the time," she said, smiling. "I can look under the name." She was pretty, which was distracting, because she kept looking at him, and he didn't like pretty girls looking at him with their perfect skin and their watchful eyes that never missed a thing. He always felt that they were mocking him.

"I'm sorry, Mr Bentley," she said, and she did look sorry. Sorry and puzzled and a bit embarrassed. "I can't seem to . . ." She disappeared under the counter, again, checking through the drawer where the processed packets were kept, and appearing moments later, looking flustered.

"They might come in tomorrow's delivery," she said.

Bentley stared at her. "I asked for overnight development," he said. "Days ago."

"I — I've checked right through," she said.

Mr Doran is waiting for those photographs. I can't tell Mr Doran they've been lost. He'll think I'm trying to get more out of him. A cold sweat broke out on his forehead.

"Look again," he said, his voice strangulated by the constriction in his throat.

"Mr Bentley, I've emptied the —"

He slammed both hands on the counter and the girl gave a little squeal. The sudden fear on her face made him feel ashamed, but he also felt a guilty excitement: this was power. "Look again," he repeated.

The pharmacist came down from his raised work area at the back of the shop. "What's the problem?" he asked.

An elderly couple shuffled off to the left, out of reach.

"You lost my photos. I need them." The words came out in short bursts; he couldn't seem to catch his breath. "I need them tonight."

The pharmacist eased the frightened girl to one side and said, "Bentley, you say?" He was short and skinny and balding and Bentley thought if he didn't hurry up he might snap the little twerp like a twig. He riffled through the packets in the drawer and shook his balding head.

"They're not here, Mr Bentley," he said.

Bentley lost it. "Listen, you stupid little shit!" His saliva sprayed in the chemist's face, but although the man stepped back, he didn't wipe it away. "You've got my fucking film and I *want* it!"

His eyes slid nervously from Bentley's face. "I can call the lab, if you like — see what's causing the hold-up."

A dread certainty struck Bentley. *The police have it. The lab called the police and told them they were* suspicious of the content of the film and the police had taken it away. *Oh, God. Doran is going to kill me.* "No," he said, afraid. "Don't bother. It doesn't matter." He leaned off the counter, looking for a way out. The elderly couple cowered as he looked at them; they were blocking the narrow aisle and he turned the other way.

Perhaps it was something in his expression, or perhaps he made the connection with the name, but the chemist said, "Wait a minute. Are you *Monica* Bentley's son?"

Bentley looked again at the chemist. He was older by almost twenty years, of course, and he seemed to have shrunk, but with a sudden unpleasant jolt, Bentley recognised the chemist as the man who had made up his prescriptions. The man his mother had asked for advice on topical applications and diet. He had advised her to go to her GP, had handed her leaflets and charted the young Jake's progress week by week, until Jake had refused to go into the shop any longer.

"Never mind," Bentley said. "I — I'll come in tomorrow." Knowing there would be no tomorrow. He couldn't bear them looking at him. His skin prickled and burned as if it was breaking out. Sweat stung his face and trickled down his back. He walked unsteadily to the door and groped for the handle.

"Your mother was in yesterday," the chemist called after him. "She picked up your prints."

He turned back, but had to lean against one of the shelves for support. "She —" Emotions crowded in on him: relief that he should have had a reprieve, fury that his mother should interfere as she always interfered,

270

and worst of all, a humiliating, unmanning desire to weep.

"Jake, are you all right?" the chemist asked.

He couldn't reply, couldn't look up, even, in case he saw the girl looking at him. He could not bear to see either contempt or pity in her eyes.

CHAPTER
THIRTY-TWO

The parking bays were all full when Jake Bentley arrived at the Pan American Club bar at seven-thirty. He drove around to the main parking lot at King's Dock and tried again to think about how he would handle this interview. He had argued with his mother; had accused her of spying on him and she somehow managed to turn it so that he was in the wrong. She had been thinking of him, saving him the time and trouble. And then she had cried. He hated it when his mother cried; without saying a word, she made it about all those cold wet days he had dragged her to Ainsdale, the extra expense of their seaside trips, the hours spent in doctors' surgeries.

So, as he stepped across the threshold into the moody darkness of the bar, he was nervous. He had gone for the black chinos and jacket, but changed into a white T-shirt at the last minute. He *wanted* this job — had spent his whole life building towards it — and he wasn't about to throw it away because he turned up to interview looking a shade too Goodfellas, when the occasion called for something more sophisticated.

He shrugged some of the tension out of his shoulders and walked inside, hands relaxed at his sides, scanning the room right and left. The bar was housed in an old warehouse with brick arched ceilings and steel Doric columns. This part of the building was dark. The stone-flagged floor space was divided on one side into long booths with bench seats and high wooden panels, back-lit with diffuse lighting. The rest of the space was taken up with horseshoe-shaped velveteen sofas and circular tables. The height of the sofa backs reflected the bar's emphasis on privacy.

He wondered if he should take a stroll around. They might even be up on the mezzanine, in the restaurant area, then he saw Mr Doran beckoning him over to one of the circular tables. He shook hands with Bentley and even smiled as he waved him to a seat on the sofa next to him. "You know John Warrender."

Bentley nodded and Warrender eyed him coldly. *Cop's eyes, cop's attitudes, cop's arrogance. Well, screw you,* he thought.

"Beer, Mr Bentley?" Doran asked.

There were half a dozen opened bottles on a tray. Bentley picked one at random and nursed it in both hands. His eyes kept straying to Warrender, who watched him without expression. Bentley wondered if he should take the photographs out now and hand them over. He could feel the wallet as a small bulge in the inside pocket of his jacket and he was anxious to be rid of it.

Doran took out a packet of cigarettes and offered it to Bentley. Bentley shook his head, then cursed himself: timid was not exactly the image he was trying to project.

"Those things'll kill you," he said, with more bravado than he felt.

Mr Doran looked at him, the cigarette unlit in his mouth, and Bentley blushed a little. Doran struck a match from the small complimentary pack in the ashtray and took a draw before answering.

"There's worse ways to die, eh, Mr Bentley?"

Alarm fluttered just beneath Bentley's rib-cage. *Should I apologise?*

"You're right, though," Doran said, narrowing his eyes against the smoke. "I gave up six years ago. Haven't lapsed once — till this week." He shook his head. "Pathetic, isn't it? If my wife found out . . ."

"Place like this, you can always tell her it's second-hand," Bentley suggested.

Doran smiled. "Told you he was no slouch." Warrender glanced at his boss, then back to Bentley.

"Bloody hell, John! Lighten up." Doran jerked his head, indicating his chief of security. "He's a worrier," he confided. "He's worried about them snapshots. Did you have any trouble?"

"No," Bentley said. "No trouble. Only, they thought they'd lost them at first." *Talking too much, Jake. Talking way too much.*

"But they hadn't," Doran said.

"No." *Why don't you tell him your mum picked them up for you? Let him think he's got more people to worry about?* Because he knew that Doran was as worried as Warrender — he wasn't stupid. "No," he repeated, and clamped his jaw tight to stop himself running off at the mouth again.

274

"So . . ." Doran spread his hands and Bentley suddenly realised that he was waiting for the photographs.

"Oh!" Bentley fumbled his beer bottle onto the table, almost knocking it over in his hurry. He took the wallet from his pocket and handed it over, noticing too late that he'd made a big wet thumbprint on the cover.

Doran sifted through the shots like they were holiday snaps. "These aren't bad." He held up one of the pictures. "I'm guessing that's Megan Ward."

Bentley nodded. It was a series of three: Megan locking her car, then walking up to the house.

"This is very good, Jake." Doran raised his bottle to toast Bentley's skills and Bentley followed his lead, chugging a few grateful swallows, unaware that Doran was watching him closely.

"You know, we do a bit of surveillance work, Jake. Maybe you could give the lads a few tips."

"Sure, Mr Doran," he said, beginning to feel happier. *Jake. He called me Jake — twice.* He took another mouthful of beer.

"We could use a smart guy like you." Doran paused, scrutinising him carefully. "You know it wouldn't be smart to keep extra copies." Although he continued in an informal conversational tone, Bentley felt the temperature drop a few degrees. "It wouldn't be a good move to ask the lab to run off a set of prints for your Auntie Edith in Stalybridge." He smiled, but Bentley sensed the razor-sharp threat underlying it.

"No, Mr Doran. I wouldn't do that," Bentley said. "I really —" *No. Don't say it. Don't tell him how much you really admire him.* He gathered himself and said, "I just want to work for you." He bit his lip, remembering Mr Doran's earlier remark about "fan-boys", but it was all right. Mr Doran laughed and handed him a fresh bottle of beer.

"That's flattering, Jake. I'm . . ." He seemed genuinely moved. "I am — I'm flattered."

He slipped the photographs back into the wallet and held them up. A big shaven-headed flunky appeared from the shadows and took them. "The top picture is Megan Ward," Doran said. The man grunted and left, disappearing through the double doors to the windy sweep of roadway outside the bar.

Doran rubbed his hands. "Now, how about some scran?" They ordered food and more beer and Mr Doran told stories about the old days. "Before you were born, mate," he said, laughing.

Mr Doran laughed a lot, once he unwound a bit. He had even, white teeth and a rich infectious chuckle. Bentley couldn't help being a bit star-struck. Mr Doran was so . . . he didn't have a word for it — he could make waitresses smile, he was always watching to make sure you had enough to drink, and he told good stories. Cool — maybe that was the word. When he laughed, you just wanted to laugh with him. And when he spoke, people paid attention.

"I used to be in your line during the eighties," Doran said. "Strong-arm, protection, body-guarding."

Bentley gazed at him round-eyed. "We've all got to start somewhere," Doran said, with a wink to Warrender.

276

Bentley's heart swelled with the possibilities. Mr Doran was telling him, Jake Bentley all of this. Maybe — but he didn't dare allow his thoughts to gather form — it was enough right now to be talking to Mr Doran as an equal, a friend, even.

"One time," Doran said, "one of the local union bosses was giving us aggro. Said the militants were shaming the working classes — public transport brought to a standstill, unemptied bins, de-dah, de-dah ... 'Rats roam the streets of Liverpool,' he said. 'And not all of them go on four legs.'" He shook his head; it obviously still rankled. "Scabby bastard." He took a swig of beer. "Trouble was, he was persuading some of his flock to bleat the same song. Now, I don't condone violence, Jake. But there's ways, you know?"

Bentley nodded, taking a pull on his beer. He was beginning to feel at one with the buzz of conversation in the restaurant. Opposite him, the cocktail bar was lively with traffic and the bartenders were hamming it up, warming to the evening performance for the female custom. The backdrop behind the shelves of liquor glowed from amber to pink to green and turquoise in a lulling cycle of colour.

"You had a quiet word?" Bentley said.

Doran laughed. "I haven't got your persuasive bulk, Jake, mate," he said, with an admiring glance at Bentley. "Never did have. Nah, what we did was, me and a few ... colleagues went round to his house in a bin lorry. Tipped a week's-worth of rubbish on his driveway. His car happened to be parked on it at the time."

Bentley laughed and Doran joined him. "Should've seen his face. He kept shouting 'My car! My car!' I went up to him and, you know what I said?" He could barely get the words out for laughing. "You've gotta stop talking garbage, pal."

Bentley laughed even louder. He felt a glow of happiness like he had never felt before.

The big shaven-headed guy came back in and stood a little way away from their table, like a waiter respectfully awaiting instructions. "Excuse me," Doran said.

They went off to one of the booths to the left of their table and Bentley looked over at Warrender. He had almost forgotten that the security manager was with them. Warrender stared blankly at him, but by now Bentley had the measure of him. He raised his beer bottle in salute and took an insolent swig. *If the boss likes you*, he thought, *it doesn't matter a tinker's cuss what the hired help thinks.*

Doran returned, all smiles. "My car! My car!" he said, waving his hands in mock horror, which set Bentley off laughing again. He apologised for the interruption and sat next to Bentley on the sofa, watching the flunky disappear again into one of the booths. "Some of them need a crib sheet on how to take a piss," he said, and Bentley laughed too loud and too long.

Slow down, he thought. *You've had too much to drink and you're acting too friggin' grateful. Don't make a tit of yourself.*

Doran picked up a couple of bottles and handed him one. They kept coming, cold and fresh, and the empties were taken away, so he'd lost count.

The conversation came around to the grotesque hike in house prices since Liverpool was named as European Capital of Culture.

"Time was," Doran said, "working-class people like you and me lived in the city centre. You had the tenements and the artisans' cottages and courts around Duke Street and Mount Pleasant. Affordable housing."

"'S' all gentrified, now," Bentley said.

"Ever thought of moving into town, yourself?"

Bentley snorted into his beer bottle. "I couldn't afford a barrow on Bold Street, the prices they're charging now."

"See?" Doran said, looking to Warrender for affirmation. "Ordinary working men, pushed out to the sticks while the yuppies — poncy incomers from the south most of them — swan in and take over." Warrender was as unresponsive as ever, so he turned back to Bentley. "But you know what, mate? It's not the price they're charging that matters, it's what you're earning."

Bentley's brow furrowed. "Same diff, isn't it?"

"Not if you're earning double what you're used to."

The alcohol had slowed his thought processes. How could he earn double? The gym didn't pay that kind of money even to the manager. His frown deepened, his lips almost forming the question, then he saw that Mr Doran was smiling. *I've got the job!*

"Mr Doran," he said. "I don't know what to say. I won't let you down." He offered his hand and, though he seemed surprised, Doran took it — even put an arm around him and gave his shoulder a squeeze.

"I know you won't, mate."

The voices around Bentley became a meaningless gabble, the music swelled and subsided, but Mr Doran's voice remained sharp and clear. "We're organising security on an apartment block in Duke Street right now," Doran said. "You should get your name down before the dinkies get wind of it and they double the price."

"Dinkies?" Bentley echoed.

"Double Income, No Kids. A hundred and sixty-five K would get you a fourth-floor apartment with two bedrooms, hardwood floors, designer fitted kitchen and bathroom. Very high specs. Trust me," Doran said. "You'll get double the starting price in two years."

The figures made Bentley's head spin: from mildewed rental to loft apartment living overnight. He was grinning so much his jaw ached.

"D'you wanna see?" Doran asked. "I could get one of the lads to drive your car home for you, and I'll drop you after we've checked out the place."

Bentley thought about it: he couldn't drive — not with all he'd had to drink — and he wanted this evening to go on. He wanted Mr Doran to talk to him about his new job and all the things he could do and have. Patrick Doran's voice was warm and strong; it was like listening to a story — a story where he was the hero and a happy ending was guaranteed — but he was

280

beginning to feel disorientated by the drink, even a little queasy.

"You could give us your opinions on the security arrangements while you're there," Doran added and Warrender bristled a little.

That decided him. This was work. And if he pissed Warrender off and got himself a nice new gaff into the bargain, well — that was just how his life was since he'd met up with Mr Doran, wasn't it?

"Let's do it." He got to his feet and the room shifted sharply sideways, but Mr Doran caught him by the elbow.

"Whoops!" he exclaimed, laughing. "Don't know about you, mate, but I'm a bit over my usual limit."

It made Bentley feel better that Mr Doran was feeling the effects too, but he made a real effort to walk a straight line to the door. Warrender drove, while Doran and Bentley sat in the back. Warrender didn't look like he'd taken to the role of chauffeur too well. Bentley relaxed, enjoying the soft give of the upholstery and the expensive smell of leather. Mr Doran's own Beamer; he, Jake Bentley, was riding in Mr Doran's Beamer. He remembered that he hadn't handed his own car keys over to Mr Doran, but it didn't matter — he was pleasantly buzzed and he had a new job, a job with prospects. And he had just spent the whole evening with Patrick Doran himself. He would pick up his car tomorrow — what the hell . . . he'd take a taxi into work to hand in his notice.

The building site was surrounded by high steelhoard fencing, but Bentley could see a five-storey warehouse beyond it. Mr Doran took a flashlight out of the boot of his car and handed another to Warrender.

"You'd be better off with some perimeter lighting, here, Boss," Bentley said.

"Are you taking notes, John?" Doran asked.

Warrender shot Bentley a venomous look, but Bentley sensed that the power he held was already beginning to wane and he found that he could quite comfortably look the ex-cop in the eye; he even smiled to himself as Warrender opened the personnel door in the vehicle access gates.

Doran led the way across the broken remains of a cobbled street, into the building. It smelled of damp and algae and crumbling mortar. "You need to use your imagination here, Jake," he said, shining the flashlight onto the damp walls and soggy mortar oozing like paste from between the bricks. "Think Albert Dock — think Pan American Bar," he added with a flourish.

Bentley peered doubtfully into the damp darkness of the building. With its arched ceilings and the steady drip of water somewhere in the distance, it reminded him of a cave. "I'm not sure about this, Mr Doran," he said. The floor was slimy underfoot and the smell was getting to him.

"The Albert Dock was in a much worse state than this place," Doran said, walking on into the dark, his flashlight racketing off the walls and brick arches of the warehouse. "Salt water's corrosive, you know."

"Oh." Bentley followed unsteadily, with Warrender taking up the rear. They had made a good job of the Albert Dock, and property in the city centre was bound

282

to go on increasing in value, he reasoned, trailing after the bobbing light of Doran's torch. They went on, down a slippery stone staircase into the bowels of the building. Warrender was a solid presence behind him. It was oddly warm this far underground, a machine ground incessantly somewhere off to their right in the shadows and he began to feel claustrophobic.

Doran stopped unexpectedly and Bentley almost bumped into him. "See those pits?" Doran said.

Bentley saw a series of deep holes, lit in turn by Doran's torch, each about ten feet in length and maybe four feet across, edging the brickwork of the outer wall.

"Once they've filled those with concrete, this place'll stand for another hundred years," Doran said.

"Great," Bentley said without enthusiasm. His stomach was really starting to roil now. The persistent stench of rot and the constant churning of the machine he couldn't see reminded him just how much he'd had to drink. He swallowed, trying not to think of the filth and the stink and the rats. There were always rats. "I'm not feeling so good."

He turned and came up hard against Warrender. The security manager handed Bentley his torch, then patted him down. "What the hell d'you think you're doing?" he demanded. Warrender shoved his face into Bentley's, but still he did not talk. Then he spun Bentley around, turning him to face Doran again so fast that Bentley almost lost his balance.

"Hey — watch it!" Bentley warned. The flashlight in Warrender's hand lit up Doran's face and the coldness of his expression made Bentley reconsider any reprisal.

"Now," Doran said, his voice icily cold, "Explain why you lied to me."

"*Lie?*" Bentley was dizzy and disorientated.

"I must warn you that I have to accept your first response," Doran said. "And wrong answers *will* cost you points."

It's a joke. Bentley almost laughed with relief, but the look on Mr Doran's face stopped him dead. He stared at Doran, horrified. "I didn't," he said, his voice rising. "I swear, Mr Doran, I didn't lie to you."

Doran sighed and took a folded yellow envelope out of his pocket. Bentley recognised it immediately as the envelope his photos had come in and he began to shake. *Oh, God . . . Oh, God, you stupid, dumb —*

"This was in your car," Doran said.

Bentley realised that the reason his car keys were still in his pocket was because they didn't need his keys to get into his car. His mouth dried and he felt suddenly very sick. "It's off an old set," he said weakly.

Doran shook his head. "You're only making things worse," he said. "Look at the date."

Bentley eyes filled with tears of desperation so that he could barely read it.

"See that little box where it says number on the roll?" Doran went on. "The girl's ticked thirty-six, which means there were thirty-six exposures. Now, I've counted them over and over, but I can't make the numbers match. There's only twenty-four snaps in the wallet you gave me, Jake."

"Mr Doran —"

Doran held up one hand to stop him. "Is this where you say, 'It's not what you think?' 'Cos frankly, Jake — that's clichéd."

Bentley looked at his shoes and concentrated on not throwing up over them. When the nausea subsided, he said, "I got in a few shots before I realised who the guys were that called at Sara's house." His voice trembled a little, but he thought he sounded under control. "If I'd known they were your men, I would *never* have taken them." He dared a fleeting glance at Mr Doran's face. Went on, "I didn't want you to think —"

"That you were trying to shaft me?"

Bentley nodded miserably. "I thought — I knew — it would look bad."

"You know what looks worse?" Doran waved the empty envelope in Bentley's face. "This."

Bentley blinked, trying not to flinch.

"I think you kept the pictures back as insurance, in case I didn't give you the job."

"No Mr Doran — I swear!"

"So where are they?"

Bentley closed his eyes and groaned involuntarily. "I burned them. The prints and the negatives." He passed a hand over his face, wiping away tears.

"I think you gave them to the police," Doran said calmly.

"No!"

"On your knees, Bentley." These were Warrender's first words to him.

"Mr Doran. I was stupid. I should have been honest with you. But I didn't tell the police. If I told the police, wouldn't they be here by now?"

"Get on your knees."

"I feel really sick," he said.

Warrender raised his hand. He held a gun. Automatic.

Bentley tried to hold himself steady, but he felt weak with sickness and fear. "Please, Mr Doran," he begged, tears coursing down his face. "You've got to believe me. I burnt them. I was afraid I'd get stopped and the cops'd find them, so I burnt them."

"Shame you didn't burn the envelope then, isn't it?"

Warrender pushed the gun barrel into the back of his head. It felt cold, and this time when Warrender said, "On your knees," he went down. The floor of the cellar felt slimy against the palms of his hands.

Warrender drove the barrel hard into the base of his skull. "Get your hands where I can see them," he snarled.

"I don't want to die," he said, trying to take the pathetic whine out of his voice, trying not to breathe too deeply because it made him want to heave, trying to stay alive just a few minutes longer. "I could be useful to you, Mr Doran. I really could."

"You might be right," Doran said.

Bentley felt the pressure ease a little and he thought. *There's hope. Keep talking. There's hope.*

Then Doran said, "But I can't trust you."

He was falling. He didn't feel the impact, but he could smell damp earth, could taste the grit in his mouth. *Oh, you friggin' idiot, Jake!* He told himself. *You fell in the pit. Get up, you wuss. Get the fuck up!* But his legs wouldn't work. He told them to move, but they wouldn't. And he felt cold, like he had been plunged into water, into ice, and the shock had taken his breath away. He saw the wink of the two flashlights some way above him.

They know I'm here. They'll call for help.

Then the lights were gone. He tried to shout, but though something bubbled in his mouth, no sound came out. *Oh God! I don't want to die. Don't let me die here. Please, don't —*

The distant mechanical noise grew closer and Bentley stared up into the darkness. He saw a glimpse of orange as one of the flashlight beams bounced off the machine. He saw the barrel of it rotating, round and round, a slow, steady, solid sound. And then it stopped.

What he saw next was in flashes of torchlight, like dancers frozen in action by strobe lighting: the machine. Orange. Mr Doran's face. The machine. A stalactite, white, smooth. Orange again. The machine's barrel. Tilting. Grey sludge. Heavy and thick.

He tried to scream but he choked on blood. He tried to move, but the bullet Warrender had fired had severed his spinal chord. He tried to close his eyes, but his eyes refused to obey. His mouth filled with cement. Then his eyes and nose and ears were blocked with the heavy, burning mix. It sealed the gaping wound in his throat and buried him under the weight of concrete a full horrifying minute before he died.

CHAPTER
THIRTY-THREE

"This is wrong." Naomi Hart was driving one of the firm's cars, headed towards Megan Ward's bolt-hole in Rodney Street.

"You heard what the boss said." Foster grabbed the door handle to steady himself as she made a sharp right.

"I heard him, and he's wrong."

They passed the clock tower of Liverpool University's Victoria building as it struck the quarter-hour. Nine forty-five and the evening briefing had concluded only minutes earlier.

That morning, Foster and Hart had gone home to sleep as Rickman ordered, but they were both back on duty by late afternoon and they had been allocated night watch on Megan.

"Yeah, well, he's the boss," Foster said. "You're not supposed to agree with him all the time." She scowled and he added, "Look on the bright side — it's brass monkey weather, and it looks like rain; at least you'll be inside in the warm."

Hart gave him a disgusted sideways glance as she made the final left turn.

"You can get your head down, if you like," he said. "I'll keep an eye on her."

She sighed, easing in to the kerb by Megan's house. It was cold and bright, a gibbous moon shivered pale over the rooftops, and the imposing façade of the Anglican cathedral, just visible at the end of the road, glowed pale pink in its light.

"I don't know why you're so against this," Foster said. "You don't exactly like the woman."

They got out and Hart looked at him across the roof of the car. "I don't. Don't like her. Don't trust her. Which is kind of the point." The air was fresh and green with new spring growth and Hart took a calming breath. "She's liable to flit and you *know* we won't be able to track her down." She pressed the remote on her key fob and locked the car down before starting across the street. "She's as slippery as a greased weasel and she can magic money out of thin air — she's already admitted defrauding Patrick Doran of over a million and a quarter pounds."

"Doran's a crook!"

"So is she."

Foster dipped his head: he couldn't argue with her on that one.

"And God knows how many other poor fools she's ripped off," Hart went on.

Foster waited for a car to pass before following her to the other side of the road. "If this is about me having a bit of a flirt —"

"*God!*" Hart threw her hands up in frustration. "This isn't *about* you. I'm just saying — mess her around and she could disappear. Permanently. We'd lose a potential prosecution against Megan and maybe Doran as well."

"You think I hadn't worked that out?" he said, feeling a surge of anger. "Give me some credit, Naomi."

Hart looked off down the street for a moment or two. "All right," she said. "I'm sorry. But I'm sick of baby-sitting. I'm sick of being nice to her. I'm tired of her whole 'woman of mystery' bullshit."

"Personally, I find it kind of sexy," he said, recovering a little.

She shook her head, exhaling loudly in frustration. "I give up." She made as if to move on, but he stopped her.

"Hey," he said, "I might be skirt-chaser, but I'm not a complete idiot."

Surprised, she said, "That's not what I think."

They looked at one another for a few seconds and Foster thought, *Okay — that's a start*. He nodded, acknowledging the implied — if rather back-handed — compliment, and slid her a sly look as they walked on. "What — you don't think I'm skirt-chaser, or you don't think I'm an idiot?"

She smiled, then bit her lip, a look of annoyance flitting across her features, though whether it was directed at herself or him, he couldn't tell. "You're incorrigible," she said.

"You wha'?"

"A dead loss."

"You haven't heard my best chat-up lines," Foster said, leaning on the doorbell, then taking a step back so that Megan could get a good look at him from the sitting-room window. She buzzed them in and was waiting for them at the door of the flat.

"Are we set?" Megan asked.

She seemed keen — even excited — which struck Foster as odd, given that she was about to part with more than a million pounds. He looked at Hart and Hart shrugged.

"Don't look at me," she said.

Foster sucked his teeth. *One step forward, two steps back — that's Naomi for you.* "We're all set," he said.

Megan pressed the speed-dial key for Doran on her mobile but Foster took it from her and cancelled the call before it connected.

"We need to discuss game play, first," he told her. "The meet is at midnight on Church Street," he said. "By the statue of the Moores brothers. He comes on his own. No muscle."

Megan shook her head. "I decide the venue and the time."

"Sorry, Megan," Foster said, "This isn't open to negotiation. We've got civilians to think about. Public safety. So it's our rules or not at all." Megan remained silent, apparently thinking it over, and Foster told her about the security arrangements and the presence of armed officers. "Church Street is pedestrianised, so we won't have to worry about traffic," he explained. "It's after the pubs close, but before the clubs empty out, so there won't be much foot traffic. There'll be a police van stationed at the Bold Street end — which is normal, that time of night — only tonight it'll be full of our lads."

Hart tutted and he said, "By 'lads', I mean 'officers', of course."

"Got it all worked out, haven't you?" Megan said.

"We've done this kind of thing before," Foster confided. "So, d'you wanna make that call?"

Doran felt sick and exhausted; part of him said that Bentley was a harmless fantasist who would have been useful for a middle-ranking job, that the occasional kind word would have been enough to keep him sweet. The more pragmatic part of him said that Bentley would quickly have tired of menial work and tried to use his knowledge about Sara Geddes's death as a lever. Doran had seen and heard enough during the course of the evening to know that like most fantasists, Bentley's ambition exceeded his abilities. If he had taken Bentley into the firm, there would come a point when he would think he deserved more. More power, more responsibility, more money. And Doran would not be held to ransom.

He answered his phone on the second ring. Caller ID showed "number withheld". "Doran," he said.

"Mr Doran." A woman's voice. "My name is Megan Ward."

He felt the blood drain from his face. He tapped Warrender on the arm, then clicked the phone into its cradle and switched to "hands free".

"Go ahead, Miss Ward," he said, repeating her name for Warrender's benefit.

Warrender shot him an alarmed look and his hands closed tightly on the steering wheel. After a pause, Megan Ward spoke.

"Am I on speakerphone?" The voice was clear and calm, a hint of northern — Lancashire, maybe.

"I'm driving," Doran said. "What can I do for you?"

She laughed. "*You* do for *me*? Nothing, Mr Doran." Her voice hardened. "Now pull over — I prefer to talk privately."

Warrender glanced at him and he nodded. The line disconnected and he snatched the phone from its cradle. "What the hell is she playing at?"

"Just that," Warrender said, sliding the car to a halt at a bus stop. "She's playing you like a sodding violin."

"Why is she calling now?" Doran asked, not expecting an answer. "Why this precise moment?" Bentley's body was still cooling under half a ton of concrete and Megan Ward, the bitch who had caused this whole sorry mess, had decided that this was the most opportune time to call him.

"Coincidence?" Warrender said at last.

"I don't like coincidences," Doran said. "They're usually bogus and they're almost always bad news. You're sure Bentley wasn't under surveillance?"

"Only from my men," Warrender said.

Doran knew better than to expect a fulsome reassurance. Warrender stated the facts as he saw them without embellishment; it was one of his strengths, and one of the reasons he had survived so long in the firm.

The phone rang in his hand and he flinched. He pressed the "answer" key and said, "Miss Ward. What do you want?"

"Now, that's a more honest question," she replied.

Doran waited, thinking that if he ever tracked Megan Ward down, they would have a long and painful discussion.

"I want to talk," she said.

"You could've picked up the phone."

"I just did." He heard amusement in her voice.

"I'm listening."

"Of course you are," she said. "After all, I have your money."

Doran breathed through his nose, trying to keep from smashing the phone against the dashboard.

"I'll meet you by the Moores brothers' statue in Church Street at midnight," she said.

"I decide when and where," he interrupted, unwittingly echoing her own words to DS Foster.

Again he heard that soft laugh. "You're forgetting who has the power here, Mr Doran. Since I have the money, that would be me."

"Why?" he said. Every survival instinct told him that this was not right. "Why are you even here? You could've vanished by now." He hesitated, wondering if what he was about to say was too revealing. "We thought you had."

"And you're doing everything in your power to find me. I don't like being watched. I don't like being hacked — no hacker ever does.

"I intend to live a long and remunerative life, and I suspect that will be difficult with your hounds on the scent — you really should keep them on a tighter leash, by the way."

"Meaning?" He knew very well that she meant Sara Geddes, but he wasn't about to discuss it on an open line with a faceless voice.

"Meaning your boys over-stepped the mark. Now I understand that you're upset, and I'm willing to make a deal. You call off the dogs, I give you your money back."

"As simple as that?"

"Actually, it's rather complicated for me . . ." She paused as if working through the logistics. "But that's my problem — one I'm willing to cope with for peace of mind."

"What's to stop me coming after you anyway?"

"You're a business man. A pragmatist. You have a good business, a reputation, the prospect of making a fortune with the current upsurge in Liverpool's economy — why waste your time and resources on a costly vendetta?"

Doran almost believed it himself. He could see how Fay might have been taken in by Megan Ward's smooth line in chat. Megan Ward in her male persona, he reminded himself and felt a small flare of anger, like a bubble of acid bursting in his stomach.

"You're an intelligent man," she went on. "You'll learn from your experiences, get trained specialists to maintain your computer security, make sure I don't happen again."

"*I don't happen*", Doran thought. "*Happen*", like she was some kind of natural disaster. He held back, even though he wanted to rage at her. She *was* a disaster: for him, for his family, and for his business.

"It's a deal," he said through gritted teeth. "How will I know you?" He took out the photograph Bentley had given him.

"Don't worry," she replied, "I'll know you."

Doran felt a premonitory dread at the words, spoken so coolly, but with a rim of fire behind the ice. He visualised again that long, agonising conversation he would have with Megan Ward. He would take great pleasure in puncturing that inflated ego.

"Midnight, then," he said, with barely an edge of anger in his voice.

"Make sure you come alone," Megan said. "I'm not the gregarious type."

Megan hung up, looking pleased with herself. "Let's get down there now," she said, checking her watch. "I like to suss out the terrain."

"Sorry, Megan," Foster said.

Her forehead creased, then she seemed to understand. "You're worried he'll show up early as well — catch your 'lads' on the back foot?" She stole a glance at Hart when she used the words "lads".

"That an' all," Foster said. "But the thing is, Megan, you're not going."

She laughed, then seeing Foster's expression, she said, "You're serious, aren't you?"

"It's too risky," Hart said. "If Doran really did send those heavies to Sara's house, you could be in real danger."

"Well, yeah . . ." Megan frowned at her like she had tentatively suggested that Harold Shipman might have been a bad man. "Why d'you think I wound him up like that?"

"Because that's what you do?" Foster said, then smiled. "You did ask."

"Doran is bad news," Hart said.

Megan began to make a sarcastic remark about the combined intellect of the Merseyside Police Force, but Foster spoke over her. "The local scalls do not mess with Patrick Doran or his employees," he said. "They'll shove industrial strength fireworks up the exhausts of police cars. They'll launch assaults on copshops — but they *do not mess* with Patrick Doran."

Megan sighed heavily, but she stopped trying to interrupt.

"His site protection is second to none. Know why?" Neither Hart nor Megan ventured a suggestion. "Because if he catches them, the lucky ones go home minus a few teeth. The ones who really piss him off are liable to lose a couple of fingers."

A muscle jumped in Megan's jaw.

"There's a story doing the rounds that he took one guy's finger for breaking into one of his sites and stealing a couple of laptops. Just the one finger, mind — he wasn't all that pissed off. Only he took it in four stages: fingernail, first joint, second joint, knuckle joint."

"All right," Megan said, her face white. "I get the picture."

But Foster wasn't finished. "He made the poor sod recite an oath before he hacked off each bit — 'I swear I will never steal anything ever again in my miserable life. I will tell my miserable low-life friends what happens when you mess with Mr Doran. If I go to the police, I will die in a thousand little pieces.' Poor bastard still wakes up in the night screaming those words."

"For God's sake, Sarge!" Hart exclaimed.

"No, she should know this," he said. "You should know this," he said, turning back to Megan, "'cos we're protecting you from this animal. We only know this as rumour, because they don't come to us. They don't go to a lawyer — they don't even go the hospital, half the time. They just crawl under a rock and wait till they've healed and then they stay the hell away from Patrick Doran."

Megan looked at him. "You think I don't know what Doran is?"

Foster had fought in Kuwait in 1991. He had seen palls of smoke boiling over sabotaged oilfields. Dark and swiftly changing, shifting and eddying and with the occasional glimpse of something within — a flare of white-hot flame, maybe. Megan's grey eyes had taken on that same strangely luminous darkness. "I know what he is. And I am going to meet him — you can't stop me."

"Yes," Foster said. "We can. And if I have to handcuff you to stop you going, I will." Megan's fury

298

was fleeting. The smoky threat in her eyes dissipated, as though she willed it from her; she relaxed her shoulders and composed her features into a semblance of careless indifference. "Fine." Her tone was light; she even smiled a little as she turned and headed for her bedroom.

"Sorry, Megan." Hart barred her way. "You'll have to take the spare room, tonight." Foster framed a question as Megan drew herself up, ready to argue. "Fire escape," Hart said, her tone apologetic. "We can't have you slipping off to a midnight assignation without us, can we?"

Megan glanced back at Foster, her face flushed, all pretence of indifference gone. He spread his hands, echoing Hart's apology and she stamped off to the second bedroom without another word.

She had stipulated that he should come alone, but she hadn't said anything about communicating with his team. Doran used his bluetooth earpiece — a toy he had barely used until now — and did a visual sweep of the area, reporting back to Warrender. He had men posted at either end of the pedestrianised area, at Bold Street and Lord Street. Extra men had been deployed at the side roads off Church Street. They would catch Megan Ward, no matter which escape route she tried.

He saw her some fifty yards away, standing under the bronze statue of the Moores brothers, founders of the Littlewoods empire. They appeared to be striding out on a brisk walk, engaged in friendly conversation. The road was deserted except for one or two couples strolling towards Hanover Street, where they might pick up a taxi.

She clutched her sports bag tightly by the strap slung over her shoulder.

"She looks nervous," Doran said. "She should be." He scanned left. "Shit — there's a police van up by the traffic lights."

"I'd be more worried if there wasn't," Warrender said. "It's a nightly feature. Just keep close by the shops and they won't catch you on their surveillance cameras. And use the statue to cover you when you're taking the bag off her."

Doran edged right, approaching from her blind side. There was nothing he could do out here in the open, especially with a police van parked at the top of the street, but his stomach roiled with hatred for Megan Ward, and as he drew closer to her, his hands opened and closed compulsively, his breathing came shallow and fast and he began to feel light-headed so that he had to slow down and start taking deep, calming breaths. She turned and looked in his direction as he slowed. He faltered, then turned quickly right towards the Bluecoat Chambers.

"Fuck," he said, "*Fuck!*"

"Boss, what's happening?" Warrender asked. "Talk to me. Do you need help?"

"I need my fucking head examining," Doran said, walking on, turning right at the end of the short side street, heading down the hill. He saw two of his men standing in the shadows, uncertain what to do. He snatched the bluetooth from his ear and fumbled the phone from his pocket. "It wasn't her, John," he whispered, cupping his hand over his mouth. "And if it wasn't her, it must have been a cop."

CHAPTER
THIRTY-FOUR

The house was quiet and dark when Jeff Rickman pulled into the drive. A couple of the window sashes were open a crack on the first floor, where the boys had their bedrooms, and a fine misty rain fell like dew, coating everything in a thin film of moisture. He had interviewed the young officer drafted in as Megan's look-alike and she was baffled.

"One minute he's walking towards me, the next, it's like he's seen a ghost."

"Could he have recognised you?" Rickman asked. "Are you sure you haven't met him, stopped him for speeding — anything at all?"

She shook her head emphatically. "I've never seen him before."

Could Doran have known she wasn't Megan? He closed his eyes for a second and the ground seemed to spin under him. He needed sleep, and as he reached into his trouser pocket for his house keys he fantasised about sliding between the cool sheets and falling into oblivion.

He was almost inside the door when he realised he hadn't turned on the car alarm. He pressed the remote on his key fob and the alarm chirruped, the indicator lights flashing in unison three times. Immediately he heard a door open on the first floor landing, and light spilled into the hallway.

Fergus appeared at the head of the stairs, his face bright and happy. His hair was tousled, as if he had been asleep, but he looked wide awake now, and ready to talk. Rickman sighed. So much for making a surreptitious entrance.

Fergus thudded down the first few steps until Rickman put his hands up and shushed him. His nephew tiptoed the rest of the way and launched into a whispered description of his evening.

"It was *awesome!*" he said. "Jeff came with us. And Mum. And Dad."

"Fergus —" He wanted to say that he was tired, that they could talk about it in the morning, but he had never seen his nephew so animated and the boy had waited up especially to tell him what a good time he'd had — to let him know that Rickman's absence hadn't ruined his birthday. He even seemed pleased that Simon had gone with them.

Rickman exhaled, smiling. "Kitchen," he whispered.

"I won the junior race," Fergus said, as soon as Rickman had shut the door. "And I almost beat Jeff. Dad came fourth."

"That's —" Rickman got no further because Fergus was in full flow.

"He used to take us go-karting sometimes when we went to Nan and Grandad's in Cornwall and he *always* beat us then."

"Well, he's getting old," Rickman said. "Warm milk?"

The boy looked offended.

"Suit yourself." Rickman took a bottle of milk from the fridge and fetched a milk pan from one of the cupboards. Fergus sat and watched as he poured milk into the pan. "Well, if you're having one . . ."

Rickman kept his back to the boy as he smiled. "Just as easy to make two," he said, then flicked the gas to high and turned around. "So did they give you a trophy?"

"A rosette thing," Fergus said. "It's upstairs." He stood, screeching his chair across the tiled floor.

"Let's not disturb the others," Rickman said. "You can show it to me tomorrow." Fergus looked a little disappointed and he added, "I hope you saved some cake for me."

Fergus jumped up. "You should see it, Uncle Jeff!"

Rickman poured warm milk into two mugs and placed them on the long bleached oak table while Fergus lifted the cake box from the fridge and opened it with a flourish.

"Wow." Rickman was impressed; the cake was a Spiderman design, the face of the superhero realistically worked in black-and-red icing.

"Mum's idea," Fergus said, suddenly abashed. Rickman understood. "I told her I was too old for kids' stuff, but —"

"That's mums for you," Rickman said. "It is good, though, isn't it?"

Fergus beamed at him and launched into an explanation of Spiderman's special powers, while Rickman cut two wedges of sponge.

They sipped their milk and ate cake while Fergus gave him a minute-by-minute, turn-by-turn account of his go-karting triumph. At the end of it, he looked tired and Rickman said, "Think you could sleep now?"

Fergus nodded, his eyelids drooping. "You should have been there, Uncle Jeff," he said. "It was —"

A sudden hammering at the front door made them both jump. Rickman frowned, getting up and placing a reassuring hand on his nephew's shoulder. The doorbell rang out loud and long.

"Stay here," Rickman said. He walked to the front door, his heart picking up pace. If Doran had realised that the woman waiting for him was actually a police officer, how would he react? A million-and-a-quarter was a lot of money to lose.

The knocking and ringing continued and Rickman placed his hand flat on the door, as if somehow he would be able to sense a threat. "Who is it?" he called.

"Jeff! Oh, thank God — Jeff!"

Rickman exhaled. Simon. His brother almost tumbled through the door when he opened it. "For God's *sake*," he objected, "What the hell are you playing at?"

Simon grabbed his arm. Rickman hadn't seen him so agitated — so lost — since last autumn. His grey hair had grown out a little and it hung in wet ringlets around his face and neck. "You have to come with me," he insisted. "I'll take you. You've got to see." He stared wildly at Rickman, his blue eyes wide and unfocused.

Rickman resisted his brother's attempts to tug him out of the house. "Simon, it's two o' clock in the morning." He pulled free and took Simon by the shoulders. Simon had always been lean and rangy, crackling with nervous energy, burning off everything he ate, but now Rickman felt a give and softness under his hands; one of the side-effects of the head injury, the doctors had told him. Disinhibition didn't only mean a propensity for saying the first thing that came into your head — it meant impulsiveness in all things: eating too much, expressing anger and frustration in petty rages. And calling at your brother's house at two in the morning.

"Come inside," he said. "We'll talk."

"He doesn't know," Simon muttered. "Talking won't do any good." He looked up at his brother and repeated, "Talking won't do any good."

Rickman pointed him in the direction of the sitting-room.

"I never should have left," Simon continued, half to himself.

Was he talking about leaving home? That was twenty-five years ago. Why was he flashing back to their childhood now, of all days?

"I shouldn't have left," Simon muttered again. "He needs help." He pulled away from Rickman, towards the front door.

"I could do without this right now, Simon," Rickman said, maintaining his grip of his brother.

He saw Tanya on the staircase. She clutched the collar of her dressing-gown tightly around her neck. Behind her, Jeff junior stared at his father, his eyes blank and expressionless. Rickman tried to smile reassurance and Tanya shivered.

"Come on," Rickman said.

Simon twisted to look into his face. "Is it a crime?"

"I don't understand you," Simon," he said, trying to hide his irritation. "You're drenched — come through into warm."

Simon pushed him away, held him at arm's length, searching his face as if he would find there the answer to all the confusing questions that had troubled him since his accident. "Jeff, you have to listen," he said. "I killed somebody."

Rickman stared at him, shocked. He heard a small sound and looked past Simon. In the shadows at the far end of the hall, Fergus stood motionless, his arms limp by his sides. He saw in his nephew's face fear and unhappiness and bewilderment that the world could be so terrible, and it was like looking at an image of his younger self.

Fergus had seen too much already — heard too much. He bundled Simon into the sitting-room and closed the door. "What do you mean you killed somebody?" he asked. But Simon was gone again, wringing his hands and looking distractedly about him.

"What I did." He nodded. "That's why. It's a punishment."

Rickman peeled off his brother's jacket. The thin cotton was soaked through. Simon was trembling, but his skin felt hot through his shirt.

The fire was almost out, and Rickman added a fresh log, pulling an armchair close to the hearth and making Simon sit down.

"Now," he said, crouching next to his brother's chair, "tell me why you're here."

"I *told* you." Simon's kingfisher-blue eyes flashed angrily. "I *killed* somebody."

"How?" Rickman demanded. "How did you kill them?"

"In the car. An accident. I —" He flinched as if seeing the impact. "It was too fast — I should've —"

"Simon, you were go-karting with the boys. You're just confused."

"No!" Simon pushed his wet hair off his face in a gesture of frustration Rickman recognised from when they were boys. "Not then. I was in a *car*."

"You drove here?"

Simon frowned. He was drifting, his concentration almost exhausted. "Can't drive — not allowed . . . The head . . . drama?"

"Trauma," Rickman said.

Simon's head bobbed compulsively. "Why — can't — I — remember?" He balled his hand into a fist and drove the heel of his hand into his forehead again and again.

Rickman caught Simon's wrist and held it. "Because of the head injury," he said, staying calm, placing his hand over Simon's closed fist. "It's *not* your fault."

Simon turned his tear-stained face to him. "It's no one else's." Fresh tears sprung to his eyes and he turned his head away.

308

"No," Rickman said. He did not accept this. He would not. "You said yourself you can't drive. So how could you have caused this accident?"

Simon stared at a spot three feet away, still avoiding his brother's eye, but Rickman could see that he was trying to work this one out. He stopped struggling and slowly, Rickman released him.

"I see him." He sounded incredulous, and yet adamant. "His eyes —" He buried his face in his hands and sobbed.

Rickman stood and took his mobile phone from his pocket and found the number for the central control room at Liverpool Police HQ. "DCI Jeff Rickman," he said. "Give me the duty manager."

He watched Simon while he waited for the inspector to pick up the phone. Simon wiped the tears from his face with his palms and began muttering again. Most of it was incomprehensible, but Rickman thought he heard the word "drink" or "drunk" a couple of times. He heard a rattle and some distorted conversation at the other end of the line, then DI Michaels announced himself.

Rickman knew him by reputation: he was efficient and ambitious. "Quick check," he said, responding in kind to the inspector's crisp manner. "Any RTA fatalities this evening?"

"None," Michaels said.

"No hit-and-run incidents?" Rickman held his breath as he waited for the answer.

"No." Michaels sounded more guarded. "Why?"

"It's probably nothing." Rickman glanced quickly at his brother. "I'll get back to you if there's any cause for concern." He broke the connection.

Simon's muttering had subsided to the occasional whispered word, his chin nodded as if in time with a pounding in his head, and Rickman guessed he was having one of his migraine attacks. He needed to talk to Tanya. Simon didn't look like he was going anywhere soon, so with a final backward glance, Rickman left the room, closing the door softly behind him.

He had his hand on the stair newel when he saw a light at the end of the hall: *Oh, God — Fergus.* He hurried to the kitchen; Tanya, Fergus and Jeff junior were all in there, hands wrapped around mugs of hot tea, huddled together as if against an impending storm.

"I'm sorry," he said, feeling an outsider, an intruder in their troubles. "Tanya, I need to talk to you."

She lifted her lovely brown eyes to his. They had developed a down-turn of sadness over the months he had known her, but they held a beauty and warmth he responded to.

"They've seen the worst," she said, her voice heavy with grief. "They can hear what you have to say."

Jeff junior met his gaze, that same empty look in his eyes as before, but there was a hint of challenge in the way he lifted his chin. Fergus bent his head and stared into his teacup, blinking back tears.

"Simon's accident," he said. "Was anyone else involved?" He felt almost guilty that he had not asked the circumstances of his brother's accident before now, but last autumn things had been complicated.

310

Tanya blinked: the question was not what she had expected. "A tyre blew out, she said. "He hit a tree. Nobody else was hurt."

He nodded. "And —" He glanced at the boys again. "Was there any suggestion — Did they think . . .?" His finger went to the scar that cut across his right eyebrow. "I'm sorry, Tanya." He tried again. "Had he been drinking?"

Again, she looked puzzled. "Simon is teetotal."

"They checked?"

"Before the operation. His blood alcohol was zero."

Rickman exhaled relief flooding him like sudden sunshine. He thought he understood. He thought perhaps he could make sense of what Simon had told him. "I think it's okay," he said. "I need to take Simon out for a while. Will you be all right?"

He drove Simon along empty roads. Only an occasional police car or taxi swished by them in the mizzly rain. A faint mist hung over the city and the trees, some with fat spring buds just opening, dripped heavier droplets onto the pavements and verges. The traffic lights seemed to change in their favour, oddly silent without the accompanying roar of traffic, and they sailed through Penny Lane and onto Smithdown Road.

The look on Tanya's face as they drove away from the house made him wonder how long she could go on, meeting crisis after crisis.

Simon stirred and Rickman said, "Do you know where we are?"

He didn't respond, but he sat up and looked out of the window, his agitation growing as they approached the top of the hill nearing the junction with Lodge Lane. Rickman turned left, glancing again at his brother. Simon seemed to repeating something over and over, softly, as though the words comforted him.

Lodge Lane was much changed since their childhood: many of the shops that had burned down in the Toxteth riots of '81 had never been replaced, but the left-hand side of the road was much as they had known it.

"There!" Simon shouted.

Rickman braked hard, stopping in the middle of the road. A single cab rattled past in the opposite direction. The driver gave them a cursory glance, but didn't slow down.

"He was there," Simon shouted excitedly. "Right there." He pointed to a spot ten yards in front of them. His breathing was rapid, close to hyperventilation.

"Just breathe slowly," Rickman said. "Slow, and steady. Tell me what you see."

Simon stared, his eyes wide, his hands gripping the dashboard. "He's lying on his side. His right leg is bent the wrong way." He gave a short, snorting exhalation and Rickman put a hand on his shoulder. "There's . . . stuff." He began taking a breath between each word. "On — on the road."

Even in the artificial light of the street lamps, Rickman could see he had lost colour and there was a sick sheen on his face.

Simon tried again to control his breathing, then said, "His . . . eyes are — open."

"Simon," Rickman said. "This is important. Do you remember when this happened?"

Simon nodded shakily. "My . . . seventeenth birthday."

Rickman relaxed, waiting for his brother to grasp what he had said.

When the realisation came, Simon repeated more calmly, a look of wonderment on his face, "My seventeenth birthday."

"Dad took you for a drink to celebrate," Rickman said.

"He'd been drinking before we went out. God, he was so pissed . . . We went to The Boundary pub on the corner of Smithdown and Lodge Lane. We could have *walked* it in five minutes, for God's sake — but he had to take the car."

Rickman pulled over to let a delivery truck pass them.

"The kid walked out. There was plenty of time." Simon's eyes widened, still fixed on that spot in the road. "Dad hit the accelerator instead of the brake." He shuddered. "He could have stopped, but he hit the wrong pedal. The kid — I saw his face — it was . . ." There were no words to describe the horror of that moment. "He hit the windscreen and . . ." He released his grip on the dashboard and his hands slid into his lap.

"You didn't kill anybody, Simon," Rickman said. "You didn't hurt anybody. You didn't do anything wrong."

CHAPTER
THIRTY-FIVE

Doran turned left onto Paradise Street and walked down to the Radio Merseyside offices. Its grey concrete frontage was rendered darker and more drab by the smoked glass windows. The receptionist's desk was lit, but the main lighting had been switched off; only the late shift and security staff were in the building. The Merc's engine purred softly, almost inaudible over the laughter of a group leaving the Moat House Hotel, pouring tipsily into taxis and shouting their goodnights. He saw nobody else.

He slid into the passenger seat and closed the door; Warrender looked at him and then away, knowing better than to speak at that moment. The steady thrum of the car's engine felt like a pulse of blood in his heart, his neck, his throat.

"Was it the police?" Doran said, at length.

"You're sure it wasn't Megan?" That was Warrender's style — questions and counter-questions.

"I'm sure," Doran said.

"Then probably, yes, it was the police. I can find out easy enough."

"Do it." Doran pushed his fingers through his hair. *What do they know? What has she told them? Why the hell is she hounding me?* They listened to the thrum of the engine for a couple of minutes. *Oh, God — what if Bentley was being followed?* The engine stuttered and then picked up the rhythm again.

"What do I do now?" he asked.

"Get a lawyer."

"I can't *afford* a lawyer. And I can't claim my own money back without implicating myself."

"In what?" Warrender asked. "There's no proof of anything — nothing on record."

Doran shielded his eyes despite the dark: the streetlights seemed to dazzle from the damp road surface. "The tax records," he said. "They were on the office network."

Warrender fell silent again.

"I'm looking for *advice*, here, John." Doran's employees all knew the danger when he adopted this particular tone.

"Talk to Keiran Jago," Warrender said. "He'll fix it — you might end up a bit out of pocket, but you'll get the bulk of it back — and you'll stay out of prison."

Doran glanced sharply at his Security Manager and Warrender stared back, his cop's eyes flat and empty. They had killed a man only hours before and yet Warrender showed no signs of emotion or agitation.

"It's what you pay me for," he said, as though he had read Doran's thoughts.

"Your cold, cold heart?" Doran said, half-joking.

"My honesty," Warrender said.

Doran was almost afraid to ask the next question: Warrender's honesty might be too much for him in his present state. "What if Bentley *was* followed?"

"He wasn't."

The certainty in Warrender's voice was reassuring, but Doran needed more than a reassuring tone. "What makes you so sure? If he was working with the police —"

"If he was working with the police, they wouldn't have offered you a bag of cash, they'd have arrested you. Because they would have the photographs and they would know that he went onto a building site with you and me, and never came out again."

Doran glanced over his shoulder; talking about cops with them so nearby made him nervous. "Let's go," he said.

Warrender gunned the engine and they took a left up Duke Street. Neither man looked in the direction of the new development, nor spoke as they passed the site. They had dealt with such matters before, and only referred to them when it was absolutely necessary. Once they were over — once they knew they had covered the bases and were out of danger, they were done with, history. And both Warrender and Doran were men who looked to the future. They did not forget, but they knew how to keep a bond of silence, and this had forged a trust, if not a friendship that had endured more than twenty years.

"It might be an idea to send the lads on holiday for a bit," Warrender suggested. He meant the men who had been involved in Sara Geddes's death.

"How's Danny taking it?" Doran asked. Technically, Danny was the one facing a possible murder charge.

"He's pleased with his bonus — they all are," Warrender said with a sly glance at his employer.

"So, there's no need to send them away, is there?" Doran said.

"They'd be out of the way."

"Getting rat-arsed and bragging to the first scrubber they pick up and take back to their hotel. No — I want them near me. The police have got nothing — no eye-witnesses, no forensics, nobody with a sudden urge to confess."

Fay was waiting at the door when he arrived home. She looked pale and tired, her blue eyes had lost their sparkle over the last week, but she looked determined, and prepared to fight if she had to.

"Not now," he said, walking past her, heading for his office; he needed a drink and some quiet.

"If not now, when?" she demanded. "You're never *here* Patrick. What the hell is happening to us?"

Doran wheeled on her. "It's already happened, Fay. It happened as soon as you began your little internet fling."

"It wasn't a fling."

"What? Because it wasn't consummated?"

"I was — lonely. I fell into conversation."

Doran remembered her as a young girl, still with the country bloom in her cheeks, serving drinks in a bar down town. She was lonely then, and desperately homesick, though she tried to hide it. That was in the days when his emotions had not been so blunted, when he had been aware of her presence even before he saw her, could feel her like an electric charge making the hairs on his skin stand up. He had seen her loneliness and fallen into conversation.

"'Fell into conversation,'" he muttered. "Would you have fallen into bed if you'd got the chance?" That was cruel and he saw the injustice of it in the flush that rose to her face.

"She's a *woman*, for God's sake! How can you be jealous of a woman — a — a *fantasy*?"

He stared coldly at her. "A fantasy," he said. "That's really what I needed to hear."

"You're twisting my words," she said. "I meant that the person I conversed with was a creation — like a character on TV. It wasn't real."

"But this is," he said. "This" — he spread his hands as though the mess they were in was visible, tangible — "this is real. And if it doesn't bankrupt us, it might end with me in prison."

Her eyes grew round, filled with apprehension, and she put a hand to her throat. "What have you done?"

"What I've always done," he said. "What was necessary."

Fay knew him better than anyone; she knew that Megan Ward had taken their money, she knew that Megan Ward was missing, that Sara Geddes was dead. She nodded to herself. *She knows*, he thought. He watched her, waiting for her response. The only people he cared about on this earth were Fay and Maura and the boys. He couldn't imagine life without them, didn't think he could live in a world without them. But he would not apologise and he would not beg.

"You've always provided well for me and the children," she said, and his heart began thudding thickly in his throat. "You've been a good husband and father."

This was it: this was the build-up to telling him to leave. He clenched his jaw and looked into her face. *He would not beg.*

She held herself erect, her hands clasped in front of her, her face pale and solemn. He had never seen her more poised or more beautiful. He wanted to stop her, to walk away so he wouldn't hear the words; and yet he remained, unable to move, unable to use persuasion or threats or force, because he loved her. He knew he was a bad man, that he had lost the knack of reading her because he had done so many things that required coldness and distance, but he loved Fay more than he loved life itself and if she told him he must go to prison, that he must atone for the terrible things he had done, he thought perhaps he would.

"Do what is necessary," she said, calmly and clearly.

For a moment he was stunned, then he felt a rush of gratitude, relief and confusion and he looked at her, unable to speak. His legs felt weak and he didn't trust his voice.

"But I don't want to know about it," she went on. "And I don't want the children to know."

He relaxed, exhaling in a long rush of air. He moved in close and put his hands on her shoulders. She didn't pull away, but he saw a dull resentment in her eyes.

"I didn't start this," he said.

"I know." She sighed, looking away from him. "I know, Patrick."

He slid one hand to the back of her neck and pulled her to him, kissed her forehead and then left her.

No eye-witnesses, no forensics, nobody with a sudden urge to confess. He intended to make damn sure of it. He might be a bad man, but he was a good husband — Fay had told him that, and he believed in Fay more than he had ever believed in himself — and he would protect his family no matter what it took.

The ward was quiet. Most of the patients slept a narcotic-induced dreamless sleep that would carry them untroubled and unrested through the night, tumbling them from their beds the next morning exhausted and hung-over.

Nathan Wilde sat in the nurse's office, sipping a cup of coffee. Without the gel and styling mousse to give it structure and form, his hair lay flat to his scalp. He had barely eaten in the days since his arrival, and he looked thinner and less florid than when he had first been admitted. He flicked nervously at the join between the cup and the handle with his thumbnail, sending out a series of ringing notes, like a tocsin.

"Warlock infected the system," he said, his voice low and calm, though it trembled a little as he added, "He was everywhere. That's where the bugs came from."

The nurse took a breath and he corrected himself. "I mean where I *thought* they came from." He glanced swiftly at her face. "I got into his head — or he got into

320

mine . . ." He stared past the nurse into a puddle of light from a spot-lamp on her desk. He felt lost and baffled.

The nurse sighed. "Nathan, we talked about this: it isn't possible for somebody to get inside your head." She raised her voice, as she always did when the patients said something she didn't understand. Nathan had noticed that in the last day or two; it was like emerging from a fog, seeing people take shape out of the muddle of voices and images and terrors. This was her quirk: shout, and the crazy people will hear you better; shout and they'll hear your voice over all the others clamouring for attention in their heads.

"I'm trying to explain," he said. It was like working out a three-dimensional puzzle in his head — when a piece slotted into place in one dimension, it was hopelessly misaligned in another. "WiFi," he said. "They jump the gap."

The nurse folded her plump arms across her chest. "Are you seeing bugs again?"

Like it was a choice — like he'd been caught having a crafty smoke in the bog.

"No," he said. "The *signals* jump the gap. You don't need a connection. He got in and he knew . . ." What was he trying to say? That Warlock knew how he thought — exactly how he would defend the network?

The steady *ping ping ping ping* of his thumbnail against the cup handle sounded like a church bell pealing an alarm, a ship's bell warning of danger. *Yes,* he thought. *That was it.* He tried again. "Warlock gets inside your head . . ." He faltered. "I think that's what happened. But I didn't mean to kill Sara."

The nurse drew up a chair and sat next to Nathan. "Sara?" She leaned forward, eager, attentive.

He hadn't remembered the name before, but now he couldn't understand how he had forgotten it. "Sara Geddes."

The nurse's shoulders slumped. "Sara Geddes," she repeated. "The woman who's been on TV every news bulletin for the past week?" She rolled her eyes. "Nathan, you were in *hospital* when Sara Geddes died."

He knew he was right. Sara was Warlock's guardian. And Warlock had let her die, but it was Nathan had sent the wolves to destroy her. "I'm not making it up," he said.

"I know. But it's not *real*," she said, her voice loud and adamant again. "You didn't *do* anything."

Nathan smiled, but tears stood in his eyes. "Sometimes doing nothing is the worst sin of all."

CHAPTER
THIRTY-SIX

The mood in the Incident Room was subdued. Many of the team had worked a double shift to be there at the hand-over, and a one o'clock finish with an eight-thirty briefing hard on its heels was not good for team spirit or tempers.

Tunstall heaped three spoons of coffee into a mug and added another three of sugar before pouring hot water onto the granules. DC Reid snoozed at his desk, his head resting on one hand; the rest of the team sat or perched or leaned on furniture, steaming mugs of coffee in hand. Some had brought a breakfast of pastries or chocolate bars, which their more squeamish colleagues watched them eat with queasy distaste. Conversation was minimal and the atmosphere of despondency hung over them all like fog over the Mersey.

Tunstall turned away from the tea tray to face the room and discovered that there were no chairs free. He muttered, "Bloody hell," and lumbered over to a filing cabinet, complaining about the accommodations. Even the arrival of Naomi Hart didn't trigger the usual rustle caused by the men noticing her and trying to make her notice them.

"Blimey," she said. "Did somebody die?"

"Hopes and dreams, Naomi," Foster said. "Hopes and dreams." He'd had a preliminary briefing from Rickman and was more up to speed than Hart, who had taken sole responsibility for Megan Ward when Rickman called him in at seven.

"There you go again," she said. "Coming over all philosophical." He smiled, leaning with his back against the wall. "Some women find that very attractive in a man."

"But they don't know you like I do," she said, wafting past him in search of coffee and a place to perch during the briefing.

Rickman came in moments later, his manner brisk and businesslike. His grey suit looked smart and uncreased and he was smooth-shaven and fresh, despite having had only two hours sleep. Simon had stayed the night and needed to talk.

Rickman looked around the room at the sagging figures of his team. "Okay," he said. "We took a chance — it didn't pay off."

"What the hell happened, Boss?" Garvey asked. "I know we weren't spotted — was he tipped off, or what?"

"I don't know, Garve," Rickman said. "But he didn't fall for Megan's double."

"I knew it," Tunstall said bitterly. "Dozy chuffing woodentop blew it."

Hart looked over at him, an eyebrow raised. "Wasn't so long ago you were a chuffing woodentop yourself, Chris," she said.

324

Tunstall glared at her angrily, his jaw working, and Rickman stepped in. "It's more likely Doran knew who he was looking for. Somehow, he knew what Megan looks like."

"He has been watching her place," someone offered.

"Only *after* she cleared out," Hart said. "But we *do* know somebody who's been hanging around for weeks, taking pictures."

"Bentley," Foster said. "We confiscated his photo album, but —"

"It wouldn't be hard to hide a few, and I expect Patrick Doran would pay good money for a snapshot of the woman who stole his cash and made him look an idiot."

"Bring Bentley in," Rickman said. "See if you can get anything out of him. If he has held back any of the photographs, he's in breach of his bail conditions."

"It's not going to help us with Doran though, is it, Boss?" Garvey asked. "He's never going to fall for a second attempted hand-over of the cash."

Rickman tilted his head, recognising the truth of Garvey's assessment. "We've got the money," he said. "We've got a record of Doran's undisclosed earnings lifted from his own computer hard drive. The Inland Revenue is considering the evidence now — and we're just waiting for the go-ahead on an arrest. But you're right: it doesn't help us with the Sara Geddes enquiry. So —" He looked around at the team, rallying them. "We need new angles, new leads."

Hart was first to respond. "What about Megan?" she asked. "Why's she so keen to talk to Doran?" She kept her eyes on Foster, although the question was addressed to the entire team.

"Doran was a bit of a scall in the eighties," Foster said, leaning off the wall. "Maybe he pissed her off."

"How? By nicking her Barbie doll? She'd have been barely out of nappies in the mid-eighties."

He shrugged. "He did something to her family, then."

"But we don't even know her real name, so tracing her family history is pretty much a non-starter," Hart said.

"You've had a lot of contact with her, Lee," Rickman said. "Didn't you get anything useful?"

Foster shook his head. "She's slippery — and she's really cheesed off."

"Can't we put pressure on her?" Hart asked. "She said she had more on Doran."

"You know what happens when you squeeze something slippery," Foster said. "It oozes right out of your grasp. Carrot and stick might work, though."

"Meaning?" Rickman asked.

"Are we charging her, or what?"

Rickman rubbed the scar that bisected his right eyebrow; he thought he saw where Foster was taking this. "Offer her a reprieve on the fraud charges if she's forthcoming with her intel on Doran?"

"She was *really* brassed off we wouldn't let her make the meet," Foster said. "And her temper didn't improve any when she heard Doran had wimped out." He rolled his eyes comically. "The *language*." He tutted prissily and a few people chuckled.

Rickman ignored the ham act — that was just Foster trying to raise morale, as he always did. "The Fraud Squad doesn't seem to be in a mad rush to charge her," he said. "We could probably strike some kind of deal — imply that we're doing her a favour." He smiled a little. "It'd be sort of poetic — conning her into giving us something for nothing. But I'd want something up front from her."

Foster nodded, satisfied, and leaned back against the wall. "I can work on that."

Hart shot him a disgusted look, but remained silent.

The phone next to Garvey rang and he picked it up. "Sarge," he said. "Nolan." Nolan was baby-sitting Megan. "Says it won't wait."

Foster weaved through the obstacle course of tables and chairs, standing and seated officers, to get to the phone, while Rickman continued. "The oil rig accident," he said.

Rob Voce cleared his throat. "I've come to a dead end on that one, Boss," he said. "I just can't find anyone who recognises the family in the photo." He had sent copies of Megan's family grouping to Aberdeen and Dundee. "It happened too long ago —" He shrugged helplessly. "Half the rigs have been decommissioned —"

"Find another way in," Rickman said. Voce looked ready to argue but Rickman forestalled him. "Reid will help you."

Reid opened his eyes and jerked upright. "Ar'ey, Boss — why me?"

"Because of your charming phone manner," Rickman said. A few laughed — Reid's "phone manner" amounted to a slight slowing of his jack-hammer scouse delivery and curbing his more colourful turns of phrase.

"Fresh eyes, new evidence," Rickman said, more seriously. "Talk to each other — you're not in competition — this is a team exercise." He was aware that several of the team saw this as a career case, and that was fine, so long as it didn't get in the way of the investigation. He saw a few exchanged glances, some a little shame-faced.

Foster hung up and Rickman said, "Lee, as soon as the briefing finishes, I want you and Naomi to go and talk to Megan."

"That could be a problem," Foster said. He looked dazed, even a little punch-drunk.

Rickman hadn't time to frame a question before Foster added, "Megan's disappeared."

The Incident Room erupted into noise: exclamations of disbelief, questions as to how she got away, expressions of outrage and dismay.

"All right." Rickman's voice cut across the tumult of voices. The noise died down and he asked, "When and how?"

"Twenty minutes ago. She used the fire escape from her bedroom."

Jesus! Rickman would be asking the officer on duty why they allowed Megan unsupervised into a room with a way out, but for now, he had more practical considerations on his mind. "Get the sketch of her circulated to uniform division, together with her car make and number." Foster nodded. "Bring Bentley in, see if you can keep him clear of Jago for a bit — find out if he sold any photos to Doran.

"Doran is still our prime suspect, so the rest of you will concentrate on him; talk to your contacts, informants, drinking buddies — anyone who might have a story to tell — if they knew him in the eighties, they might have something that would help us to identify Megan."

He looked around the room; what he feared most was apathy — a conviction that no matter what they did, they couldn't make a difference. He thought he had averted that possibility for the moment. He waited until they were all looking at him; he saw disappointment in the expressions of some, determination in others, but in all of them, he saw exhaustion.

"We're tired," he said. "All of us. Mistakes are made through tiredness. Now that could count against us, or we could make it work for us." He saw puzzlement register on a few faces. "If *we're* tired, you can bet Doran is, too. We just have to be ready to catch him when he stumbles."

Kieran Jago didn't look like a lawyer. You might take him for a labourer or a club bouncer. His father had been both in the early years of their emigration from Ireland. Jago was tall and broad. He wore his sandy hair cropped close to his skull, he shaved every other day and only ever showed a faint glistening of brownish stubble, like a sprinkling of sugar on the russet-coloured skin of his face. His sharp green eyes missed nothing.

The desk sergeant had put him in one of the consulting rooms; they were more comfortably furnished than the interview rooms and did not contain audio equipment. Jago paced the small space impatiently, checking his watch every minute or two and occasionally tapping his breast pocket as if to check that his cell-phone was still safely in place.

Foster opened the door and he turned, instantly adopting his professional persona: calm, unsmiling and watchful.

"What can I do for you, Mr Jago?" Foster asked. He was wary after their first bruising encounter, but this time he had more ammunition, a strong case against Bentley and the possibility of a charge of conspiracy to pervert the course of justice, so he could afford not to sound too deferential.

"My client is missing."

"There's a lot of that going around," Foster said, thinking *could this day get any worse?*

"Am I supposed to know what you're talking about?" There was the merest trace of Liverpool-Irish in his accent; years of university training and the services of a voice coach in the early days of his career had buffed his accent to a rich, mellow burr.

"It was kind of an 'in' joke," Foster confided. He offered Jago a seat and the solicitor accepted, taking one of the pink upholstered chairs and placing it a

330

couple of feet from the table. Foster took another and they sat at a slight angle to each other.

"We would like to question your client on a matter related to Sara Geddes's death."

"Specifically?"

"Let's talk about that in the interview room, eh?" Foster had known men like Jago in the marines: they appeared calm, but they were on a slow burn, and when they blew, you'd better dive for cover — fast. You had to watch the eyes if you wanted early warning. Jago's flashed green for danger. "Part of Bentley's bail conditions was that he should sign in at the station desk every morning," Foster said, "so he's got three hours before he's in breach of that condition."

"I've told you, he's gone — vanished."

"Then he's in trouble."

"I think he is," Jago said, with a sincerity and concern that made Foster look at him again, surprised.

"We've got officers out looking for him as we speak," Foster said. "We'll see what they turn up." He was about to get up, but Jago stopped him. He sat forward in his chair, one finger raised, his attitude earnest, even eager.

"I want to put in a missing person's report."

Foster laughed. "That's good," he said. "That's really funny."

Jago sat back in his chair, his eyes flashing a warning again. "I am registering a legitimate concern for my client. I expect you to act upon it."

"We don't usually put out a missing person alert on an adult male with a criminal record who's gone

331

AWOL. Your client is facing further charges of stalking. It doesn't take a degree in psychology to work out why he's gone."

"You're saying you won't look into it?"

"Oh, we'll look into it, all right — he's an absconder — we *always* look into them." Jago shook his head angrily and Foster added, "He's done a runner, Mr Jago. Get used to it."

"I can't believe he'd do that."

"Are you *disappointed* in him, Mr Jago?" Foster couldn't resist the sarcasm. "Oh, wait — you didn't stand bail for him did you?" There was no bail set, and Foster knew it, but the question was enough to wind Jago up.

He sucked his teeth, staring Foster down. Foster held eye contact, wondering how far he could push it before Jago went over the edge.

"I can't believe it," Jago enunciated carefully, "because he has no reason to abscond. The complainant is dead."

Foster felt a flare of anger. " 'The complainant' has a name — it's Sara Geddes. She was attacked outside her own home while your client looked on and did nothing. Which doesn't look too good for him, I've got to tell you. And the fact he's now done a bunk looks even worse."

"My client — whose name, by the way, is Jake Bentley — has been discounted as a suspect in the attack."

Foster smiled. *He's trying to say they're all just people — Sara Geddes, Jake Bentley, Patrick Doran as well, for all I know.* "He's done a bunk because he doesn't want to face the stalking charge. I suspect he already knows why we want to question him on this other matter, an' all. The CPS are willing to back us on this one." Jago seemed unmoved, and Foster eyed him curiously. "Are you gonna see it through to the end?"

"Yes," Jago said, without hesitation. "I am."

Foster lifted one shoulder. "Whoever's paying your bills might not see it in the same light." Again, he saw subdued anger in the tense set of Jago's jaw.

"I told you — I'm working *pro bono*."

"If you say so. But who recommended Mr Bentley as a client?"

He didn't answer the question, but Foster thought he saw a flicker of amusement in the lawyer's eyes. "Mr Bentley is a man who's been dealt a rough hand in life," Jago said after a moment or two. "I'd've thought you would have more sympathy."

"Yeah? Why's that then?" He expected Jago to start preaching the usual partisan doctrine of common experience, cultural heritage — Irish immigration, English repression, the dual religions of football and church — but Jago was a man of surprises.

"I'm not talking about *The Beatles, Ferry 'Cross the Mersey* and all that me-eye." The Irish tones became masked by a sharper edge of Liverpool in his accent. "That cheery scouser crap is rooted in a mythical culture of a different millennium," he went on, emphasising each point with a jab of his finger. "I'm talking about Liverpool as it is now, in the twenty-first century: expansion, new money, Urban Splash, The Tate Gallery, European Capital of Culture."

"Sorry, mate." Foster said, adopting a bored expression. "You lost me after 'mythical'."

Jago, in full flow, ignored the deliberate insult. "The city is experiencing a renaissance — an affluence it hasn't seen in generations — a new confidence that should benefit all of its citizens —"

"Are you thinking of getting into local politics?" Foster interrupted. "I mean, is this your campaign speech or what?"

"The point I'm making," Jago said, his voice icily calm, "is that with all this growth and development, you'd think there'd be enough to go around. But d'you know what Liverpool means to the people I represent? Not the celebrities and the football stars — the little people — people like Jake Bentley?"

"I've got a horrible feeling you're gonna tell me," Foster said.

Again, Jago ignored his needling tone. "Liverpool — their home, the place they were born, and where they'll probably die — means dirt," he said, "poverty, drugs, street crime, burglary."

"And doing the odd freebie sets the world to rights, does it?"

Jago responded to the sneer in his voice. "I may be idealistic, Sergeant, but I'm not naïve: you don't redress the balance with a few *pro bono* cases. But for each person I've helped I can at least say I did *something* — I didn't sit back and say it's all too much."

334

"You can't justify theft and violence by bleating inequality," Foster said, feeling a fresh burst of anger. "I do this job every day. I deal with the 'little people', as you call them, every day. Victims of the Jake Bentley's of this world."

They stared at each other for some moments with mutual dislike.

"Are you going to instigate a missing person report?" Jago demanded.

"Talk to the desk sergeant," Foster said, getting up, ending the discussion. "He'll take the details."

CHAPTER
THIRTY-SEVEN

It was a long and arduous day; frustrating and tiring. A community police foot patrol located Megan's car, parked in a back alley behind one of the new glass-and-steel office blocks at the back of Hatton Garden. Garvey and two others set up surveillance, waiting to pounce, should Megan appear.

When the owner finally showed up at six-thirty p.m., Garvey was at first incredulous, then furious, to see a man walk up to the car with self-conscious insouciance.

"She's only gone and sold it on, hasn't she?" he told Foster later. The proud new owner was an architect who was more than pleased at getting an Audi TT Roadster, barely eight weeks old and with under a thousand miles on the clock for six thousand pounds below showroom cost.

"Any chance he's connected to Megan?" Foster asked.

"He looks legit," Garvey said. "Got himself a bargain, though."

"How did he pay? We could maybe trace a cheque."

"She was very specific," Garvey said. "Cash only."

"Is he mad or what? She could've stolen the car."

Garvey shrugged. "She had all the documentation, and anyway, he said she seemed such a *nice* young woman." His tone conveyed astonishment and disgust at once. "She fed him some line about an ex-boyfriend showing up and wanting to whisk her off to Venice to live."

"I suppose they don't have much use for cars there." Foster said, with a comical look. "I just can't believe he fell for it."

"He said she seemed genuinely excited. He got swept up in it." Foster gave him a sceptical look and Garvey spread his hands. "She's plausible," he said.

"Oh, yeah," Foster agreed. "That's our Megan's middle name." A thought occurred to him. "Any sign she did actually go abroad?"

"We've alerted airports and port authorities. All we can do is wait and see."

The oil rig inquiries were stalled, too, after a promising start: two riggers who thought they might know the mystery family — but they couldn't remember a name. They did give DC Voce the name of a man who was friendly with the family. Reid made the call and got an answerphone message. Further inquiries came up with the less than welcome news that their man was away on a camping holiday in Europe.

So the rollercoaster continued, the adrenalin highs and serotonin lows: lack of sleep was becoming a real problem for some of the team, Foster among them. He drove home, slamming through the gears, disgusted with the day and with himself for ever having liked Megan Ward. Hart was right: Megan was no more than a cheap hustler who got off on manipulating people. Sara Geddes had trusted her, had opened her heart and her home to her, and in all likelihood she had been murdered because of Megan's selfish need to get one over on the other poor sod. He didn't believe it was about money — for Megan, it was about the thrill of the hunt: finding the mark, winning their trust, proving she was smarter and faster and more ruthless.

He knew that much of his bad mood was down to the hours he was working. Sleep — or the lack of it — was beginning to obsess him. He fantasised about it, imagining himself in bed, the alarm clock stuffed under shirts in the deepest drawer of his dresser. He could feel the texture of the sheets, the soft, dreamy give of the pillow as he lay his head on it. He had twice nodded off at his desk during the day, and sounds and light were beginning to take on the heightened quality of a dream.

He had knocked off immediately after the evening briefing, switched off his mobile, and driven straight home. There was nothing in the fridge — not even milk for a cup of tea, but he was too tired to stop to pick up even the basic necessities; if he could just get a couple of hours rest, he felt everything else would be fine.

He had to drag himself from the car to the front door and only the promise of sweet dreamless sleep got him there. The security light was out and he turned to the street to find his house key. He found it, slotted it into the lock on his second attempt and pushed the door open. Something moved at the edge of his vision and he felt a shock of adrenalin. He stared into the patch of darkness and saw nothing. Sleep deprivation, waking dreams. He laughed softly to himself. *You're hallucinating Lee*, he told himself, turning back to the doorway.

A blur of shadow rushed at him and he reacted instinctively, swinging right and taking a step to the side, using the attacker's momentum as he grabbed a handful of clothing and continued the forward motion, following through with a shove in the middle of the back. His co-ordination was slightly off and he used too much force: the shadow fell through the doorway, clipping the edge of the door as they went down and Foster fell too, landing in an untidy heap with his assailant.

The attacker groaned and Foster realised his mistake. "What the bloody hell?" he said angrily, getting to his feet and dusting off his trousers. Megan Ward was slower to move. She groaned again.

"Jeez, Foster," she said, rolling onto her back and propping herself up on her elbows.

"You're lucky I didn't break your stupid neck, creeping up on me like that. And it's *Sergeant* Foster to you."

"Oh," she said, in a mock-injured tone. "And I thought we were friends."

"What d'you think you're playing at?" he demanded.

"I just wanted to get in off the street without drawing too much attention to myself," she said.

"That worked well, didn't it?" He scowled down at her, feeling furious and confused and bitterly disappointed that his plans for an early night had been ruined.

Megan smiled a little ruefully, touching her forehead lightly: it was beginning to swell where her head had caught the door frame. She checked her fingertips for blood and gave a slight shrug at finding none. "It's been that kind of day," she said, getting smoothly to her feet and slapping the grime from her hands. She wore her dark-brown hair tied back and tucked under a woollen hat. She opened the vestibule door and walked down the hallway to his flat door.

The adrenalin rush, the weariness, the frustrations of the day hit Foster with a force that winded him for a moment. He shut the front door and bent forward with his hands on his knees to catch his breath.

"Are you all right?" Megan asked, taking a step towards him.

"This isn't a game, Megan," he said, ignoring her question.

"I know."

"So why are you even here?"

She batted her eyes at him, playfully. "I thought you might protect a poor damsel in distress."

"There you go again." His voice echoed up the uncarpeted stairs. "Making a joke of it — you walked *away* from police protection."

Her mouth curved into a smile and she came closer. "I don't want *police* protection."

"No," Foster said, brushing past her, "Forget it. I haven't got time for this shit."

"What?" She seemed genuinely surprised.

"I'm not one of your marks," Foster said. "Don't mess me around. Half the team is out looking for you

— which means we're at half-strength investigating Sara's murder."

"Sara was my friend." Her eyes seemed to cloud: slate-grey, with the promise of rain. "That's why I'm here — I want to help."

Her sincerity was a little late in coming and Foster gave her a bitter look. "Yeah? Well, we don't want your help."

It seemed that Megan had come with something to say, and she didn't intend to leave until she'd said it. She clenched her jaw against his words, frowning, then she gave a little nod as if to say, I *deserved that*, and went on with stolid determination: "If I hadn't been so self-absorbed, I'd have known that Bentley was stalking Sara and not me. I got away in time because of that mistake, leaving Sara to face the consequences of my actions. I owe her — I know that." She seemed to struggle with her emotions again for a second. "I want to make it right."

"By running away — again?" That stung. He saw hurt flash in her eyes and then she blinked. "Oh, now I've hurt your feelings," he said, sarcasm dripping from every syllable.

"I meant it when I told you I don't want police protection," she said. "You can't get at Doran the way I can."

"And how d'you think you can 'help'?" Foster asked, curious despite himself.

"I can get the information you need."

"See," he said, "that's why we don't trust you. First you say you've *got* evidence, *now* you say you can get it."

"I didn't lie to you." Her voice was a little shaky. "I gave you his tax records — I gave you over a million pounds, for God's sake!"

She kept talking about it like it was her money. "You did do that, I admit. We've got enough to charge him with tax fraud and false accounting. And we're grateful." He opened the front door and gestured for her to leave with a sweep of his hand.

The phone started ringing behind his flat door and she said, "Aren't you going to get that?"

He glared at her while the phone rang on, and finally fell silent as the answerphone kicked in.

She took a breath — she even seemed to lean backwards in her determination not to be budged. "I can get you more," she said hurriedly.

"More hints, more mystery — more bullshit." He took a step away from the door, intending to drag her out if necessary.

Her eyes widened in alarm. "Doran has used his firm to commit a number of armed robberies," she said quickly.

Foster hesitated.

"I can give you everything you need."

Foster smiled and shook his head. "Yeah? When would that be, then? When you've finished playing your computer games? You should market your ideas, honest to God — Nintendo'd lap them up."

"I'm more of an *X-Boxer*, myself," she said, coolly. They stared at each other, Foster trying to figure her out, failing miserably. A door opened then slammed on the first floor, and Megan glanced up towards the source of the noise. She stepped back into the shadows cast by the staircase as footsteps clattered down the stairs.

Foster greeted his neighbour with a laconic, but friendly "All right," and held the door for him as he went out. He stood there for a few moments longer, undecided. If he let Megan walk now, they would lose any chance they had of getting Doran on anything bigger than fraud. He was fairly certain the businessman would have effectively covered his tracks after the abortive attempt to hand over the tax money, so all they had was Megan's evidence — if it existed. He let his head drop onto his chest. *Sod it — only one way to find out.*

He shut the door and walked down the hall to where Megan still stood, watching him quietly. He walked past her and slotted the Yale key in the lock and she said, "You believe me?"

He looked at her, curious to know if this need to be believed was any different from how she felt when she was working on some poor sucker during one of her scams. He winced, a little offended. "I don't *believe* you, Megan. But like the man said — it's good to talk."

He led her to the kitchen: he needed coffee, and plenty of it. She seemed to sense this and didn't attempt to talk to him while he brewed up: not the usual instant stuff he drank, but a strong filter blend.

The warm, nutty aroma reminded him he hadn't eaten since breakfast, and his stomach cramped momentarily in complaint.

Megan pulled off her hat and shook her hair free; it tumbled, thick and glossy, to her shoulders. Foster thought it an overly theatrical gesture. He sweetened the coffee and handed a mug to Megan and they drank the hot black liquid for a minute in silence, at opposite ends of the small space, both standing, though Foster leaned against one of the units for support.

"Okay," he said. "What's your proposal?"

"All I want is a chance to talk to Doran," she said, watching his face carefully.

Foster stared at her uncomprehendingly. "What the hell d'you want to talk to him about?"

"Sara," she said simply.

He laughed. "D'you think you're gonna get a confession out of him, Megan?" he said, leaning off the counter. "You're a rank amateur when it comes to men like Doran. You can't just walk in and do a Lone Ranger with men like him — he's dangerous — seriously dangerous. Hard-nosed scouse scalls are scared of Doran — what makes you think you can get him to talk?"

"As you keep pointing out," she said, with a self-critical smile, "I know which buttons to push — and I don't mind being afraid." She gave a little shrug. "I spend half my life being afraid."

"Your choice — you chose this life!" *What the hell does she want — sympathy?*

344

"You're right," she said, easing past him to place her cup in the sink. Her shoulders looked thin and frail beneath her jacket. "I chose this life. But only because it was preferable to the fear I couldn't control."

"Oh, *what?*" Foster stared at her back. "More bullshit riddles." He expected an angry response, but when she swung around to face him, she was smiling.

"I don't expect you to understand," she said. "But I won't give you anything until you let me have a shot at Doran. I don't mind being the lure," she said, eager, now. "I know I can make him talk — but I need your help to bring him in."

"You're willing to use yourself as bait?" Foster said. "I knew you were a thrill-seeker, but suicidal? Doran isn't soft, Megan — he'll want something more than the pleasure of your company. You haven't got his money any more — we have — and my DCI isn't about to part with it on your say-so."

"I have money," she said.

He thought about it for a moment. "You don't think the fifteen thousand you got for your sportster will do anything for him?" He watched her reaction. She seem surprised that they should know about her car sale. She began to deny it but the attempt was half-hearted and he interrupted.

"You might be invisible, Megan, but when you own things — even better, when you *sell* things — suddenly *ping!* you're all solid and substantial again."

She chewed her lip, but said nothing.

"The fifteen thousand will only aggravate him," Foster told her. "It'd be like dripping acid on a burn."

"I'll get more," she said.

"More what? More money?" She nodded. "Just like that?"

She inclined her head. Such things were easy for Megan Ward. He looked into his coffee cup, but the black slick of liquid held no answers to this puzzle of a woman.

"Let me get this straight," he said. "You want me to help you set up a sting operation with a man you are convinced is a murderer, using stolen money? If it wasn't so crazy, it'd be hilarious."

"How else would I get it?" She wasn't faking her confusion.

He shook his head. "You're unbelievable."

"Do you never bend the rules, Sergeant?"

He took a breath. How many times had Jeff Rickman accused him of failing to see the rights and wrongs of a situation, only the path of least resistance. What was the word Jeff used? *Expedience*, that was it.

She continued looking at him and he said, "This isn't about me — it's about risk. It's too risky. For you and for me."

"This could be the biggest arrest of your career," she said.

"And the last. Helping you — especially on some bird-brained scheme like this — is way outside my remit. It's against orders, against the wishes of my boss. If we pulled it off, they might give me a medal, but they'd have to kick my arse out the door right after."

"Funny," she said, tilting her head and looking at him like she'd never really seen him before. "I never thought of you as a Jobsworth."

"Don't try to mess with my head, Megan. I know I'm a lot of things — but I'm not a coward — and I've got nothing to prove to you," he added quietly. He finished his coffee and leaned past her to place the cup in the sink. They were close enough that he could feel her breath on his cheek, could smell the warmth of her perfume. She smelled of apples and spices and sweet hay. She didn't move. *Point to Megan*, he thought, feeling himself liking her again. Not wanting to.

He folded his arms and leaned against the counter beside her. "You're asking too much," he said. "I don't even know who you *are* and you're asking me to lay my job on the line."

"You want to get to know me?" she asked. "I'm not that easy to define."

"I'm not saying I want to get to *know* you, I'm saying I don't *trust* you."

"Well," she said slowly, "I can't do much about that." She moved towards the door, and Foster followed her.

"So you'll leave it alone?"

She smiled. "I can't do that, Sergeant."

He took hold of her arm and he saw a spurt of anger in her eyes. "You can't go up against Doran on your own," he said.

"Looks like I've no choice."

"I'll arrest you if I have to."

"On what charge?" She tried to pull away from him but he held her.

"I dunno — assault."

"I'm the one with the injury," she said. The bruising on her forehead had turned an angry purple.

"All right — for being a suicidal bint, then."

She puffed air between her lips. "I may be a thrill-seeker, but I'm not suicidal," she said, throwing his words back at him.

It was one jibe too many. The pointless activity, the disappointments and frustrations of the day came rushing back at him in a tidal wave of exhaustion. "Okay," he said letting go of her arm, "you want to kill yourself, don't let me stop you."

She rubbed her arm, looking him in the eye, and he could see her struggle with her pathological need for secrecy; he also saw a little gleam there that said maybe she was fighting an urge to slap his face.

"I gave you the money," she said. "I gave you the chance to get Doran — you blew it." There was raw emotion in her voice.

"I'm tired, Megan," he said. "Do what you like — just leave me out of it."

"I *can't*," she said, her eyes magnified by tears. "I can't do this alone."

"So don't do it."

"I can't just walk away from this," she insisted.

"Why not? You've been walking away all your life. It's what you do — it's what you're good at — what makes this any different?"

She opened her mouth to speak but he stopped her. "Do me a favour — don't give me that crap about Sara. You walked away from her knowing you'd been rumbled. You didn't warn her, and you didn't try to draw them away from her."

"Don't you think I regret that?"

Foster was too tired to argue any more, he didn't want to hear any more of her self-justification and he couldn't stand to see her trying out her cheap grifter tactics on him. "Get out," he said.

She shook her head, tears spilling onto her cheeks. "This *is* for Sara," she said. "I'm not so bad as you think."

He looked away, not wanting to be influenced by her tears. "You don't know what I think," he said.

"Only what you've told me: that I'm a hustler, a cheat, a thief and a liar — you're right — I'm all those things. But I did care about Sara." She fell silent and he looked at her again. Whatever it was she wanted to say, she wasn't finding it easy. She sighed. "But it isn't just about Sara," she said.

He waited and she sighed again.

"Patrick Doran killed my brother."

CHAPTER
THIRTY-EIGHT

"Gareth was ten years older than me," Megan said. They had moved to Foster's sitting-room and now sat either end of a chocolate-brown sofa. Megan nursed a glass of whisky — not the good stuff — Foster still wasn't sure if he trusted her, and he wasn't going to waste his good stash on someone who might be taking the Mickey out of him. He propped his feet up on a low table in front of the sofa. A state-of-the-art hifi and a single leather chair placed square in front of a widescreen TV were the only other articles of furniture in the room.

"He was ace with computers, electronics, anything like that. He just knew how things worked." She laughed a little tearfully. "He was going to be the next Bill Gates."

She fell silent for a while, and only took up the story again when Foster leaned forward to place his empty coffee mug on the table.

She smoothed a line along her eye-socket with the pad of her thumb. "He got into trouble, hacking into commercial concerns, messing with their databases, sending rude messages on their global email services. He didn't blackmail anyone or gain from it financially, it was —" She seemed lost for words for a second. "For Gareth, it was an interesting intellectual exercise — he liked the challenge."

"How old was he?"

"Fifteen, the first time he was caught. They gave him a warning, confiscated his computer and put him on a community service order. But Gareth never —" She frowned. "You have to understand — he didn't live by other people's rules. Gareth had his own way of seeing the world. He couldn't see the point of taking away his computer — he didn't really see that he'd done anything wrong. He was even banned off the school's network, so he had to drop his ICT course." She sighed. "He did the community service when it suited him. He started using internet cafés, library computers — any way he could get access to the internet."

"And it wasn't just for the intellectual exercise this time," Foster said, taking a swallow of whisky and feeling it hit much harder than it would normally.

"He cracked some government mainframe. Got into their satellite systems, managed to change the direction of one of the satellites." Megan paused. "It caused a communications blackout that could have been dangerous — military repercussions."

"You computer types might be clever, but you're not very smart, are you?" Foster said. "I bet they had him for breakfast."

Megan lifted her chin in acknowledgement. "He was put in a Young Offenders' Institution for two years."

Foster knew about Young Offenders' Institutions: they could take a boy apart piece by piece and

351

reconstruct him into something his own mother wouldn't recognise.

"I can't begin to explain how devastating it was for my mother and me," Megan said. "Mum wasn't strong — after Dad died, we looked to Gareth for everything — and when he went away, she fell apart."

"You can't have been more than a toddler," Foster said.

"I was six years old. I had to take over from Gareth as carer — Mum couldn't cope. But I didn't really know how to help. I was too young to understand depression. I was even less well equipped to understand how that place changed Gareth."

Foster nodded; it was as he had thought.

"I thought it was bad when they put him away; it was worse when he came back."

"Drugs?" he asked.

Her eyebrow twitched into a momentary frown. "He used amphetamines to keep awake, nootropics to enhance memory, weed to chill." The names seemed to come easily to her and Foster wondered how much of Megan's web surfing was drug-enhanced. "But what happened to Gareth wasn't chemically induced," she went on. "It was in here." She tapped her chest, just over her heart. The frown returned and she stared into her whisky before taking a sip. Her hand was shaking.

"When he got out, the government offered him a job — working on systems security." She smiled bitterly. "Ironic, huh? He turned them down — he said it was the government fucked him up, and he wasn't about to start helping them." She looked hurt and confused and bewildered. "They gave him a chance and he was so messed up, he couldn't take it."

The doorbell rang and Megan jumped. Foster checked his watch: nine-thirty. His sitting-room looked out onto a small concreted back yard and a high brick wall. He saw Megan's gaze stray to the window. There were two possibilities: police business — or Doran. He placed his glass on the floor beside him and got up, gesturing with the flat of his hand for Megan to stay put. At the door of his flat he could hear nothing, so he turned off the light and opened the door fast, keeping behind and to the side of it, using it as a shield.

The hall was empty.

The doorbell rang again, longer this time and with a couple of extra spurts at the end. It was dark, and the broken security light meant that he couldn't even see the silhouette of the caller, to gauge height and potential threat.

He crept to the end of the hall and the figure on the doorstep shifted their weight. He saw no more than a vague form behind the glass. He had no choice — he went to the door and called, "Who is it?"

"Open up, Foster, for God's sake! It's bucketing down." It was Hart.

Foster opened the door, trying to decide what he was going to tell her.

"Where the hell have you been?" she demanded.

"Here."

"Well, why don't you answer your damn phone?"

He thought guiltily of the phone call he had left unanswered.

"And your mobile's switched off."

"Sorry," he said. "Is it urgent?"

"Let me in and I'll tell you." The wind, gusting in bursts, whipped her hair around her face and sent rain in spatters against her raincoat; he realised he was gripping the door, effectively forming a barrier to her.

"Naomi —" He really didn't know what to tell her. His shoulders sagged and he said, "Ah, bollocks."

"You know, I usually get a better reception than this," Hart said, ducking her head against a blast of rain-soaked wind on the back of her neck.

Foster glanced over his shoulder. Hart caught the gesture and said, "Oh, right. I'm interrupting."

"It's not what you think," Foster said, opening the door wide. She stepped in out of the rain, shaking water from her hair.

"Let me guess," she said, evidently enjoying his discomfort. "Kieran Jago's PA came over to kiss and make up."

He winced. "It's more complicated than that."

She puzzled over this for a moment, then seemed to decide that the statement was indecipherable. "Sorry to drag you away, from . . . whatever it is, but we've had a possible sighting of Megan. The boss thinks she's more likely to talk to you."

"He's not wrong."

"And I was so *nice* to her . . ." She caught something in his expression and stopped. He jerked his head in the direction of his flat door and followed her through his narrow hallway into the sitting-room.

354

"Megan." It was hard to gauge from her tone what Hart was thinking, but her hand went to her hair. As far as Foster was concerned, she had nothing to worry about: Megan was a good-looking woman, but even wet through, Naomi Hart had the edge on her.

Megan looked relaxed, she sat back, one arm resting along the backrest of the sofa, an amused expression on her face. "Am I in the way?" she asked. "'Cos, you know, I could leave." The openness, the vulnerability she had allowed Foster to see was gone.

Hart regained her composure and matched Megan's cool tone. "We've been looking all over Liverpool for you, and all the time you were here. In Sergeant Foster's flat." Foster heard the accusation in her voice.

"She was here when I got back. She wants us to try again with Doran," he said.

"There's no way Rickman would agree to that," Hart said.

Megan looked up at him and tilted her head as if to say, "You see why I came to you and not the rest?"

Foster switched his attention to Hart. "Wait till you hear what she's got to say."

Megan gave a short laugh but refused to talk.

"O-kay," Foster said. "I'll tell her, shall I?"

"No." Hart took off her wet coat and draped it over the coffee table. "I want to hear this from Megan." She sat at the far end of the sofa and folded her hands in her lap with polite interest. "Only — can you give us a brief character summary, first?"

"I don't know what you're driving at," Megan said, offended.

"You're hard to keep track of," Hart explained. "I mean, you change personalities like changing a hat. You'll play the innocent or the flirt, the lonely housewife or the hard-nosed journo — whatever gets you what you need."

"The roles I adopt are functional," Megan said. "I know who I am."

Hart spread her hands. "Do tell!"

Megan flipped her a contemptuous look. "I don't have to explain myself to you," she said.

"You seemed to be doing all right with Sergeant Foster, though."

Megan looked away from her, an angry smile on her face.

"He'd've been pissed off, finding you on his doorstep," Hart went on. "Only way to get round him would be to play the vulnerability card. What was it? Lonely orphan? Kindred souls?"

"That's *enough*." Foster saw Hart's surprise at his annoyance. She didn't know how close she had come to the truth — how could she? Nevertheless, he felt stung by her words.

"Don't tell me she got to you," Hart said.

Megan glanced from one to the other. "You're letting him down, Constable." Her expression softened into amusement. "He's supposed to be the one with all the snide remarks."

"I'm clocking twelve hours a day, on average," Hart said. "This particular twelve-hour day, I've spent running around like an idiot, looking for you. I'm cold, and I'm wet, and I'm tired. You've messed us about

356

from the start. Tying up police time, selling us one line after another. Playing your tedious mind games. We're trying to find Sara's killer, Megan. Your friend's killer. You're making our job harder. Worse than that — you seem to think it's a huge joke. So forgive me if I'm not playing my role to your satisfaction. I can't turn it on and off the way you can."

Stung, Megan snapped to an upright position, ready to argue. Hart exhaled impatiently and Foster decided to take control. "Look," he said. "Like I said, I'm not one of your marks." Megan raised an eyebrow and he forged ahead, determined to get her back to where they left off.

"Just to bring you up to speed, Naomi — Megan's brother, Gareth, got caught hacking back in the eighties. The Youth Offenders' Institute mangled him a bit and he came out bitter and hard. Is that about the size of it?"

Megan seemed offended by his assessment, she looked at him round-eyed and made no reply.

"What?" he demanded.

"I thought that was a private conversation," Megan said.

"I might be a sucker for a vulnerable woman," he said with a sly glance at Hart, "but I'm not stupid. I want a witness to this."

Megan seemed to be conducting an internal argument. She stared at him, apparently undecided whether to tell him the rest or walk out.

CHAPTER
THIRTY-NINE

"Gareth used to baby-sit for Patrick Doran — their eldest child — Maura," Megan said.

They had called a truce over whisky and dry crackers, which was all he could find in the cupboard.

"Doran treated my brother like family. Gareth was nineteen years old, studying programming part-time at Liverpool Polytechnic, as it was then. Doran had started in business a year or so earlier — security work to begin with — but he saw the potential of the electronics market and expanded into burglar alarm systems, CCTV and corporate surveillance work.

"Doran has a way of finding kids like Gareth: vulnerable, impressionable — easy to manipulate. He knew all about Gareth's history — said it didn't matter. 'New opportunities, new life', he said."

"How very liberal-minded of him," Hart commented. Foster had turned the TV chair around to the sofa, and Hart had taken it, facing Megan, openly sizing her up, and he was struck by how typical this was of her — meeting life head-on: he admired her for it, it matched his own philosophy.

"Until then, Gareth had been earning one-fifty an hour plus tips in a bar. He hated it — long hours and no time to tinker with his computer. Doran's job offer seemed like a dream ticket: a chance to learn about the new technology at double what he was getting in the bar. Doran paid extra for 'special projects'."

"What were these 'special projects'?" Foster asked.

Megan put down the whisky glass she had been nursing for the past ten minutes as though she had discovered a worm in the dregs. "Hacking," she said. "He wanted information from competitors' systems — potential clients, mostly. Doran would put in a more competitive bid and pinch the contracts from under the oppositions' noses." She shrugged. "Standard cutthroat business practice.

"Gareth adored Patrick Doran — you have to remember our father died when Gareth was fourteen — Doran seemed to really take an interest and Gareth responded to that." She sighed. "I don't know if he was showing off or just shouting for more attention, but Gareth told Doran he could infect the rivals' computers with a virus — slow them down, weaken them — even program them to relay sensitive information to Doran's system."

"Someone twigged?" Foster asked.

"No!" she seemed outraged by the suggestion. "Gareth was too damn smart for the plodding systems analysts the other firms employed."

Foster waited and she went on, "They could have cleaned up: always having the jump on the other guy; slowing their systems so they haemorrhaged cash till there was nothing left. But Doran is greedy; he saw an account that was already on a rival firm's books and he wanted a piece of it — if that meant stealing it, what did he care?

"It was a money run — one of the big supermarket chains — coming up to Christmas, you're talking big money. They had the route, the names of the delivery team, times of day. All of it. Doran sent a hand-picked team of his own. They moved in — knew exactly when and where to hit them — but it was messy. The rival's crew fought back — hard. They nearly didn't get away."

"You sound all disapproving," Hart said, and Megan smiled bitterly.

"Unlike computer fraud, armed robbery isn't a bloodless crime."

"Tell that to Sara Geddes."

Foster shot Hart a warning look. He had heard more from Megan in the last hour than she had told them in two nights, and he didn't want her to clam up just because Naomi Hart couldn't get a hold on her temper.

Hart rolled her eyes, but she got the message. She sat back and took a swallow of whisky, leaving the questioning to Foster.

"When was this robbery — do you know?"

"1989 — that was when Gareth got deep into Doran's murky world."

"What are we talking about?" he asked. "More armed robberies?"

She shook her head. "Doran was scared off by the near-miss with the money run. He went for softer targets after that: point of delivery, private addresses. Burglary, mostly. This went on for months. Then Gareth found a big account on a competitor's books, providing security at a diamond dealers' event. Scores of them were scheduled to attend, buying and selling millions of pounds' worth of diamonds."

Foster frowned. "I wasn't in The Job, then, but I think I'd remember a robbery on that scale."

"I told you," Megan said, irritated by the interruption, "Doran went for soft targets. The dealers had each donated an amount towards security — he picked one out from the list of contributions."

Foster felt a prickling of unease: this was beginning to sound familiar.

"Mr and Mrs Orr, an elderly couple running a family business," Megan went on. "They lived in West Kirby. Their shop was in Liverpool, but the event was taking place in Shrewsbury. They were sure to take their day's purchases home with them. By this time, Gareth was getting a share from the robberies. The greater his involvement, the bigger the share."

"So he wasn't just giving Doran info?" Foster asked.

"Alarm boxes could be tricky, even then," she explained. "If they needed Gareth to get them inside, he was paid extra."

Foster felt another stab of recognition. "And Gareth was called in to get them into the jeweller's house."

She nodded. "He disabled the alarm. Normally he would go home at that point, but Doran was worried there might be more gadgetry inside — an alarm on the safe or something."

"Doran was there?"

"Doran and John Warrender, his Chief of Security —
there are some things he doesn't trust to the lower
forms of life in his business."

"1989," Foster repeated. He glanced at Hart, who
seemed to have mellowed over her whisky, and was
listening intently. "Warrender was still in The Job, then,
wasn't he?"

"He quit in 1990, I think," Hart said.

So, John Warrender had been moonlighting for
Doran well before his retirement — committing
robberies at night and no doubt investigating them in
the day. Megan's suspicion of the police apparently had
some foundation.

"They should have been straight in and out," Megan
told them. "They had an electronics expert, Doran was
an experienced safecracker, and he'd even brought
along a cop, in case anyone turned up asking awkward
questions. The couple were safely tucked up in bed for
the night, but they didn't reckon on Mr Orr's prostate
trouble. He got up in the night, saw a light on
downstairs and went to investigate."

"I looked into the old man's face," Gareth told her
years later, "and I thought, *Why am I even here?*" It
would be a long time before he began to understand
the gradual accumulation of wrong moves and bad
choices, the faltering steps that led to a giant stride into
the nightmare that followed.

It took just minutes to find and crack the safe,
embedded in the wall behind some books on a shelf in
the dining-room. The safe was empty, except for a few

362

valuables and documents. Doran turned on the old man, furious.

"Where are the stones?" he demanded.

The old man shook his head and a lock of silky white hair fell into his eyes. His face was smooth, clean-shaven and he had the delicate colouring some people acquire in old age; powdery white, but with a hint of pink high in his cheeks. His nose was straight and thin as a blade.

Doran sent Warrender upstairs to keep the old woman quiet while he and Gareth tied the old man to a chair. Doran made Gareth bring the dining chair into the hall, so that Mr Orr's wife would hear them. Gareth placed the chair on the waxed wood floor and stood back, while Doran did the rest. He remembered the warm rum colour of aged wood all around them, the smell of wax polish and the slow tick of a grandfather clock.

Gareth found his gaze drawn to the man's pyjamas; dark blue with white piping around the collar. The detail seemed unbearably poignant and Gareth suddenly wanted to cry.

"Where are the stones?" Doran repeated.

The old man shook his head and Doran hit him hard in the face. Blood spurted from the old man's lip and Gareth was startled to feel some of it spatter, warm on his face.

"Mr Doran —"

Doran wheeled on him. "You *fucking* idiot. Keep your mouth *shut*."

He had said Doran's name, and it could not be unsaid. Gareth blinked and stood still, afraid to attract Doran's attention again. He had identified them all, and Doran's fury at him was transferred to the old man.

Doran turned back to the old man. "I asked you a question. Don't make me repeat myself."

Mr Orr spat on the floor at their feet, a gobbet of blood and saliva that turned Gareth's stomach.

"I took them to the shop." Although his voice shook, he looked Doran in the eye, contemptuous and angry. "They're in the vault."

Doran hit him again. "Wrong answer," he said. "Your vault is on a time lock. It won't allow you access till eight-thirty tomorrow morning. So. Where — are the stones?"

Doran asked that question again and again. Each repetition was followed by a blow with his gloved fist to the old man's face. The third blow broke the old man's finely chiselled nose.

The crunch of cartilage and the grunt of pain from the old jeweller were too much for Gareth. He felt like a dreamer who had woken from a nightmare to discover a massacre taking place in his home. He turned to flee, but Doran caught him and spun him around, pushing him down. He fell on his knees in front of Mr Orr and stayed there.

"Please," he begged. "Just tell him. For God's sake, just fucking *tell* him!"

The old man sobbed and shook his head. He heard Mrs Orr begin keening somewhere upstairs, then a slap, followed by silence.

The defence would point to the bloody hand-print on Gareth's jacket as evidence that he had not been alone in the Orr's house that night. But the jury was not convinced. They held Gareth responsible for what happened next.

Doran asked again, "Where are the stones?" And again. And again. And again. Each refusal to answer was punished by another blow to Mr Orr's face, until the old man couldn't have answered if he tried, because the blood filled his mouth, and the bruising was so severe he could not have formed the words. Gareth closed his eyes against the horror of it and covered his ears against the sound of fists on bloody flesh, but also against the awful coldness of that single, cold, repeated question.

He felt a sudden burst of pain in his leg. Doran had kicked him. He opened his eyes and brought his hands away from his ears.

"Get the wife," Doran said.

Gareth looked into Doran's face and saw ... nothing. He had thought that the face of evil would be furious, rabid, gleeful in its destructive rage. But looking into Doran's face he saw a total absence of feeling that chilled him more than rage or even insanity could.

They brought the old woman downstairs. She was in her nightdress and she looked tiny and incredibly frail. Gareth saw the fold of her gown tremble and he looked away, shamed by what he had witnessed, that he had come to this.

Doran stood in front of her husband, blocking her view until the last moment, then he stepped away. She groaned, sagging at the knees, then struggled to free herself from Warrender's grip. Gareth knew she wasn't trying to get away, only to reach her husband and help him.

Doran told Gareth to fetch another chair and they made her sit. Warrender stood behind her, his big hands on her narrow shoulders, and she fixed her eyes on her husband's face, her lips trembling, but a look of such determination on her face that Gareth was afraid for her.

Doran stood in front of her, his hands at his sides, and Gareth saw a drop of Mr Orr's blood fall from the tip of Doran's finger and splash onto the floor.

"Where . . ." he repeated for the last time, "are the stones?"

Gareth heard Mr Orr groan — or it might have been Gareth himself.

The old woman braced herself and Gareth looked at her, tears streaming down his face. "Please," he said. "He's . . . he'll . . ." He was afraid even to say it, now. He knew that Doran would kill them both, and he knew that it was his fault.

Her eyes turned briefly from her husband to Gareth and he saw fear for herself and pity for him.

Her cheekbone cracked under Doran's fist and her head snapped back. She slumped and Gareth covered his face, again, sobbing.

There was a silence, then Doran said softly, "Fuck."

Gareth felt himself being hauled to his feet. "Shut up," Doran said. His voice was devoid of all emotion.

Gareth wiped his face with the sleeve of his jacket and did as he was told.

"Neck's broken," Warrender said, trying to sound dispassionate, but Gareth saw that he was shaken.

A look passed between Doran and Warrender and it seemed they had come to an agreement. Doran dipped into his pocket and brought something out. At first, incongruously, Gareth thought it was a comb. Then he heard a click and a switch-blade flicked out.

"You first," Doran said, handing the knife to Gareth.

He stared at it in the palm of his hand: a bone-handled knife, antique, probably. It seemed sinister, monstrous. He stared at it and wondered how many lives it had taken. "N-no," he stuttered, offering it back to Doran. "I don't want it."

"I'm not *giving* it to you, moron," Doran said, with the same cold emptiness. He glanced at the old man. Mr Orr's breathing was harsh, stentorian. "You'll be doing him a favour," he said.

Gareth's eyes widened. "No," he said again. He wanted to say, This isn't me — this isn't who I am.

"You said my fucking *name*, you little prick," Doran said. "This is your fault. You're in this as much as we are."

Gareth shook his head. No. They could not make him do this. It didn't cross his mind to use the knife to protect himself, or the old man. He offered it again to Doran, and when he refused, Gareth placed the knife on the ground. Doran glanced at Warrender.

Gareth fell, lights flashing behind his eyes, his ears ringing. Warrender had punched him in the side of the head. Gareth curled into the foetal position, waiting for the kicking to start.

"Open your eyes," Doran said.

He curled tighter.

"Open your eyes you pathetic little shit."

Doran was holding a gun. He pointed it at Gareth's face.

"Now — pick up the knife."

It was a couple of feet away from him, the bone handle gleaming dully in the warm light of the hallway. He licked his lips. *Please, God, I don't want to die.* He told himself he would be a better man — make up for all the bad things he had done, if only they let him live. He didn't know how this would be achieved. Didn't really know what he meant by it. He couldn't think past the barrel of the gun in Doran's hand. But he knew, for the first time since he had been released from prison, that he wanted to live.

"I cut him," Gareth told her all those years after the terrible events of that night. "I cut Mr Orr. I told myself that Doran made me. I told myself I had no choice — that Doran was going to kill him anyway."

"'Do it', Doran said, and I thought, *Okay, I'll do it. See what I can do. Come near me, I'll do it to you, as well.* Once I started, I couldn't stop. I had the old man's blood on my clothes, in my hair — it was dripping off me, but I couldn't stop."

"He held a gun on you," Megan said. "You were out of your mind with fear —"

"God, I wish I could say that," he said. "I wish it was true. I wish I had been out of my mind, so I didn't have to remember what I did — didn't have to accept *responsibility* for what I did. But I knew what I was doing. I knew it was wrong. Those two years in the Youth Offenders' Institute tore something out of me. I don't know if I believe in the soul, but something *human* in me was gone, and I couldn't get it back."

"Gareth . . ." she said, trying to understand. But he didn't want that — didn't feel he deserved it.

"You know what terrified me? You know what made me give myself up to the police?"

"Guilt?" she said, and he had to look away; her trust was too painful to see.

"Out of guilt, yes, but also because of the rage I felt. When I cut that old man, I got back at everyone who ever hurt me. I got back at Dad, for not being there. At the system, for putting me away. At the lads who tormented and bullied me in that hell-hole. At the screws who let them, at Mum for being so damn helpless . . ." He hardened his voice so it wouldn't break. "At you, for needing me."

He saw the shock on her face and knew how much he had hurt her, but she had to know who he really was. "The rage didn't stop after I killed that man," he said. "It burned inside me, turning everything to ash. I didn't know what to do. And I was afraid of what I might do."

CHAPTER
FORTY

Rickman had waved Tanya and the boys off at six a.m. Tanya wanted to avoid the worst of the traffic on the M6 south. They had decided to visit her parents in Cornwall.

Fergus offered his hand. "Bye, Unc," he said, avoiding Rickman's eye. He had been badly frightened by Simon's outburst, and even now, Rickman sensed he was apprehensive.

Rickman dipped inside his jacket pocket. He had been dressed and ready for work for the past half hour. He handed Fergus one of his police business cards. "In case you need me," he said.

Fergus stared at the Merseyside Police Authority crest, then looked up into his uncle's face.

"That's the number for the Bat Cave," Rickman said, pointing to his mobile number.

Fergus smiled.

"It's always switched on."

"Batman — always on the job," the boy said, still smiling, running his finger over the embossed logo.

"So, whenever — okay?"

Fergus nodded, pocketing the card.

Tanya closed the tailgate of their hired SUV as Fergus climbed into the front passenger seat. "We'll call in before we leave the country," she promised.

Rickman nodded. "Don't worry. I'll take care of things this end."

Tanya slipped into his arms and he felt the contact like an electric shock. She kissed him lightly on the cheek. "Thank you," she whispered.

He checked all the doors and windows before leaving; the house felt empty, too full of echoes. She had promised to come back. This time. But how many times could he expect them to return? Simon had no use for them, and seeing him was damaging for Jeff junior and Fergus. He was fearful that next time, or the time after that, they would not return, and the prospect of losing them so soon after they had come into his life terrified him.

He put out word that he wanted everyone in for the morning briefing, and the Incident Room was packed end-to-end by eight-fifteen. The mood was very different from the day before: there was a buzz of excitement, and the fatigue that had infected the team the previous day was banished by energetic speculation and gossip. It seemed clear there must be new evidence. Tunstall was taking bets on a body having turned up.

"If there's a body, we'd have heard about it by now," Reid said.

"It's got to be a body," Tunstall insisted. "Why else would Tony Mayle be here?"

"I dunno." Reid shoved a stack of untidy paperwork to one side and staked his pitch on a desk near the back of the room. "His lot've been looking at Megan's computer, haven't they?"

Tunstall grunted, unconvinced. "Tony Mayle's the boss — he doesn't do house calls 'less it's for a body — and a fairly interesting one at that."

Foster passed him on the way to the tea table. "Nice one, mate," he said. "If you wait about thirty seconds you could say that to Rickman's face."

Tunstall flushed. "Oh, hell, I didn't mean —"

Foster moved on and Tunstall blundered off to find a quiet corner to sulk.

Naomi Hart was already brewing up, squeezing out a tea-bag before dropping it into the metal bin tucked away under the table. She looked rested and fit, her creamy skin suffused with healthy colour, her blonde hair twisted into an artfully careless knot. It shone lemon-gold in a narrow band of pale spring sunshine that sliced through one of the high windows.

"All right?" Foster said, by way of a friendly greeting.

"Pretty good," Hart said. "I had a very . . . entertaining evening."

Foster eyed her. "I grow on people."

"So does athlete's foot." A smile twitched at the corner of her mouth. "And anyway, Megan provided most of the entertainment."

Rickman called the briefing to order before Foster had the chance to reply.

"Let's get started." Rickman's voice carried clear and strong over the general chatter. "We've a lot to get through." Within seconds everyone was seated — or at least out of the line of view of their colleagues — and an expectant hush fell.

"Megan's real name is Ceri Owen. She has — or had — a brother, Gareth." There was a stirring of recognition from some of the older members of the team, and the name Gareth Owen became a murmured echo around the room. "She claims he's dead, but the night team has instigated a search: if he *is* dead, he almost certainly died in prison. We should have confirmation one way or the other before the end of this briefing."

"Where is Megan — um — Ceri?" Garvey corrected himself. "Did you locate her?"

"She located me," Foster said dryly. "Where she is now is anyone's guess. But she did give me her mobile number."

"Good of her," Garvey said.

"You have to remember, she's not under arrest," Rickman said. "We can't detain her if she refuses protection, and we can't compel her to tell us where she's living. Lee —" He stood aside and Foster stepped up, coffee mug still in hand.

"First off," he said, "I vote we carry on calling her Megan — I can't get my head round this new name." There were nods of approval, and Rickman agreed it would be simpler to stick with the name they knew.

Foster outlined the basic facts of his interview with Megan.

"She just showed up at your place?" Garvey sounded almost envious.

"It's my animal charm, Garve," Foster said. This caused a ripple of laughter.

"Whatever her reasons for approaching Foster," Rickman said, picking up the thread before people started to stray off-topic. "We've got a lot more background than we had twelve hours ago. We need to make the most of it."

Voce, gaunt and serious as always, asked, "Does that mean I'm off the oil rig enquiries, Boss?"

"Consider the rigs decommissioned for now."

Voce gave a wan smile.

"We need to concentrate on checking out Megan's story," Rickman went on. "If there is any evidence against Doran — we need to find it." Gareth Owen had done time, while Doran had prospered, and Rickman believed in natural justice.

"Why didn't the jewellers just tell Doran where the diamonds were?" Reid asked. He looked brighter this morning, Rickman noted: apparently Voce wasn't the only one cheered by the news that the rigs had been reassigned to low priority. "They must have been insured," Reid went on, "Why risk their lives?"

"They'd given the diamonds to their son for safe-keeping," Rickman said. "He lived about half a mile away in Caldy. The Orrs were afraid that Doran would go after their son.

"He went straight to the shop, as arranged, the next day. When his parents didn't show up, he went to investigate. He found the bodies — their own son — he walked in on a scene that must have looked like a bad day at an abattoir. Mr Orr had been stabbed and slashed twenty times peri- and post-mortem. His wife was stabbed five times, post-mortem."

There was a silence as the team absorbed this information.

"The court record shows that Gareth Owen claimed to have left the house empty-handed. But valuables and a small amount of cash from the safe were never found. Now, we have to bear in mind that all this is hearsay — and from an unreliable source, at that — but if Megan *is* telling the truth, the missing items could give us a way to prove Doran's involvement."

Foster held up a set of prints. "I've got photos and sketches of the stolen jewellery and a gold watch. I'll pin them on the board after."

"Why didn't Gareth just tell the police about Doran's involvement?" Reid asked.

"Megan says he did," Foster said. "But Doran and Warrender had airtight alibis. They said it was a grudge accusation from an embittered and frustrated kid. Both testified against him. Made it look like they had been investigating him within the firm. They had records of money going missing, break-ins at property protected by their security systems — they even used his hacking activities against him — kid didn't stand a chance."

"They got away with murder." Rickman looked at Reid, seated on one of the tables at the end of the room. He was still young enough to be shocked by the failures of the system.

"Warrender was rapped on the knuckles for moonlighting — he took early retirement just after the trial," Rickman said. "Doran was exonerated."

"There must've been blood everywhere," Garvey said. "How come forensics didn't find anything on them?"

"Mr Orr's blood was found on Gareth's clothing and under his fingernails — the DNA evidence was conclusive," Rickman said. "There was no physical evidence to link Doran and Warrender to the murders. But Gareth waited until the next day to turn himself in, which would have given Doran and Warrender plenty of time to clean up." He found Tony Mayle in the throng.

"Tony —" Mayle looked over at Rickman, waiting calmly for the DCI's question. "Could there be trace evidence present that wouldn't have shown up in the eighties?"

Mayle thought about it for a moment. "There's a possibility of transfer of skin cells from Doran's knuckles to Mr Orr —"

"Nah," Foster shook his head. "They were all wearing gloves."

"So how did Gareth get blood under his fingernails?" somebody asked.

Rickman looked to Mayle for an explanation.

"Trying to wash it off, most likely," Mayle said. "The natural response to so much blood is to strip off what you can and try to wash off the rest."

A spark of excitement in the Crime Scene Co-ordinator's eyes made Rickman say, "What?"

"Doran tied up Mr Orr?" Mayle asked.

Foster nodded.

"What did he use?"

"I don't get you."

"Rope or tape?" Mayle demanded with uncharacteristic urgency.

"Dunno, mate . . ." Foster glanced at Hart and she shrugged. "You'd have to check with the evidence store."

"Tape can be difficult to manage wearing gloves," Mayle explained. "So, they take their gloves off — leaving a nice crop of epithelials on the tacky side. If Doran did that —"

"It's been fifteen years," Foster said, doubtfully.

"Depends how the evidence was collected and stored — we didn't have the protocols then that we have now — but DNA is remarkably resilient," Mayle said, "and we can get a profile from a single cell using LCN. We stimulate the DNA present to replicate until we have enough to produce a DNA profile," he said, misreading Foster's baffled look. "— And you *really* aren't interested, are you?" he added, with a laugh.

"I'm interested," Foster said. "If it helps send Doran down, I'm interested."

"How long will it take? Rickman asked

"If we find what we need . . . It's a delicate process," Mayle admitted. "We would have to send the ligatures to the Forensic Science Service for analysis — it could take a while."

Rickman looked around the room. They were tired, but hyped — he saw eyes dimmed by overwork and lack of sleep, those that weren't glazed with exhaustion glittered with an unnatural, almost fevered, excitement. "If Megan's story is true," he told them, "the whole nature of this investigation has changed. We could be in for the long haul." A few shoulders sagged.

"Brace yourselves," he said, "But *pace* yourselves." He saw one or two nods; a few nervous glances from the younger members of the team. "We leave the Forensic Science Service to do their analysis. In the meantime we investigate Doran — see if we can find any cracks in his defences. Then, if the forensic evidence corroborates Megan's story, it'll be just one more strand in the case against Doran."

"What d'you want us to do, Boss?" Foster asked.

"Circulate pictures of the items stolen from the Orr's house — antiques dealers, pawn shops, whatever. Talk to contacts — it could be someone who was unwilling to talk fifteen years ago is more inclined to help us now. Find out anything you can about Megan's brother, Gareth. Talk to the investigating officers on the Orr murders — and I want to see the case file."

"Boss —" Tunstall's voice boomed out over the buzz of approval of this rallying speech. "I've been thinking, Boss," Tunstall said.

Reid jumped up and offered his place to Tunstall. "You have it, mate," he said, with fake concern. "You don't want to overdo it."

Tunstall glared at him. "You're a cheeky perisher, Reidy."

"Let's have your thoughts," Rickman said, deadpan over the muted jeers and laughter of the team.

Tunstall was nothing if not robust. "Megan says she wants justice for Sara." He said, tearing his attention with some reluctance from Reid, who had returned to his seat and was trying to control a fit of laughter. "Way I see it, Boss," Tunstall went on, doggedly, "this was never about Sara. It's about revenge for her brother. I bet she's been after Doran since she was a kid."

"Fair point," Foster said. "But Megan claims she was sent away during the trial. The first she heard about what he'd been banged up for was when her schoolmates started having a go at her in the playground."

A fax machine whirred into life on the desk next to Hart and she angled her head, trying to read the text as it slid out from the rollers.

"Megan and her mother moved away and she says her mum never talked about her brother after that," Foster said.

"Makes no odds *when* she decided to have a go," Garvey chipped in. "She'd want to get back at Doran sometime or other."

"She says she didn't even know the name of his firm," Foster said. "He changed the name after the trial — mud sticks and all that."

"So why'd she come to Liverpool?"

"I dunno —" Foster raised his voice a little, exasperated. "The vibrant night life? The footie? The fabulous waterfront? I can think of a million reasons."

"It's a question worth examining," Rickman said. "We've no reason to believe she's telling us the truth." Rickman thought he understood Megan's desire for anonymity, but he wondered at the casual lies, the fabrication and sloughing off of identities. Perhaps it

379

was all about control: she wrote her own narrative, and in doing so, rewrote her past.

"She was setting Mrs Doran up for a two hundred-pound scam for nearly two weeks," Foster said, his impatience getting the better of him. "Why bother with two hundred quid, when she could have over a million? Fact is, Megan didn't even know she was talking to Patrick Doran's wife till Fay Doran mentioned his business in one of her emails."

Rickman frowned. Could Foster hear himself? *"Megan says"*, *"Megan didn't know"*? Defending her — speculating on her motivation?

"But what makes you think Megan's telling you the truth?" Garvey insisted.

"She's lying."

Everyone turned to Hart. She held the sheet of fax paper in her hand, and she looked almost as shell-shocked as Foster. "This fax is from HMP Manchester. Megan's brother is alive. He's currently working out a twenty-year term for the double murders of Mr and Mrs Orr."

Foster frowned. His lips formed a question, but he didn't utter it, and Rickman called the team to order to distract attention from his friend. "On-going matters," he said. "Bentley has gone to ground. He hasn't reported for work, hasn't been back to his flat. His car was found on the car park at King's Dock — wheel clamped. It's been there for twenty-four hours or more. He hasn't contacted his dear old mother and get this — she's upset because they argued about some photos she picked up for him from the local chemist."

It took a moment for the possible significance of this to sink in. Once it did, there was a mutter of interest from the team. *First objective achieved.* Foster had evidently been shaken by the revelation that Megan had lied to him, and Rickman owed him this and much more for the times his friend had covered for him. *Now we just have to bag and tag Doran,* he thought, *and I'll be happy.*

"Does she know what was on the pictures?" Hart asked.

"She says not, but I'd like someone to go and interview her. She hasn't seen him since she gave him the prints."

CHAPTER
FORTY-ONE

Lee Foster clattered down the concrete stairs at the back of Edge Hill Police Station, with Rickman's advice still ringing in his ears. "Don't make the mistake of identifying too closely with Megan, just because you have some shared experiences."

Too late for that. She'd played him like a fish on a line. It hurt his pride more than his feelings — or so he told himself. His first task of the day was to interview Bentley's mother, but another took priority. He sat in his car and keyed the fast-dial for Megan's cellphone.

"You're a bloody liar, Megan — Ceri — whatever the hell your name is. You played me like one of your marks, and I —" He stopped himself in time: *and I believed in you. Is that what you were going to say? Bloody hell, Lee — how old are you?*

There was a pause, then he heard Megan's warm, slightly accented voice. "Good morning, Sergeant Foster."

"Don't piss me about," he said. "You made me look like a tit. I can't *believe* I defended you in front of my boss and thirty other officers."

"Including DC Hart, I take it?"

"*Hart?*" Foster raised his voice, but it was muffled by the car's sound-proofing. "What the hell has Hart got to do with it?"

Another pause, then she laughed softly. "Don't be coy, Sergeant."

He covered the mouthpiece and said, "*Fuck*," softly. Was it that obvious?

"If you were a mark, I'd make you explain why you're so upset — so I was sure what it is I need to defend or invent or deny. But you're *not* a mark, and I'm not 'playing' you," she said. "I'm assuming you've checked my story and found Gareth." She paused. "My brother is alive. But far from well. The last time I saw Gareth, he looked like an old man. He might not be dead yet, but it's only a matter of time."

"It's only a matter of time for all of us," Foster said. "Don't try that double-speak with me. I was educated by Jesuits."

"Gareth has Hepatitis C," she said, her voice calm and clear. "His liver is swollen to twice its normal size. He's dying."

Foster took a couple of breaths. "If this is more of your crap —"

"It's a matter of medical record," she said. "He's dying. But he's been dead ever since they murdered that poor man and his wife. He —"

Foster interrupted before she could say any more. "Don't bother getting all revved up for the big sob story," he said. "I'll call you back when I've checked the facts." He broke the connection, fuming, partly swayed by the emotion in her voice and cursing himself for an idiot for having allowed her to get to him again. He made a quick call to the Incident Room and gave instructions, then turned the car out of the car park in the direction of Walton.

Megan had made him look a pillock in front of the entire team. He recalled how lightly Megan had flattered and flirted, and how easily he had fallen for it, and he burned at the memory.

"Bloody hell, Foster," he groaned, accelerating through the lights and almost hitting the back of a post office van, pulling in at a sub post office. He braked hard, swerved and moved on.

The shops were just opening for business on Townsend Lane. A florist moved tiered stands onto the pavements and stacked them with buckets of flowers: grandstands of primary spring colours — irises, daffodils and tulips — others he couldn't name. Tile shops and kitchen cabinet makers occupied premises that used to be tenanted by cut-price grocers and discount clothing stores — "Cash for vouchers" on notices in their windows.

Foster had left Liverpool at sixteen and vowed never to return. That was at the end of the eighties. The Militant Tendency had been kicked off the city council, two major riots had ravaged Toxteth and unemployment was tearing down the very fabric of Merseyside's economy.

He did come back, on compassionate leave, in 'ninety-seven, when his mother got sick for the last time. He left the marines and built a new career in the police. He told himself it was just for a year or two, until she was on her feet, but he had stayed on after she died. He found he liked the new clubs that had sprung up around the city — liked the buzz, the noise of building work a constant in the city centre. Surprised, also, to find that he liked the feel of solid ground; the river was close enough and wide enough so that he didn't feel hemmed in, and the sense of belonging that had once been a burden came to be a comfort. Strange, now that he had no family ties in the city.

He drove past the narrow strip of garden, planted for the Victorian merchant house-owners on the edge of Newsham Park. Lawns and shrubberies acting as a fire-break between the wealthy middle-class homes and the smaller, more pinched properties on the other side of Shiel Road.

A few miles on, he drove down Priory Road, which separated Anfield Cemetery and Stanley Park. The wind was in the wrong direction today and the stench of the meat-rendering factory hung over the faded blue roof of the stands at Goodison.

He saw Kieran Jago's logo on a shop sign between an empty shop-front and an estate agent's office. Jago's firm had thirty branches in all, with two or three solicitors acting out of each office, another fifteen at his headquarters in town; so he asked himself again, why had Jago taken on Bentley — represented him personally? He understood why Bentley wanted Jago: he was the best, and everyone wanted the man himself. Scally car thieves or white-collar fat cats caught with their hands in the till, they all wanted Kieran Jago.

Because he was the best. But why would Jago be even remotely interested in a loser like Bentley?

Doran was the common factor. It was the only explanation that made sense. That being the case, why had Jago come to the police when Bentley disappeared? He seemed genuinely concerned for Bentley. *And your judgement is really spot on right now, isn't it, mate?* he thought. Well, maybe it wasn't, but there was no denying Jago had been quick off the mark. He must be used to his clients jumping bail from time to time — probably even had contingency plans to track them down before the cops cottoned on.

So, Foster thought, *What makes this one so different? The man who was paying the bill, maybe?* He imagined that Doran would be the first person Jago told about Bentley's disappearance. Had Doran seemed less than heartbroken at the waste of his money? Jago, of all people, must have some idea just how far Doran would be willing to go to protect himself.

He scooted left on Queens Drive and found the sharp turn off the roundabout at Rice Lane. Concealed under the ugly concrete of the flyover, only locals, postal workers and cops knew this entrance into Walton Hall Park. So many parks. It hadn't seemed so when he was a kid: the Liverpool he remembered, before his spell in Black Wood, was grey and weary and dusty.

The Bentleys' house overlooked the park. It wouldn't be long before spiralling prices and the chance to make a killing persuaded the owners to sell. Solid Edwardian, open parkland to the rear, close to arterial roads and convenient to the city centre: they were fast becoming prime property — fortunes had been made on houses like this in recent years.

He pulled up outside a well-maintained house with a door so pristinely white it could only be uPVC. The front door opened almost as he rang the doorbell. Mrs Bentley was small and neat, a human reflection of the house in which she lived. Her hair, though grey, was styled into a fashionably short cut and she wore discreet makeup.

"Have you found him?" she asked, slightly breathless, as if she had run to the door.

"Found who?"

The hint of anxiety was replaced by irritation. "You are the police, aren't you?"

Foster caught a glimpse of steeliness that warned him that this was a woman not to be messed with; the kind of Liverpool matriarch that had fed and clothed their families by working two or three part-time jobs when their men could find none.

"DS Lee Foster," he said, showing his warrant card. "No, I'm sorry Mrs Bentley, we haven't found him, yet."

Something crumpled in the woman's face. Her hand went to her mouth and she made a sound somewhere between a gasp and a sob.

"Let's go inside, love." The endearment broke protocols instructing respectful forms of address, but Foster knew she would respond.

She nodded, still with a hand to her face, and turned. He gave her time to collect herself, which she did by making tea and showing him through to the

387

sitting-room at the back of the house. The back garden was tiny, walled in on three sides, no more than two strips of soil either side of a path to the back gate. But the borders were massed with lemony primroses and stiff spikes of plump grape hyacinths, tangled with the hairy stems of poster-red and violet-blue anemones. She had tubs and containers, window boxes and hanging baskets in tiers of colour that reminded him of the florist's shop on Townsend Lane.

"How do you think I can help?" she asked, placing a neatly laid tray of tea and biscuits on a table and handing him a cup. She seemed calmed by the ritual of preparation and caring for her guest.

"You know the photos you mentioned," he said. "We talked to the chemist and he said Jake didn't react well when he thought they'd lost them."

She gave him a sharp look. "I haven't got them, if that's what you think."

"No," Foster said, quick to reassure her. "Of course not." He guessed that Mrs Bentley was like many of her class who had never done a dishonest thing in her life — sensitive to even a whiff of suspicion.

"I gave him the pictures as soon as he got here."

"And he was still . . . upset?" What the pharmacist had said was that Bentley had been aggressive and threatening, but it wouldn't help to tell Mrs Bentley that.

"He said they were important."

"Did he say why?" She seemed uncertain and he added gently, "You must be worried sick, him going off like this —"

"That's the *point!*" she exclaimed. "He wouldn't *do* that — he wouldn't go off — not without telling me."

Foster nodded, sympathising. "That's why we need to know more about the pictures."

She nursed her cup, half-turned towards the window, watching the sun chase across the narrow strip of garden, lighting the flowers in a mosaic of colour. "He's always been a solitary boy," she said. "Likes his privacy. That's why he got upset over the pictures — he says an artist doesn't share his work with anyone until it's perfect."

Foster guessed that Bentley hadn't told his mother about his illegal activities with his "art". "Is he any good?" he asked.

"Hard to say," she said, with the merest hint of annoyance at her son's secrecy.

Foster grinned. "It'd drive me up the wall — I'd be sneaking a sly squint at them, given half the chance."

Mrs Bentley stared at him for longer than was comfortable.

"That's why people don't trust the police, Sergeant," she said with a look that put him in no doubt that his megawatt smile was wasted on her. "I cleaned empty offices stuffed with secrets for thirty years and *never* felt tempted."

Foster left the house feeling like he had been hoisted physically from his chair by the scruff of his neck and booted out of the door.

He smiled to himself, perversely cheered by the exchange. Old women and young girls — opposite ends of the spectrum. Neither responded to his charm. He knew it, but could never resist trying anyway. His cell-phone rang as he fired the ignition. It was the Incident Room. He listened in silence for a few moments, then pressed the "end call" key and rang Megan.

"You pass," he said. "This time. End-stage cirrhosis of the liver."

"I'm so pleased to set your mind at rest," she said, coolly, but she couldn't disguise the slight edge of anger in her voice.

"There I go again," Foster said, with sincere regret. "Putting my big foot in it. I didn't know you two were close."

"I've only seen him twice since he was sent to prison, but we were. We were close," she repeated softly.

Foster made a mental note to find out exactly when she made the visits.

"Gareth looked after me, when our father died," she went on. "Mum couldn't cope. The Gareth I knew as a child was kind and gentle and caring — he saw that I was fed and clothed, remembered birthdays and thought up ideas for treats. Then he went into the youth offenders' unit, and it was like someone had flicked a switch."

"But he's been in prison, what — nearly fifteen years?" Foster said. "Why the sudden concern?" He sucked air through his teeth. "Sorry — I didn't mean that to sound so —"

"Brutal?" She laughed softly. "It's all part of your dubious charm, Sergeant." She left a couple of seconds' silence, then he heard her sigh. "I tried to make contact with Gareth in prison, but he wouldn't see me — never replied to my letters. So I got on with my life, earned a living."

"Yeah, robbing people blind."

"Bad blood, Sergeant." He heard the smile in her voice. "You know, I really *didn't* know who Fay Doran was when I first got her order. When I snouted around a bit in her computer files and found Doran's firm, I was shocked — stunned, even. And of course I wanted to do something for Gareth. The detention centre took away some of my brother's humanity, but Doran finished him for good. Gareth didn't stand a chance once Doran got hold of him."

"So it *is* about revenge," Foster said, thinking of Tunstall's remarks in the briefing.

"Not revenge," she said "Justice. For Gareth, for Mr and Mrs Orr, for Sara — and who knows how many others? Men like Doran don't stop — ever."

He wished he could see her face. "What do you want, Megan?"

"An admission of guilt. I want him to admit to me that he killed Mrs Orr. I want him to admit that he beat Mr Orr to the point of death. I want to hear it from Patrick Doran that he incited my brother to murder."

"And how d'you think you'll get him to do that?" he asked, hearing the emotion in her voice, knowing for sure that in this, at least, she was sincere. "He may be a Catholic, but I'd bet a year's salary he's never even confessed it to his priest." He recalled their earlier conversation and said, "You and Gareth are plotting something, aren't you?"

"I told you," she said, "I've only seen him twice since he went to prison."

She didn't say they weren't plotting, though, he thought. "He coached you, didn't he?" Foster said. She didn't answer and he kept pushing, determined to get one — one that he could at least half-believe. "The stuff you passed on to the Met, stealing Doran's cash, planting the logic bomb in your computer — that was all down to Gareth, wasn't it?"

"It's a lot to get through in two forty-minute visits," she said.

Foster smiled to himself. "But when you told him who you wanted to shaft, I'll bet he found a way. Email, chat rooms, instant messaging — there must be a dozen different ways — I'll bet you learn fast."

Megan laughed, and there was real delight in it. "I'm not the only one," she said.

Foster left a silence, then said, "Well?"

Another laugh, subdued and self-deprecatory, this time. "He wouldn't help me with Doran," she said. "Told me to stay the hell away from him."

Foster was sceptical. "The Fraud Squad reckoned you were just a talented amateur before this lot."

"*Amateur*," she repeated. "I might have to make them regret saying that."

"How come you got all hi-tech and Mastermind if Gareth wasn't helping you?"

"Gareth tracked my activities after he told me to lay off Doran. I suppose next to him, I *was* an amateur. He got in touch — actually, he took control of my entire damn computer — put this ugly great fire-breathing dragon up on my screen. I thought I was going to have a heart attack. Then, *he* was there — Gareth — his face, anyway. He'd managed to set up a live link: don't ask me how he got the hardware — I still don't know, but that's my Gareth, always resourceful." Her voice sounded watery, close to tears.

"And he said he'd help."

He heard a choked sound, somewhere between a laugh and a sob. "He said I was going to wind up in prison." She paused a moment. "What was it *he* called me? A clueless wannahack, leaving a cyber-trail so wide he could follow it blindfold in the dark. He told me to leave it alone, or he'd shut me down. I said I'd go and buy another computer, start with a new identity. I'm afraid I played the guilt card — I wasn't about to stop, so he had no choice."

"I *knew* it." Foster slapped the steering wheel in triumph.

"Just so you're clear, it was under duress," she said. "He'd have made a cracking teacher, though." Unexpectedly, her voice broke, and she coughed, clearing her throat. "The upshot? I'm getting better at this all the time."

Foster sighed. "You know we can't let you do whatever you're planning with Doran. Even if he trusted you, my boss wouldn't risk a civilian being hurt in a sting operation like you're proposing."

"You're not calling the shots," she said.

"Look, you said yourself, there could be others on Doran's casualty list. He's not gonna think twice about adding you to it."

"So, I'll have to be smarter than he is."

"Bloody hell . . ." he breathed. He remembered the worried look on Mrs Bentley's face when she said, "*He wouldn't do that — he wouldn't go off — not without telling me*"; and he was finally convinced that Bentley's mother and Jago could be right — that something bad had happened to Bentley.

"Sara's stalker?" he said, knowing he shouldn't be talking about this to a civilian, especially not to Megan Ward.

"Bentley. What about him?"

"He's gone missing."

"Doran?" she said, at once.

"I don't know — maybe. The thing is, I don't want you taking any stupid chances."

"So you won't help me?"

"We can't — he's too —"

"I don't care about the police," she interrupted. "I asked you. Won't you help me?"

"I can't. Megan, I'm sorry —" But she had already gone.

CHAPTER
FORTY-TWO

The twins were fractious; the natural consequence of a difficult few days and a weekend treat of burgers and cola at McDonald's. Declan had taken Frankie's Game Boy and Frankie was demanding it back. "It's mine!" he yelled. "Give it back!"

His brother mimicked him, dancing and dodging just out of reach and Frankie turned to his mother to arbitrate. "*Mum!*"

Fay Doran sighed. "Give your brother his Game Boy," she said.

Declan got in a couple more feints before handing it over. "You're rubbish, anyway."

"*You're* rubbish!" Frankie shouted back, his face red, his hands balled into fists.

"That's *enough*," Fay said.

"Rubbish," Declan muttered as one last parting shot. "Am *not*."

"Right," Fay said. "Go to your room."

"But *Mum*," Frankie complained, wide-eyed with the injustice of it, "he called me rubbish."

"I will not act as negotiator in your little war," she said, firmly, hearing her own mother's intonation and even (God help her), the very words her mother would

395

use when she and her brothers and sisters had pushed the boundaries too far. The boys looked at each other, appalled at being banished, each hating the other for having caused their banishment.

Fay watched them slouch out of the room, uttering dire threats against each other from the corner of their mouths. Maura was on the way in and she held the door open, letting them walk under her arm. A look of understanding passed between the girl and her mother, a moment for which Fay was disproportionately grateful.

"What's up with Jekyll and Hyde?" Maura said.

"They're both after being Hyde," Fay replied. She glanced at her husband, who seemed to be oblivious to the noise and argument.

The trouble was, they had all been affected by Patrick's mood. Maura became especially affectionate, bringing him cups of tea and kissing his brow as if he were an invalid; the boys, confused by the tension in the air, mistook it for bad feeling, absorbed it like little sponges and took their aggression out on each other. Fay remained quiet and watchful, keeping the boys out of his way and making sure he ate regularly. Occasionally, she would brush her hand against his, or squeeze his arm in passing. Sometimes he would return the gesture, sometimes not, but he would always make eye contact, to let her know that they were okay, that he had ceased to blame her.

Fay contented herself with this as she watched Patrick toy with the shepherd's pie she had made, trying to tempt him to eat with his favourite meal. He separated the mashed potato from the meat, as if searching for something.

The phone rang and Doran clattered his fork against his plate. Maura sprang to the phone on the kitchen wall. "Probably Gray," she said, then chirruped, "Doran residence." She sounded confident and happy, and Fay felt a pang of anxiety for her daughter. Maura might be perverse and obstinate, but Fay recognised the underlying insecurity she herself had experienced as a teenager. She would rather have died than admit that she was lonely and frightened when she first came to England, and Maura was the same, pretending that everything was fine, that the storm cloud that seemed to gather over their house was no more than a passing shower, that Daddy was just over-worked. Maura had never had a money worry in her life and Fay, who had grown up poor and got out early, wanted desperately to protect her daughter from the privations she had endured. Fay had been forced by circumstances to make the transition from girl to woman too fast, and she wanted things to be different for Maura.

Maura chatted happily for a minute or two, and Doran went back to his food, taking a forkful into his mouth and chewing mechanically.

"For you, Dad," she said, holding the phone out to him.

Doran frowned. "Who is it?"

"Megan . . . someone."

He stood, scraping his chair loudly on the tiles. His face was white and Fay recognised both anger and fear in his expression.

"I'll take it in my study," he said.

Maura held the receiver in her hand, looking puzzled and a little frightened. "Daddy?" she said.

He walked out without looking at either of them, and Fay took the receiver, closing her palm over the mouthpiece and slipping her free arm around her daughter's shoulders. "It'll be fine," she said, her voice warm and soft.

She listened until she heard her husband pick up the phone in his study.

"Ward?" he said. "What the hell —"

Fay quietly replaced the receiver. She didn't want to know. Did *not* want to know.

"What the hell did you say to my daughter?" Doran demanded.

"Nothing, Mr Doran." Megan Ward sounded shocked, a little breathy. "Idle chat — girl talk — that's all."

"You do not speak to my family. Are we clear?"

"Yes," she said. "Yes — I — I'm sorry."

He took a moment to get his own breathing under control.

"I wanted to explain to you about yesterday —"

"You set me up," he said, "and you want to *explain*?"

"I didn't — I didn't set you up, I swear, Mr Doran. I wanted to make the meet. They stopped me."

"They?"

"The police."

"Why should I believe you?"

"Because I'm telling you the *truth*."

"What do they want?"

"I don't know." She was havering now, he could hear it in her voice.

"You're lying. The police show up, you don't. There's got to be a reason." Did they know about Bentley? Had the double-dealing bastard given the police copies of the photographs outside Sara Geddes's house?

"They don't tell me anything," she insisted. "I'm just a scammer they've got over a barrel."

"D'you think I came over on the last ferry?"

"No, Mr Doran." She seemed to be struggling to find the right words. "Look — I'm guessing, but I'd say they were onto your tax . . . stuff."

Doran sat, lowering himself carefully into his chair. This was one of those good news/bad news scenarios: the good news — that the police didn't know about his involvement in the Geddes woman's death and Bentley's disappearance. The bad news — they probably knew that he owed a couple of millions in back-taxes. Did they know about the insurance accounts? Did they know just how much Ward had stolen from him?

"Have you been talking, Megan?" His voice was syrupy.

"No — God, no!" Her breathing sounded tremulous and watery. "Mr Doran, I just want my life back."

"So we do have something in common, after all."

"I'm way out of my league," she went on. "I wanted — I want to give it all back."

His heart skipped a beat. But even as the adrenalin surged into his bloodstream, he noticed she was avoiding saying outright what she intended. *"Give 'it' back"*, she had said. *"Tax stuff."*

"Can we talk freely?" he asked.

"I don't know." She sounded both weary and excitable, almost feverish with terror and very close to breakdown. "I *told* you —" she insisted. "They don't tell me anything."

Okay . . . he thought. *Okay . . .* The adrenaline still fizzed in his system, and with it, a tiny glimmer of optimism.

"The tax man can be very . . . accommodating, so I've heard," she said, as though she had read his thoughts. "The bigger the sum, the more accommodating he can be. You must know that."

Of course he did. He read the financial pages of the newspapers: forward tax contracts with the Inland Revenue had effectively allowed the wealthy to operate outside the tax system for years, but it looked like those days were gone. He shook his head impatiently. He was getting way ahead of himself: the important thing was to get the money back and worry later about how to avoid the tax man getting his hands on it. Jago would know a corporate tax lawyer, someone who could minimize the damage.

"You want your life back?" he said.

"Yes."

"Then I want all of it."

"Every last penny." She sounded fervent; he could almost picture her with her hand on her heart. He let her sweat a little while.

"When I see full restoration, you're off the hook."

She gave a grateful sob.

"But —"

Fuck. "But — *what?*"

"A certain department is all over your network like a bad dose of MRSA."

"Don't do this," he said. "Don't piss me off, Megan."

"I'm not messing with you, I swear. Look, why don't you check with your computer experts and I'll call back."

The line went dead and Doran stared at the receiver. His scalp felt tight, as though his brain had swollen, pressing against the plates of his skull, and stretching the skin, till it felt like a ripe tomato, threatening to split. *She hung up. Suffering God, the bitch hung up on me!* What if she didn't call back? What if she vanished for ever with his money? If he failed Fay and Maura and the boys ... "Oh, God," he groaned, replacing the receiver and putting his head in his hands. His face felt cold and damp with sweat. He clutched his hair, tugging it at the roots, desperate to feel something other than this mind-searing terror.

"No," he told himself. "Don't you fucking give up now, Patrick." He had tackled hard men, who tried to muscle in on his turf, scallies sneaking onto his sites to steal building materials and heavy plant machinery. He had seen off the competition, both legitimate and gang-financed. He had faced a murder prosecution and got off free and clear; he had clawed back from the losses of the stock market collapse in the mid nineties, and he would *not* be bested by a fucking *woman*.

He inhaled and wiped the sweat from his face. He would not fail. It became a mantra. Failure was not an option.

David Manning was working late, as he had done since Doran brought him in to sort out the mess Nathan Wilde had left. When Doran phoned, the technical forensics expert was installing firewalls, prior to reinstating records, checking programs line by line for viruses and God alone knew what else.

"How's it going?" he asked. He knew he sounded strained, but he was counting on Manning putting it down to the general screwed-up state of his business.

"We're getting there, Mr Doran." He sounded as calm and unruffled as he always did.

There was an awkward pause, Doran not sure how to ask what he needed to know without telling Manning he had defrauded the Inland Revenue, and that he thought the Fraud Squad were after him. "Good," he said. "Great."

"Was there something specific?" Manning asked.

"No, not specific . . . um, actually —" Doran laughed, hating the nervousness in it. "It's rather a vague enquiry. Have you noticed any . . . unusual activity?"

"Warlock?" Manning said, suddenly sharp.

"Or anything of that sort." There was another pause, this one pregnant with significance.

"We have had a rather persistent visitor — he comes in by a back door, has a rummage around, then drops off the radar before we can trace him."

"Bloody hell, Manning — you're supposed to be locking these bastards out!"

"As I explained," Manning said, his voice calm and conciliatory, without for one moment sounding apologetic, "we're getting there, but Warlock created so many points of access that your system, in layman's terms, is leaking like a colander. We have to find each hole in turn and plug it. You'll have to accept a certain level of insecurity until we find all the back doors."

Doran almost laughed. He had been living with the worst kind of insecurity ever since he found out that his money had been stolen.

"I have somebody working on the sub-routine that opened the hatches, so to speak," Manning went on. "She's almost cracked it. When she does, we will be able to block the virus that let Warlock in."

"Can't you just de— ..." Doran found that he didn't have the right terms in his lexicon. "I don't know — de-bug the system, or inoculate, or whatever you call it?"

"Warlock has created a virus that modifies itself from time to time, as it replicates," Manning said. "Just as a real virus mutates and stays a step ahead of our immune systems. Effectively, we *do* need an inoculum — something that will recognise parts of the virus program that remain unchanged and will disable it before it has the chance to attack your network. Which is why we need to understand the program so that we can lock it down."

Doran waited for Megan's return call with an even stronger determination to find her and pay her back in slow, exquisite stages for what she had done to him.

The phone rang within thirty seconds of him having hung up, and he got the creepy feeling that maybe she had been listening in on his call to Manning.

"Somebody's been poking around," he said, determined not to let her have the first word. "But who's to say that isn't you?"

"Me?" Her voice went up an octave. "D'you think I'm crazy?"

"Do *you* think I'm stupid?" His voice was a low growl. He heard her breathing and liked the sound — shallow, and scared.

"If I thought that," she said, "I wouldn't be talking to you, now. I'd be in South America, or Mexico, living the high life."

Doran thought about it: he didn't know where she was; she had his money, and yet she was still around, still trying to bargain with him. So, maybe his reputation did count for something.

"Anyway," she added, apparently unable to bear his silence, "— even if you don't trust me —"

"Oh, I don't," he interrupted.

She went quiet for a moment and he had a mental image of her biting her lip nervously. "You don't have to trust my word to see that the police are taking an interest in you," she said, after he allowed the silence to stretch a little longer.

"True enough," he said, "I've seen the evidence with my own eyes."

"So the worst possible thing would be to move the . . . to ship the — items into existing . . . storage units."

God she's crap at this! He decided to play along. "Okay," he said. "Leave it where it is. Give me the access codes, passwords — what have you."

"Fine. That's a great idea." She sounded hugely relieved and Doran was perversely suspicious. "I'll send them by courier — I guarantee you'll have them within the hour."

She was talking too fast, sounded too glib.

"You're giving me your guarantee?" he said. "You gave my wife your guarantee — and that ended well, didn't it?"

"But —" *Please*, he thought, *don't insult me by sounding offended*. "I — *really* I don't want any more trouble," she stammered. "You can trust me, I swear."

That settled it. "Sure I can," he said. "When I have everything in my hand: cash, codes, passwords, print-outs, disks, copies of any documentation."

"Documentation?"

"You trashed my computer system, stole my money, fucked up my life — are you expecting me to believe you didn't steal sensitive documents and files?"

"You'll have them," she said, meekly. "Within the hour."

"Delivered by you."

There was a shocked silence.

"My security specialist will check everything is in order," he said. "And as soon as I have clearance from

405

him, you can go. Of course, if there's even a whiff of something rotten, you'll be standing right in front of me, so we can sort out any . . . shortfall there and then."

"Please, I —" Her voice took on a whining, tearful tone.

"You want your life back?" he said. "Those are my terms."

CHAPTER
FORTY-THREE

Foster arrived in the Incident Room at seven p.m., straight from a management meeting with Rickman, in preparation for the briefing. The Fraud Squad were concerned that their surveillance of Doran's network had been discovered, and there was a high probability of vital evidence being destroyed. They would move in on Doran's office at four a.m. in a joint strike with the Fraud Squad, get what they could from documentary evidence, see if they could make a deal with Warrender.

Megan's brother had refused to speak to them, but Rob Voce had tracked down his solicitor, who had agreed to an interview. The forensic evidence from the case had been preserved, but not in ideal conditions, and Tony Mayle feared that the samples had deteriorated too much to yield anything useful. He sent them to the Forensic Science Service, anyway: articles of blood-spattered clothing; the murder weapon; the duct tape that had been used to bind Mr Orr. It could take a month for the results to come through; because of the poor state of the evidence and the possibility of contamination, Rickman had assigned it low priority.

Foster watched the steady drift of people into the room with a sick feeling of inevitability. An early arrest meant they wouldn't get Doran on the major charges — certainly not on Sara's murder. Jeff Rickman was hopeful that they might still get something useful from the DNA evidence relating to the Orr murders, but Foster, for once, was pessimistic.

It had rained all morning and into the afternoon; cold hard drops, as big as pennies. The sky, grey and dark, seemed to loom just above the rooftops, sullen and heavy. The River Mersey turned dun-coloured under the cloud cover, as brown and muddy as the water that sluiced off the building sites in the city centre and silted up the sewers.

The team worked through it, turning up their coat collars and running to or from their cars, shaking the rain from their clothing before stepping into houses. Any who had the option concentrated on office work, sweating over reports or making one call after another, enquiring further into Doran's past, into the circumstances of Warrender's early retirement, and Gareth Owen's prosecution and imprisonment.

At two p.m. the rain slowed to a drizzle, and by three, it had stopped altogether. This was noted only by the unfortunate and unimaginative who had been unable to find an excuse to remain indoors. In the grey surroundings of the ill-lit Incident Room, the late show of April sunshine went unremarked; people kept their heads down and amassed names and dates, possible interview subjects, sources of information, banking them for action when they had more energy.

Mostly, they worked quietly, only a murmur of voices in telephone conversation, or officers in twos or threes, taking a short break to make coffee or tea. At the tea table, chat was directed away from the enquiry: Liverpool's home game, their position in the league, a comedy show somebody had seen on TV. Nobody felt like talking about the enquiry, because nobody wanted to admit that it had stalled.

Megan Ward had been their best link to Doran, but with Megan out of the equation, all they had was a little over a million-and-a-quarter of Doran's money, which he seemed reluctant even to admit was his, let alone collect.

The evening briefing was due to start at seven-thirty and the room was beginning to fill. Garvey was among the first, carrying a lightweight plastic bag containing a tray of takeaway food. He found an empty desk and plonked himself into the chair with a sigh, opened the container and savoured the aroma, then began forking the food into his mouth, a serene look on his face, as though he was listening to his own personal celestial choir. Foster didn't know how he could do it — shut out the noise and growing clamour of the place.

Reid swooped down on Tunstall who had just unwrapped a steaming portion of pie and chips, stealing a few chips and moving on fast, before Tunstall could grab him. "You bloody gannet!" Tunstall yelled through a mouthful of food. "Buy your own!"

"Keep it down, you two," Foster warned. "This isn't play-school."

He sensed Hart, off to his left, but avoided looking in her direction. He couldn't stand to see triumph — or worse, sympathy — in her eyes.

Reid made another swoop, but Tunstall was ready, swivelling his chair and guarding his food like a dog with a bone. Reid persisted until Foster raised his voice.

"Are you two deaf?" he said. "You'd do better sorting out the mess on your desks. Reid, you've been skiving indoors all day, haven't you?"

"Not skiving, Sarge," Reid said.

"Well, whatever you call it, you've had plenty of chance to sort out this crap." Foster lifted a newspaper and sweet wrapper and fanned a number of unfiled reports that lay hidden beneath.

"Sarge," Reid said, and began sifting through the mess.

Foster moved on, prowling the jumble of desks and peering over shoulders.

"He's in a bit of a strop, i'n't he?" Tunstall said. "Who's rattled his cage?"

Reid glowered in Foster's direction, as he threw the newspaper and wrapper in the bin. "Multiple Megan, who d'you think?"

Tunstall laughed. "*Multiple Megan*," he repeated. "Nice one, Reidy. He really fell for it, didn't he? Reckon he's losing his touch with the ladies?" He spoke a little too loudly, underestimating the carrying power of his Widnesian boom.

Foster turned. "You what?" he demanded.

Tunstall turned bright red. "Just saying — we'll soon catch up with the latest," he said, while Reid crouched behind his computer monitor, stifling a fit of laughter.

Foster kept watching until Tunstall threw away the remains of his meal and settled at his desk, then he continued prowling. There wasn't anything he could do — Megan was well out of their reach and he didn't expect to see her again. But he couldn't help wondering, what if she decided to follow through with Doran? *She'll end up dead, that's what,* he told himself. The text messager on his mobile phone beeped and he rummaged in his pocket, turning the lining inside-out in his hurry to retrieve it.

"Access URL below," it read. He scrolled down the screen, his heart picking up pace. Three Ws and a web address. He looked around the room, seeking out Naomi Hart, now.

CHAPTER
FORTY-FOUR

They agreed to meet at the car park on the edge of Chavasse Park. When Patrick Doran and John Warrender arrived, the place was in darkness, the attendant long gone. Partly concealed from the road behind hoardings, it was a temporary space, prime land, sandwiched between the Crown Court and the police headquarters, compulsory purchased for the Paradise Street project, waiting for the developers to move in. Doran wondered if Megan thought that the proximity of law enforcement and legal process would protect her.

The cupolas of the Liver Buildings, half a mile away, glowed ghostly white across the broad expanse of Strand Street and the black waters of Canning Dock. One of the clock faces was visible; lit in a garish yellow, it showed eight p.m.

The car park's surface was pitted, covered in limestone chippings and hard-core that had sunk in places. Doran drove one of the firm's cars, loose grit popping under the wheels of the Merc like bubble-wrap. The odd stone pinged against the wheel arches. He parked on the far side of the attendant's wooden shack, and set the lights to "park". The engine idled softly; neither man spoke. Cars passed in a steady stream on Strand Street, a hundred yards or more away, but few came down Canning Place: the shops were closed, the courts long since adjourned for the night, and there were no decent pubs or clubs within easy walking distance.

A car approached, driving slowly. Orion, Doran noted automatically, light-coloured — silver, maybe, or white, difficult to tell in the artificial light. It drove on, but returned minutes later and turned into the car park, splashing through puddles at the entrance — an arbitrary structure built from two-by-four struts, painted black and yellow. Hornet stripes — a warning to the unwary. The car's headlights flashed and dipped on the uneven surface.

"It's her," Doran said, feeling a tingle of anticipation. "You're okay with this?"

Warrender nodded without looking at him.

"This is just me and you, John. We get the money, and whatever else she's got. She doesn't walk away."

Warrender's eyes flicked in his direction, then followed the car as it drew close. "Hard to walk away on broken legs," he said.

Megan drove her Orion in a wide loop, switched off her headlamps as she completed the hundred-and-eighty-degree turn, then drew up next to Doran's window. Doran pressed the electric window-wind at the same time Megan did, and each looked at the other without speaking as the motors whined. She looked different; younger than the photograph Bentley had given them. She wore her hair down, dark brown and silky, the shorter sections touching her jawline, the rest breaking at her shoulders. She was what his mother called "fine boned", and Doran couldn't help thinking how easily the cartilage of that pretty nose would crack.

"Passwords, documents, account numbers," Doran said, holding out his hand.

"You wouldn't expect me to have them with me, would you?" She sounded different, too cocky.

Warrender ducked his head to get a better look at her.

"You said you wanted to meet face to face," Megan said. "I'm here."

Doran smiled. "You're asking for a slap."

Megan stared back at him. "Check your on-line account."

He took out his phone and scrolled down his mobile phone book, recalling the number for his account and holding Megan's gaze as he waited for the line to pick up. He listened to the recorded message, then keyed in a couple more numbers.

Megan clicked her tongue. "It's all machines, these days, isn't it?" The tip of her tongue showed between her teeth for the briefest moment. "Don't you just love it?"

Doran glared at her. *Definitely asking for a slap.* The mechanical voice gave him his account balance and a muscle jumped in his jaw. He saw the gleam of recognition in her eyes and resented it.

"Seven hundred-and-fifty thousand," he said, breaking the connection. "Not enough. Not near enough."

414

"A gesture," Megan said. "So you know I'm for real — and that I have your money." Doran searched her face for the lie. "I told you — the Fraud Squad are all over your network. You don't want that kind of money in your account if you want to keep it."

"You're looking after my interests," he said, placing a hand on his chest. "I'm touched. So, what are you proposing? That I should set up another account?"

Megan smiled pityingly at him. "Mr Doran, when I wiped you out, it took me less than thirty minutes. That's every account — transfers authorised and executed."

He blinked — so, even if she did return the money, he wouldn't be able to trust it to stay put. She could move it around as easily as most women rearranged the furniture. His heart thudded slowly. "I want cash," he said.

"I'll take you to it."

Not a moment's hesitation. It troubled him that she seemed to have anticipated his demand, but since she agreed, and since even Megan Ward couldn't make hard cash vanish in an instant, he thought her foresight was no bad thing.

"Now," he said.

"After we've talked."

"You want to *talk*?" He looked at Warrender. This wasn't part of the deal.

"She's wired," Warrender said.

Megan slammed her car into reverse and for one horrible moment, Doran thought she was leaving. Then she stopped again, leaving just enough room to open the driver's door. She swung her legs out first, fifties starlet-style. Long legs, Doran noticed. Good legs. She stood in one smooth motion. She was wearing a skirt suit and blouse. She slipped off the jacket and draped it over the bonnet of her car, standing in the parking lights. Then she unzipped her skirt and let it fall, stepping out of it and placing it on top of the jacket. She was wearing stockings — what Fay called "stay-ups", with an elasticated rim around the top. She looked through the windscreen, holding Doran's gaze as she unbuttoned her blouse, taking her time, an eyebrow arched, a small smile playing on her lips. She shrugged out of her blouse and held it between her finger and thumb, spreading both arms and turning slowly, three hundred-and-sixty degrees. Warrender's eyes slid up and down her body, but Doran looked away, disgusted. Had she no self-respect?

"She's not wired," he said.

Warrender opened the passenger door. "We'll see."

Megan stood her ground as he walked up to her. Doran got out and leaned on the open driver's door, his gaze flitting from Megan to Warrender. His security manager reached past Megan to pick up her clothing.

It must be seven degrees out here, he thought, *and she isn't even shivering.* She waited with one hand on her hip while Warrender checked the seams and lining of the suit carefully. After a few minutes, he shook his head. Megan gave him a pert smile, and held her hand out. He sneered at her, bunching her clothing in his fist, then letting it fall into the still-damp chalk dust of the car park. Megan's smile never faltered.

416

"Get in," Doran said.

She shook her head. "I prefer to use my car. And I prefer to talk to you in private."

"That's not going to happen," he said, feeling a reluctant glimmer of respect for her.

"Then you won't get your money."

Warrender looked at Doran, waiting for the signal to grab her, but Megan picked up her skirt, apparently unconcerned and shook some of the dust off it before stepping into it. Doran's eyes were drawn to her despite himself. He couldn't work her out: she seemed afraid on the phone — but now . . .

"You know you can't force me into transferring the money," she said.

"You think so?" She wasn't cool-headed, just too thick to see when she was way beyond the danger zone.

"I'm not saying you wouldn't try," she said, "But unless your technique has improved, you're known for killing your torture victims before they have the chance to talk."

Doran felt a sudden chill. *Who the fuck is she? What does she know?* He made an effort not to look at Warrender. "So," he said, a splinter of ice in his voice, "Maybe I'll just kill you."

The air between them seemed to hum. "Your choice," she said. But you still wouldn't have your money." Her grey eyes, almost black in the dark, held his, unwavering.

It was his move. While she was alive, there was a chance of getting his money back; when he had his money, he could think about payback — for now, he had to play along, but he also had to play smart. "Search the car," he said.

Megan finished dressing as they checked out the sun-visors, the door pockets, the upholstery, the glove compartment, under the seats.

"Clear," Warrender said. "What about the laptop?"

"I'll need it to get the rest of your money back," Megan said.

Doran thought about it. "All right, but it goes in the boot."

Megan shrugged, and continued buttoning her blouse, maintaining an insouciance that made her look elegant despite the white streaks of damp chalk on her skirt and jacket.

Warrender placed the laptop in the boot of the car, and Doran caught his eye. She wasn't going to have this all her own way.

CHAPTER
FORTY-FIVE

Detective Sergeant Foster looked over Naomi Hart's shoulder, trying not to crowd her. She clicked on the Internet Explorer icon and quickly highlighted the Liverpool Police Authority address in the dialogue box at the top of the screen, over-typing it with the web address Megan had sent.

"Virtualhero.net," Hart read. "Sees herself as a righter of wrongs, does she, Sarge?"

"I doubt it," Foster said. If nothing else, Megan was honest about her dishonesty. "It's just a wind-up about a conversation we had."

Hart clicked the "go" button next to the dialogue box. "She seems to've taken it to heart, though."

He shrugged, and they waited for the screen to load. It went dark and Foster stole a look at Hart. Her face was slightly flushed, the nape of her neck pale and slender. She seemed to notice his scrutiny and turned, a small frown of annoyance creasing her forehead. "What?"

"Nothing. Just wondering why you keep calling me Sarge," he said, to cover for the fact that for a moment he had been lost in admiring her. "I mean, I thought we were on first-name terms."

She turned away again. "Don't know what you mean, Sarge."

Foster sighed. "Would it help if I said I appreciate it?"

She glanced at him, suspecting sarcasm. "Appreciate what?"

"You not telling me I told you so."

She hesitated, then nodded, her silence saying far more than words.

"Look," he said, "I know I acted like a dickhead."

She seemed taken aback. After a moment, her expression softened. "We all do, from time to time," she said. "So long as you don't make a habit of it."

"I'm working on it."

She slid him a sly glance. "It'll take a while before I let you live it down, though."

Foster rolled his eyes comically and Hart smiled. Letters began to appear on the screen. "I think we're in," she said.

The letters were in gothic style, pulsating in red and gold. When the word was complete, Hart read, "Warlock. Is that her web handle?" She caught Foster's look and said, "Her handle — nickname — whatever."

"Beats me," he said.

Wisps of greyish light, ethereal as smoke, drifted across the screen, gradually taking form and solidifying into a figure in a midnight blue cloak with pointed hood; a sinewy hand gripped the gnarled staff traditional to wizards throughout folklore. The figure turned, its cloak trailing glitter, shimmering, like stardust. The Warlock had the archetypal white flowing

420

beard and sharp nose; the grey eyes though, were, without doubt, Megan's: intelligent, amused, but with the heat of passion behind them.

"It's her, isn't it?" Hart breathed, staring into the eyes as if trying to find Megan beneath the mask.

"Yeah," Foster said, his chest tight. "I think it's her."

Rickman arrived for the briefing with a document wallet tucked under one arm. "New development?"

"You could say that." Foster stood to one side to allow Rickman a clearer view, just as the bushy eyebrows drew down into a frown and the figure began to speak.

"Turn up the volume, Naomi," Foster said.

"Volume?" Hart blinked. "Lee, I don't have speakers on this machine."

"Bloody hell! Why didn't you say?" he demanded, missing entirely Hart's reversion to his first name.

"You didn't *tell* me you wanted sound," she said, indignant.

Rickman stepped in. "When you two have finished arguing, you might want to follow me." They glanced guiltily at each other, then hurried after Rickman. He led them to his office, where he swivelled his laptop so that all three could see the monitor. "Do your stuff," he said.

Hart accessed the website again and the same introductory sequence loaded. "Don't worry, it doesn't look like you've missed anything." Hart sounded huffy and Foster felt a little shamefaced — that had always been his trouble: mending bridges, then tearing them down before anyone got to set foot on them.

She accessed the control panel and turned up the volume as Warlock turned to face them. "I'm playing the guilt card again," it said, or rather, *they* said — it sounded like a congregation, reciting a prayer in unison. Foster thought he could hear Megan's voice, undisguised, among the female voices in the upper register. The image seemed to flicker and stutter and for an instant, Warlock's face changed, and Foster thought he saw Megan, smiling, sharing the joke. He felt light-headed and sick.

"Will you save me?" the myriad voices chanted.

What the hell had she done?

"What's that about?" Rickman asked.

"Nothing," Foster said. "Something I said, earlier."

"Another of your cryptic conversations?" Hart asked.

The screen went dark and, alarmed, she reached for the mouse. Rickman stayed her hand, and a moment later, they saw two faces. The lighting was poor, but Patrick Doran and Megan Ward were both easily recognisable.

"We've got visual," Rickman murmured.

The screen was split into four, all showing the interior of a car. Two images, one of Megan and one of Doran, filled the top half. The lower half of the screen was divided into a view through the rear windscreen on the left and the front view on the right.

"She's off her head," Foster murmured. "No, scrub that — *I'm* off my head, thinking she'd let it go."

"She came to you?" Rickman said.

"No," Foster continued scrutinising the images, trying to work out the location from the blurred exterior shots. "Phone call. I should've known a girl like that would go it alone."

"She's a *woman*," Hart said.

"And it seems to me she's been making her own decisions for some time now," Rickman added.

Foster rounded on him. "And why *is* that? It's not like she had a choice, is it? Her mother in and out of hospital with depression. Her brother in prison; Megan spending half her young life in care." Rickman, of all people should understand that.

"Whatever her reasons, we have a situation," Rickman said evenly. "We need to work out the best way to deal with it. How's she sending the images?"

"WiFi." The question was directed at DC Hart, but Foster answered.

They both looked at him, surprised.

"I'm a fast learner," Foster said. "So I'm told." Uncomfortably aware that it had been Megan who'd told him.

"She's using more than a laptop for this bit of technical wizardry," Hart said. "Miniature cameras and a link to the internet at the minimum — but you'd still expect to see some wiring, a bit of cable." She stared at the screen, trying to penetrate the grainy darkness of the image. "She must have some serious kit."

"Paid for on somebody else's credit card, I'll bet," Foster said, filling the silence because he couldn't stand the sound of his heart pounding in his ears.

"Where are the cameras?" Rickman asked, scanning the three images. He had seen the minicams Traffic Division used, and there was no way they could be hidden on the dashboard of a car. "Doran isn't stupid — why doesn't he see them?"

They stared at the screen, trying to find some sign. Hart began to shake her head, then froze. "The infra-red detectors for the alarm!" she exclaimed.

"I still don't . . ." Rickman said, squinting harder.

"You're not supposed to. Look at the angles: left to right, gives you Megan in the driver's seat; right to left, gives you Doran. She's replaced the infra-red sensors with wireless minicams. She must have the front-view camera fixed to the mounting for the rear-view mirror. God knows where the fourth camera is."

"She's set herself up as bait. Stupid cow *is* suicidal," Foster muttered.

"Is this live?" Rickman asked.

"There's no way of telling," Hart said.

"When did she text you?"

Foster continued staring at the screen, sweating. This was torture. What the hell kind of person gave you a link to her abduction and didn't give you a single landmark?

"Lee?"

He shook himself. "What?"

"The text —"

"Sorry, Boss. Um, I dunno — ten — fifteen minutes ago?"

"I think we have to assume it's live," Hart said.

"What do we do, Jeff?" Foster asked. *Say you'll help her.* Normally, he'd have said it straight out, but Naomi's presence in the room stopped him.

424

"The way I see it," Rickman said, his attention focused on the screen. "We can try and locate her, move in, and interrupt what might be a perfectly amicable conversation."

Foster swallowed. "Good idea. Let's go with that."

Hart glanced at him, less than impressed, then she turned to face Rickman. "Or," she said. "There was a definite 'or' in what you just said."

Rickman tilted his head in apology to Foster. "Or we can sit back, watch the show, see how it ends."

In the Incident Room, people gathered around Naomi Hart's computer monitor as though it were a TV screen showing the FA Cup final, live.

CHAPTER
FORTY-SIX

"They're on the move," Foster said. The view through the windscreen see-sawed wildly, showing black sky, a few orange flashes, then white road surface, too blurred to make out any detail. Finally it fizzed and blacked out entirely.

"Shit!" Foster resisted an urge to rattle the monitor, but only just. "We'll never find her now."

"We've still got the rear view," Rickman said, "It looks like a rough surface — give it a minute to settle down."

As they watched, holding their breath, Patrick Doran turned to Megan. His blue eyes looked almost black on the screen, his dark Irish good looks marred somewhat by lack of sleep.

"You wanted to talk," he said. "Shall I pick a topic or have you got something in mind?"

She turned right onto a made road surface — or so Foster guessed, since the rise and fall of the rear view ceased.

Megan glanced in the mirror. "When I'm sure Mr Warrender has stayed put, I'll tell you."

Rickman reached for his desk phone and put a call through to Special Ops to request armed response back-up and aerial support. "They need a location. Lee? Naomi?"

Hart and Foster peered at the screen.

"It's so damn *dark*," Hart complained.

"Wait a minute." Foster pointed to a low, white-tiled frontage, reminiscent of a 1960s public toilet, just visible through the rear screen. "Isn't that the fire station at Canning Place?"

"Could be," Hart said, doubtfully, then it was gone from the view-finder.

The car slowed at traffic lights, sweeping right. The forward view was still blank and the rear showed them nothing but a glare of blue-green against darkness, as they passed the lights.

Foster pushed his fingers into his hair and left them there, almost crazy with frustration. "Woah!" He leaned in to the laptop. Had the windscreen view just flickered? But the right lower portion of the monitor remained stubbornly dark. Just as he was beginning to despair, he saw a sparkle, a flash, and then the twin domes of the Royal Liver Buildings appeared on-screen, their granite frontages reflecting so much from the spotlights that they seemed almost to fluoresce. "Oh, you beauties," he laughed.

No need to explain to Rickman, he saw them as plainly as Foster did. "They're heading north on Strand Street," he said, talking into the phone to the comms officer who was relaying his instructions. "Just shy of the Liver Buildings."

"Wait wait wait," Foster said, falling easily into surveillance mode. "She's now turned right right right into — Where the fuck is that?" he asked Hart.

She peered at the monitor. The camera gave virtually nothing left or right of the windscreen, and the camera's depth of field was equally poor: sodium flare from the street lights on a wet road surface, together with the blinding dazzle of approaching headlamps from an oncoming car made identification difficult.

"James Street? — or Brunswick?"

"No, Brunswick is one-way, the wrong way," Foster said.

"Shit — sorry, Lee — the picture's hopeless. Oh, God, and now she's turning left."

Rickman hooked a map out of his desk drawer and Hart spread it out next to the laptop. "The eye in the sky has been deployed," he told them.

"Left again," Hart said. "Could that be Dale Street?"

"Right right right," Foster said, his gaze fixed on the computer screen. The car turned right again at the end of the street, and a frontage he thought he recognised came into view. "I think . . . Is that . . .?" His eyes darted right and left, looking for a definite point of reference, but the image was out of focus. "I *think* that's Exchange Station." He stared harder, as the car swept towards an arched building with an iron clock fixed to the side of the building. "It is. It's the old station." The façade had been renovated and the iron gates at the wide, Norman-style arches painted and gilded. It was unmistakable.

"What's the time?" Hart asked.

"What're you on about?" Foster demanded.

"The time — on the *clock*." Hart grabbed the laptop and swivelled it towards herself. "Eight-twenty," she said.

Foster checked his watch. "We're on real time," he said.

"Tithebarn Street," Rickman said into the receiver. "Keep well back."

"Heading right right right into —" Hart checked the map. "Hatton Garden."

"They have eyeball target," Rickman said.

Foster and Hart exhaled in unison. "What now?" Foster needed action.

"Organise three teams," Rickman said. "Tell them to get to the city centre, fast. Surveillance only. I want constant radio contact. The comms room will organise a frequency so we can talk to each other and to the eye in the sky. Armed Response is already in the area — we do *not* want to get in their way."

"So what *do* we do?"

"We watch and wait — see how the mop flops."

Foster stared at Rickman. "Are you smoking wacky baccy, or what?"

"I need you here," Rickman said.

Foster looked ready to argue, but he seemed to change his mind and satisfied himself with a resentful look. "I'll get the troops rallied, then, shall I?"

"Sir —" Hart recalled Rickman's attention to the computer, and Foster slipped out of the room.

"I'm putting you on speakerphone," Rickman said to the helicopter pilot.

Hart found the control panel on the computer and turned the volume up to maximum.

"Satisfied?" Doran asked.

"Not yet," Megan said. "But since it's harder to hit a moving target, I feel a little safer."

"I gave you my word, Megan."

"But you're a ruthless man, Mr Doran," Megan said.

He looked at her, his face closed, the only hint of emotion a slight twitch of the muscle along his jaw. "I prefer to think of myself as practical."

"So I really don't need to worry, once I've returned your money?"

"Of course not." It was said smoothly, without hesitation.

"He's lying through his teeth," Hart said.

Megan looked directly into the camera, almost as if she had heard.

"She knows," Rickman murmured.

The helicopter pilot's voice, muffled and crackling, broke in from the speakerphone. "Target turning right right right into Dale Street."

"Where the hell is she going?" Rickman asked, but Megan was talking again.

"I'm more of a dreamer, myself," she said. "But I do have a practical side — I have made contingency plans."

"Meaning?"

"Your money is stored in a high-security facility, requiring fingerprint and retinal scan analysis." She tilted her head. "Which should guarantee I'll stay alive at least long enough to get you your money."

"Failsafe," Rickman urged. "Tell him you have a *failsafe*." But she didn't.

"I told you," Doran said, sounding controlled, patient, sincere. "All I want is my money."

Megan sighed, a long, relieved, grateful sigh.

Shocked, Hart said, "She's as good as told him he's free to do her in after he's got the cash."

Rickman shook his head. "She's laid the bait. Doran just took it."

"Foster's right. She is suicidal."

Rickman stared at the screen. "I don't think so. But she is putting a hell of a lot of trust in us doing our job right."

They were still in the business district; traffic was minimal on Friday night: the bars, cafes and restaurants that served the office workers were closed or empty.

Hart squinted at the screen. "Isn't that the Brunswick pub?"

Rickman looked closer, catching a glimpse of the brightly lit Victorian ale-house as it slid past. They were on Tithebarn Street again.

"Confirmed," the helicopter pilot said. "Target seems to be circling the business end of town."

Hart smiled. "Clever."

Rickman frowned in question.

"She's using office networks — piggy-backing their WiFi signals," she explained. "The networks don't shut down just because it's the weekend — this is when they get all their number-crunching done."

"So long as it keeps us in touch," Rickman said, willing Megan to be careful.

Megan kept her eyes on the road. "Would it be 'practical' to betray a boy who looked up to you?"

Doran said, "That would depend on the circumstances. I gather you have a particular example in mind?"

"My brother."

He glanced over at her, curious. "Ward . . ." The corners of his mouth turned down. "Doesn't ring any bells."

"My real name is Ceri Owen."

The seat creaked as he turned fully to face her. "Gareth," he said softly. "I should have seen the resemblance."

"Don't see why." Megan's voice was light, flippant. "I mean, you don't visit, you never call, you never write . . ."

He remained twisted in his seat, so that Rickman and Hart could see only his profile: snub nose, hollow cheeks, jet-black curly hair.

"What do you want, Ceri?"

"I prefer Megan."

The seat creaked again, as he moved closer, as if to get a better look at her face.

She didn't look at him. "The question is, what do *you* want, Doran?"

He smiled, spread his hands as if to say, *It's simple.* "I want my money back."

Megan tutted disapprovingly. "We really can't do this unless you're honest with me."

Doran settled back in his seat, and stared stonily ahead, and she drove on, this time looping in a wide figure of eight, but always keeping within the business district. The traffic was halted in Castle Street: a function at the Town Hall. The floodlighting illuminated a crowd that had spilled out from the ballroom onto the balcony. They stood sipping champagne and chatting, women in ball gowns, men in evening suits, stark against the creamy sandstone.

"So," Megan said. "The truth: what *do* you want?"

"I want to put my hands around your throat and choke the fucking *life* out of you," he said.

She nodded, apparently unperturbed. "That's understandable. I, on the other hand, want you to admit what you did to my brother. But, since we're being honest, I should also tell you that I want to take a gun and put a bullet in your brain." Her tone was matter-of-fact, and without rancour.

He blinked, evidently shocked, and turned to look at her again.

Megan acknowledged this with another brief nod. "Good — we're clear on our objectives." She glanced at him. "You have the advantage of strength — I doubt if I could fight you off — so what happens next really depends on the choice you make: money or revenge. I don't have a gun, so it's pretty clear I'm not going to kill you. But I'm a hacker. I don't need a *real* gun — not while I have a virtual gun to your head. So, if you want your money, you should act nicely and make no sudden moves.

"Oh, and since I have the advantage, you should probably tell me what I want to hear."

Doran's jaw worked so hard he looked like he might break a tooth, but after half a minute, it seemed he decided to play along. "Gareth blew his chances and he went to prison for it."

"What 'chances'?"

"What the hell does she think she's doing?" Hart said.

"So far, she's playing it smart," Rickman told her. "Letting him know what she knows, so he's really got nothing to hide."

"But if he tells her, he's going to have to kill her."

"That's what she's gambling on," Rickman said, keeping his eyes on the screen.

"What 'chance' did my brother *ever* have with a shark like you?" Megan demanded, emotion creeping into her voice.

"He could have been a senior manager in the firm," Doran said.

Megan sighed, changing down the gears, cutting through a narrow side street. "You're veering from the truth again, Doran. And frankly, your money trail is getting cold."

For a moment, it looked like Doran might grab the wheel and force the car into one of the high walls of the side street, but then he exhaled and made a deliberate effort to relax the fingers of his hands. "Okay," he said, "you want the truth?"

Megan lifted one shoulder. "It's all I've ever wanted."

CHAPTER
FORTY-SEVEN

Doran looked at Megan for a few seconds. "What the hell," he said. "If it gets me my money, I'll say whatever you want."

Rickman sucked air through his teeth. "He's onto her." He glanced at Hart. "He's making it clear he feels coerced. If she asks him a leading question now, the CPS will throw this evidence out before it gets within spitting distance of the magistrates' court, never mind the crown court."

"I want . . . the truth," Megan repeated with slow, deliberate emphasis.

"Okay . . . Good . . ." Rickman purred the words, talking softly as though he had a radio link with Megan. He willed her to stay cool, to make use of her manipulative skills.

"The truth . . ." Doran said it as though trying to remind himself what it meant. "We should have walked out of there with a hundred thousand pounds worth of diamonds; all we got was blood on our hands."

"Gareth wasn't the only one who screwed up that night."

Doran stared at her. "*He* killed the old man. He admitted it at the trial. And he *never* appealed against his sentence."

"Because he accepted his part in it. What about you? You're not denying you were in the Orrs' house when they were murdered?"

"You sound like a cop."

Unexpectedly, Megan laughed. "Well that would be because I'm in the surreal position of asking you about a murder — two murders — and I'm not really sure of the social niceties of this situation. For some reason, it didn't come up in social studies role-plays at GCSE."

Doran watched her as they continued in a perpetual loop, going round and round the city centre, like a car on a very slow Scalextric track.

"Come on, Doran," Megan said. "You saw me naked. Where would I be hiding a wire?"

Rickman glanced at Hart. "I didn't see that — we didn't get that, did we?"

Hart gave him a sideways glance. "Maybe she knew who'd be watching and wanted to preserve her modesty."

Abashed, Rickman looked again at the screen.

Doran nodded. "So this is just — what? To give you peace of mind?"

"Let's say I've heard Gareth's side — I wanted to hear yours."

He frowned, hesitating, as if he wasn't sure exactly where to start, or what to tell her. "Two people ended up dead. That was — unfortunate," he said, after a full half minute. "But your brother ended up in prison, and that was stupid — unnecessary. He walked into that police station. Nobody made him."

"He couldn't *live* with what he did," Megan said, her voice raw with sudden emotion. "How do you?"

Doran stared at the road ahead. They were approaching the Town Hall for the third time. A burst of spring rain spattered the windscreen, and the party began to move indoors, their laughter and exclamations just audible in the bubble of isolation within the car. The spotlights and the reflections of traffic lights and street-lamps on the building gave it an almost festive glow.

"I have a beautiful family, a nice house, I have —" he snorted "*had* — a successful business." He stared at the Town Hall building. "I have the respect of people like them." He lifted his chin, indicating the few remaining revellers on the balcony.

"And that helps you sleep at night?"

He smiled, and there was something like regret in it. "The *pills* help me sleep at night."

"You love your family," Megan said. "Didn't it occur to you when you tortured Mr Orr in front of his wife that they had a family? You do know their son discovered the bodies? You have sons — how would you feel if your sons were forced to look at what you did?"

"I did what I had to."

Rickman held his breath.

"You *had* to kill her?"

"I slapped her — just the once."

"You broke her neck."

"As I said, it was —"

437

"Unfortunate. Yes, I remember. So, you killed her — accidentally, I'll concede that. Is that why you felt you had to murder Mr Orr?"

"I *didn't* —"

"You put the knife in Gareth's hand. You held a gun to his head."

"All he had to do was cut him. One small cut."

"What — to show *willing*?" She sounded bitter and angry, and Doran responded, turning towards her.

"To *protect* him."

She slammed on the brakes and a car behind them screamed to a halt just in time. The driver sounded his horn and drove around them as they faced each other angrily.

"To protect *yourself*. Gareth said your name — he told me. You took two lives to protect *yourself*."

"No," Doran said. "It wasn't just for me."

Megan gave a short, humourless laugh.

"Use your head," Doran said. "You're involved in a crime, you don't report it. All he had to do . . ." He seemed at a loss for a moment. "It was a token gesture — I'd have done the rest."

Shocked, she sat back, letting her hands slide off the steering wheel. "You'd have done him the *favour* of killing Mr Orr? And, what was the plan? That you'd go back to being father figure and mentor?" She was almost breathless with incredulity. "Did you *really* think that Gareth was the sort of person who could torture and murder another human being and pretend it never happened?"

"He could be a free man, now," Doran said, dogged, even a little resentful. "Top of his profession."

Megan shook her head.

"I — *liked* the kid," Doran insisted.

"He's dying." Megan's eyes filled with tears. "Gareth is dying."

Doran said nothing.

"My brother is dying — is that '*unfortunate*'?"

"He did this to himself."

Megan wiped her eyes. "Yeah," she said tiredly, "that's what he keeps telling me." She put the car in gear and they continued on, past grey buildings on wide roads, twisting, circling, returning again and again to the same landmarks, the same questions, each pass bringing something more sharply into focus, a building more readily recognisable, a truth more transparent.

"What about Sara?" she asked.

Doran sighed. "It was an accident. They were supposed to take your computer, grab you, if they could find you."

"Did they think Sara was me?"

He shrugged. "Who knows what goes through the minds of men like them?"

She stared hard at him "I'm sure a man like you could hazard a guess — I mean, you're not so different, are you?"

"Your friend's death was an accident," he insisted.

"But you gave the order."

"To search your flat, yes." He was clearly losing patience.

"You say you're a practical man, but with all these 'accidents', it seems more like incompetence."

"Stop," Rickman murmured. "Leave it, Megan."

Hart tensed, anticipating Doran's reaction.

But the anger they had seen building up in the man seemed to dissipate all at once, and he was cold and still. "Oh, you'll find I can be quite efficient, Megan." Again, the muscle in the line of his jaw seemed to ripple, and then he said, "I've been very patient, but now I'm bored, and I'd like my money."

Megan's eyes flicked to the camera, and reading her expression, Rickman thought for a moment that she might try one more time. "*Don't*," he said.

Minutes later, Megan parked outside a nondescript building; low-rise, with steel-frame windows and pitted grey concrete — six or seven storeys of unremitting ugliness.

"One of the little banks had its regional HQ here," Megan explained. "Before they got swallowed by a global giant. The basement strong-room is impressive, and with the additional technical security do-dads these guys have, it's probably as safe as the Bank of England."

Doran ducked his head to get a better view. There was no company logo, no name on the building, not even a street number. "A bit low-key, isn't it?"

"Its anonymity adds another layer of security," Megan said. "I bet even you didn't know of its existence."

440

"Which makes me suspicious," Doran said. "Maybe I'll step inside with you."

Megan smiled. "You're welcome to try."

As the car door opened, the chopper could be heard as a distant buzz. Rickman warned the pilot and he ascended into the cloud cover. Megan walked away from the car without looking back.

Doran was out of the car in seconds, and Hart and Rickman were left looking at the empty car interior. Without the helicopter, they were effectively blind. "Does anyone have eyeball target?" he asked.

His speakerphone crackled, and then Voce confirmed that he could see the car as well as Megan and Doran. The slightly echoing sound of a relayed radio connection gave his voice a weird quality, as if it was coming from a distant and lonely landscape, and Rickman was reminded of the faint voices and vague shapes that made up Megan's web of connections on the internet. "Keep them in sight," he said. "But do not approach."

Doran was by Megan's side in seconds; he kept close as she approached the double doors under a mean and sodden-looking concrete canopy. She pressed the buzzer and it was answered instantly.

"Can I help you?"

"Melanie White," she said, without preamble.

Doran looked askance. "You can call yourself Mickey Mouse, for all they care," Megan said. "So long as the biometric checks match."

A pause, then, "Good evening, Ms White. Would you please identify your companion?"

"Patrick Doran," she said. "He'd like to come in with me."

"I'm afraid that won't be possible, Ms White. It's against protocol."

"I understand, but —"

"Our rules are not open to discussion or negotiation, Ms White." He managed to sound reasonable and immutable at once. "The protocols are absolute."

"Listen, pal," Doran said. "We're not leaving till —"

Two large and extremely useful-looking security men appeared from nowhere, and Doran broke off, startled. They wore the navy blue uniforms more typical of hotel porters than security guards, but they were definitely not the type to argue with.

Megan's smile of apology was tinged with amusement. "Looks like you're waiting in the car," she said.

On the computer, Rickman and Hart watched Doran slide back into the passenger seat. His hair was wet and he wiped a hand over his face to remove some of the rain before dipping into his coat pocket.

"Now what?" Rickman said.

Doran pressed a fast-dial number, and in seconds he was connected. "John, I'm in a side street off Tithebarn." He glanced around, trying to find a sign. "Can't see a street name. It's on the right, though, just after Exchange Street. Get close, but stay out of sight. I'll be needing you any minute, now."

A CCTV camera caught a light-coloured Mercedes travelling slowly up Tithebarn Street three minutes later. The car pulled into the bay next to a bus stop. One of the surveillance teams drove by and confirmed that the driver was John Warrender. Tithebarn Street was one-way, and Warrender was in position to follow as soon as Megan turned out of the side road.

"She's on her way out, Boss," Voce said, after another ten minutes had elapsed.

Megan placed two sports bags on the ground and waited for Doran to get out of the car to check them. When he nodded, she got in and started the engine as he finished zipping up the bags. Doran went around to the passenger side, but the door was locked. Megan pressed the electric wind on the window.

"Flag a taxi," she said. "You can afford one, now." She gunned the engine and screeched away from the kerb.

Doran ran after her to the corner, carrying the sports bags. He dropped one and waved Warrender over.

The Merc roared across four lanes, headlamps still out, nearly clipping the rear end of a hackney cab. The driver pulled down his window and swore long and vociferously, ending with a two-fingered gesture.

Warrender pulled up at an angle to the kerb and Doran threw the bags on the back seat, piling in after them. "Move!" he yelled.

They fishtailed from the kerb, ran a red light, narrowly missed a second collision and forked right, heading towards the museum.

"Shit!" Warrender scanned the cars ahead. "Where did she go? Did I take the wrong turn?"

Doran leaned forward, gripping the front-seat head-rests for support. "There!" He pointed to a light-coloured Orion at the traffic lights. She was indicating right. Behind them, unnoticed, armed officers in an unmarked car. Voce followed, two cars back. The helicopter descended through the low cloud and established visual contact again.

Megan swept right in a tight loop; it looked like she might take the tunnel turn-off at the roundabout, but at the last moment, she cut left, heading past the wedge-shaped building at the bifurcation of Victoria and Whitechapel. In recent years, it had been the offices of the Labour Party, now it was a fitness studio. With its tiered windows brightly lit, it looked like a liner, docked in the mizzly streets of the city.

This was the busy end of town, and traffic was heavy. Megan's Orion dodged left, then right, squeezing between two buses. From there, she reached the lights as they changed to red, and drove through, merging with the flow of traffic turning right. Warrender blasted the Merc's horn, and drivers turned, bewildered.

"Don't lose her," Doran warned. "Don't you lose her now."

Warrender turned the wheel, mounting the kerb and edging past the knot of traffic. A group of girls, on the start of a night out, squealed as he drove at them, scattering them right and left. Car horns blared and police sirens began to wail, causing more confusion.

Drivers looked around, trying to gauge the direction of the sound.

Warrender bumped the Merc down onto the roadway and gunned after Megan. She was near the crossroads with Victoria Street now, and he had to weave in and out of traffic to catch her. As she reached the junction, he was on her.

He drew level with Megan's car in the middle lane.

"Ram the bitch," Doran said.

Warrender swerved right and both cars skidded on the wet surface, turning ninety degrees to face the on-coming traffic. The Orion bumped the kerb, the rear end mounting it and continuing its slow spin until it hit the sandstone balustrade of the car park for the municipal offices. The car shuddered and stalled.

Megan reached for the door handle, but the side collision jammed it against the balustrade, and she had to scramble across and out the passenger side. Doran was out of his car.

She ran to the wall; the drop into the car park was steep. "Do it," Doran shouted. "It'll be like shooting fish in a barrel."

Panicked, Megan turned, facing the solid bank of headlights: traffic heading towards the tunnel entrance at the end of Victoria Street. She saw shock and concern on the faces of pedestrians. Someone even called, "Are you all right, love?"

"Get down!" she screamed. "He's got a gun."

A second car drove out of the mass of traffic to her left, bumped onto the pavement, and headed towards her. Megan turned wildly. She was trapped between

Doran and this new threat, and Doran was reaching into his pocket. She turned again to the wall, and looked down on the branches of London planes, just beginning to show tender spring shoots. Then the driver of the second car shouted to her.

"Get in!"

She looked towards the car, then to Doran, in an agony of indecision. His hand came out of his pocket.

"For fuck's *sake*, Megan, will you get in?"

She whirled back. "Foster?"

She ran, keeping her head low, using her car as a shield. Doran shouted something at her back. As she reached Foster's car, he raised his arm. As she pulled open the passenger door, he took aim. As she dived in, he fired on them. She bumped her cheekbone against Foster's arm, and simultaneously, something grazed the sleeve of her jacket, embedding itself in the upholstery with a soft *thud*.

Foster ducked, muttering, "Fuck," under his breath, then he jammed the car in reverse and, keeping his head down, yelled into his radio as he drove. "Bastard's shooting at us. Request assistance! Request assistance! Firearms back-up requested! *Now!*"

Motorists crouched down, car horns blared, pedestrians screamed, diving for cover. Doran advanced, arm raised, and the drivers nearest the kerb began to panic, steering their cars right, trying to avoid the line of fire. Doran fired twice, and two holes appeared in the windscreen. Megan screamed, crouching lower. The sirens were closer, but seemed to be hampered by the

446

traffic. The helicopter clattered overhead, its PA on, its spotlight on Doran.

"Foster?" The radio was barely audible over the noise. "Lee, what the hell are you doing?" It was Rickman.

"Stay down," Foster yelled "the cavalry's arrived."

"Police," the PA system boomed. "Put down your weapon and lie face down on the ground."

Foster didn't wait to see if Doran obeyed. He continued along the pavement, engine screaming as he reversed at speed. There was no way out at the next junction, traffic was massed against them; these drivers, unaware of events around the corner, irate at their inability to turn into the flow, edged forward, blaring horns. Some got out and peered over the traffic, trying to get a better view. Foster carried on, scraping the car's undercarriage on the kerbs as he bumped off then back on at the far corner.

The police cars closed in, slowly forging a way through, and Doran turned and ran back to his car.

The next turning was one-way in their favour and Foster spun the wheel, rattling them both as he came down off the kerb again and manoeuvred into the flow of traffic. "I think we lost them," he said, his breathing ragged. "It's okay, you can sit up."

She did. "Shit, Foster!" she gasped. "Shit shit shit!" She hit him hard in the shoulder. "I thought it was them. I thought you were —" She bent forward, hiding her face in her hands and Foster slowed down, reaching out to her. His hand hovered for a second, then he gently placed it on her back. She was shaking, and he could feel the fevered heat of her fear through the thick wool of her jacket.

"I'm sorry," he said.

Rickman's voice sounded loudly from the radio. "Foster, for God's sake! Get out of there. Leave this to Armed Response."

"The boss," Foster said. "I'm playing hookey."

"Foster," Rickman said again. "Come in."

Foster flicked the switch, turning the radio off. They had almost reached the end of the road and he put both hands back on the wheel. On the corner, he caught a glimpse of the rear end of a Mercedes, its tail light out. "Oh, God . . ."

Megan saw, and her eyes widened.

"Hold on," he said. He turned into the oncoming traffic on Dale Street. It was sparse, here, but he had to swerve to avoid two cars, and he heard a dull crunch as another braked sharply and a fourth car rear-ended it. He turned left, tearing up Vernon Street, the new grey sets buzzing beneath the tyres. They hit a ramp and heard a screech as the sump hit the bricks. Cresting the ramp, the car lifted a foot, then clanged down onto the road again, sending sparks flying right and left. The street was just wide enough for one car, and Doran was close behind them.

"Bloody loony must've done a U-turn into the traffic," he muttered, keeping an eye on the Merc in his rear mirror. Behind it, flashing lights: the ARVs were in close pursuit.

At the Travel Inn, a businessman looked on in horror as they ploughed through his luggage, scattering it.

Doran followed after, and they heard the man's dismayed yells diminishing as they raced on.

Foster saw steel hoardings jutting out at the side of the road and jigged the wheel right.

Warrender, at the wheel of Doran's car, was slower to react. He caught the steel hoarding at an oblique angle. It shuddered, teetered, groaned, then crashed onto a following police car.

"Oh, crap." Beyond the hoardings, Foster saw traffic barriers on both sides of the junction, three feet high, guiding traffic right. "Hold on tight," he yelled, spinning the wheel, burning rubber, heading into the chicane. He scraped the side of the car against the barriers with a scream of tortured metal and starburst of bright white sparks. Megan held the hand grip over the door, her eyes tightly closed, her lips pressed together. They shot out of the junction into a pulse of traffic.

Warrender fought with the wheel of the Merc, desperately trying to correct the right swing caused by the collision. He oversteered, hitting the traffic barrier at the head of the junction, avoiding a head-on impact, but colliding with the second barrier, ending with the car wedged within the chicane. More police cars howled down the street, the last of which, seeing the problem, reversed out onto Dale Street and screamed down Moorfields to block off their escape route. The police helicopter hovered as armed officers surrounded Doran's car.

CHAPTER
FORTY-EIGHT

"You got your confession," Foster said. They were parked in one of a cluster of interconnected streets in Kensington. Named after the London district by a planner with a sense of humour, the narrow terraces lacked gardens and their front doors opened directly onto the street. Many of the houses were empty and boarded up, some had SOLD signs tacked to the red brickwork. Refurbs; inward investment from southerners with a mental image of a place that was far from the reality.

"You heard?" she seemed surprised.

Foster flicked on the radio. It was still hot with noise: Doran and Warrender arrested, chaos in the city centre. "My all-seeing eye — well, ear, if you want to be accurate." He turned down the volume, leaving just enough so he could keep an ear open in case they sent search parties out for him and Megan.

She nodded. "Is it enough — I mean, will it be?"

Foster shrugged. "A case like this, it isn't any one thing. But it all adds up: the stuff you gave us on his tax fiddles will help."

She grimaced apologetically. "I never did come through with that other stuff, did I?"

"The fact he took a couple of pot shots at you in front of about a hundred witnesses — that's almost as good as."

A smile sparked in her eyes. "Always glad to assist the police in the fight against crime."

"Yeah, right . . ." Foster looked at her. Her jacket was smeared with white powder, her cheek-bone red and swollen where she had hit it. The bruising on her forehead from her previous injury was fading and she had covered it fairly effectively with make-up. "You're okay, though?" he said.

She found the bullet-hole in her jacket and poked a finger through it. "He's ruined my suit." She laughed, and Foster noted the tremor in it.

"Seriously," he said. "You're okay?"

She looked into his eyes and he saw warmth and gratitude. "I'll be fine. What about you? Your boss didn't sound too pleased."

"I'll survive." He glanced around the car's interior. The holes in the windscreen had already begun to crack in a spider's web of fine fissures; the side panel and frame had been shunted inwards by the impact with the barriers, and the glove compartment flap was askew. He found two bullet-holes in the upholstery. He didn't like to think where the third had ended up. "Not sure the wheels'll make a full recovery," he said.

She laughed, this time sounding more steady. "I hope you weren't attached to it, because —" She pressed the flap release to illustrate her point and a jumble of items fell out of the compartment onto her lap.

Foster reached across, knowing what was there, not wanting her to see it, but she slapped his hand away. "We don't know each other that well," she said, lifting the items and turning to put them on the back seat. Foster got a faint waft of her perfume as she leaned across; a delicate, warm fresh scent.

An A to Z of Liverpool slipped as she placed it on the seat, revealing a sheet of artists' paper beneath it. It was Sara's sketch of her.

She picked it up and turned back. Foster saw in her face that she recognised it as Sara's work; he also believed absolutely, and for the first time, that Megan's affection for her friend had been real.

She seemed to sense his scrutiny and tried to make light of it. "Sergeant Foster!" she said, "I'm touched."

"Yeah, well don't start looking at wedding dresses just yet."

She studied the paper again, her eyes shining.

"Why d'you do it?" he asked.

"I had to get Doran," she said simply, still studying the picture.

"Not Doran — this hacking lark. What d'you get out of it?"

She looked up from the sketch. "The challenge. The game."

"Hacking bank accounts isn't a game," Foster said.

She seemed surprised. "But it *is*. It's all about the search — the *quest*. It's about belief and play: you have to believe that the system *can* be hacked, and then you just have fun with it. You just keep at it till something gives."

"And you walk off with a pot full of money."

She lifted one shoulder. "Sometimes. But that's not the point — the point is, you got past their security. You found a way in. You saw the number patterns and reconfigured them to your own mosaic."

"But you weren't even into hacking till recently," Foster said. "From what I've seen, you were pretty low-tech, by hacker standards. It was more about into making people do what you want."

"Not *making*," Megan said, "Persuading. Violence is for morons."

"Cheers, Megan." Violence was part of his job. Was he now hearing what she really thought of him? And all the rest — the flirting, the pretence at identifying with him — was that just another of her scams? Had she *persuaded* him to do what she wanted?

She looked into his face and seemed to read the insult he felt. "Don't you have an expression, 'necessary force'? That's not violence — that's containment."

"Now you're patronising me," he said, "And if violence is for morons, what does that make your brother?"

Something flickered across her face, like fleeting pain, and he instantly regretted what he had said.

"What Gareth did was unforgivable," she said. "He knows that. It's why he never applied for parole, never tried to take the case to appeal — because it's unforgivable and even if society forgives him, he can't forgive himself. He could have been anything he wanted, and he blew it. But Doran helped him along the way and he deserves to pay more than anyone."

Foster couldn't bring himself to apologise, not after what Gareth had done, but Megan had no part in that, and he wanted to take away some of her pain. "You've done what you set out to," he said.

"Yeah." She smiled to herself. "And then some."

"Give it up."

"Give what up?" She flushed and then paled; he put it down to fear of the unknown — fear of the ordinary, perhaps.

"This," he said. "This crappy life, moving from town to town, never belonging anywhere."

"You say 'belonging', I hear 'ownership'," she said. "I don't like to be owned."

"Why've you always got to see the negative? Belonging is about sharing, being involved, giving something of yourself. Having a place where people know you and care about you. But it does mean you've got to put something into it as well."

"Who are you trying to persuade?" she asked, "Me, or yourself?"

"What?" Foster asked, affronted.

"You keep people at bay. It's not a criticism," she added, as if expecting an argument. "It's just the way we are. We can't change it; why make ourselves miserable trying?"

"We?"

She inclined her head. "Me and you — we're two of a kind."

He wasn't sure he liked being included in her cosy circle of two. "We're on opposite sides of the law."

"Fine line," she said, teasing. "Genius and lunatic, crook and cop."

"Admit it," Foster said, "Your heart's not really in it."

She laughed, astonished. "What do you mean? I'm *good* at this."

"Who d'you think you're kidding?" Foster demanded. "You gave up a whole load of money to a charity."

"I couldn't very well keep it!" she exclaimed.

"See what I'm saying? You staged this little drama tonight —"

"Doran killed my friend. He put my brother in prison."

"The two people who made you feel you belonged."

She frowned, refusing to concede the point. "And now I've honoured my debt and I'm free to slip away."

"But you're still here."

She batted her eyelids at him and gave him a seductive pout, self-mocking. "I like you — and I'm trying to corrupt you."

"I'm incorruptible," he said.

She held his gaze, the mocking sparkle in her eyes now directed at him.

"You even gave back Doran's money," he said. Something chased across her face, too swiftly for him to capture the look. "Let's face it, Megan, you're crap at this," he concluded, "— too much conscience."

"I can be ruthless," she said, her tone a little hurt, but still teasing.

Foster snorted. "You know why you're an internet scammer and not a con artist?"

She narrowed her eyes at him. "I've a feeling you're going to tell me."

"When you actually meet the people you steal from, you feel bad about it. On the internet you can kid yourself they're as phoney as you are, but face to face . . ." He sucked air between his teeth. "Different pot of scouse altogether."

She looked offended.

"Added to which you've got a lousy poker face. I can read you at fifty yards."

She smiled. "Yeah? What am I thinking now?"

He shook his head. "I'm serious. The Fraud Squad are watching you. They gave you a by this time because they're grateful. But as the wise man said, gratitude has a short half-life. If you carry on, they'll nick you — and soon."

She frowned, studying his face. "You're letting me go . . ."

"I've got nothing on you."

"Well, I'm not about to argue," she said, still surprised.

"Computer fraud isn't my department." The way Foster saw it, Doran was a crook and a killer, he saw his job as protecting the innocent. "Anyway, like you said, Doran owes you."

"I don't want to land you in more trouble," she said, "I mean, the car . . ."

"All I've got to say is I stopped at a junction and you jumped out and legged it. These streets are like a rabbit warren."

Her eyes hadn't left his face. "I have a sizeable pot of money set aside. And I've got a really sweet idea for a scam." She was joking, but only to hide the fact that she was serious.

Foster hesitated, then laughed. "Stop — I don't wanna have to arrest you," he said.

She shrugged. "I'm just saying, we could have a good time."

He looked into her mocking grey eyes and saw a kind of longing. He could almost see himself doing it. Almost. "Thanks all the same — I've got a life here." He thought about Rickman. "People I care about. People who care about me."

She lifted her chin. "The blonde bombshell."

"Naomi?" he said, surprised. "No. Not in a million years."

She sighed. "You men are so dense."

"Naomi?" he repeated, and she nodded, amused.

"I don't know why the hell I'm telling you."

"*Naomi*," he said a third time, under his breath. "Blimey."

"One of the advantages of a solitary existence," Megan said, "is you get plenty of time to think." She lifted her shoulder. "It's also one of the disadvantages."

He nodded, still trying to get to grips with the idea.

"Piece of advice from someone who knows?" she said.

He narrowed his eyes, expecting a sudden switcheroo; Megan doing what she did best, confirming your expectations, then knocking them down: *How could you even think Naomi would be interested?* But she didn't. She didn't switch positions or make fun of him. She remained serious.

"Secrets aren't a good basis for a relationship," she said.

"I don't get you."

"Sure you do." She cocked her head in one side . . . "I wasn't wrong about you, was I?"

"How d'you mean?"

"You *were* in care."

He didn't answer. Didn't need to.

She held his gaze for a moment. "That other stuff I promised you on Doran? Tell your techies to check out the smartchip on my bogus card," she said.

"The credit card — we checked that —"

She shook her head. "Tell them to look underneath the smart chip. You'll find a SIM card for a mobile phone. In the address book, they'll find a list of PO boxes. Each box has a CD-ROM with some info about Doran's activities — the heists, the time sheets, dates, maps — even the names of the crew. Someone will be willing to talk."

"He had them on his computer?"

She shook her head. "Doran's too smart. He emailed his security guy and the crew with times and dates."

"Warrender . . ." Foster said, almost to himself.

"Doran wiped his emails," Megan explained, "but deleted files are easy enough to find if you know where to look. John Warrender didn't even bother to delete his emails. Maybe he planned to use them as his insurance policy against the vagaries of the employment market. But I think he was just sloppy."

458

She smiled and Foster understood. Warrender was as much to blame for the death of the jeweller and his wife as Doran and her brother had been. And now he would pay.

"Thanks," he said, feeling a little stunned.

"It should make up for the car," she said.

"Oh, yeah . . ." He smiled at the thought. "Why now? I mean, you've been giving us the run-around on this stuff from the start — we weren't even convinced you had anything."

"Rule number one for the scammer: keep 'em guessing. Like you said, a case like this, it's the accumulation of evidence — now you've accumulated some more." She waited a moment, then added, "And you did save me." She held his gaze, her eyes dancing with humour.

"Beat it," he said, grinning. "Before I cuff you and take you in."

She opened the car door, still smiling, but he put a hand on her arm to stop her. "Don't forget this." He offered her the picture, Sara's sketch of her.

"Keep it," she said. "As a memento."

"I can get a copy," Foster said, still holding the pencil sketch out to her. "You should have it. We took your other stuff back as evidence." He meant the shoe box. She had left it behind when she disappeared from the flat in Rodney Street.

"Take it," he insisted. "It'll remind you who you are."

She took it from him, then kissed him on the lips, slipping her hand behind his head. He nearly caved in at that touch, breathing her scent and feeling the warmth of her hand on his neck. She drew back, her eyes searching his.

"Pity," she said, as if she had found an answer in the taste of his lips.

He watched her tuck the picture carefully inside her jacket and zip it up, then she walked away into a dampness that was more mist than rain. He waited until she had turned the corner and was gone from his sight before reaching for the radio receiver.

CHAPTER
FORTY-NINE

The team had been debriefed at eleven p.m. and sent home for a few hours sleep. Fraud squad officers raided Doran's offices and home at around midnight, taking away computers, bank records, and whole filing cabinets of paperwork. By morning, some of it had already begun to corroborate Megan Ward's claims.

Detective Sergeant Lee Foster stood in front of DCI Rickman's desk, to all appearances contrite and subdued. It was seven-thirty a.m. and the morning briefing was due to begin at eight.

Rickman stared at Foster and shook his head. "I won't waste my breath going over the lunacy of what you did." He had already had a long and angry conversation with Foster about the risks he had exposed himself to.

At the time, Foster had countered that Megan would probably be dead, if he hadn't. "Look on the bright side," he said. "Doran's not gonna worm his way out of the charge of attempted murder on a police officer."

Rickman eyed his friend, furious at what he'd done, and what could have happened, yet, even more infuriatingly, he could understand it. Understanding Foster's actions confused the issue. This should be a straightforward matter of discipline; Foster had breached it, and should be held to account. But it was also a matter of conscience and emotional attachment, promises made and broken. And the common bond between Foster and Megan, which Rickman, even with his desperate childhood and the secrets it imposed on his relationships, could only understand imperfectly.

"You let her go, Lee," he said at last.

"She hadn't done anything wrong."

Rickman laughed, angrily. "She's a thief, a con artist and a hacker — how's that for starters?"

"You know what I mean." Foster at least had the good grace to look uncomfortable. "She was the victim. She risked her *life* to get that confession out of Doran. What was I supposed to do, tell her 'Ta, very much, and by the way, you're nicked'?"

"It's not your job to decide the rights and wrongs, Lee."

"I know," Foster said, avoiding his eye.

Rickman took a breath and let it go. "There'll be an investigation," he said. "Out of authority — Manchester CID has already been mentioned."

Foster nodded.

"You disobeyed a direct order."

Foster looked up quickly. "I don't expect you to lie for me."

Rickman held his gaze. There was no suggestion of accusation in Foster's clear blue eyes, no hint of a favour owed, yet Rickman knew that the sergeant had done far more for him in the past. He had risked career and even liberty to ensure that a murder did not go unpunished.

"I asked you to organise back-up surveillance," he said. "That's the truth — they needn't know any more than that."

Another nod. "Thanks, Jeff."

"But you should not have been in the car alone."

"Not enough officers available with surveillance training," Foster said.

"And," Rickman went on, "you should not have used your own car."

"You know how it is," Foster said. "Never enough firm's cars to go round when you need them."

Rickman paused. He had primed Foster on the most pressing issues, as the ACC had voiced them to him, but the next point was far more tricky. "You'll have to explain how Megan got away."

Foster's eyes glazed and he staggered a little. Rickman began to get up, but the sergeant waved him away. He touched his fingertips to his forehead lightly. "I think I might've had a touch of concussion," he said. "I was pretty shook up in the car chase."

"You're nothing if not resourceful," Rickman said, acidly.

"Case of having to, way I was brought up," Foster said.

A sharp rap at the door preceded Hart's entrance. Rickman suppressed an impulse to bawl her out for not waiting: it wasn't something he usually insisted on, and his irritation was with Foster, not Hart.

"Sorry, Boss," she said, apparently sensing his displeasure, nevertheless. "I found this in my stack of phone messages." She held up a pink slip. "It's from a Doctor Pickering — she's a consultant psychiatrist at the Royal." She tried not to glance at Foster. "Said it was urgent. She left a mobile number, so I called her. She has a patient named Nathan Wilde. He works for Doran — as a computer whiz."

Rickman felt the stirrings of excitement.

"He says he's got info relevant to the Sara Geddes murder investigation."

Rickman hardly dared ask: psychiatric unit, claims to have information regarding a murder — was this just another crank? But the psychiatrist would be more than capable of judging if the claim was genuine, surely? He asked the question.

"Why didn't he come forward earlier? It's been nearly two weeks."

"He's been off his head on drugs. Amphetamine psychosis, according to the psych — but he's been asking to talk to someone about the murder for days, and they finally realised he wasn't hallucinating or whatever."

"Is he confessing to the murder?"

"No, he says Doran sent some heavies to 'deal' with Warlock. He was quite specific about the name."

Rickman exhaled in a rush. For a moment, he thought they had lost Doran as their best suspect. Then another depressing thought hit him. "CPS won't wear it," he said. "A witness out of his mind on drugs . . ."

"Maybe," Hart said. "But Warlock hasn't been mentioned on the news reports. And Wilde says he can give us the names of the men Doran sent out to take care of Megan."

Rickman smiled. "Lee — get over to the hospital and take a statement," he said. "I want those men brought in — see if they'll talk."

"Looks like we're not gonna need Jake Bentley, after all," Foster said.

"Any sign of him?" Rickman asked.

"Not that I've heard."

Hart shook her head. "He's gone."

"What about the post office boxes listed on the SIM card?"

"Just like she said," Foster put in. "Names, dates, stolen route lists, maps, the lot."

"We've got him." Nobody spoke for a few seconds, but the excitement in the air was palpable. "Fetch Doran," Rickman said. "Take him to Interview Room One — I'll take this myself. Hart — you can sit in." Foster was about to protest, but Rickman interrupted. "He tried to *shoot* you, Lee — I don't want you anywhere near this."

Foster conceded reluctantly. "Can I at least bring him up from the cells? I want to look the murdering bastard in the eye."

Rickman nodded. "But go carefully." He picked up the phone and called Kieran Jago to let him know that his client was about to be interviewed.

They walked down the concrete fire escape in silence, their footsteps echoing up the stairwell.

"I understand you being pissed off with me," Foster said.

She didn't answer.

"Well say *something*, even if it's only to call me a wanker."

"Did you let her go?" She didn't look at him.

"She got away," he said, carefully.

"Did you let her go?" she repeated.

Foster remembered what Megan had said about relationships needing to be founded on honesty.

He sighed. "I let her go. But we've got enough evidence to put Doran away for life," he added.

"So it was a trade-off?"

"Kind of."

They had reached the bottom of the stairs and Hart put her hand out to open the fire door.

"She wanted me to go with her." Foster kept his head down. He didn't want to see what was in Hart's face, right now.

Hart let her hand fall. She was silent a moment or two, then she asked quietly, "Why didn't you?"

"It's complicated."

"Complicated," she said. "Fine." She walked on through the door, putting distance between them.

He followed her. "Woah — wait up. I'd like to explain — to try, anyhow." The idea terrified him, and he hoped it didn't show.

She turned back to him, but only for a second. "There's really no need."

He wasn't sure if he felt relieved or disappointed. Maybe there were too many secrets between them. And anyway, he had never mastered the art of confession.

They had arrived at the custody suite.

"When's his brief due to arrive?" Foster asked. The custody sergeant was Phil Fordham, an officer of thirty-plus years experience. He was bald and slight, but he had a black belt in Aikido, and had single-handedly put down more drunks and druggies with a side-step and an arm-lock than most men twice his size.

"Depends who he appoints," Fordham said.

Before Foster had time to frame a question, the sergeant went on, "DCI Rickman's just been on the blower. Mr Jago has withdrawn his services." His expression did not change, but Foster sensed he was having a rollicking good laugh at Doran's expense.

"I'll go and tell him the good news, should I?" Foster said.

DC Hart signed Doran out, while the custody assistant, a civilian, opened Doran's cell. Doran had washed and shaved, and his black hair was slicked back, still wet. The custody assistant handed Doran his shoelaces and tie and they gave him time to get himself together.

"Is Jago here, yet?" he asked, threading laces through the eyelets of his shoes, and addressing the assistant like he was one of his employees at morning roll-call. He gave no indication that he recognised Foster.

Foster said, "I'm afraid Mr Jago has declined."

Doran looked up at him, surprised and Foster said, "We can ask the duty solicitor to sit in, if you like." He saw Doran thinking through the implications as he finished tying his shoelaces: Jago refusing to represent him looked bad — it looked like he thought Doran was guilty. Worse than that, guilty or innocent, it looked like he suspected Doran was not going to walk away from this — even with the best legal representation. As he looked at Doran, Foster wondered, too if the solicitor's fears for Bentley had consolidated into a firm belief that Doran was responsible for his client's disappearance.

Doran was uncooperative. He agreed to be questioned without a solicitor present, but Rickman was sure this was only so that he could gauge exactly how much they knew, ready to build a plan of attack. He answered "No comment" thirty-five times during the course of a twenty-minute interview.

"We are about to take a statement from an employee of yours." Rickman thought he saw a momentary jolt of alarm flash across Doran's face. *He thinks Warrender is cutting a deal.* Rickman might exploit that lack of trust later. "Nathan Wilde says you sent men to Sara Geddes's house."

"He's a headcase."

"He was," Rickman said, calmly. "But now he's making a lot of sense."

"A headcase and a druggie."

"Mr Doran," Rickman knew there was nothing to be gained from pursuing this line: Wilde was likely to be deemed unreliable. The real promise lay in what they could get out of Doran's heavies — if they could trace them. "The Fraud Squad is sifting through your records, as we speak. We have specialists working on data extracted from your computer network at various times over a considerable period of time." Doran paled slightly at this. "This data implicates you in a number of armed robberies. Now, you are already charged with assault with a deadly weapon, and two counts of attempted murder, so, it would be in your interests to cooperate."

"Sorry," Doran said. "Did I miss the question? I might've nodded off."

Rickman gritted his teeth, and reminded himself that they hadn't expected a confession from Doran, but since they already had one recorded on Megan's website, they didn't really need it. He debated whether to tell Doran and decided against it — he wanted to be sure that Technical Support had extracted everything they needed — the last two weeks had shown him just how easy it was to tamper with computer data, and he didn't want Doran's computer technicians having a go at Megan's site.

"Tell me about Jake Bentley," Rickman said.

Doran watched him coolly, his blue eyes showing no flicker of recognition. "Who?"

"He was coming to you for an interview," Rickman said, risking the bluff — Bentley's mother hadn't known who her son had arranged to meet the night he disappeared.

"Bentley?" Doran frowned. "Like the car? Never heard of him."

"Why did Megan give you money?"

He shrugged. "Maybe she likes me. I'm a likeable guy."

"I believe she was returning money from your illegal operations."

"Impossible," Doran said, with a tight smile. "My business is legit."

"Mr Doran, we counted the money in the sports bags we found inside your car. There was one million pounds of real money, and another two million in counterfeit." Doran blinked. His eyes, red-rimmed and bloodshot, widened a little.

"The counterfeits were pretty obvious — they looked like they'd been done on a laser printer. Probably just there to add weight to the bags and pass cursory inspection in poor light."

Doran looked grey — physically ill; he loosened his tie and leaned his elbows on the table.

"A million?" he said. The plea in his voice unmistakable: this had hit him hard.

There was more, Rickman thought. *Jesus, how much did she get away with?* "A million . . ." he repeated.

Foster arrived back at the station with Nathan Wilde's statement shortly after. He was favourably impressed with the systems analyst, and had passed on the names for other members of the team to check. Rickman gave him a run-down of his interview with Doran, and Foster asked, "Just how much d'you think she got?"

"From the look on his face?" Rickman said. "She's bled him dry."

"There was a million in the two bags we found in Doran's car. There's another one and a quarter million from the initial sum she turned over to us," Foster reminded him. "It's not a bad haul."

"It's nowhere near what Doran was expecting. I thought he was having a heart attack, Lee."

Foster whistled. "But if she's got so much already, I'm wondering why was she so desperate to take a look at that VISA card?

Rickman's pushed his fingers through his hair. "Oh, hell . . . Did we miss an account?"

Foster shook his head. "Tech support got all the encrypted numbers off the magnetic strip." They fell silent, picturing the card, trying to visualise any other information Megan could have gleaned from it.

"The card number!" Rickman exclaimed.

"No —" Foster said. "They checked the card number — there was no such account."

Rickman picked up the phone and punched in the number for Tony Mayle. The Crime Scene Coordinator picked up on the second ring. "Tony? Jeff Rickman. When Megan gave you the encryption code for the credit card, what did you check it against?" He listened. His heart hammered against his rib-cage and he broke out in a sweat. "And they traced all of those accounts? You're sure they got all the money from them?"

He listened to Mayle's reply, thinking, *We missed it. It was right there, under our noses the whole time, and we missed it.* "Shit. Tony — I want you to use the encryption key on the card number — the embossed number on the card, yeah. Call me back when you have something." He hung up.

"Tech support only checked the numbers on the stripe," he told Foster. "They didn't check the card number itself."

Megan worked with intense concentration. Her computer screen was black with white lettering. She was working in computer code, at the level she envisaged as inside the mind of the machine. She accessed bank codes, downloading them direct to her laptop hard drive, using a USB connection, and manipulating the information with software she had developed under the tutelage of her brother. The computer's light reflecting off her face gave it a sickly grey tinge. Her eyes darted from keyboard to screen, to laptop.

A warning beeped, and she realised someone was trying to access her account. She typed commands as they tried to shut her down.

Rickman's phone rang. It was Mayle.

"We've found another account. She's using some kind of firewall. We can't get in — and neither can the bank." He spoke in a low, urgent voice. "We've traced the location of her computer to a hotspot in the city centre."

"Give me the location." Rickman made a note, tore off the sheet of paper and after a moment's hesitation, handed it to Foster. "Don't screw this up, Lee," he said. "Take Garve with you — and Hart." The message was clear: Megan did not get away a second time.

Megan had several programs running simultaneously, one of which temporarily denied the bank systems manager access to the computer network, fencing off a small area only, so as not to trigger a total freeze on the system — a security tool to prevent hackers taking control of the network. She finished by transferring a large sum of money by anonymous file transfer protocol, using a re-router. The account she sent it to would be effectively untraceable.

Foster, Hart and Garvey found the hot-spot with no problem: it was an internet café with WiFi access. Located in the city centre, next door to The Courts pub, it was in sight of the Crown Courts.

Garvey took the back; Hart and Foster went through the front door. Foster scanned the room and located her immediately, sitting in the far corner, her computer angled so that the other customers couldn't see what she was doing. He walked over and grabbed her by the shoulder.

"Hey!" The girl turned around, alarmed and angry. "Get in the queue!" she said.

The manager came over, a man in his late thirties, dressed in combats and a T-shirt that read, "GONE PHISHING". His clothes smelled faintly of the bitter-sweet aroma of cannabis resin. "What are you playing at, mate?" he demanded.

"Well, it's not Game Boy." Foster and Hart both showed their warrant cards. Foster pulled a photocopy of Sara's sketch from his pocket. "We're looking for this woman."

The manager looked shifty.

"Where is she?" Foster said.

"Sarge, take a look at this." Hart was standing next to a computer which appeared to be in use, even though nobody was at the keyboard. Images, numbers, rows upon rows of figures and symbols flashed on screen, too quickly for the eye to register exactly what they were.

"Who's using this?" Foster asked.

The manager looked at the faces of the two officers and decided it would be wise to be helpful. "She left half an hour ago," he said. "She booked the computer for two hours, but left after five minutes. Paid extra for me to keep the link open."

"What's she doing?"

He glanced from one to the other again and licked his lips nervously. "She's using it as a relay."

Foster only just managed to keep his hands off the man and his bad-smelling, bad-spelling T-shirt. "So where . . . is she?"

The manager took a step back. "I — I don't know," he stammered. "She could be anywhere."

Nobody paid much attention to the blonde, waifish student with the short haircut; her face was a little long for the hairstyle, and her eyebrows rather too dark in contrast with her hair colour, but the other students were more concerned that she had tied up two machines in the University of Liverpool post-grad computer lab. She typed studiously at her computer, apparently unaware of the other students, and of the bad feeling from a cluster of three, waiting near the door, glowering at her. These computers were many times more powerful than the undergrad computer labs dotted around the campus, and could be configured to use a variety of computer languages, by simply typing in a password and the language required.

The lab housed thirty work stations, the flow of students in and out of the centre numbered in the hundreds per week. The student finished her download and dutifully logged out of the system, collecting her shoulder bag and jacket as she left, giving a shy smile to the boy who took her place.

She had startling blue eyes, the kind of shade that can only be obtained from an optician specialising in contact lenses. Her bag contained a laptop and a carefully rolled picture in a cardboard tube. The laptop would be required to access her bank accounts, when she reached her destination; the picture was a reminder of who she was. But for now, as she stepped out into the press of students, making their way to lectures, she was just another face in the crowd, unknown and invisible.

Also available in ISIS Large Print:

The Dispossessed

Margaret Murphy

There's a murderer out there getting personal . . .

Bled to death and left in a rubbish bin, the teenaged prostitute is just the first victim.

DI Jeff Rickman's investigation into the Afghan refugee's sordid death leads first to the heart of a community who can't — or won't — talk to him. Then the investigation comes home to Rickman's own private life. As the body count starts rising he is framed for a crime he didn't commit. A murderer is trying to make things personal. Very personal.

Is he on the trail of a serial killer? Or something even more sinister?

ISBN 0-7531-7329-8 (hb)
ISBN 0-7531-7330-1 (pb)

Weaving Shadows

Margaret Murphy

Clara Pascal returns in a new thriller from Margaret Murphy

Barrister Clara Pascal thought she was taking on a simple child custody case . . .

Still traumatised by her own recent experiences as a kidnap victim, Clara works hard to keep the shadows of the past from affecting her friends, family and work. But the dreams don't get any easier and the past won't go away. When a local woman is brutally murdered Clara finds herself amidst a crime investigation that she wants nothing to do with. Her client is a convicted killer — so why does Clara think he's innocent?

Risking her career, her reputaion and her life Clara sets out to prove her case while a killer comes ever closer to making her the next victim . . .

ISBN 0-7531-6971-1 (hb)
ISBN 0-7531-6972-X (pb)

Darkness Falls

Margaret Murphy

"Dark, gripping, horrific crime tale." **The Bookseller**

Clara Pascal had it all: she was a high-flying barrister, devoted mother, envied and admired by her peers. Now, robbed of everything that gives her life meaning, she lies chained to the stone wall of a cellar — and her kidnapper will not tell her what he wants from her. As Clara passes from fear to anger to despair in her dark prison, DI Steve Lawson leads the Cheshire police team working to find her. The police team frantically knocks on doors, follows up wisps of leads, bullying and begging witnesses for help, but it seems that Clara Pascal has disappeared without a trace. And Clara, at last, begins to suspect why her jailer has kept her alive for so long.

ISBN 0-7531-6981-9 (hb)
ISBN 0-7531-6982-7 (pb)

ISIS publish a wide range of books in large print, from fiction to biography. Any suggestions for books you would like to see in large print or audio are always welcome. Please send to the Editorial Department at:

ISIS Publishing Limited
7 Centremead
Osney Mead
Oxford OX2 0ES

A full list of titles is available free of charge from:

Ulverscroft Large Print Books Limited

(UK)
The Green
Bradgate Road, Anstey
Leicester LE7 7FU
Tel: (0116) 236 4325

(Australia)
P.O. Box 314
St Leonards
NSW 1590
Tel: (02) 9436 2622

(USA)
P.O. Box 1230
West Seneca
N.Y. 14224-1230
Tel: (716) 674 4270

(Canada)
P.O. Box 80038
Burlington
Ontario L7L 6B1
Tel: (905) 637 8734

(New Zealand)
P.O. Box 456
Feilding
Tel: (06) 323 6828

Details of **ISIS** complete and unabridged audio books are also available from these offices. Alternatively, contact your local library for details of their collection of **ISIS** large print and unabridged audio books.